The author, Paul Carlin, was born in 1960. He divides his time, as much as possible, between his home in Nottinghamshire and France. *A Lawyer's Story* is his second novel.

Paul Carlin

A Lawyer's Story

AUSTIN MACAULEY PUBLISHERS™

LONDON • CAMBRIDGE • NEW YORK • SHARJAH

A CIP catalogue record for this title is available from the British Library.

ISBN 9781528921053 (Paperback)
ISBN 9781528963282 (ePub e-book)

www.austinmacauley.com

First Published (2021)
Austin Macauley Publishers Ltd
25 Canada Square
Canary Wharf
London
E14 5LQ

This is a work of fiction. The law firm Wilfred Farrelly & Cholmendlay, Solicitors and Commissioners of Oaths, in its different forms, is a figment of the author's imagination as are all the characters said to work in it at various times. Names, characters, businesses, places, events, locales, and incidents in *A Lawyer's Story* are either the products of the author's imagination or used in a fictitious manner. Any resemblance to actual persons, living or dead, or actual events is purely coincidental. Any opinions expressed and thoughts are those of the characters and should not be taken to be those of the author. It should not be inferred that the author approves of any acts or omissions on the parts of any of the characters.

Part One
January 1947 – Nottingham

Prologue

His arm rose like a cobra to the snake charmer's tune. With the tips of his fingers, he flicked the unguarded light bulb and its dull hue was thrown around the sparse room. The shadows in the corners kept their secrets, but he could see enough to tell him that three beds stood empty. He was alone, just as he'd expected. Alone, that was, save for the prone figure in the fourth, the one directly before him. He smiled and stood quite still, as if frozen to the spot, stretching the moment as far as it would go, branding every little detail into his memory, to be recalled later for his future pleasure.

The scent of stale urine and vomit hovered over the whole picture. Her long, grey hair lay in matted clumps over a once-white pillow. Eyes clasped shut, her mouth lolled open. Saliva had trickled down deep wrinkles running from that rancid, sour mouth, leaving a crusty trail. A soft sheen of perspiration lay like a death mask on her creased yet skeletal features. Her tube-like, scrawny neck was half covered by a grubby sheet. He visualised his hands squeezing, his thumbs pressing down hard into her windpipe until her eyes were forced from their sockets. But his arms remained behind his back, his fingers tightly entwined, lest he lost control.

Yes, this was his moment; those sweet, glorious seconds when the anticipation beat the actual deed, when his mouth was dry, his pulse raced and an exquisite, tender tingling massaged his whole being.

It was only when the silence was broken by smashed crockery and a curse in the adjacent kitchen that he blinked, ran his tongue over his lips and walked slowly over. As he did, his silhouette, cast by the light of the stilled bulb, crept across her like a creeping paralysis. He stopped, just for a heart-rending moment, as her death-like stillness made him think that for once he'd miscalculated and was too late. Leaning over, he placed two trembling fingers on her neck. A soft and slow pulse beat faintly but unmistakably against their moist tips. He smiled once more.

'Ethel, my dear. Wakey, wakey.'

Her eyelids edged open, roused by his soft and suave expertly honed diction. She whimpered as her head turned slowly towards him. Milky eyes gazed up at him, her look puzzled. Music from a gramophone record drifted in from the kitchen. Debussy. He had never thought it a particular favourite but today, with its haunting melody, it was quite acceptable and, in its way, quite apt. Finally, the muscles in her lined face relaxed, she breathed out and her thin, chapped lips formed a smile.

'Doctor Farrelly.'

Her scratchy voice was weak, barely audible over the tinkling piano. 'Praise the Lord it's you. I'm so glad you're here. I'm so tired…so very…very tired. Please, don't let the nurse near me, will you? Keep her away, won't you? Please…'

She stopped talking and her derisible, pathetic words drifted into the shadows. He knew her prattling would cease. His curled lips, complete silence, knitted eyebrows and eyes like black slits boring into hers would make it so.

'Doctor?'

From his medical bag lying on the floor, he slowly pulled out the syringe, the needle and the vial, not taking his eyes from her. 'Relax, Ethel my dear, not long now,' he murmured as he took the cap between his thumb and finger and removed it from the end of the needle. He pushed the needle into the vial before gently pulling back the syringe, still gazing into her eyes as he did. Looking away, just for a moment, he shivered as the large dose of clear, but syrupy, liquid morphine slowly filled the whole of the cylindrical chamber.

He placed the syringe delicately on the tip of his thumb, letting it lie between two fingers. Dragging his eyes away from her, he held it up against the light, inspecting it. The silver tip of the needle glinted in the muted, yellow glow. Blood rushed through his veins, energising him further, powering him on, driving him towards his purpose. Beads of perspiration felt cold against his forehead.

He looked down, sensing a change in her – a sudden awareness, heavier breathing. Her wide, haunted eyes were staring at the needle. Her lips moved but no words emerged. She started to squirm, struggling to push herself up, struggling to get away, her eyes pleading to him as she did.

But this was his time. And she was spoiling the moment. His moment. She should be subservient, powerless against his will. She was his, to do with as he pleased. And so he struck her cheek with the palm of his hand. And smiled at the satisfying crack.

'Ethel darling, please,' he whispered.

The music still floated into the room. *Clair de Lune*. That was it.

'No…no…please no.'

With a clenched fist, he struck her again, this time rendering her silent as her head jolted to the left. He nodded, placated, and took the bed sheet between the thumb and first finger of his right hand. It slowly peeled away to reveal a white night dress, yellow stains down its front, hanging off her emaciated body. A crimson pool, vivid against her grey skin, had formed at the base of her nose. He laid the syringe by her side and delicately dabbed the blood with his handkerchief. Satisfied, he pushed up her right sleeve. Gripping her puny wrist, he twisted her arm to reveal a network of blue veins lying translucent just under the white skin and pushed the needle against the most prominent, leaving a barely visible mark.

'Ethel,' he whispered, shaking her bony shoulder, 'wake up, my dear.' He shook her again, this time violently. 'This is something we should share.' She groaned as her eyes creaked open.

'That's better.' He pushed the tip of the needle against the mark left on her arm.

'No…no, please.'

'That's right, Ethel. You know what it is you can feel, don't you? And I am going to be the last person you will ever see.' He smiled, his best smile, the smile that he reserved for those precious occasions when it was truly justified.

Wide, saucer-like eyes stared into his, as if begging for her pitiful, purposeless life. Her lips moved. He held up his hand again; further words were unnecessary. Still smiling, he thrust the needle into the vein and depressed the syringe, forcing the poison into her body. He peered into her eyes, drank in her terror as her pupils shot from right to left. His whole body trembled. This was how it had to be, how it was meant to be. This was how he had decided it should be. The music still drifted in, the music of the angels. It thundered in his heart as another pointless existence was about to be brought to an end.

With a slight moan her head fell to one side. Such joy! Such bliss! What it was to give the little nudge that tipped someone into oblivion. To be responsible, to be the actual cause, was to be God. This was the power that caused his blood to pump through his veins. This was what led to the exquisite conviction that he was all powerful, that he was untouchable, that he should decide who should die and when. Death was what he lived for.

His pulsating chest gradually settled. His pounding heart calmed. He drew out the needle and stood up. It wouldn't be long now. His shirt under his jacket stuck to his back. He took out a clean handkerchief from his trouser pocket and dabbed his brow. He would go back and change his clothing. In a little while, they would call him again and he would be asked to return. It was then that he would attend to the practical matters and sort out the money.

He walked away, his work done for now.

Chapter 1

John Farrelly, solicitor of the Supreme Court and newly appointed junior partner in the firm Wilfred Farrelly & Cholmendlay, Solicitors and Commissioners for Oaths, lay on his back, eyes clasped shut. What had woken him, he couldn't be sure. A baby's screaming ricocheted around his head, mingling with the whisky-induced throbbing. The sickly odour hanging over the room, not totally hiding the underlying reek of mouldy damp, caught in his throat. This, most definitely, was not home.

Broken fragments of the previous evening sidled into his head; snapshots of events and people, snatches of conversation, Frankie Laine and Perry Como, the smoky smog, the dark corners. Finally, she was there, in his mind's eye. He had found her; Ava, his Ava. James was whispering in her ear. Her face, that perfect face, was bathed in laughter as she looked round. John's heart lurched as her eyes landed upon him and she came to his side.

'Where have you been all night, tonight of all—'

'Hush, honey,' she had purred, sliding her arm through his, stopping his whining. 'I'm your birthday present.'

The mattress beneath him suddenly shifted and the sucking of bare feet padding on sticky linoleum told him that it was not a dream and that he was with her and not alone. Ice-cold air nipped his arms and chest as he pushed himself on to an elbow. His hand groped under the pillow, seeking his spectacles, nearly poking himself in the eye as he scrambled to get them on.

She drew apart the blackout curtains, allowing in the dank, grey light of the early January morning, and he stared at her head, her arms, her legs, her back. Ava. His Ava.

Who was he kidding?

She lit a cigarette and threw back her head. Permed, platinum blonde hair settled on her milky-white shoulders. Smoke plumed towards the ceiling. Still in the cream slip she had slept in, she leaned over a table and buffed a porthole into the ice on the inside of the window. Presumably the resulting scene was the back yards and outside toilets; that's what Mother had told him in that disapproving tone of hers was to be found behind these two-up two-downs. The window rattled as the rumble of a train on a nearby cutting momentarily drowned the child's wailing. Ava suddenly shivered and turned. He quickly looked away, feeling a hot blush sweep over his face.

'Dear God,' he muttered, taking in his surroundings. In truth, there was little to take in. His white shirt with its starched collar hung limply off the back of a wooden chair by the table, his unravelled bowtie at its foot, while his dark jacket lay crumpled across the bed. Matching trousers lay spread-eagled on the floor, partially covering a well-thumbed magazine. The open page extolled the virtues of Dolcis shoes, the drawing of the smiling woman indicating that true happiness was attainable on payment of ten shillings. If that was right, he would make his Ava the most contented girl in the whole of Nottingham.

The room was small and square; to the right a fireplace in which lay black and grey ashes and to the left, a small wardrobe of dark wood. Next to that, the site of the screeching, the baby's cot. Chipped, dirty cream paintwork told of its age. A moth-eaten bear and a doll, its pale blue eyes staring glassily out of a grimy face, lay on the floor by its side. Had she mentioned the kid? If she had, he hadn't been listening. It couldn't be any more than a couple of years, although he was no judge. Fat little fingers gripped the bars, its round face smudged with tears. The faded pink romper suit hung loosely off its tiny frame. He caught its eye, and the wailing ceased just for a moment. He quickly turned away, unable to communicate in any way with this alien life form and the noise cranked up again.

He watched, incapable of looking away, as Ava wrapped her arms around herself and rubbed the back of her left leg with her right foot. Once more he was transfixed; by her back, long and straight, the goose bumps on her shoulders, pencil-lined perfect legs giving the appearance of stockings.

He said nothing, barely breathing, in case she looked around and said something that destroyed the illusion that she was his and that he was more than a temporary dalliance. It occurred to him that despite the grime of the room, the poverty and the general wretchedness of it all, this was a place where last night he had been truly happy. It was a place which was foreign to everything he had ever experienced. For the first time in his life, he had felt love other than by way of family duty. His heart had soared to the heavens and back, he had been cleansed. Life wasn't to be found in the dry pages of the law books; life had been here, in his arms. James had been right; work should be to an end, not the end.

'Time to go, honey.'

The words weren't said in an unkind way, but still they sliced through him. He thought of his mother telling him it was time to start the daily five-mile trek to the grammar school as she fastened his duffle coat. But this woman was worldly wise in a way that his mother was not. Ava could read his mind. It seemed that his thoughts, that private area where he could hide from the world, were not his own anymore. She now shared them. She had bewitched him, made him lose all measure of control, all sense of propriety, so that he was hers utterly and completely. She had taken his mind, turned it into mush and casually moulded it into something which provided her with a passing amusement. And she could read what was left. And that's what she was doing now.

She turned and stubbed out the cigarette in an overflowing ashtray on the table. By its side stood a large porcelain ewer in a matching bowl. Lifting the ewer with both hands, she tipped in some water and splashed her face and arms.

'My, that's cold.' She laughed and looked at him for the first time that morning. 'John, baby. Time to go, I said.'

He stared back into her soft blue – almost grey – eyes, hypnotised by the exquisite beauty of her face. He was unable to peel his eyes away, the novelty not blunted even though he had been seeing her twice each week for three months now. He yearned to stroke her pastel, flawless skin, seen now for the first time without makeup. Dazzled, he was the first to blink and look away. He fell back onto the pillow, his hands linked behind his head. 'I c…could—'

'Sorry sweetie. I'm busy today, people to see, places to visit. You know that. I told you. John, baby, don't look like that. You know I've got to find work. I need something other than the club.'

He should have left then, whilst he still had some dignity. But he couldn't help himself. He couldn't leave without getting something sorted; he had to know when he would see her again, when he would get his next fix. The thought of dragging himself away without knowing was too much to contemplate. Without that, the days would just lie in front of him, grey and lifeless, until she deigned to call him when she wanted something, giving him that brief moment of euphoria. Until then she would occupy his every thought.

'Anyway, you're the lucky one. You've got work today. Tell me what you'll be doing?'

'Oh,' he replied, 'a c...couple of completions, that's about it.'

'Now, you did explain that – that's when the house is actually bought and sold. Am I right?'

He laughed, despite his certain knowledge that in less than ten minutes he would be alone in the cold street and he would feel as wretched as it was possible for any man to be. 'S...something like that.'

She bent down and picked up her handbag from where she had placed it the previous night and fished out what turned out to be nail varnish. She then sat on the bed, her back to him. The child still sobbed.

'You solicitors make everything so complicated. Why can't it be like be like buying some apples or even chocolate? You wouldn't even need to ration houses. With all the building there'll soon be enough to go around. So what's the difficulty?'

As she said this, he sat up and watched her repair chipped nail varnish, the deep red shade at odds with the whiteness of her fingers and the merest pink of her nails. He leaned towards her. 'Ava. You have to c...carry out searches and—'

'What do you mean, searches? Oh, never mind.' She turned her head and looked at him quizzically before going back to her nails. 'You are just what I would expect a solicitor to be like. If I'd never met one, that is. But it's odd really; you're not like any other solicitor I've ever met.'

'And how m...many have you m...met?'

She laughed. 'You wouldn't believe who comes into the club. They just tell me what bitches their wives are and presume I'm something they can buy.' She laughed again before adding quietly, 'they'd never leave them though, never in a month of Sundays.'

'I d...don't think that you're someone who can simply be bought.'

He bit his lip and grimaced. The words had come out too quickly. He'd appeared too eager. She slowly drew the small brush down a nail before holding up one hand, fingers splayed, and carefully examined the results. He touched his lip with the tips of his fingers, making sure he'd not drawn blood. She gently blew on her nails and, apparently satisfied, started on the other hand. It was a full minute before she replied, her words little more than a whisper. 'I don't want anything heavy, John. And deep down I don't think you do either. Just think about the scandal. I can see the headlines now: "solicitor shacks up with a hostess who works in a night club and who just happens to be an unmarried mother.'"

'Ava, darling. I wouldn't m…mind. Honestly. I'd g…give anything.' He cursed his inability to keep his desperation from his voice. He thought of holidays in Barmouth as a child, pleading for an ice cream.

She pulled a little mirror and compact from her handbag and deftly dabbed powder onto her cheeks.

'And just think of the better quality of l…life you'll have, both of you.' He waved an arm in the general direction of the baby.

'So, I'm something that can be bought? Anyway, we've been through all of that. I've told you, I'm not going to be here much longer. Once I've got something more than the club and earned enough, we'll be out of here so quick you won't be able to…oh, I don't know… but I'll be able to make my own way thank you very much.'

She stood and pulled a chord near the door but the dingy, yellow light bulb hanging from the ceiling made scant difference to the dank, colourless room. Her hand dipped into the dark interior of the wardrobe before emerging with a light blue dress. Finally, she smiled at the crying child. 'Be with you in a mo, sweetie.' She then stopped and studied the dress, a frown casting a shadow over her perfect features. 'It'll just have to do,' she said quietly, as if to herself, as she ran her fingers over a milky stain on the shoulder.

'Ava, why can't you just think about it? You'd have no n…need to w…work at all. You could give up the c…club. I hate the way they paw over you as if you're some k…kind of m…meat.'

She glanced at him. 'Honey, you've obviously forgotten that's where you met me.'

Pulling the coarse fabric of the dress over her head, she sat down on the bed again, her back to him. 'Do me up, there's a love.' John tugged on the zip before taking hold of her shoulders and trying to turn her so that she faced him.

She stood up and pulled away. 'Now, out of my bed please. I need you away before Mam realises I've had someone back. She's terrified that she'll have another one to look after.' She placed her mirror on a mantelpiece over the fireplace and took lipstick out of the bag which she pulled across her lips. 'Got to look my best today, you never know, today could be the day. I was talking to your brother last night. He suggested a job in a hospital or a nursing home. So, that's where I'm going to look. Now, he is a dish, that brother of yours, I must say. You'd never guess that the two of you were twins.'

He felt her gaze in the mirror fall upon him. 'I feel so alive when I'm with him,' she continued. He was determined that she would see no reaction but felt the deep blush burning his face, betraying his hurt.

'So your brother is your twin? You're both twenty-four?'

'Y…yes. W…why?'

'He seems younger in some ways, and yet older in others.'

'W…what do you m…mean?' He sounded, even to himself, like a moaning child.

'Well… last night, he was bounding around the dance floor like a debutant. I know it was his birthday bash, and yours as well I suppose, but he seemed so…well, so young. And yet, he…well, I suppose he was looking out for you like an older brother might. He doesn't seem like a doctor.' She laughed once more. 'You two are an odd pair.'

'James is engaged you know.'

'Well, things can change…' she said quietly, once more as if to herself. She then turned and looked at him. 'Anyway, you will be as well once you've found the right girl.'

'Perhaps I h…have.'

'No, you haven't.' She looked back at the mirror. 'The two of you are so different. He's just so…so glamorous, I suppose. You know, he reminds me of the American soldiers, the Parachutists who stayed at Wollaton Park during the war, before they went to France. They were so…oh I can't think of the word. I loved the way they talked, the way they kissed.'

She turned around. 'I could have married a Texan, you know. We were sweet whilst he was here and he said he was going to come back for me. He wrote a couple of times after it was all over, but that was it, baby or no baby.'

John looked away. Suddenly her occasional slight American lilt, something that he had always found so alluring, made him want to gag as a vision of her with another man hit him between the eyes.

'Your brother reminds me of him. He can make a girl feel a million dollars with just one look.'

He looked back at her. She was playing with him, as a child might pass the time with an old toy on Christmas Eve. He just couldn't compete. His thin, chiselled face, framed by sandy bordering on ginger hair, was no match for James's film star looks.

She wasn't being deliberately unkind. It was hardly her fault she had succumbed to James's charm just like everyone else.

'I bet he's always got something on the side whereas you…well, you've never done anything like this before, have you? Why, I don't believe you've ever been with a girl before. A girl can always tell.'

He cringed at the certain knowledge that she was able to read him so completely. He thought of the time in the lower third, of his father calling him into his study, knowing his son had failed Latin, without a word being spoken.

'You d…don't know that at all.' It sounded so feeble.

'Yes, I do, sweetie. Trust me. Now, up please.'

He dragged himself out of bed and pulled on his trousers, nearly stumbling in his efforts to keep an air of sophistication, and then forced his feet into his shoes. His desperation grew, as if fuelled by the humiliation, and he persisted. 'When can I see you again?'

She laid a cool hand against his burning cheek. 'Oh, I'm sorry, honey. I'm going to be busy during the day and working every night at the club, both this week and next. Perhaps I'll call you from the club one night next week and you can buy me a drink.'

He slowly put on his shirt and tie, his mind whirling, stretching out the task. Suddenly he strode the two steps to her and again grabbed her shoulders and forced her around. 'Ava, you d…don't understand!'

'Hush, sweetie. Don't let Mam hear you.'

'Surely you c…can see what it would be like? No scrimping for m…money. No having to flirt in the c…club with somebody you d…detest.'

She smiled, taking his hands from her. 'Oh, it's not so bad.'

'It's so d…damn awful!'

'Hush, I say. And don't swear in front of the baby.'

'Ava—'

'John. I want to make my own way. Me and my baby. I'm not going to rely on any man. It's the surest way to disappointment.' She walked towards the window. 'One day I'm going to be famous. You see if I'm not.' She wrapped her arms around herself before speaking again, this time her tone hushed, telling herself where her future lay. 'And then I'll be away from here so quickly, me and my baby, away from the queueing, the rationing, away from the cold, away from the misery of it all.'

She turned around smiling, as if back in the present, and put a finger against his lips, stopping him from saying anything else. 'Now, off you pop, honey.'

He leaned forward wanting to kiss her lips and she deftly moved her head to one side so that their cheeks brushed. 'Careful of my lipstick. It's expensive. I'm not putting it on again. Now you'll make me late if you're not away soon.'

As if suddenly conscious of the sobbing baby, she pulled away and moved to the cot in the corner of the room. 'Elizabeth. Poppet. What's the matter? Isn't Momma giving you any attention? Come here.' She picked her up and lifted her over the side. The noise lessened to a sniffle as she planted a kiss on the baby's forehead.

'Ava, is it of any c…consequence to you how I feel?'

She turned, the baby on her hip. 'Honey. Of course it is. You're very sweet and you're very kind. You're not like the rest. It's not that I won't see you, but I can't be doing with anything serious. I told you that at the start. That suited you then if I remember correctly.'

'Well, it doesn't s…suit me n…now!'

'There's no need to shout,' she hissed. 'And what about me? What if it does suit me? Or doesn't that matter?'

'I just d…don't understand you. Any other girl would d…die for what I can offer.'

'And what's that when it's at home? Anyway, I'm not any other girl. Or perhaps you're just like the rest and think your money can buy me?'

'Ava, I d…didn't m…mean that. It's just that we c…could be so happy. I just know that I'm right.'

'John, that's enough! If you don't stop, I will refuse to see you. Please back off. I'll call you. Now go. Please!'

Still holding the baby, she pulled open the bedroom door with her free hand. 'Go quietly, will you.' She placed her lips lightly against his cheek and gently pushed him through the open door and on to a dark landing.

He stared as the door closed in his face and stood for a moment before forcing himself to leave. The stairs were partially lit by a dull light which came through the glazed window in the front door below. He went down, as noiselessly as shoes against uncarpeted steps would allow.

At the bottom, he found himself in a small hallway with the front door before him. Down a corridor he heard a noise; splashing he thought. An old woman with her back to him was plunging clothes into a sink. Lank white hair fell onto painfully thin shoulders under a threadbare green cardigan. Through a gap in a door leading off the corridor, he looked into the subdued light sliding through half-open curtains into what appeared to be a living room. Bed sheets lay crumpled on the floor. He raised his eyes in the direction of the room where he, Ava and the baby had slept, before opening the front door and going into the grey morning.

The icy grey cold slapped him in the face as he pulled his jacket around him and walked slowly along the cobbled street. Two or three shrieking children chased a ball. Even at this early hour, women were huddled around open doors. A group of men stood at the corner of the street, sucking greedily on cigarettes. He only had thoughts for one person; a woman who he would wager was not thinking of him at that moment.

Chapter 2

James Farrelly placed his medical bag by his feet and lit a cigarette, shielding it from the biting wind with cupped hands. He stood still, quite still, taking in the moment, as the calming tang of the tobacco swept through him. It was only then that he knocked twice on the hardboard panel of the front door. As he waited, he breathed out slowly, wondering whether she was already dead. He turned and looked up and down the street, stamping his feet.

The early afternoon slate-grey sky and grey smoke, billowing from the chimneys, complemented the street's squalor. A grey day in a grey street of a grey town. Sherwood Avenue, typical of Nottingham's suburbs, stretched into the gloom, heading off towards the city. It was no different to hundreds of others, with its soot-stained, orangey-brown bricked pre-war semis lining each side of the street, wedged behind tatty, falling wooden fences. Late Christmas decorations still twinkled in the odd window, as if the occupants were trying to suck out the last morsel of festive cheer, but generally those living within their four walls were merely existing under the austerity and misery of what England had become after the war. It wasn't just food that was rationed – it sometimes felt as if happiness, good humour, even the occasional smile, were all regulated. Too much and you may get used to it. And we'd won the damn war.

He muttered under his breath as he rapped the door twice more.

Squealing pasty-faced brats clutching and mimicking make-believe guns scrambled over the bricks piled up across the road, where a similar house would have stood, but for the Luftwaffe. More than eighteen months had passed since it all finished, but the gap was still there, like a missing tooth in a punched mouth. A man and woman walked down the street, huddled into their coats, staring at the ground and taking no notice of the bread van as it rolled slowly up the street, one lamp not working. As it reached the couple, it backfired. They did not look up, just scurried on. The kids still sprayed their imaginary bullets around, oblivious. They were right, it was just a game. And you had to treat it as such lest you drown in the sea of melancholy.

But it was a game he was winning.

Jesus. Where was she? He pulled his coat around him before banging three times against the door with the outside of his gloved right fist. Taking a step backwards on to the tarmacked area between the house and the fence, his eyes raked across the building before him, fearing irrationally, just for a moment, that they weren't in.

Two pebble-dashed houses had been bludgeoned into one several years ago. As he well knew from many a previous visit, the rooms downstairs had been converted, albeit loosely, into large bedrooms. That only left room on the ground floor for a small hallway and the kitchen. Ernie and Nurse Dolores, as she was now known in the neighbourhood, existed upstairs. The caring, such as it was, was administered downstairs. Four beds were stuffed into each of the two rooms, so space for eight patients. In the two years he had known them, there had never been more than four at any one time and they hadn't lasted long. He smiled.

A light suddenly flickered through the stained glass at the top of the door. 'Comin'. I'm bloody comin'. Oo is it?'

'You know darn well who it is, Ernie my good fellow,' shouted James airily through the door, surprised at the relief he felt.

The door edged open. James picked up his bag and stepped into the hall. The single bulb hanging from the ceiling created just a pool of lemon-like light, but left the man's features in semi darkness. The only items in the small square area were a coat stand in a corner and a mirror on an otherwise bare white wall. Doors went off to the left and right and a narrow passage headed off in front of him. Stairs alongside the passage led up into darkness. The musty odour in the hall could not quite mask a stench of chip oil. James nudged the door shut with the sole of his shoe. 'Don't want to let the cold in do we, Ernie? Or you might catch your death in here.' He laughed. 'How is our patient?'

'I'll fetch 'er, Doctor,' said the man, his voice flat and emotionless. James rolled his eyes as the man lumbered along the passage and through a door; he was clearly too stupid to understand the question. James grimaced as he was assailed by a stronger whiff of what they were eating. Music from a gramophone drifted into the hallway. *Debussy again*, he thought, humming along.

A woman, small, wiry and bird-like, shot through from the direction of the fatty odour. James's eyes widened as they rested on a gold chain and watch glinting in the half light, hanging from the front of her blue tunic.

Her high-pitched squawk cut through the gloom. 'He said I could have it.' So that was her plea to his unspoken charge. She moved out of the shadow of the corridor and he found himself staring into black beady eyes. He delved into his memory bank of deaths where Dolores had played a part. The last male death here had been that rather disgusting old man, he of the porous bowel, and that was at least two months ago. He couldn't recall the name. Then again, he rarely could. And Dolores may have been keeping her treasure hidden until she felt it safe to reveal it to the world, although she wasn't normally reticent in showing off her spoils, ill-gotten or otherwise.

'Anyway, you took your time.'

'People to see, Dolores, my dear, people to see,' he replied, smiling down at her. 'Now, if you'll just give me a minute, I'll get on, shall I?'

The woman darted through a door to his left as he leisurely took off his trilby and coat and hung them on the coat stand, fighting the need to go straight to the purpose of his visit. Catching his reflection in the mirror, he stooped in front, took a small comb from the inside pocket of his jacket and smoothed it through his black, brylcreamed hair from its left side parting. Maybe it was the pencil line moustache, maybe it wasn't, but it was true what they said; he could have been Clarke Gable's better-looking, younger brother. He pulled his Windsor knot tight to his throat and ran his forefingers down his moustache.

'Capital,' he murmured to himself.

His heart again began to beat just a little quicker and the butterflies in his stomach grew as he savoured the final moments before dealing with the second part of the task. He smiled at his reflection and followed the woman.

The room was now lit by just a candle, placed on a wooden cabinet next to the bed in the near corner. The grey day seeped through the windows, adding to the murk. He placed his bag on the floor and pulled his jacket around him; it was no warmer here than it had been outside. Ashes lay in the unlit hearth. The corpse lay on the bed, covered to the neck by the grubby white, torn sheet. Fighting the need to meet its glassy stare, his eyes flicked over everything but. Nothing had been moved. Three other beds, empty and bereft of bedclothes, stood pushed together in the corner at the room's far end. The room, as he well knew, had little by way of comforts. No pictures or prints adorned the plain, white walls. Blackout curtains hung limply by the windows. No chairs were positioned by any of the beds. The linoleum flooring, dirt ingrained into its pitted surface, was curling up at its edges.

Next to the candle sat an ashtray and next to that a glass. False teeth, white plastic objects fixed to the end of a sickly, pink palate, floated in discoloured water. 'I thought only right and proper to show some decorum,' said the woman, looking at the candle. 'She was flesh and blood when all's said and done.'

And electricity costs money, thought James. 'Quite right, Dolores, my darling,' he said, looking at her, 'there'll be a place reserved in heaven for you after all.'

He lay his cigarette in the ashtray. A thin trail of smoke meandered upwards. The unsmiling woman stood by the bed, arms crossed. She looked seventy although MacPherson had once told him that she was about fifty-five. Grey hair pulled tight into a bun at the nape of her neck framed a thin, sallow face, almost yellow in the light of the flickering candle. Her nurse's garb did not extend as far as headgear. Wafer-thin lips, high, prominent cheeks and those large, black eyes gave her, he fancied, a look of menace. It was a face which, he felt, rather suited her.

'Well?' He trained his eyes on her, still fighting the need to look at the body.

She stared back. 'In the night it started. Her breathing's what I noticed. I sat with her and she eventually dozed so I went upstairs. First thing this morning, our Ernie said she was worse. Seems to me that she's had a stroke. That's when I sent him out to the telephone to call you and you—'

'I meant, my dear, what happened after I left?'

'I left her to rest for a couple of hours and when I came in to look upon her, she was barely breathing. That's when I sent my Ernie out to call you back. I checked an hour ago and she'd gone.'

'Okay, Dolores. Let me take a look. Feel free to finish your meal, won't you?' His eyes locked into hers. She met his gaze but didn't move. His hands were pushed deep into his jacket pockets, fists clenched, fearful lest she should notice their trembling. He had to say something, anything, to break the spell. 'Was it too much trouble to close her eyes?' The words came out too quickly.

'My work's finished once they're gone, as if you didn't know.'

James picked up the cigarette and took one last drag, inhaling deeply, before drilling the nub end into the ashtray. He perched on the edge of the bed and leaned over, finally allowing himself to take notice of the prone figure lying there.

The grey hair still lay over the pillow. Glassy eyes gazed up at him. He stared back, now unable to tear himself away from this vista of death. The lips, a blue tint just visible, had sunk over the gums and into the mouth. He gently placed two fingers against the neck for the second time that day, but didn't need the stone-like stillness to tell him that life had long gone. The perfect silence was always the tell-tale factor. To him, death had an exquisite solitude all of its own. To sit by a corpse was to be with God; that's what caused the butterflies in the pit of his stomach, his heart to race.

The need to be alone with this body was becoming overwhelming. But to find an excuse to get the woman standing there to leave would look odd, could even reveal something of what he felt, of what he needed. With the tips of his forefingers he slowly drew down the eyelids, his heart thudding against his chest as he performed this sweet, final act, the act of extinguishing life for evermore. It was the tranquillity, the perfect peace that let him place everything in its proper order, to hone his explanations. He had always thought that was his gift from God. That was why he was so good at his job. That was why he was successful.

He needed to camouflage his heavy breathing. And, as ever, there was the need for cash – not that there was any indication that that the body below was a route to untold riches.

'Relatives?'

'None. Or at least none who could be bothered to come and see her.'

'I don't recall anything about a will?'

She bit her lip. 'There was no need. She'd nowt to leave.'

He looked into the nurse's eyes. 'But you think you're taking what she has left, I presume?'

'Ernie helped her write a letter saying that in return for looking after her 'til her end, we could keep what she had.'

James looked down at the body once again, rubbing his chin. How long had the old witch had her? Dolores, if asked, would half the time, thus doubling the risk in an effort to make him look elsewhere. A lengthy stay without visitors was always a good sign. He really ought to know how long. He was getting complacent. It was about a month. They'd just put up the decorations in the surgery when MacPherson had mentioned, in a rare moment of sobriety, that Nurse Dolores had a new customer. So – no one visiting over Christmas. A positive sign.

He slid his hands under the sheet and pulled out a bony right hand. This was the point where, with a practised eye, he valued her. He always left such matters until his return; it had always seemed to him to be rather unseemly to be calculating the proceeds whilst preparing somebody to meet their maker.

Rigor mortis had already started. No rings, no watch. Nothing. No surprise there. As ever he went to the left hand last. What priceless gems he had found embedded into ring fingers in the past. Nothing there this time. 'I see you beat me to it, Dolores, my darling,' he said quietly, as if to himself. Bending his neck, he studied that third finger. No blemish so there probably never had been a wedding band, an engagement ring. 'Another victim of the Great War, eh?' He looked up briefly. 'Husbandless and childless.'

'I told you there was nowt.'

James hooked his fingers under those of the corpse's and scrutinised closely the nails. As with the lips, he found the tell-tale blue tint. That, together with the history of nausea and breathing difficulties, confirmed that this woman had died of morphine poisoning. Dolores's theory of a stroke was nothing more than something for him to scribble on the death certificate.

'Cashbooks?' he asked.

'Fifty-seven pounds, twelve shillings when she came. My nursing charges have to come out of that, mind.'

Once more James stared up at the woman standing in front of him. She had crossed her arms again. He reached down for his bag and undid the strap, not taking his eyes away. He then pulled out a wad of forms attached to a clipboard. 'If anyone takes an interest, Dolores, how much morphine will they find clogging up the old dear's organs?'

'Morphine which you prescribed. And you told me to give it her. Aren't I right?'

'That all depends on whether you mean me personally or the surgery of which I am junior partner. A very junior partner.' He laughed.

'Don't you be getting too clever with old Dolly, my lad. I know a lot about you; there are those that would say too much.'

He slowly rose to his feet, flung the clipboard onto the floor and stared down at her, his eyes boring into hers.

'Ernie!' she screeched. James suddenly smiled. She breathed out, her shoulders slumping just slightly.

'No need for that, Dolores. We'll settle at about twenty-five pounds each, shall we?' He saw her purse her lips and look quickly at the body before running her hands down her face.

'Look. I've had to deal with this one over all Christmas. I can't get staff. He's useless.' She flicked her eyes towards the door. She then stopped for a moment as if in thought before continuing, the words tumbling from her. 'We've got a new one. She's got creeping paralysis and her mind's addled. She's next door. I reckon she's worth summat. There's summat about her. Take just ten quid now and we'll go halves next time. It'll be worth your while, just you see. Come on, let me show you.'

James quickly placed the flat of his hand in front of her. 'Let me take a look for myself, eh my dear?'

'Then have this.' She delved into a cupboard further along the wall and brought out a saucer on which was welded a candle which she lit with the wick of the other, before handing it to him. 'Don't want you switching on the lights and waking her now. I had little enough sleep last night with this one.' She nodded in the direction of the body lying below them.

James headed through the gloom, the candle in one hand and his medical bag in the other, towards the door on the other side of the room, a door he had been through on many occasions in the past. In a bed pushed into a far corner lay a body-shaped bundle. He walked over slowly, staring straight ahead, not wishing to wake up what was there, although he had little doubt that the body would already be riddled with morphine. Nothing would rouse it before morning.

An elderly woman lay on her side. Only one half of her face was visible, peeping out from under the bedspread. Her breathing was shallow but regular. He cursed under his breath as his toe stubbed something protruding from under the bed. Bending, he pushed the candle in front of him and saw a pair of metal callipers. So, a cripple as well as a lunatic. The creeping paralysis, if what he had been told was true, was advanced. Possibilities. Possibilities.

Holding the candle in one hand, he stood and looked down at her. Thick white hair had been permed in the not-too-distant past. An indication of wealth or some relative or other with too much time on their hands? Too early to tell. The eyes were closed. Jowls of ashen fat rolled from the cheek, collecting under the chin. Pale lips quivered just slightly as she breathed. A thin, flaky trail of sputum had dried at the corner of the mouth.

James, still pondering Dolores's comment as to her wealth, gently raised and slowly pulled away the top sheet between a thumb and forefinger before lifting the podgy fingers spread out next to the woman's face. He had come across the left hand first, but that disappointment was tempered by the gold wedding band and bracelet. He had not expected to find an engagement ring. She, or indeed James himself, was not likely to see that again. Anyway, there may be something here. The fact that the engagement ring had gone meant it was of some value. Dolores may have finally struck gold and—

'Help me.' His heart leapt and he nearly dropped the candle as the woman's fingers closed around his own, their grip surprisingly strong. Her voice was faint but firm.

'Good afternoon, my dear,' he replied quickly. 'I'm so sorry to disturb you. My name is MacPherson, Doctor MacPherson. The nurse has asked me to pop by and see how you are. I was just about to take your pulse, little realising that you were awake.'

'Help me.'

'And that is exactly what I'm here to do, my dear.'

'You don't understand. I should not be here. I …' A fit of coughing caused the woman to spin onto her back and ram the handkerchief, which she had been clutching in her right hand, into her mouth. Gasping, she tried to push herself up but fell back, as her body convulsed with the coughing. The accent was not local; there was no evidence of a deprived Nottingham existence here. Her chest heaved as the coughing subsided. Light blue eyes, full of life, stared at him.

'So where should you be, Mrs…?'

'Harris. Mrs Edie Harris. And I should be at home, my home.' Tears welled in her eyes. As she dabbed her face with her handkerchief, four white tablets rolled out from under the handkerchief on to the top sheet. 'See. See what she's making me take. Sleeping pills.'

So, Dolores was already pumping morphine into her, or at least trying to. This was not like any dementia he'd come across. If the corpse next door was any guide, Mrs Harris may not be returning home. It wouldn't take Dolores long to discover that her form of treatment was not being taken.

He stared at damp, glistening patches under the woman's eyes and thought of the Christmas Eve afternoon he'd buried alive John's hamster. Even now, years later, his skin tingled as he recalled his brother's tears. Pressing his face into the newly dug, damp earth, telling him he would be made to eat the rotting carcass if he so much as breathed one word to their father had quickly wiped them away. As he had pulled him to his feet, urine trickled down his brother's leg from under his knee-length trousers. For James, that had completed the experience.

'How about I talk to the nurse about your pills? I'll just take your pulse, my dear.'

'Where's my doctor?'

'I'm your doctor – while you're here, that is.' James smiled at her and took her wrist between his thumb and forefinger. 'Now, my dear, this home to which you wish to return.'

*

'And how has she ended up here?'

'That woman from the County Welfare Organisation asked before Christmas if I had room. She brought her the day after Boxing Day. You've not gone and woken her now, have you?'

'Fear not, Dolores. To my surprise she came round and was reassured to find a doctor ministering to her. She'll sleep like a baby tonight. However, we do need to talk about her medication.'

'Why? What are you planning?'

'Dolores, my dear.' He placed his hands on her bony shoulders. 'That poor old lady is probably in a degree of pain. A stronger dose than normal?' James flicked his eyes towards the dead body on the bed, raised his eyebrows, and smiled.

'If that's what you reckon, Doctor,' she replied quickly.

'I'll see to it. Now, I believe we settled on ten pounds for my services today?'

'So, you agree with me then? She is worth something.'

'She's not worth that much, Dolores. Don't raise your hopes too high. If she was our route to untold riches, what would she be doing here?' He smiled and bent down and whispered in her ear. 'But between us, we should be in pocket. So, perhaps you would leave the wedding ring on her finger for the time being.'

She shot out of the room and he picked up the clipboard. Her explanation was as good as any and, as he stared at the body below, he scrawled 'cerebral haemorrhage, due to myocardial degeneration' under the cause of death before signing it. The woman came back, clutching a ten-pound note.

'Thank you, Dolores. For that you now have one death certificate.'

She snatched it from him and held it near the candle, squinting over the words. 'I see it's Doctor MacPherson who's signed it.' She laughed, a shrill cackle, and he was taken back to the fourth year in the High School and the first scene in *Macbeth*.

'How is the old soak today?' she asked.

'Sleeping this lunchtime off.'

'Presumably, he won't remember signing this, will he?'

'No Dolores. He won't remember today; which is of course why his signature is here.' He picked up his bag. 'Another funeral where you'll be the only one in attendance.'

'She wanted to be cremated.'

'I don't think so, my dear. We don't want any complications, do we? And with that, I will bid you a good afternoon.' As he got to the door, he stopped and turned. 'You say you can't get staff. I may just be able to help you there.'

Smiling at her, his best smile, he walked back out into the darkening day.

Chapter 3

He'd parked the Bentley around the corner; he'd thought it best. Newly formed frost, lying on its black and polished exterior, glistened in the yellow light from a street lamp. Visions of twitching curtains filled his head as his shoes clipped on the whitened pavement. It was probably his imagination. Nonetheless, his overcoat collar was turned up and not just because of the cold.

He laid a gloved hand on the gate and turned quickly, glancing up and down the tree-lined avenue. God, he could have done with a drink. Cold breath swirled around his face. The street was deserted. Detached houses stood in their private grounds. White smoke from their chimneys chugged gently into the inky black, moonless night sky, smudging the ice-like pinpricks of the stars. Curtains masked the lighted downstairs rooms, hiding the occupants from the rest of the world. Did austerity bite here? Or were they somehow exempt?

He turned back, scrutinising the house before him. Two large windows each side of the front door, two floors; it was a house which smacked of wealth. Sleeping in the darkness expected of an unoccupied building, it nonetheless stood proud, taking its rightful place amongst the affluence, indifferent to its emptiness. Illuminated by the streetlights, the path towards the front door bisected the front garden. He bent to examine footsteps in the snow; one set in and one set out, small as if those of a woman, the edges firm so made since last night's downfall. Long strands of grass, poking through the white blanket, and undocked roses hinted perhaps at neglect or more likely an inability to provide the necessary care. He squinted through the gloom before spotting the large, cylindrical plant pot standing in a corner of the porch. He smiled as he recalled the telephone conversation yesterday evening.

'Doctor MacPherson, you say?'

He had stubbed out his cigarette in the nearest of the two ashtrays on the desk in the surgery. Her soft voice floated down the line. He had expected an old hag. 'Yes Miss Stott. My surgery is on

Mansfield Road and I've taken on responsibility for old Mrs Harris. I understand that you were party to the decision to relocate her.'

'Yes, there was no choice, I'm afraid. Her eccentricity was concerning the neighbours. Her son, I'm afraid, is simple. There are doubts over her ability to look after him as well as herself—'

'What about other relatives, I was under the impression that she was blissfully wed?' His fingers drummed gently on the desk.

'No. She's a widow. She lost her husband a couple of years ago and she's gone downhill since. The neighbourhood find her quite eccentric. Actually, I'm glad you've rung. One of the neighbours brought Denis, that's the son, to see me last week. There had been concern about him being on his own. I've contacted a cousin of his in Lincoln who has agreed to take him in. One thing I do need to discuss with you is Edie's wish not to have visitors. Denis simply doesn't understand his mother's sudden antagonism towards him and her reluctance to let him visit. He—'

'I'm sure—'

'No let me finish. I had to read out the one letter he has received from his mother – written by the nurse or someone who works there given the writing – saying she did not want him or anyone else to visit. It was particularly hurtful.'

He picked up the Webley. Its sleek barrel glinted in the light from the streetlamp slipping through the window. Its cylinder clicked with a satisfying snap as he nudged it round with the tip of his thumb.

'Yes, that is a great shame and is despite and contrary to our advice to Mrs Harris. For some reason, she seems to hold her son responsible for her placement in the home. Look. I'm dealing with her medication, but she does seem to have taken a shine to my colleague, Dr Farrelly, who looks in on her from time to time if I'm not available when he attends others there. I'll see if he can talk to her. I'm sure it can all be sorted out.'

'Well, I'm sure that would be a comfort to Denis…you do seem to be going the extra mile, Doctor MacPherson. May I…err…enquire as to the purpose of your enquiries?'

He put down the handgun, the clunk against the oak desk echoing around the surgery.

'Of course, Miss Stott,' he replied, pouring a measure of whisky from the three-quarter empty bottle, 'how remiss of me not to enlighten you straight away. Mrs Harris was concerned as to how long she was to stay in the nursing home. In fact, she has indicated several times since arriving at the establishment a desire to return home. I am of the view that, for the moment at least, her level of understanding is such that such a course of action would be premature. I understand she has been diagnosed with Progressive Disseminated Muscular Sclerosis – creeping paralysis by its usual name – which explains the double incontinence, the mobility issues and the slowness of intellect. I'm sure you understand that the combination of all those problems render such an eventuality rather unlikely.'

'Well, that's not what—'

'Can I say, Miss. Stott, that your decision to send her to the home reflects excellent clinical judgement.' The whisky slipped down his throat, burning a path as it went.

'Well…thank you, it's always—'

'Tell me, how did you become aware of Mrs Harris's sad plight?'

'Well, I happen to be the secretary of the County Welfare Organisation. We are a charitable body who step in to lend a hand when people are unable to care for themselves and there are no relatives able to help. We try to arrange care for such people. Edie's son and one of the neighbours have been doing what they could but—'

'And how did you come by Nurse Dolores's establishment?'

'We've found in the past that she's able to take people on urgently and at a most reasonable cost. We weren't sure about Edie's finances but we've now got her passbook so we can pay the fees for a few weeks at least. And it gives Edie a chance to recuperate and, if necessary, us the chance to find somewhere suitable for the long term.'

He emptied his glass. 'Fear not, Miss Stott. Edie will be properly cared for at the home so you may take your time in finding an alternative placement.'

'Well, that's very—'

'The purpose of my telephone call was to make arrangements to collect one or two items.'

'Oh, a visit would be a little difficult at the moment. With Denis gone, the house is empty.'

He poured the rest of the contents of the bottle into his glass. 'Edie has advised me as to the trinkets that would make herself feel at home. Both myself and Nurse Dolores really feel it would help her settle and perhaps lead to her being more receptive to visitors.'

He took a sip.

'Miss Stott. Perhaps if I could be allowed access to the house, I am quite willing to personally pick up the items that she requires.'

'Oh, I'm not sure…perhaps I should be there.'

'I don't want to put you to any trouble. With my duties at the surgery, it'll be quite late. Perhaps you could leave out a key?'

'Well…if you're sure, Doctor MacPherson. According to the neighbour, the house could do with a spring clean so please forgive—'

'Absolutely no problem at all.'

'It's awfully kind. Perhaps we can talk again when your colleague has had chance to speak to Edie…or perhaps I might come. She knows me and—'

'At present, that is not medically advisable, Miss Stott. She needs to settle in a little more. We'll sort it, never you fear.'

The conversation ended in agreement. Edie would stay where she was for the foreseeable future and arrangements would be made for further funding to cover the nursing fees. He ascertained where the key would be left, further remonstrations that the length of the working day did not permit a visit at anything other than unsociable hours finally ensuring that he was able to visit the house alone.

James had put down the telephone, linked his hands behind his head, and smiled. He had read once more the letter from the cousin telling the old woman that Denis was safe and how it would be a such a comfort to let him see her and blathering on about not understanding why the nurse would not let him visit.

The couple of weeks waiting for the opportunity to create the chance to come here alone had been frustrating. But the letter revealing that the house was empty had provided the opportunity he sought. Dolores's reluctance to allow relatives to poke their noses where they weren't wanted and her censoring of correspondence had borne fruit, as it so often did.

James bent down staring at the myriad of indentations in the snow in front of the pot and nodded as he realised who had made them. He took off a glove and lifted one edge of the pot, smiling as his fingers felt the cold metallic ridges. The key was under the pot, just where the interfering hag had said it would be. With one more glance behind into the freezing night, he found the lock, turned the key and slipped through the open door. The *thud* as it closed behind him shut out the world. He was left standing in a darkness tempered just a little by the mottled yellow streetlight passing through the glazed semi-circle window at the top of the door.

It was the stench which hit him first; the underlying damp of the cold, empty house mingling with something far more pungent. He blinked as his eyes adjusted to the gloom.

And then froze.

A small, dark shape shot across his foot, fur bristling against the bottom of his trousers. James kicked out and it scuttled into the darkness. Scrambling in his jacket pocket, his trembling hand fished out a box of matches. As the flame fizzed, three pairs of green eyes stared at him. He breathed out. No one had thought to mention them. But it explained the odour.

He turned around slowly, the match held in front of him until he found a light switch. As the hallway was suddenly engulfed with a bright light, three cats shot away. Two more were eyeing him cautiously from the gloom at the top of the stairs to his left. One stood up, arching its back, hissing. He pulled his coat tight, the cold as numbing inside as it was outside, and tried to put the stench of cats' urine from his mind.

The hallway was a square, spacious area and surprisingly empty given what he saw down the corridor. A thick green carpet lay from wall to wall. Against one side was a small table on which stood a lamp. Items of mail were leaning neatly against its base. He picked them up and flicked through them. Nothing was of interest save for the penultimate letter. On the reverse was a command to return the letter to a firm of stockbrokers if undelivered. He nodded, almost imperceptibly, filing away the information, and replaced the letters.

Doors led off to each side. He presumed the kitchen was at the end of the corridor in front of him. Boxes lay against each wall, a multitude of items spilling out. Curious, he picked his way through the narrow gap, pushed open the door and flicked on the light.

Here, the acrid smell was if anything stronger. Any number of cats were milling around empty bowls near a door, which presumably led to a back garden. One bowl was half-filled with water. So, somebody was still coming in to pick up the mail and feed the cats. He picked up two of the bowls and filled them with water before placing them back on the floor.

He cast an expert eye over the kitchen's contents. Against one wall was an oven. He grimaced and put his hand to his throat and thought he was going to gag. Its surface was caked in fat. A frying pan stood on a hob, coated by the same substance. Conversely, a large refrigerator hummed in one corner. Squalor and luxury side by side. Cupboards ran around two walls. Once more he was surprised, this time by finding neatly stacked jadeite dishware on their shelves.

He would not certainly have had the old woman as a follower of fashion. A table in the corner of the room was littered with newspapers, most, James noticed, more than six months old.

But other matters were swimming around his head. Ensuring the house remained in darkness save for the room he was in, he traced his steps back into the hall and wandered into the other rooms on the ground floor, making a mental inventory of what was there and its likely value. Separate dining and living rooms were generously furnished. Brentwood furniture in both rooms again reflected a surprisingly modern taste. Red and white floral patterns covered the sofa and chairs. Similarly decorated drapes hung by the windows. He whistled under his breath on spotting a television set standing in a corner of the living room, its wooden surround matching the rest of the décor. These were not rooms which indicated a need for thrift. His original hunch may have been correct.

But that did not paint the whole picture. On the sofa and chairs, most of the wooden flooring, in fact every surface, lay piles of newspapers and magazines. James made his way around noting that some were a number of years old. 'Invasion Starts, British and Yanks storm into France' was a particular headline which blared out at him. More boxes, again crammed, stood against the walls.

His eyes caught a number of photographs standing on a dresser in the dining room. Family photographs, family pictures. He picked up the nearest. A family sitting on the bench at Llandudno in 1932, a man in a shirt and tie lying back, leaning on his elbow, trousers rolled up to his knees, a youthful Edie sitting up and smiling sweetly, a young boy looking at her – Denis was it? Then another; Great Yarmouth 1946, Edie on her own, hand clasping a walking stick. A third, Great Yarmouth again, 1939. This one was of a husband and wife walking down the promenade, a distance between them, Edie with an arm linked in the crook of the boy's. James pursed his lips, staring at him. He had pictured when talking to that rather sickly woman from the County Welfare Organisation the previous evening that the son was older, in his late forties, perhaps inadequate, pining for dear old mother. He should have checked the age. This boy was no more than twenty. The eyes were staring listlessly at something behind the photographer. He was exactly as she had described: simple. His mother had dressed him in his jacket and cravat as a little girl would dress a doll. The boy, thought James, was a person to whom things happened, not someone who would interfere. Rubbing his chin, he wondered where exactly the boy was staying and, of greater importance, who was looking after him. He put down the photograph, glancing over many others of a similar nature, and reminded himself of the purpose of the visit.

He headed upstairs. More cats skulked stealthily in the gloom above him. The main bedroom was at the back of the house, just as dear old Edie had said. The door gave only slightly as he pushed. Putting his full weight behind the door, he was able to create a gap just large enough to squeeze through. Switching on the main light here was less of a worry; it could not be seen from the street. Whilst he could easily explain his presence, his natural inclination was for privacy. What the light revealed was a complete mess which the clutter downstairs had just hinted at. More boxes, dresses on rails, any number of magazines occupied every bit of available floor space. The only surface not covered was the large bed in the centre of the room. Tousled sheets lay randomly on the bed; it was unlikely that anyone had been in the bedroom since it had been used as such.

His eyes flicked quickly over the scene before settling on the large oak wardrobe in the corner. He nudged various items away with the toe of his foot and pulled open its heavy doors. All manner of clothes, dresses, skirts, cardigans hung neatly before him. A strong smell of lavender swept out, overpowering just for a moment the cats' odour. Holding the clothes to one side, his eyes widened. Her safe was in the corner, attached through the back of the wardrobe to the wall, just as she had said when he'd spoken to her about the need for security. He took from his inside pocket one of the letters which Dolores had secreted from the old woman and on which he had written the code. This was a week ago when the dear old woman's desperation to return home had reached new levels. The dial clicked precisely with each turn and the small but heavy iron door swung smoothly open.

His hand delved in and pulled out the contents. A number of envelopes and packets of various sizes fell to the floor. Having swept away several dusty magazines, he placed them on a bureau opposite the bed. He bit his lip and ran his moist palms down the front of his coat. Fortunately, the envelopes were open, the gum having dried long since and, carefully he drew out the contents. Time stood still. He stopped thinking about the cats. He stopped pondering the hoarding. His fingers flicked nimbly through the documents, now oblivious to the cold.

The first two envelopes contained share certificates; South African gold mining companies. He'd read that gold was the safest of currencies and whilst no expert, he was willing to wager everything he had that these were worth a bit. His heart racing, he gently placed the certificates back in their envelopes.

The next three envelopes nearly brought tears to his eyes as he poured over the title deeds to three properties. He quickly deduced that dear old Edie was the owner of houses in London, Great Yarmouth and Buxton – all mortgage-free given that the deeds were not held within the dusty vaults of any bank.

His hands now trembling, he picked up one of the smaller packages. There were seven in all. The one he selected was lighter but something within moved. He held it to his ear and gently shook it, listening with rapt attention to the delicate tinkling. The smaller packets were securely fastened and he realised that he could leave no sign that the safe had been disturbed or all his plans, all his careful arrangements, may come to nought. But he needed confirmation, he had to have confirmation. He needed to see with his own eyes, feel with his own fingers the icing on this particular cake. He needed to touch the evidence that presented his route out of the squalor of life in post-war Nottingham. One open packet would surely cause little suspicion. And so temptation prevailed.

He tenderly pulled open the flap of the envelope in his hands and lowered the resultant opening against the surface before him. A gentle chinking against the bureau made him catch his breath. Mouthing silently a prayer, telling God that from now on he would direct all his energies towards Him, he lifted the envelope.

James's eyes lit up, his heart hammered against his chest, his mouth went dry and he had to stop himself from shouting out loud. Twelve diamonds lay before him, twinkling in the light. His eyes were drawn straight to two in particular, their pink hue speaking of untold wealth in a way that words never could. He picked up each of the other small packets in turn, gently shook them and listened in each case to the same sweet sound, a chinking like the chiming of a cash till.

He stood up and moved around, stepping between the boxes, circling the room, again and again, his hands behind his head, thinking and thinking and thinking some more. His heart raced, every part of his body tingled with the excitement of what he had discovered. He suddenly stopped, catching his reflection in a body-length mirror in the corner of the room. Wild eyes from a flushed face stared back at him. A vision of life on the Italian Riviera, somewhere he had heard that the war hadn't touched, a life of utter luxury, a life where his will was supreme, all played in his mind. It talked to him, tempted him, told him this could be his.

39

But so near and yet so far. He sank to his knees and buried his head in his hands pushing the vision out of his mind. What use were visions? Dreams were just that: pointless fantasies, the foibles of the weak and feeble. His fingers slowly slid down his face and he looked up. He was met with a stony, calculating stare. The idea, not even that, the inkling which had nudged its way into that thinking when he had first laid eyes on the old woman lying helpless in the bed, now began to crystallise into something with a form, something of substance, something he could mould.

He imagined chess pieces on a board. His opponent was in darkness. The pieces began to take the appearance of the people around him. They stared up at him as he picked them up and dropped them onto squares of his choosing. Suddenly, it was all too easy. He could see the way to win the game. He looked up triumphantly at his opponent. And found himself once again looking into the mirror.

The visions, the dreams, the fantasies suddenly went, as though he had slammed a door on them, to be opened again at the very end, when he had succeeded. Now, all that was left in his head was a black void. A calmness descended, rational clinical thought took over. He slowly stood and looked down at the bureau. What if the boy and his cousin returned? What if they took it all away? No, that wouldn't happen. The boy, he was certain, did not understand the riches that lay here. No other relatives had made any great effort to visit. So long as the old woman didn't return, the contents of the safe would remain where they were. Mind, it wouldn't hurt to alter the code.

James put the diamonds back into their envelope. That envelope was placed at the back of the safe. There was no temptation, none at all, to keep anything. They would be his soon enough. The rest of the packets and envelopes were returned and the iron door was pushed shut.

He then sidled out of the house, put his collar up and scurried away into the black night.

Chapter 4

John scooped up the scraps of paper on the large mahogany desk in the centre of his office and slumped into his leather chair. He switched on the lamps at each side and glanced at the messages, mainly commands to ring various clients, apparently alarmed at the apparent lack of progress in their affairs. Several beige cardboard files were scattered across the desk, their contents spilling out. He stared at them and placed a cold hand on his throbbing forehead, the price of yet another heavy night.

A fire crackled in a hearth to his left. It was hot, too hot. He pulled himself to his feet to take off his overcoat and stared into the mirror on the wall by the coat stand. The face of a boy stared back. He hadn't shaved but no one would notice. His ashen complexion had a sheen of perspiration as his hangover continued to bite. He swallowed, fearful that last night's beer was about to end up on the red and green carpet. Dragging himself back to his desk, he avoided his father's stony stare from the large portrait hanging over the fireplace. Along the wall opposite ran a large bookcase, any number of legal tomes behind the glass doors. The walls and the book shelves were of a dark oak, giving the room and thus John an aura of capability which he readily conceded had not been justified since that night three months ago when James had taken him to the Blue Light Club and John had seen for the first time that there was a life outside studying and then practising law.

He got up and stepped across yet more files lying on the carpet and stood at the window behind his chair. His second-floor room looked down on Nottingham's Market Square. Snow was falling, just as it had for most of the last week. Queues of housewives, heads wrapped in scarves, snaked towards the butchers. Those at the front bunched under the veranda, the sloped plastic roof protection from the snow, the close proximity of the person next to them scant protection from the biting wind. A woman stood by the stone lions in front of the similarly pillared Council House. She wore a dark calf-length red coat, like blood against the lying snow. Her features broke into a broad smile as a man in a trilby nearly slipped as he slid towards her. He steadied himself and kissed her on the cheek. With her arm through his, they moved towards the café, the café where John had first spent time alone with Ava. Even from his room, John could make out through its condensation-covered window the ghostly shapes of people sitting at the tables, waitresses buzzing this way and that. It and others dotted around the square, would be full as shop and office workers took their eleven o' clock break. Most mornings, before that night, he would have been one of them. But it was different now. Now he just hid away.

Memories of that first date slipped into his mind, tormenting him with recollections of the smell of her perfume, her infectious laugh and the feeling of standing ten feet tall as he basked in the glory of the admiring glances in Ava's direction of every other man. That was the night that he realised that he had to be with her and that he could not concentrate on anything other than her. He had pestered her for another date but soon found that his ration was two evenings each week, and one of them was while she was at work in the club giving him only fleeting opportunities to talk to her. His presence in the club was only tolerated on those occasions because he bought more than his fair share of overpriced drinks. But to see her was everything. He had even been prepared to endure the humiliation of sitting alone in that grubby hole while she threw herself at anybody who was prepared to put money in the pockets of the owners. The bitterness ate further into him, consuming him like gangrene, bit by bit.

A booming voice from outside the door to his office – his father laying into the articled clerk – caused John to physically jump away from the window and the winter's scene. Scampering to his desk, nearly going his length as he slipped on one of the folders on the floor, John frantically crammed pieces of paper back into the files on the desk and tried to pile them into something vaguely coherent and organised. His attempt at orderliness was in vain as his father burst through the door. A large man in terms of height and girth, his black suit and black brylcreamed hair, just a touch of grey at the sides, reinforced the impression of dominance. Dark eyes peered out of fleshy cheeks. Folds of wobbling skin fell over his starched white collar. To John, his frame filled the doorway, blocking off his only means of escape.

'And where the blazes were you last night? Your mother was worried sick!'

John said nothing. He thought of his father's voice carrying through the rest of the building, of the typists in the pool below sniggering as they were made party to this latest dressing down. They had been right all along. He was lightweight, too weak to hold down the position of solicitor in his father's firm. And allowing his son into the firm would go down as the only mistake his father had ever been known to make.

'I…err…I stayed with a friend…the roads were a n…nightmare…I err didn't want to disturb—'

'I hope to God you were not with that slut who your damned fool brother knows?'

To hear of her being spoken of, even in such a way, hit him like a slap in the face. It was an acknowledgement that she existed, that she was real and that last night she would have been doing something. Whatever it was, it was with somebody else, not with him. A vision of her in the club, sitting on a stool by the bar, flirting with anyone who walked in, taunted him. It was one of the characters in *Othello* who had uttered the words 'green-eyed monster'. Until now he had not understood their true meaning. Now he certainly did; in fact he was living it. Had he been with her last night, he would have stood up, faced his father, shouted back, telling him and the world that he was a man who had a woman.

Who was he kidding?

'Err…no. I d…don't know who you m…mean.'

'How many more times have I got to say that people such as ourselves do not mix with the likes of her…'

And so it went on; the words flowing around him like the never-ending snow on the dull winter's day. There had been a time, not so long back, when he would have kept his distance from the lower classes, when he and his father would have been as one on such a matter. Things had changed since those simple times. He had always presumed that one day he would marry. He had done nothing to bring such a state to fruition, merely presumed that it would happen, in the same way that he had ended up working in his father's firm. Those vague and distant half plans had been blown away by a wind of change that had taken his breath away, made his eyes water, made him cower lest he be swept off the face of the earth. For the first time, he had found love. And love, like some kind of illness, did not recognise boundaries, striding through man-made obstacles without a backward glance, caring not whether polite society approved, ambivalent to the carnage it left in its wake. And more than that, it was disinterested as to whether it was returned. To him, at this point in time, it was an illness, an illness of the cruellest kind: invisible, hiding all outward signs, but utterly destructive, as disabling as any injury it was possible to suffer.

He imagined his father's face if he gave voice to the idea that this person in the gutter who was not like us, was not one of us, had stolen his heart. 'I…err…I…I'm not c…courting.'

'For God's sake, boy! Will you stop taking me for a fool!'

'I'm not, Father, h…honest I'm not.'

'In this office, you call me "Sir", you blithering idiot! How many more times do you need to be told! In any event, I am not taking valuable time out of my day to discuss the niceties of office titles! Thompson – that's Mr Thompson to you – telephoned me this morning to tell me that you still have to complete on his lease on the shop up the Mansfield Road…'

John sank back once more in his chair as if forced back by the power of the tirade, meekly nodding and agreeing at the right moments and promising that he would work all the hours that God sent to bring everything to order. Finally, his father left, leaving room for Ava to slip back into his mind, as if it was her personal fiefdom. Three weeks one day had passed since that night and the memories once more assumed prominence. It was an act, he felt, that should be marked as a rite of passage. He was now a man. But it didn't seem that way. In fact, she had made him feel more of a boy then he had before. But what would he not give just to hear her voice?

A light tap at the door brought him round. He knew his father had not returned; light taps on the door were not his father's way. 'Come in…oh, morning Shirley, what now?' The secretary's tight smile could not hide the sympathy in her blue eyes. John noticed a slight blush on her face.

'I am sorry to disturb you but James – I'm sorry, I mean your brother – telephoned. He said if you could meet him at twelve at the usual place. He said that you would know what he meant.'

'Thank you, Shirley. That's fine.'

The girl smiled again and bustled out of the room. James – the one invitation he was not likely to decline. He opened the file which happened to be in front of him and forced his eyes to read the two-page letter from the buyer's solicitors. Words such as "retained piece of land" and "restrictive covenant" hovered in front of him but their collective meaning remained elusive. Pushing the file away, he stood up and took his trilby and coat from the stand in the corner of the room and scuttled out of the building before his father was aware of his absence.

Chapter 5

If anything, the snow was heavier. Driven on by a howling wind, it masked the world in a white overcoat, making everything invisible, covering his footprints. He breathed it all in, glad to be out of the claustrophobic office. The slow walk through the back streets began to blow away the hangover. All too soon he was before the camouflaged white walls of the Trip to Jerusalem, said to be Nottingham's oldest hostelry. Hewn in the days of the crusades from the rocks underneath the city's castle, it stood there like an old friend. He pushed open the heavy oak door and stamped his feet.

He was met by a fug of cigarette smoke and a wall of heat, momentarily taking him back to the Blue Light Club. The muted glow from the lamps gave the honey-coloured, uneven walls the appearance of sand. It was lunchtime and busy. Steam rose from discarded coats, pink glowing faces downed their pints of Shipstones. Voices bombarded him from all sides: 'Will it ever stop snowing?' 'Power cuts tonight, duck,' 'Better get some candles.' He levered his way through the crowd towards the bar where he stood, coins in hand, trying to catch the eye of the two women serving.

The elderly one barked orders to her younger companion as they moved rapidly up and down the length of the bar, pulling pints and taking money. It was the younger one who finally glanced in his direction and raised her eyebrows. John opened his mouth, but before he had the chance to say anything, she looked behind him, a smile erupting over her face.

'Now there's a sight for sore eyes.' John immediately recognised the deep voice.

'Long time no see, love,' said the woman behind the bar.

'I'd be in every day if I knew you were here, my dear.'

In the crowded public bar, John was suddenly completely alone. He turned slowly and looked into the familiar face. His brother's deep, brown eyes were laughing at him. Six feet in height and the build of a squaddie, despite avoiding the draft, James cut a presence in the crowd which was simply beyond John. It was always the same when they met; John was the runt in a litter of two.

'Johnny, my boy! Glad you could make it.' James turned back to the woman behind the bar. 'Gladys, my darling. A pint of bitter for me and a half of mild for my little brother here. And I don't suppose you could rustle us up a sandwich? There's a love.'

'Eh, ain't you heard about rationing, cheeky?' Almost imperceptibly, she nodded. 'There's some tables free upstairs if you want somewhere quiet. I'll bring your drinks up, I'm due a break.'

'Thank you, my angel. Come on Johnny my boy, follow me. I've got a little business with which you may be of some assistance.'

John felt a tug on the arm of his coat and they made their way back through the throng onto the narrow and steep stairs that took them up to the second floor. James led them into a snug dominated by a roaring fire, the only furniture being a small wooden table with benches either side. Here, there was no electric light. A candle stood in the middle of the table, its flickering light creating undulating shadows on the shimmering sandstone walls. They sat down, facing each other across the table.

'This'll do nicely. A bit of privacy. Don't want all and sundry knowing our business, do we?'

John looked at his brother, his mood somehow lifting. The light of the fire and the candle created an intimacy, a barrier to the trials, humiliations and problems of the everyday world. Even the rumble of conversation in the bar below had somehow faded and could not intrude. But it wasn't just that. John never ceased to be amazed at his brother's joie de vivre, his ability to brighten up any room. James had the knack of making everybody he encountered feel as though they were the most important person in the world and that's what John felt at that very moment.

Such were the thoughts milling around his head as James chatted amiably of events of the previous few days before starting on a story of a woman who had brought her five-year-old into the surgery that morning together with a stretch of wooden stair rails through which the little blighter had got his head stuck fast. Nifty use of a screwdriver James happened to have with him and reassurance to the little darling's mother that all would be well in a couple of days had dealt with the matter. 'She needed a carpenter, not a doctor,' he said with a laugh.

John felt his melancholy lift further, as if his dark mood was powerless to withstand the shining light that was James. The woman who had served them emerged into the room carrying a tray which she placed by the candle, smiling at James. Was it the light or had she applied fresh lipstick?

'You're lucky. I've found some spam.'

'Thank you, my angel. Keep the change, treat yourself,' said James, pressing coins into her hand. John suddenly felt ridiculously flattered to be seen alone with James. Here, in James's presence, he was a proper person, a man of importance. If it were not the case, why would James be bothering with him? It didn't matter that the woman didn't notice him anymore than it mattered that Mars and Venus weren't aware of each other's existence.

'So, John,' asked James once she had gone, 'how's it been for you this past couple of weeks?'

John easily put to one side the slight he should feel, the fact that there had been no contact from James for God knows how long. He sensed that James was well aware of how things had been recently; the flutter in the typing pool whenever James breezed into the office was a sure indication that he got to know office gossip quicker than John. As John hesitated, he was given a prompt.

'The old man's been on to you again, has he?' John felt his face burning. 'Thought as much,' continued James, laughing as he pulled a pipe and pouch of tobacco out of the side pocket of his tweed jacket. The act of pressing the tobacco into the head of the pipe seemed to take up all of his attention but he continued in the same jocular manner. 'So, what's his problem this time?' James looked up. 'The ravishing Ava by any chance?'

John's heart lurched at the mention of her name and his mouth was dry. He took a sip of his drink. 'No…n…not at all, w…what makes you say that?'

James laughed. 'You look as though you've been caught scrumping apples. I gave her a lift home last night and managed to worm out of her that she'd ended up with you all night after the party. Mind, she was definitely the worse for wear at that particular bash. I've never seen her that bad. So how was she the next morning?'

'Okay I suppose, I—'

James laughed again. 'So you did stay over! Well done old boy! And the old man's upset because you were with someone you can't bring home?' John said nothing, having nothing to say.

'Come on then, tell all.'

John's mind slipped back to his childhood days; a severe father, a distant mother and a brother who veered from abject cruelty to unswerving loyalty. But, it was his brother who could put right the trials and tribulations of an all-male day school with a kind word, his brother who could induce him to reveal his deepest fears and his brother who simply listened. And so John related the story of how he had been smuggled into her bedroom and of how he had ended up in her bed. John's modesty prevented him from relaying further details but there was no need. John had an uncomfortable feeling that James did not need telling.

'So, my little brother's come of age,' said James as John's account came to an end. John gave a weak smile and looked into the fire.

'What's the problem?'

John didn't reply. He felt his brother's intense stare, felt his scrutiny.

'You're smitten, aren't you?'

Again, John said nothing, training his eyes on the fire and blinking as he felt the sting of tears. James leaned back in his chair with his hands behind his head and laughed, the long deep laugh of someone who had found something genuinely funny. 'You and Ava, eh? Who'd have thought? And knowing the young lady as I do, I suppose she's not enamoured by the prospect of a young cub following her around.'

'What do you mean?' John could not keep the anger from his voice.

James leaned forward. He put his pipe on the table, pushed the candle and sandwiches to one side and placed his hands on John's forearms. John looked into his brother's eyes, unable to stop himself. When James spoke, his tone had none of the light heartedness of earlier. 'For once, the old man may be right. Come on Johnny boy, she's not the one. Her type never is.'

'What do you mean?'

'John, she'll always be drawn to chaps with money, like a moth to the light. She's good for a bit of fun, she's one to do your growing up with but that's it. Have that fun and then move on. Good God, you can't settle down with the first one you've been with. You've got your whole life before you.'

When John replied, the words poured out like a breached dam. 'But I like her, I really do. I can make her life better. You ought to see where she's living. It's appalling. I can take her away from all of that. I just don't see why she won't take what I can offer. She's not called me since. And now I'm not sure if she even wants to see me again.'

'Girls like her are not interested in what you can offer, as you put it. She has no interest in the future, just the present and what she can get. They're all the same. Take my word for it.'

'She's not like that! She's different! And why would she ask me back if...' John stopped talking as he suddenly remembered Ava's laugh, her glance in his direction as James bent and whispered into her ear. He wanted to slap his brother. 'It's not like you think.' He blinked back tears again, unable to think of anything better to say.

James laughed again. 'Have it your own way. You'll see I'm right.'

When John spoke, his tone was subdued and measured. 'She is different. She's ambitious. She wants to move on. She isn't what you think.' John took a sip from his glass, grimacing at the reminder of last night's beer. Again, he looked into the fire, this time deep in thought. Finally, he continued. 'The old man's giving me hell over it.'

'He's going to. He sees the future of his beloved firm in the hands of a call girl,' replied James with a smirk.

'She is not a call girl! She only goes to the club to get the money to give her the chance to get away from home.'

'What about the kid? Hasn't she got a brat in tow?'

'You shouldn't speak of the baby like that. And she's a good mother.'

'Well, if that's right, she won't want to leave the child while she wanders off into the sunset with you, will she?'

'I wouldn't want her to. I was quite taken with her. A little girl. She's quite sweet.'

'Good God, there really is no hope.'

John ignored the comment before continuing on a different tack. 'I just wish he'd let me be.'

'Don't worry. Dear old pater, that sweet man, likes you. You're not an embarrassment like me.'

'How can you be an embarrassment? You're qualified. You're a doctor.'

James smiled. 'That may be the case, dear boy, but I'm not part of the firm. Am I? My decision at the tender age of eighteen not to allow myself to be sucked into the law and the whirlpool that is Wilfred Farrelly & Cholmendlay, Solicitors and Commissioners for Oaths is a faux pas for which there is no redemption. Putting me through medical school was his way of preventing complete humiliation.'

John stared at his brother. He had heard the lament before, many times in fact. Now there was an edge to James's voice, the previous bonhomie no more.

'I've often wondered. Does it bother you that you don't get on with him?'

James said nothing for a few seconds before replying, his voice little more than a whisper. 'John, dear boy. I would love to be able to say that it doesn't bother me one fig. But there are times when I stop and think what a mess I am and wonder what it would be like if I'd done what you've done and just followed him into the firm. Anyway, I've made my bed, it's up to me to make my own way. No one will help me.'

Neither said anything for a minute. Then, with his usual lighter tone James continued. 'Anyway, too late for such regrets now.' He took a sandwich and pushed the plate in John's direction. 'There may however be a way that I can help you get back in the good books of the enchanting Ava if that's what you really want.'

'How do you mean?' replied John, leaning forward.

'One of the residents at the home where she's somehow duped them into thinking that she's a qualified nurse wants to alter her will.'

'She's got a job? She's not at the club?'

'Yes, with a little help from MacPherson, but don't get your hopes up – she's still at the club. Dividing up her time so she says.'

John tried to push away the envy that gripped him. James had clearly been in her company, but he may also be a route to her.

'She's looking after an old biddy at a nursing home McPherson covers,' continued James. 'A Mrs Harris. Mrs Edith Harris. This Mrs Harris wants to leave everything she's got to Ava apparently. I would imagine that Ava is the only person who's given the old dear any attention in years. She'll no doubt change her mind in a couple of weeks if she's still around but can you deal with it? It'd get me out of a hole actually. The old girl is a patient and, at the moment, it's all left to me. It's not much but I'd rather not have it. It's all a little bit awkward. I'm going around about seven when I've finished surgery. Are you free to pop along?'

'James, I'm really behind at the moment and I was going to stay behind and try and get caught up—'

'Ava will be there,' interjected James, settling the issue.

'Is that the business you mentioned earlier? I wondered why the sudden wish to see me after three weeks of silence. You could have telephoned me.'

'People to see, dear boy, people to see. Anyway, I thought it would be nice to catch up. See how you are. See what the position was with Ava,' he smiled. 'I was going to recommend somebody else but they can't get anybody there for a couple of weeks and the old thing hasn't got long in my opinion so I thought we could kill two birds, as it were. You know, the old lady gets her affairs sorted and I'm out of an awkward spot.'

'Right, I've really got to get back.' James gave directions as he got to his feet. 'Oh, by the way. Don't tell Ava yet, old boy. Just in case the old dear wants to change her mind. Seven o'clock at the home it is then.'

Of course, he'd be there. He rubbed his chin, wondering if he had time to sneak back home to shave.

Chapter 6

The pebble-dashed house glowed in the yellow pools of light from the streetlamps and the reflection of the lying snow. John stepped out of his car and looked up and down the empty street. A white frost was already beginning to sparkle on the white blanket. The relentless deluge had finally petered out as he had walked slowly back to the office and stars were now twinkling in the bluey-black night sky. He pulled his coat around him as the cold slapped him. There was no sign of James. John reached into the back seat and pulled out his briefcase. Holding it under his arm in the way that young professionals did, he pushed open the wooden gate set in the slightly overgrown hedge and stepped carefully down the unswept path leading to the front door.

John rapped the door with the knuckle of a crooked forefinger, wincing and shaking it as the hardened wood took its toll. He turned around so that he faced the street. A dog could be heard barking in the distance. Other than that, it was quiet, as if the snow was muffling any noise. He looked in his case again, ensuring that his legal pad was there and felt for the pen in the inside pocket of his jacket. Sounds, muffled voices followed by a door shutting, punctured the silence. A man, his bulky silhouette framed in the light from the street, appeared from around the corner of the house.

'This way, duck.' John followed the man's broad back as he lumbered back down a concrete path by the side of the house and then stepped through a door into the light of a kitchen. His eyes quickly flicked over the scene. Ava wasn't there. A sooty heat hit him and he was drawn to a fierce coal fire burning in the grate on the opposite wall. A bright light was given out by one light bulb overhead. There was no light shade. A white enamel sink, full to the brim with unwashed plates, was to the right under a window which presumably looked out over a back yard. Next to the sink was a mangle. An oven stood immediately to John's right. On one of the hobs stood a chip pan with blackened fragments marooned in a white, lard-like substance. John looked away, trying not to think about the sickly smell of fat that hung over the whole room. Cupboards, standing against the walls, ran around the room. A motley collection of crockery and newspapers were strewn untidily over their tops. Bottles of various sizes, possibly medicines, stood tight against the wall. John could see through an open door opposite him into the pantry where a large ham hung from the ceiling. Another door to his left led, John presumed, into the rest of the house. The kitchen walls were a dirty cream at odds with the lemon-coloured linoleum. Footmarks and pieces of mud on the flooring seemed to fit in quite well.

In the centre of the kitchen was a formica-topped table with four chairs. The man, his heavy features accentuated rather than concealed by his dark blue overalls, slumped into one of the chairs. With one hand he picked up the folded copy of the *Nottingham Evening Post* that he had presumably been reading before being dispatched to collect John, and buried himself in the sports pages, his brow furrowed. With the other he idly picked up a lit cigarette, resting on the edge of a metal ashtray next to a mug, between two stubby nicotine-stained fingers and took a drag. Dirt was ingrained into his creases in the skin around in the palms of his hands. John's eyes settled momentarily on the man's bitten nails and red raw skin at the tips of his fingers before moving on. The sleeves of the overalls were rolled up at the elbows, blue tattoos dominating thick hairy forearms. Grey thinning hair was swept off his forehead. His ruddy forehead and bulbous nose seemed to shine in the light. A pencil was perched between his left ear and the grey unkempt hair at the side of his head.

A whimper from below the table took John's attention. In the shadows, he saw a dog, a thin mongrel, shifting its position at the slippered feet of a woman sitting at the table. Her pale, thin face seemed to him to portray misery. Tired, watery eyes stared listlessly at something above the cooker. Her hands were linked around a steaming mug. A cigarette was held in two fingers, a long column of ash hanging precariously over a second metal ashtray. She wore a blue tunic with a watch clipped to a lapel. The heads of three pens poked out of her breast pocket. Presumably, thought John, the nurse.

'I've...err...come to see one of your residents about changing her will. I believe I'm expected.' It broke the silence.

The woman looked at him, taking a drag of the cigarette before flicking the ash into the ashtray. 'That'll be Edie you need to see.'

'She's spoken to you about it, has she?'

'She's the only one we got, duck.' The man spoke without lifting his eyes from the paper.

Suddenly, John felt the chill of the evening behind him as the door opened.

'Evening, Dolores, my dear. Ernie.' The cheery voice chiming around the room belonged to James. He took off his trilby and gloves, unwrapped his scarf and sat down, placing them on the table. 'It's a cold one,' he said, not taking off his overcoat. 'Johnny, my boy, so glad you could come,' he added, nodding in his direction.

'Evening, Doctor. Cup of tea? There's one in the pot.' James's presence seemed to have breathed life into the woman. She got up without waiting for an answer and brought over the teapot, clothed in a woollen caddy, a cup and saucer.

'Thank you. And I've got something to warm us up.' James took a small bottle with amber liquid from inside his coat. 'Ernie?'

For the first time, the man showed an interest in something other than the newspaper. 'Aye. Don't mind if I do.'

The woman poured tea into the cup and topped up the mugs. 'Does he…?'

'I think he's alright, aren't you, Johnny boy?'

John would actually have said yes. He had spent the whole afternoon cooped up in his office. No secretary came in, presumably the embarrassment of his morning dressing down had seen to that, and thus he had not been part of the three o'clock tea run. Fear of encountering his father had discouraged him from venturing into the kitchen and sorting himself out – a habit he had formed when articled to his father, never having had the confidence to ask anyone to make him a warm drink.

James added the whisky to the tea poured by the woman. 'Right then,' he said, 'how's the old girl been today?'

It was the woman who replied. 'She's been sleeping most of the day. I thought you should see her though, see what's happening. Her breathing's not been good.'

'I'll give her a sedative before I leave. You've still got…?'

The woman nodded quickly. James swallowed the tea in one. 'Is she still downstairs?'

'Yes. She's lost some weight but she's still too heavy to move so I've kept her in the bed in the living room. The girl's feeding her at the moment.'

John's heart leapt at the reference to Ava. He blushed as James, smirking, glanced at him. James made no attempt to introduce John as he chatted amiably to the man and the woman. The man looked up from his newspaper and the women seemed somehow to become younger. It was the way that James had. Not for the first time, John wondered at how they could have been born of the same parents at the same time. No two brothers could ever have been so unalike.

'Right, then.' James's voice interrupted John's thoughts, 'Let's go and see the old girl, shall we? We cannot waste John's valuable time.' James smiled at his brother. That his time was considered valuable was taken by John as a compliment. Yet again, it had taken just one comment and John was as captivated as the rest.

James got up and strode through the door with the woman. John followed. They trailed through a corridor and into a hallway before entering a room through a door to the right. It was only lit by the glowing embers of a fire in the hearth and by two candles.

John was drawn to her like an alcoholic to liquor. Sitting by the side of the one occupied bed was Ava. He swallowed, trying not to stare but not able to stop himself. It had been three weeks one day, a lifetime, since he had seen her. A bowl of what appeared to be some kind of soup was perched on the side of the bed. He watched her slim, uncovered arms as she rhythmically took the spoon from the bowl and delicately placed it against the old woman's mouth and then brought it back again before repeating the action. As if drawn by the heat of his passion, she looked up. And smiled in the direction of James.

'Ava, you really are a gift from the Lord.'

'Why, thank you, Doctor.' Even in the semi-darkness, John fancied that the hint of a blush lit up the flawless white skin of her face.

'So, how do you think our patient is getting on?'

Now, it was unmistakable; she did blush. The look she gave James was one of pride and he had done it again. A few words and she was his, just like everyone else. Now, and in front of the woman she worked for, he had asked her opinion on medical matters. With just one question he had her unquestioning loyalty. Perhaps he had it already. Perhaps he was just cementing that devotion. John wondered again why James needed it. The answer was probably that he didn't. This was just his way, the way he dealt with everybody. But Ava's look was more than gratitude for showing her value to her employer. Her eyes had stayed on James just a little too long. And just for a moment, John wanted to reach up and put his hands around his brother's throat and squeeze.

Eventually, and seemingly reluctantly, she resumed the process of feeding the old woman. The three of them stood in silence watching.

'I think she's finished.' Ava looked at James and then the nurse. James walked over and laid his hand on that of the woman.

'Edie.' His voice was a little louder than usual, thought John. 'Can you hear me, my dear?'

She turned her head slightly and her lips formed a smile as milky eyes found James. She was in a cream night dress. With her white hair, she seemed lost as her head sank into the pillow. Cheekbones pushed against tissue-like skin, its grey deathly sheen shimmering in the glow of the fire. Pale blue eyes looked out of deep hollows. The thin face did not suit her. This was someone who had recently lost a lot of weight. He wondered at her illness but didn't ask, not in front of her. A rasping sound accompanied her breathing as if the effort was too much. John felt that for the first time in his life he was confronting death.

The woman slowly drew her other hand from underneath the bed clothes and took James's hand in her knobbly, swollen fingers.

'Oh Doctor…thank you for coming. I have missed you. I…really don't like the other one as much. He smells you know. He smells of liquor.' Her voice croaked as if the words had to battle to get out. John was struck by the fact that her voice was different to the norm. Perhaps it was the rasping sound. It then occurred to him that, even allowing for her difficulties in speaking, it was accentless. The Nottingham inflection, the sound which pitched the city in the north rather than the south, was not there. This was what his mother would have called 'a person of breeding'.

'I'm here now, Edie. How are you?'

'I do feel rather…rather odd to be honest, Doctor.'

James leaned closer. 'Are you in pain, Edie?'

She closed her eyes, as if collecting her thoughts. 'I don't really feel anything, Doctor. I feel like I'm floating. I am tired. I… I do need to go to sleep. But I'm so pleased to see you. If only I wasn't so tired…'

Ava picked up the dish and looked at James.

'Edie!' he shouted but it seemed to have little effect. Despite James's efforts, she was drifting off to sleep. 'I've brought someone to see you. It's about your will. You know you wanted to change it…'

She seemed to slumber as if the subject held little interest. Ava gazed at the old woman, touching her brow with her handkerchief, and then stared at James. The old woman stirred, fighting to keep open her eyes.

'Edie!' James put his hand on her bony shoulder and gently shook her. 'Edie. This gentleman here has come to alter your will. Like we said. That's right isn't it?'

She just stared through half-closed eyes at the ceiling. James turned to his brother. 'Come on let's go into the kitchen so you can write it out.'

'James! I cannot draft a will on the basis of what I've heard. I've no instructions. And anyway, I can't simply "write it out" as you say. You can see that, surely?'

James turned towards Ava, gesturing at the bowl. 'You say she's finished?'

'Yes. I think so.' She gently touched the woman's lips with a tissue from her pocket.

'You and Nurse Dolores wait in the kitchen, my dear. I wish to speak to my brother.' Ava flashed him another smile and left the room with the nurse. John's eyes followed Ava. He swallowed; she had not acknowledged him, not the once.

As the door gently closed, James pulled John over to the window. 'Look, this woman is dying,' he whispered, 'you can see that for yourself.' They both looked in the direction of the woman lying prone on the bed. The only sound was her breathing. Her eyes were closed and her mouth hung open. With her white night dress, John had the momentary impression that he was looking at a shroud.

'James. I have no idea who she wants her estate to go to—'

'Look John, she made a will without my knowledge leaving everything to me. I don't like it, it's not professional. I don't think it's much anyway. You saw how Ava was with her. You can see why she would want to leave something to her if she was able to make a proper decision. She's the only person who has showed her any kindness.'

'What about relatives?'

'If they're that bothered, what's poor Edie doing here?'

'I cannot proceed on that basis. Who are her relatives?'

'I'm pretty sure that there aren't any. She was brought here a couple of months ago after arrangements were made by the local nursing association who, to my knowledge, only get involved when there's no one else to help.'

John felt his brother's hands on his shoulders. Words drifted into his head, words beseeching him to do the right thing, the right thing by a vulnerable old lady who simply would wish to show

58

appreciation for the care bestowed upon her, the right thing for an old lady who did not have the support of a husband. And the words ended by telling him that Ava would be so grateful to the professional man who had made it all happen.

'She seemed to like you. Why does she not want you to inherit?'

'John, my boy. Who can say? But I'm not the one who does the feeding, the cleaning, the wiping. I'm not the one who has the time to listen to her memories. No, it's Ava who should get what she's got to leave.'

'What's the estate worth?'

'There's a bit there. About £100 in her cashbook. Some of that will go in nursing fees but there will be a tidy sum left for Ava. Sadly, the old dear hasn't got long.'

'Property?'

'I don't think so.'

'Can't we wait until she's a little more alert?'

'No time, I'm afraid…look at her – you can see the old dear's not got long. It's my opinion that she may not even last the night.'

'Just leave her will as it is and you are free to do as you wish with the money.'

'John, how many times? It would be a little embarrassing. Well, more than a little. Look, just draft something leaving everything to Ava. Edie would like something in saying that the legacy is in return for Ava looking after her for the rest of her days, however long that should be. It may be safer to put something in saying she doesn't want any relatives to benefit. When all's said and done, no one has bothered to come and see her while she's been here. You never know who will come crawling out of the woodwork once she's gone. If it makes you happy, have the estate to me should the gift to Ava fail in any way. That would cover all bases, would it not?'

John said nothing.

'One other thing, Johnny boy, the old girl wants to be cremated. Oh, and put in a clause giving £10 to old MacPherson. He's been good to her. Actually, he's seen far more of dear old Edie than I have. So how about you draw it up exactly as I've said and I meet you down here same time tomorrow to get it all sorted?'

'I thought you said she may not last the night.'

'We'll just have to put our faith in God.'

Chapter 7

Only the calls that simply could not be ignored had been taken. The rest were left unanswered as John had wrestled with his conscience. Veering from refusing to have anything to do with it to acknowledging that James was doing the right thing, John had spent the day pacing his office. A couple of telephone calls from James during the day enquiring as to progress, stressing the need for urgency and a newly drafted will by that evening, had simply added to his inertia.

It was late in the afternoon when Shirley tapped twice on his door. 'Your brother telephoned and asked me if I had typed the will. He said that he saw you last night and that it was something you said you would do.'

'Oh, right. It's err…nearly done,' he replied, coming away from his window to find her watching him.

'Why don't I stay late? Your brother said it was really important. He said she hasn't got long. I've not got anything on this evening.'

John slumped in his chair. 'Would you mind?' He looked up at her. 'It is next on my list, honest. I'll bring it through. And…err…thanks.'

*

Once more he found himself trailing the broad back of the nurse's husband as he trudged down the side of the house. 'It's a cold one,' said John, banging his gloved hands together, stepping into the kitchen to be met by the unsmiling stare of the beady-eyed nurse. She put down a book and drew on her cigarette as if contemplating him.

'Oh, you're reading the latest Poirot. I think *The Hollow* is one of her best yet.'

'It's alright if you like that type of thing. Old Miss Briscoe brought it in. She never did find out who'd done it.' She cackled, a high-pitched shriek which bounced off the walls of the kitchen. With a wave of her hand, she indicated John should go straight through and picked up the book, still sniggering.

His eyes shot straight to the empty chair next to her bed. He bit his lip and looked away.

'She's starting later tonight, Johnny boy. Anyway, you're here. Thank you for getting it done so quickly.' The voice came from the back of the room. James emerged from the shadows. 'Let me have a look.'

John reached into his case and pulled out the newly created document. James took it and raked his eyes across each line devouring every word, as though checking the accuracy of a prescription. To John, this desire to help others was something he had never seen before. Usually, it was only James's suave affability which allowed him to get away with an apparent total disregard for the feelings of anybody else. How many times had John seen his brother trample over other people, get his own way, and then be thanked as a smile and fitting words made everything alright?

Yet this was different. James seemed to be going to extraordinary lengths to ensure that a penniless mother got her due and that a vulnerable dying woman's meagre estate went in the way she would want if she was able to express herself. Even kindly Doctor MacPherson, with all of his problems, had not been left out. The clause to the effect that the old woman's estate should go to James if the gift to Ava failed for any reason was something he had pondered without coming to an answer. Should he ask his brother? The answer was 'no'. He wouldn't have asked his brother for an explanation any more than he would have queried a clause his father had inserted in a lease. He had once heard his mother describe him as one of life's followers, never the boss. He had always presumed it to be true. That James was mentioned in the will was in fact of no consequence – this old woman would be dead before the week was out according to James. Not that a doctor was needed to see that she was on her way out. There was no way in which Ava would not get the estate, such as it was, after the costs of the funeral, the old Doctor's small legacy and his father's fees had been paid. In fact, she may not get much at all.

'I'll just go and fetch them and we'll get on, shall we?' John looked up as James headed out of the room.

The room was in silence save for the woman's laboured breathing as James closed the door behind him. Mrs Harris's eyelids were shut tight, as if glued. Perhaps he could just try and check, just make sure that she was happy with the arrangements. He stepped slowly towards the bed. 'Mrs Harris,' he whispered. Confirmation of her instructions would settle once and for all the misgivings which lurked in the back of his mind. It was all well and good for James to ignore protocol, he hadn't been trained in the law as had John and—

She coughed. Suddenly. A deep retching that seemed to make her whole body convulse. Mucus flowed from her nostrils and sputum from her mouth dribbled down her chin. He stared, open-mouthed, his mind thrashing about, trying to think of the right thing to do. In doing so, he did nothing. It was only then that it occurred to him where he was and the people who were in the next room. The nurse. Wasn't this the type of thing she dealt with?

He backed away, not taking his eyes off the old woman. The worst of the hacking had subsided and she now lay there quietly, save for the tortured breathing which escaped her lips. He stopped, still staring at her. If she died now, there would be nothing to fret over. Her original will would stand and James would be at liberty to dispose of the estate in any way he saw fit. But then there would be the everlasting guilt, the nagging doubt that he had not done all he could for a dying client.

He slipped through the door and headed towards the kitchen. The door in front of him was closed. He was just about to push through when he heard voices.

'We've been through this! What is your problem!' His brother's hissed whisper was the nearest thing to a loss of temper on the part of James that John could recall since they were at school. 'I've told you why you have to sign.'

'I don't trust you, that's my problem,' said the nurse, seemingly not concerned who might hear.

'Damn you.' Have you not listened to anything I've said?'

'Oi, mind your manners,' said the man who John presumed to be her husband.

A momentary hush descended, the silence booming around the corridor where John stood. His face burned as he grasped that the snatch of conversation was one which was not for his ears. He stood still, his beating heart pounding, not daring to move for fear that the touch of his foot against the hard floor would reveal his presence.

'I'm uneasy about this. You're going too far.' It was the nurse who had spoken, her voice now hushed. Chairs scraped against the kitchen floor. John found his legs and scurried back. He placed himself by the window, affecting an air of nonchalance as he looked out into the street. He mopped his brow and stood absolutely still.

James, smiling, entered the room, alone, and handed him the will. 'All done.'

'What?' John glanced at the will. 'She's not signed it,' he said looking at the letters 'EH' scrawled under the woman's name. He stared at James, open-mouthed.

'Yes, she has! There.' James prodded the mark.

'James, you cannot do it like this. The testator – that is this poor woman lying here – has to sign the will in the presence of two witnesses who cannot benefit under the will.'

'John. Look at her. Medically, poor old Edie is not capable of actually holding a pen. But this is what she wants and it has been witnessed. Look.'

John saw the names of the nurse and her husband printed with scrawls underneath. 'They have to actually witness Mrs Harris sign the will. James this is not....'

John felt his brother's hands on his shoulders. 'John. This is what poor Edie wants. This is the only way she can get what she wants. Don't you think that your profession should recognise when it's right to turn a blind eye to a minor procedural irregularity in order to achieve justice. Isn't that what it's all about?'

'Yes, but—'

'By doing so Edie's able to mark the help she's been given by Ava. And I will make sure that Ava knows what you've done for Edie. They are quite close as you saw. And you may care to take on board the fact that Ava has lost her job at the club. I think she could do with the money, don't you?'

'Why? What's happened?'

'I don't know but I do wonder if she's sick of the work. Maybe you're making her think,' said James smiling.

John looked at James, bit his lip and said nothing.

'Right then, Johnny my boy, that's settled then. You keep the will somewhere safe. For both Edie and Ava.'

John put the will into his case and left, trying to convince himself that his brother was right. A settled mind was something which eluded him as he drove away. Even allowing himself the luxury of dreaming about Ava could not dispel his misgivings.

It was lying awake in bed that night, having sidled in and managed to avoid his father, that he finally decided what he would do. He had no choice. He had to do something. The proper course of action was to go and see Mrs Harris. There must be a time when she was lucid enough to be able to confirm her wishes. And if she did, he would be prepared to overlook any procedural irregularities. He would go back the very next evening. He would put a note addressed to the nurse through the door on his way into the office first thing advising of his intentions. Seven-thirty – his father would have left the office by then. Threats to report the nurse to whoever these things should be reported to would ensure he was admitted and that James was not told what he was doing. What he would do if the old woman did not give the answer he wanted was a question he would try to answer only if the need arose.

John then slipped into a light, fitful sleep.

Chapter 8

Seven o'clock.

A mist had descended. Not a pea souper but it would do. It would do very nicely in fact. Its tentacles swirled around him, caressing his face, smothering him as if in a loving embrace, cooling his fervour. Dulled, smudged blobs of orange light from the street lamps floated at intervals in the gloom. He turned up the collar to his overcoat and placed himself in the darkness between them. And watched. Watched and waited.

Ten past seven.

From the opposite side of the road he could make out Ava through the window, sitting by the bed, bending over her hands – maybe painting her nails? Apparently oblivious to her patient. He ached for a cigarette, needing to savour the soothing and familiar tang. He must refrain of course. Until later. When it was over. And when it was completely over, he could do as he wished. For now, he should just watch. Watch and wait.

Quarter past seven. The mist protected him, made him invisible. It was his friend. He craved the isolation it provided. He thought of their fifth birthday, the first time his father picked him up by the neck and threw him into the small cupboard under the stairs, into the perfect blackness. He remembered it all so perfectly, even the petty disobedience that brought down his father's wrath; that horrendous, stodgy birthday cake which made him gag and which he refused to eat. He recalled his small fists pummelling away, sinking into his father's fat, bloated stomach, his feet swinging aimlessly in the air as he was swept out of the room. 'Let him eat it! Let his belly explode! Let him die! And then it'll be just me!' His railing went unnoticed. It always did. He didn't belong there, he didn't belong with them. It was John who belonged. Not him. But in the darkness, it was so different. How he delighted as his fingers explored the small cavity, sought out the extremities of his kingdom where he was free to think his own special thoughts. It was his mother who had eventually weakened. Stupid bitch. She had let him out after his father had scuttled off to his study, no doubt feeling he had been there long enough.

Twenty past seven.

Not long now. She had picked up a magazine. How lucky she was to be the recipient of all that money. He stopped himself from laughing. Invisible people did not laugh. He would just watch. Watch and wait.

The opening under the stairs had soon become more than a place of punishment; it had become his refuge. He thought of the kitten. How could he ever forget? John's reward for examination success one year later had been a scraggy little thing that ran up your leg and had a ridiculous fascination with their mother's ball of wool. John had been in tears on one occasion when it went missing. Everyone in the house from his father down to the lowest maid had had to drop everything and look for the thing. That it was found in the cupboard under the stairs was something which made him yearn to rip it apart with his bare hands, limb by limb and cauterise its sickly green eyes with the red-hot poker Mother used to toast crumpets on a gloomy Sunday afternoon in the winter.

The cat had entered his space, his world. And if it entered his world, it played by his rules. Later, he had enticed it into the bathroom and seized it by the neck before plunging it in a sink full of water. What is so difficult to understand about that? It was at that moment that he finally understood the exquisite pleasure which death gave him. That he had left its body, limp now and like a rag doll, in his own private space under the stairs was an irony that provided an additional joy. It had been three full days before it had been found, three endless days in which everyone seemed to have lost their wits. Wasn't it obvious? Where else was it likely to be? It was his father who found it. The stench had finally settled the issue. His father's stare as he brought out the rancid ball of fur was something he would take with him to his grave. Wide-eyed anger, most certainly, but there was more. It was at that moment that he saw something in his father that his young mind could not understand. It was only as he began to get experience that he recognised the expression on his father's face. Pure fear. It was when he reached into James's world to bring out the slaughtered animal that his father realised just what he had spawned.

Twenty-eight minutes past seven.

There was Nurse Dolores, pulling shut the curtains, just as she had said she would. He picked up his medical bag, moved silently and serenely out of the shadows and glided across the snow-covered road and down the path. He stopped at the door, silent and quite still. In the stillness he could hear Dolores's shrill tone saying that she had a brew on and that Ava could leave her patient for a few minutes. Ava's clicking heels faded as they entered the kitchen. James pushed open the unlocked door and stood in the hall. Muffled voices could be heard from the kitchen mingling with strains of music which floated through the closed door. What an angel Dolores really was; she had thought of everything, absolutely everything.

Leaving the front door slightly ajar, he slid into the building and then the room. The only lighting was the lamp by the bed and the embers of the fire. But the darkness held little fear for him; he was quite able to work in the dark. He looked down at the prone body and listened.

There had been an unwanted complication that morning; Ava had managed to attract two more patients. Two more who would no doubt have their pointless existence soon brought to their inevitable end.

'She can't afford to turn them away, duck,' had been Ernie's take on the development.

'That's right. Business is business,' Dolores had agreed.

In all fairness, and he was a fair man, the £100 they would receive, although a tidy sum, would still leave them wiping up vomit when he was far away. The fact that the two new residents were safely in the other room was the compromise they had quickly reached. And so James was free to carry out his work without interruption.

He looked at dear old Edie from the end of the bed, her features in shadow. When had animals not been enough? When had it come to pass that only human life was sufficient? He could not remember. And if truth be told, he could not care less. It really ought to be tonight, had to be tonight. There was just a hint of regret that he could not take his time as he brought the prepared syringe from his bag. It was such a waste. He should have taken his time, savoured the experience and locked it into his memory. But other opportunities would arise and he couldn't linger. And so he moved forward.

*

Even wearing his coat and hat, the cold was just beginning to nip. He had arrived five minutes ago and had switched off the engine. Petrol rationing had seen to that. The deepening mist nudged the windows of his car. Was he the only person left? Had the war killed off everybody else? It really ought to have done. Who else was there for him?

He had parked down the road – no need to make it too obvious. From there, he could just make out the pebble dashing, telling him he was looking at the right house. His breath misted up the window. He had once been told it was best not to wipe the window but that didn't matter now. One last drag on his cigarette and he pulled on his gloves. A quick look at his wristwatch told him it was seven-thirty. Ava would have given the old woman her supper a while back and this was the time he was most likely to find her awake. What he was going to tell Ava was something he hadn't worked out. But when she knew what the situation was, she would see that it was for the best. He would compensate her himself if she lost the legacy.

He reached for the door handle and suddenly stopped, quite still. Screwing up his eyes, stretching his vision, he frantically ran his gloved hand over the window and leaned forward. It was James. Even in the mist he would recognise the languid gait, gliding across the road. It suddenly occurred to John that he might be too late. Had she got worse? No – old MacPherson was her doctor and James had always been particular about ensuring that he did not treat Doctor MacPherson's patients. Had James somehow found out what John had planned? He had expressly told the nurse that no mention must be made of his visit to another person. It was just a coincidence. Maybe MacPherson had asked him to help out. MacPherson certainly had his problems so that would be no great surprise. That must be it. But that didn't deal with the immediate problem. John certainly couldn't go marching in now. There was no way he would be able to bluff his way through James.

And would he want to? Why could he not be like James and just accept that what he was doing was for the best? He should trust his brother. When had James ever been anything other than a loving brother?

That first day at the High School slunk into his mind, as it so often did. The ill-fitting uniform had swamped him. At first break he had hung back in the shadows, desperate to avoid the ritual when the fags were thrown down the steep grassy bank which sided onto one of the rugby pitches. The shame of returning home and having to explain to Mother that he had muddied his brand-new attire and the anguish he would feel at the disappointment etched on her face had nagged away for weeks.

Tears had welled in his eyes as hands grabbed at his arms and shoulders and yanked him through the door leading to the school fields and to the bank.

'He's crying! He's in tears!'

Alerted to his disgrace, like sharks sensing blood, the numbers in the rampaging gang grew. The wind flew through his hair as he was carried head high to the edge of the muddy precipice. Shouts and shrieks sliced through him. Suddenly, there was silence. Total silence.

'Put him down.' James had only whispered the words. But that had been sufficient. John felt the springy grass between his feet. He walked slowly away, backwards, unable to take his eyes from the stand-off between a group of youths older than James but no bigger.

'Whose idea?' The group inched back. One of the them was thrust forward and found himself face to face with James.

'You?'

The other youth glanced behind, wide-eyed, tears rolling down his cheeks.

'Y…yes.'

James punched him in the mouth knocking him to the floor. He then bent over. As the other youth tried to scramble to his feet, James picked him up by his neck and braces and held him high above his head before hurling him down the bank. He strode down the slope, his confident steps reaching the bottom just as the youth scrambled to his feet. One punch to the side of his head was all it took to put him back onto the ground, the perfect place to receive a kick in the mouth. The youth's head flirted back, as if on elastic. Even from the top of the bank, white teeth could be seen shooting out of his mouth. Blood from the mouth rolled down his chin like red lava. James then did it again. And again. And again.

The remaining youths above the spectacle cowered, as if not able to take their eyes away but not daring to look. John had eyes only for his brother. It was not the violence that held his stare. It was his brother's face. From the intense, dark hatred in his eyes, to the twisted smile on his face, in the viciousness of the violence, John saw James's malevolent hatred for his victim. And the hatred was because of James's love for him. John may be nothing, unwanted by his parents, laughed at by the servants but he had his brother. And while he had his brother, he would never be alone.

A movement from the house brought John back to the present. He wiped his eyes and watched his brother's slow walk down the road and away from the house. How could he doubt the one person to love him? How could he have ever thought it was necessary to want corroboration of his brother's intentions? He would die rather than James realise that he had been anywhere near Sherwood Avenue tonight.

He turned the car around and drove away in the direction of home.

Chapter 9

The wind whipped around the Market Square as John stepped through the front door. Flakes of snow were flung around, white against the brooding grey sky. He held down his hat and kicked out as the front page of a newspaper wrapped itself around his leg, cursing the infernal and never-ending winter.

'Johnny boy. So kind of you to spare me the time.'

John turned around and saw James standing by the dustbins, in the jitty which ran along the side of the office. 'What's so urgent that we couldn't have met somewhere?' John glanced anxiously at his brother, fearful just for a moment that James had seen him on Sherwood Avenue the previous evening.

'Just a moment,' said James, walking ahead. John followed him across the square and up a narrow thoroughfare by Pearson Bros. James stopped outside a window a few paces up the slabbed alleyway. He bent and studied the multitude of glass jars. Handwritten labels such as Dobsons Aniseed Humbugs, Sugared Almonds, Sarasparillla Tablets, Coconut Mushrooms and hundreds of others leapt out. James took John's arm and pushed his way through a white door into the shop. Two women, both in their forties and with coiffured hair, stood behind a glass counter. Glass jars, none more than half full and some nearly empty, filled the shelves behind them. A set of scales stood on one side of the glass counter, a cash till the other.

'Hello dearie,' said one of the women, leaning over the counter.

'Ladies,' replied James. 'I'm looking for something special and I couldn't think of anywhere better to come.'

The woman draped over the counter stared at James. John stayed at the back of the shop, his hands in his coat pocket, looking at the ground.

'My brother here needs something for a special lady.' John looked up as he heard James's words. 'My dears, I wondered if you might help him out?'

'I bet I could do something for you, duck,' said the woman at the counter, patting her hair, not taking her eyes off James.

'I'm sure we can find something,' said the other, rolling her eyes and turning round to the shelves. She reached up and picked up a green and black box with the words 'Whitakers Mint Creams' emblazoned on the lid. She put them down on the counter in front of James.

'Johnny boy. How about these?'

'Um… I don't know…what…'

'We'll take them,' said James, smiling at the first woman

'That'll be half a shilling,' said the second woman.

James took his wallet from the inside pocket of his jacket and fished out some coins.

'With your ration card, obviously,' she continued.

'Of course,' he said laughing.

Out of the shop, James pushed the wrapped box into John's hands.

'Are these for A…Ava? Do you think—'

'Not for Ava, you dolt. Give them to Shirley. You can tell her that they're thanks for typing the will. And you could do with a girl – the right type of girl.' James laughed. John said nothing.

'Anyway,' continued James, 'I wanted a quick word.' They stopped in the street and as James spoke, John simply stared, oblivious to cars churning out their smoke, people walking this way and that, the biting cold.

'It was only a matter of time. I'm just relieved we'd got the will prepared,' said James.

'Last night, you say?'

'Well, this morning. MacPherson was called by Nurse Dolores before first light…. you look as though you've seen a ghost.'

'How did you get to know?'

'MacPherson told me when I got in.'

'Err…the will does reflect what she w…wanted, doesn't it?'

'Stop worrying, dear boy. There is nothing to stew about, I assure you. Come on, let's get out of the cold and have a coffee in here.'

Misted windows and cigarette smoke contributed to the clamminess which hit them as soon as they entered. James immediately headed for a free table in the corner. 'This way,' he called as John headed towards the counter. 'I'm sure they'll serve us at the table,' he added as they sat down.

Both placed hats and scarves on the table. James turned and appeared almost magically to catch the eye of a blonde-haired girl serving at the counter.

'Couple of coffees, there's a love,' his voice seemed to carry over the hum of chatter in the cafeteria.

She smiled at him, through the throng. 'Coming up,' she mouthed. After a minute, she pushed her way through those queuing, seemingly oblivious to the shouts of protest and placed two steaming cups in front of them.

'Ladies and gentlemen.' James stood up and gave a little bow to the crowd near the counter. He gestured towards a seated John with the palms of both hands. 'My solicitor here has only limited time to help with a legal matter of the upmost complexity. Please, can you forgive my pushing in?'

'Of course we can, duck,' chorused a number of female voices. The men just stared, saying nothing and James turned back to an open-mouthed John.

'You need to speak to MacPherson.'

'W…why?' replied John.

'Well, firstly, he's an executor and presumably something has to be done so that he can distribute the estate.'

'Oh, yes, of course. I n…need to sort out the grant of p…probate.'

'And secondly, you'll recall that Edie wants…wanted to be cremated.'

'So w…what?'

'Well, that means that a second doctor needs to examine the body to certify the cause of death. Both the other doctor and old MacPherson have to sign the cremation form. Nothing to worry about. No relatives to inform so everything's nice and straightforward. MacPherson put "cerebral haemorrhage, due to myocardial degeneration" on the death certificate – stroke to you and me. But it would be as well that you remind him of the legal position. As the other executor, it perhaps is one of your duties.'

'James, c…can I ask you s…something?'

'What?'

John looked at his brother's smiling face and pictured again him walking across Sherwood Avenue. What was so wrong with a doctor going to a nursing home?

'Nothing.'

*

73

The ringing of the telephone broke the silence in John's office. The clatter of the typing from down the corridor had long since ceased. He had turned away from his desk and had been staring through the window at the half moon in the frosty, but now clear sky.

'Just thought I'd bring you up to speed, Johnny boy.'

'How did you know I'd still be here? Sometimes, I w…wish I hadn't given you my private number. I'm really behind and the old man will—'

'Ernie got the cremation form from the undertakers at MacPherson's request following your call. Wilson has seen Edie and both he and MacPherson have signed it.'

'Who's W…Wilson?'

'Doctor Wilson is the second doctor I asked to view the body and sign the cremation form.'

'What happens now?'

'I need you to go to the home and drop off a letter confirming that Edie's will says she wanted to be cremated. Nurse Dolores will arrange for it to be taken to the crematorium referee first thing in the morning along with the form and the death certificate so we can get it sorted.'

'James. I really don't have time. If the old man f…finds out I'm having more time off, he'll skin me alive.'

'Well, why don't you get it done now? Get it out of the way. You could do with a break and Ava will be there.'

John sighed and put the receiver back in is cradle. He slammed shut the file he had been working on and put it back in the cabinet resolving to complete the assignment the following morning. He then took a sheet of letterheaded paper from his drawer and started writing.

*

'The nurse said I'd f…find you here.'

'Oh, it's you. Yes, we've two new ones so plenty to do. Just as well since I lost my job at the club.'

'I was sorry to hear about that.'

She looked at him. His eyes were held by the vision in front of him. Time had made no difference.

'No, you weren't.'

The two new ones, as she called them, were both dozing, one breathing heavily, the other snoring. She sat at a chair between the

74

beds and picked up a magazine. 'Anyway, I now have certain expectations. I've got some money coming my way. Dr MacPherson says it's a tidy sum so...' She looked back down at the magazine and at the advertisement for a new house with an inside toilet.

'Ava, how m...much is it that you think you will get?'

'Dr MacPherson didn't know.' She looked up. 'Don't look at me like that, I've worked hard for this. I deserve this chance.'

'I...err...wasn't inferring that you don't. But I'm not at all certain that Edie was a r...rich woman.'

Ava looked up at him once more, a look of triumph on her face. 'Well, we'll see, won't we? Anyway, if you don't mind, I've work to do.'

'I'd just come to tell you that all the p...paperwork is here so that the cremation should be able to take place. I'll start the process of getting p...probate.'

'What's that?' Her eyes returned to the magazine. 'Oh, it doesn't matter. Just do what you have to do.'

He turned and started to walk away. 'John.' He turned. 'I'll call you, alright?' He smiled and left, a little happier.

*

Once more the telephone rang.

'James. Every time I stay late, I'm d...disturbed by one of your c...calls. I've got to stay late tonight. I really have too much to do.'

'I thought I'd give you an update.'

'There's n...no problem, is there?'

'Oh no, not at all. It's just that the crematorium medical referee wasn't too happy with the documentation apparently. It's a Doctor Birkenshaw. MacPherson was saying a while back that they had had a run-in and that Birkenshaw doesn't like him. Anyway, turns out he was right. Birkenshaw thinks it's a sudden death and has referred the matter to the city coroner.'

'W...what's he said?' said John slowly.

'It's nothing to worry about. He's said that there should be a post-mortem. It's a real nuisance but it'll take place tomorrow so it shouldn't greatly delay sorting out Edie's estate.'

John felt his fingers become moist and his heart begin to beat a little quicker. In the depths of his mind, the seeds of doubt were beginning to flower. If asked, he would have found it difficult to say why. These weren't the doubts he had had over the old woman's instructions. These went far deeper. For the first time he had an inkling that what was happening was bigger than he had realised. 'You'd better keep me informed, I suppose.'

*

James poured a measure of whisky into his tea and looked at Ernie. The other man shook his head. 'I hope you know what you're doing.'

'Keep your voice down, eh? She is in the next room,' replied James. 'How about you?' he added, holding out the bottle and looking at Dolores. She shook her head and glanced at Ernie.

'So, tell me what happened,' said James, breaking the silence.

'The police were here yesterday morning,' said Dolores, quietly.

'Who?'

'A Detective Inspector Grimes he said he was. He had been sent from the coroner's office. He arranged for the body to be taken away to the mortuary.'

'Who did he speak to?'

'Well, us for a start!'

James put his finger to his lips. 'What was he asking?'

'About her generally,' said Ernie.

'It was her medication he seemed particularly interested in,' added Dolores. 'I said we got it on Doctor MacPherson's prescription at Jobsons on Mansfield Road. I can't imagine why you sent us there. They're quite organised. They'll have kept everything. Every prescription.'

'Did they speak to the girl?'

'They insisted on speaking to her alone. Anyway, I listened in but couldn't hear what was being said.'

James breathed out. 'Right. I actually came to tell you what happened today. MacPherson was invited to the post-mortem. Professional courtesy, I suppose. He'd had to forego the drink all day so he was in a bad way when he came back. His mood wasn't helped by the fact that they don't agree the cause of death.'

'I really hope you know what you're doing, lad. We could all swing for this.'

'Ernie. Fear not. What have you got to gain from dear old Edie's death?'

The other man did not reply. 'Precisely. Anyway, the present conclusion is basically that it's heart failure brought on by the congested condition of the lungs and the onset of pneumonia. He's sent off bits of various organs for testing just to confirm it. So, it's all going to plan and that's where we are at the moment.'

James smiled at the other two. Neither responded in the same vein.

Chapter 10

'I think it's Dr MacPherson you need to see.'

James took a final drag and squashed the nub end into the ashtray on his desk in the surgery and watched the ends of his fingers turn white. The telephone call that morning from the police officer saying that he wished to see James had come as a surprise. He was unnerved by the fact that he was one of the first to be seen. His optimism that he would have been one of the last or even that he had gone completely under the radar had been misplaced. He stared at the ash, marshalling his responses, assessing the man before him.

'That may well be the case, Doctor Farrelly. But I'd like to talk to you first.'

James looked across his desk at the officer who had sat down opposite him without being invited to do so. The slight Scottish burr grated. A stench of carbolic soap made James want to gag. Short grey hair made the other man look older than he probably was. His unlined clean-shaven face and clear blue eyes were almost certainly more representative of his age. For a small, wiry man, he had a knack of filling the room, blotting out everyone and everything else.

James pictured him lying prostrate, helpless, those blue eyes flicking from side to side, painfully aware of his fate. James visualised the cool cylindrical tube between his fingers, could sense the surge of adrenalin coursing through his body as the swirling syrupy liquid burst into the syringe's cavity. He saw the blue vein standing proud against the unblemished white skin, waiting for the needle's caress. And then, then, at the exact time of his choosing, then and only then, he would push just slightly and the silver tip would puncture the surface and glide in to the engorged artery and, with a twitch of his thumb, he would deposit the invading army and control would be his.

'Grimes you say.'

'Detective Inspector Grimes. The Coroner, Mr Rotherham, has asked me to look into the circumstances of the recent death of one

Edith Harris. I understand you knew, or at least had dealings with this lady.'

'I know of her, but she was Doctor MacPherson's patient. I occasionally had a word with her if I happened to call at the home.'

'Dr Farrelly, given my conversation with Dr Birkenshaw, I strongly suspect that when we get the results of the tests currently being undertaken, we will see that morphine or possibly heroin had been administered. I have no medical expertise, but I'm not aware of any condition justifying painkillers of this strength.'

'As I say, I find it hard to comment. I wasn't responsible for her treatment.'

'You may not have been responsible, but you were involved in administering the medication. Am I not right?'

James's heart missed a beat. 'Whatever makes you say that? Look, I'll do anything I can to help but I really am incredibly busy. I can only ask you to see Doctor MacPherson. When you do you will see that he has problems of his own but it may give you a better idea of the lady's condition and her treatment. Now if you would—'

'I have no intention of taking up any of your valuable time than is necessary, Dr Farrelly, but it would be very helpful if you could straighten out a few matters for me…alright?'

James met the gaze of the man across his desk. It was James who was the first to look away. It was a bluff. There was no way in which he could possibly know. He was guessing and looking for a reaction. James realised that he had been in this man's presence for but five minutes and his confidence had already been dented. He had another plan, another form of defence but had never truly thought that it would be needed. But that was for later. For now, he needed to put on a performance for the man opposite.

James smiled. 'Of course. As I say, I'll do anything I can to help.'

'Have you any idea as to the value of the estate?'

'No idea, I'm afraid. MacPherson's your man. He told me a while ago that he went round to her house at to pick up some of her belongings so he probably has an idea.'

'Bit over the top, isn't it?'

'How do you mean?'

'A doctor going all that way for such a purpose.'

'Oh, MacPherson's a very caring doctor. Can never do too much for anybody. He has his problems but that shouldn't detract from the fact that he is a thoroughly decent chap.'

James felt the blue eyes upon him. 'Let me acquaint you, Dr Farrelly, with the sums involved. A conservative estimate at this stage as to the value of Mrs Harris's estate is approaching £30,000.'

James raised his eyebrows. He was still conscious of the performance he needed to produce but once more felt his heart beating as the pace of the investigation so far hit him. 'I had an idea that the old girl was worth a bit from the odd comment that Doctor MacPherson made but I had no idea she's worth that much. Ava's a lucky girl.'

'So, you are aware of the contents of the will?'

'It's common knowledge, I believe.' Inwardly James cursed. He could not afford to make mistakes.

'I see that you could get the whole estate?'

'Me?' He laughed. 'Realistically no. It goes to Ava, a young and healthy girl and she deserves it. MacPherson speaks highly of her. Double incontinence – it's not pleasant you know. It's hardly likely that she would pre-decease an elderly woman with a multitude of health problems.'

'We'll see…have you any idea why Mrs Harris has mentioned you in the will?'

'At one point I was to get everything. Professionally that would be a little embarrassing and when I became aware that Mrs Harris had become close to the new nurse and had said she'd like the nurse to benefit I took the liberty of asking my brother, a solicitor by profession, if he would draft a new will. I presume you have been provided with a copy of that will by the coroner?'

'Do you know the girl, Ava Brownlie?'

'Not really. MacPherson got her a job at the home. I saw her occasionally when I had to go round. By chance, I also saw her a couple of times at a club where she worked as a waitress. I think MacPherson knew her from there but you would need to check.'

'She's told us that she had authority to give injections. Barbiturates I believe. Did you know about that?'

'If she did then it would be MacPherson who had authorised it.'

The officer suddenly stood up. 'Thank you for your time, Doctor Farrelly. The investigation is continuing and there are a number of people to see. I'll show myself out.'

Now alone, James pulled a half-empty bottle of whiskey from a drawer to his desk and took a swig. He then reached for the telephone.

*

'It's very difficult to see what help I can give you. I suspect I will be unable to answer most of your questions on the grounds of professional privilege. I'm sure you're aware that those rules prohibit me from divulging any information provided by a client.'

'And who is your client, Mr Farrelly?'

The telephone receiver had become moist in his fingers. His inability to suggest that he was actually acting for anyone who had not died led to Grimes attending his offices that evening. Fortunately, the secretaries had left for the evening by the time he arrived, but John was all too acutely aware that his father was just down the corridor.

'Tell me how Mrs Harris's will came to be changed?'

'I was told that she w...wanted to leave her estate to a nurse. So, I prepared a new w...will.'

'Who asked you?'

'That I can't answer. I'm s...sure you understand.'

'Had you prepared the old one?'

'No. It w...would have been unprofessional given its contents.'

'So, you prepared the new will?'

'Yes. As I s...say.'

'Mrs Harris signed it?'

'Err...y...yes, of course. L...look, is there a problem here?'

'And was she aware what she was signing?'

'Y...yes, of course, can I—'

'And her signature was witnessed.'

'Y...yes. It was all properly done. W...why do you need this information?'

'Mr Farrelly, what is the value, approximately, of the estate?'

'Err...I'm not sure. I haven't even got the grant of probate sorted yet so I haven't really looked into it.'

'A large estate?'

'Oh no...maybe a few hundred pounds. If that.'

'If I was to tell you that our understanding is that the beneficiary of Mrs Harris's estate stands to inherit in the region of £30,000, would that surprise you?'

John stared at the other man, conscious that his bottom lip was hanging down. 'Err...'

'And if I was to tell you that we expect the analysis of Mrs Harris's organs to reveal a concentration of morphine totally at odds to that we would have expected given her condition – Multiple Sclerosis I'm led to believe – would that surprise you?'

John felt his face burning. He took off his glasses and methodically cleaned them with his handkerchief, his mind swirling.

James's visit the previous night swept into his head. 'I knew you'd still be at the office. I'd picked up the receiver to call you and then thought a visit would be more sociable,' he'd said.

'Seems you can't keep away all of a sudden,' John had replied.

'Is the old man in? I presume he's left given that you didn't shoo me away.' James had laughed.

After the small talk, he'd got to the point. 'I'm in a bit of a pickle Johnny boy. I've just had a visit from the officer who's nosing into dear old Edie's death for the coroner. I think he's going to be asking everybody where they were the night she passed on.'

'And why does that put you in a pickle?' John had felt an anxious knot in his stomach as soon as James had raised the topic.

'Well, I was with a woman.'

'And why is that a problem? I'd have thought you were "with a woman" as you put it most evenings.'

'Yes, but this one's…err…a patient and I'd really rather Detective Inspector whatever his name is not get to know. For fairly obvious reasons.'

'What do you expect me to do?' John had known what the answer was going to be.

'It's just a white lie – just say that we were together all night.'

'All night?'

'I've got our story sorted. You picked me up at seven in the evening, we went to the club and I stopped with you as I was a bit under the weather and left before our dear father got up the next day.'

John had stared at his brother, saying nothing.

'Just remember it, alright?' It was not that there was any menace in James's voice. But it was the voice he used when he expected his command to come to pass. James had then got up and left, just as John was weighing up the factors for and against him asking what James had been doing on Sherwood Avenue at seven thirty the night the old woman died.

The officer's blue eyes stared back at John. John slowly put his glasses back on and returned the look. The piercing blue penetrated his head; they were reading, perusing, chewing on his every thought, scraping along the inside of his mind, sucking up information. The silence weighed heavily on John's shoulders. It was pushing him down, down into the murky depths of the events of the last week.

He was drowning in a sea of confusion. Pieces of a jigsaw floated randomly before his eyes. Each piece made a perfect sense in its own right but when he tried to fit them all together, a blackness descended stopping his mind working. What was apparent was that his brother's face seemed to be on most of the pieces. The officer's eyes were still on him, probing him, searching for information. John blinked, unable to take his eyes away and suddenly was aware of words tumbling from his mouth.

'I'm not sure what you're getting at but it may help if I was to tell you that w…we, that's my brother and I, spent that evening together. I p…picked him up at seven fifteen from his s…surgery and he was in my p…presence until he left early the following morning.'

The officer blew gently through his lips. John noticed a slight blush on his face as he leaned forward.

'Are you sure? Are you sure it was the night that Mrs Harris died?'

'Err… y…yes, quite sure. It was only a few days ago, so I can remember the evening perfectly well.'

'Just tell me about the evening, if you would, Mr Farrelly,' snapped Grimes.

John gave the story. He grimaced inwardly as the officer went over each bit, testing it, enquiring as to why this happened or that happened. Every word was judged, pulled this way, pushed that way. Their father's voice boomed in his head as he recalled holding an apple from the orchard in his small, sweaty palm. 'Don't tell lies boy. They get you in the end.' The ten lashes weren't for the theft of fruit but for lying as to their origin. His father had told him that night that he should use the truth as a shield, something he should never hesitate to use, rather than lie like his damned fool brother. Now, John's shirt under his waistcoat stuck to his back, he was desperate to undo the top bottom but kept his hands tucked in his lap lest the other man's blue eyes should feast on their trembling.

The man was standing. He was still speaking but the intensity from his voice was no more. John understood rather than heard that the officer may wish to speak to him again after he had spoken to others. And as suddenly as he had come, he had gone.

Alone, John sat still, perfectly still. Minutes must have passed before he slowly reached for his telephone. Now he had to ask.

'It's me. He's been.'

'What did you say?'

John said nothing. He drew his sleeve across his brow.

'What did you say, damn you?'

John shuddered. 'W…what you told me to say.' He heard his brother exhale.

'Good boy. You…err can't believe the scrape you've got me out of.'

John heard the click at the other end of the line. He went home but, for the first time in months, it was not Ava who occupied his thoughts.

Chapter 11

John pushed open the café door and stepped in. He stood for a moment, allowing his eyes to adjust to the dark ambiance of grey walls and black linoleum after the dazzling freshness of the bright spring morning. James was sitting in the corner by a window, as he had said he would be. Empty, copper-topped tables were dotted around the small area. In a couple of hours, the place would be heaving with the solicitors and barristers who had business in the courts. John placed his briefcase on the table and slumped opposite James.

'So, your first inquest then. Quite a day.'

'James, I really have very little idea what I'm supposed to do. Why me?'

'John, you'll be fine. Absolutely fine. And it's about time you extended yourself, old boy. You can't spend all your life buried in conveyances and leases. Makes one such a dull prig.'

'The old man would kill me if he knew.'

'Only because he would be jealous, old thing. Believe me, his regret that he never mastered the cut and thrust of litigation is something that eats away at him, corrodes him from the inside. Take my word for it. Just think, this could be just the beginning. Build up the litigation side and you'll soon be an equal partner, not just somebody who's the last name on the letterhead, like some kind of afterthought.'

John shook his head and wondered again how he'd allowed himself to be persuaded. He'd had to smuggle himself out of the house that morning wearing the dark court suit his father had bought for him on qualifying. His father's booming enquiry, about the contents of his diary that morning, as he slipped past the breakfast room had led him to mumble about a meeting at a client's home. He had then scuttled away like a frightened mouse. He had almost vomited when he had reached his car. Appearing in a public court was bad enough without the subterfuge.

Six weeks had passed since the Detective Inspector's visit and John had just begun to hope that the whole thing was going to melt away like the snow. It was last Saturday morning when James telephoned him at the office just as he was putting the final touches to a complicated assignment. Until that point and after days of contemplation, his final position was that if Ava had been fortunate enough to make her fortune then he would live with that. He just wanted the rest of the world to leave him in peace.

Despite her promise, Ava had not called him. He had been thinking about her before James's call. His heartache had dragged on but, as the days passed with no communication, he'd begun to accept that his feelings were not reciprocated and gradually his longing was numbed. Thus, as the weather had improved so had his mood. Maybe the sunny and longer days were the perfect tonic. Whereas there had been the time when she occupied his every waking thought, now…well maybe his feelings for her were not quite as acute. Perhaps James had been right; it had just been a stupid crush from which he would recover. And perhaps the time he had spent sorting out a new filing system had been a welcome distraction. Shirley had been such a help.

If his prospects had been beginning to look just a little more rosy, James's call on that blustery, but sunny, Saturday morning had soon put a stop to that. He had told John that the coroner had called MacPherson to say that there was going to be an inquest. MacPherson, the doctors involved in the post-mortem and the nursing staff at Sherwood Avenue would be required to give evidence. James was convinced that it would be right and proper for him to represent Ava. She needed someone there. James said that he had already checked with her and she had not rejected the offer out of hand.

For that reason, John found himself sitting in this awful place, with a starched collar that tore at his throat and a churning stomach, yearning for the sanctuary of his office and a life of moving property from one person to another. He took a sip of the scalding tea which had just appeared in front of him and pulled a face.

'Anyway, from what I gather, there's nothing to it.' John looked up as James's voice interrupted his thoughts.

'What do you know, you're a doctor.'

'As I understand it, old boy, the coroner is on a fact-finding mission. He just wants to satisfy himself that everything's above board so far as dear old Edie is concerned and everybody will then be happy. Ava gets the money and you milk the kudos of representing Nottingham's prettiest nurse. And make sure she's grateful – you never know where it may lead.'

James pulled a packed of cigarettes out of his jacket pocket. John shook his head as the packet was pushed across the table to him. 'You may not even have to say anything,' continued James through a plume of smoke. 'The coroner asks most of the questions. You just need to advise. You're doing the clever bit you see, which is why it's right that you're here, representing Ava.'

'God. I feel awful. I will have one.' John lit a cigarette and looked out of the window. The Guildhall was across the road. He looked away. 'That's another thing,' he started, 'I had a reporter ring yesterday. I had to ask Shirley to say I wasn't in. I don't think she was too pleased. How do the press know about this? For the life of me, I cannot understand the fascination.'

'The press have a nose for money and glamour, old boy. Speaking of which, there she is. I think that is your cue to enter the arena.'

John's mouth went dry as he saw Ava walking alone down the street towards the Shire Hall. Even from this distance he could see that she'd had her hair freshly permed. He wondered if the white top she wore underneath her red jacket and matching pleated skirt were all new. And if so where she had got the money.

'Don't worry old boy. The new outfit was my idea although I let MacPherson claim the credit. And pay the bill. She's got no beau on her trail.'

John felt his face burning. 'Stop laughing at me. This is most definitely the worst day of my life.' He stood slowly up and then felt James's hand on his arm.

'Just give it a minute, Johnny boy.' They both looked over to where Ava was standing in front of several photographers. She suddenly smiled, a sight which lit up the whole street so far as John was concerned. Men in hats and raincoats, holding notepads, spoke to her, laughing at her replies and eagerly scribbling down her words. It was then that he noticed the small mousey woman step out from behind her; the woman he had seen ironing in the hovel where they lived. Suddenly the memory of that night hit him and the longing, the utter misery that she was not his came back. He was no further forward.

James voice interrupted him again. 'As I say, give it a couple of minutes. Let the press have their fill and then you go in and grab Ava.' John turned to see that his brother was now standing, his face just inches from his own. The intensity in James's voice held him, rendered him unable to move. 'Remember what we said. The coroner will ask Ava if she wants to give evidence and will probably tell her that she is under no obligation to do so. But as we agreed, that looks suspicious. Let her talk and say what she did for Edie. It's the best way. That's what we agreed. Okay?'

John nodded. Maybe he was the one which should be sorting the strategy – if a strategy was actually needed. He bit his lip realising that he had no idea. Feeling a slap on his back and with the words 'good luck' ringing in his ear, he stepped out into the sunshine and made his way slowly to the large building Ava had just entered.

*

The three-storey building that was Nottingham's Guildhall reached into the sky. Turrets on each corner pointed upwards. Arched windows across the top two floors, reflecting fluffy white clouds, revealed nothing of its interior. The ground floor was dominated by a huge rectangle entrance of glass, again revealing nothing of what lay behind. Its original grey stone was now smeared with the blackness of coal dust and the smoke churned out by cars flying along the street on which it stood. John momentarily thought of the building meting out punishment to make up for the punishment it had endured. Two statues either side of the entrance, one brandishing a sword, the other scales, stared at him.

One or two people milled around even at this early hour, willing their appearance before the magistrates to be over. Today the building had an additional role and mercifully the photographers and reporters, attracted like maggots to a dead body, seemed to have gone back into whatever lair they had originally emerged. John trudged up the worn steps avoiding the stare of the statues and pushed through the revolving glass door and into the dark interior.

He shivered as the cool, cavernous entrance hall opened out before him. Ornate, white pillars stood to his right and left at intervals along each wall. Pictures of bewigged elderly men stood in the gaps, their bushy eye-browed, stern countenance glaring down at him, telling him he was unworthy, that this was no place for the likes of him. His new shoes clicked on the speckled grey marble flooring as he inched in, echoing off the walls, attracting people's attention. He looked around, wishing suddenly that his father knew he was there.

'Can I 'elp?'

John turned to his right. Behind a desk sat a uniformed black-haired man. Clutching a walking stick, he pushed himself to his feet.

'Err…sorry.'

'I said, can I 'elp you? You look a little out o' sorts. Is it the magistrates that you want?'

John said nothing, staring at the man, not knowing what he wanted.

'Sir?'

'Oh, y…yes…sorry. No, I'm err…looking for the Coroner's…err Court.'

'Right duck, well that'll be up the stairs to the right. Court number three 'as been set aside. It's all the interest there's bin. The beaks aren't 'appy at being pushed out, I can tell you. There's a number of folk with an interest gone up already.'

'R…right…err thank you.'

John found the stairs and slowly went up. At the top, bright red against the dark walls sat Ava, her hands clutching her handbag in her lap. She was looking at her mother, her red, glossy lips moving. John stopped and gazed, looking at her hair, her face, her neck, her arms, her legs. Why had he ever thought that somebody like him had any chance with a girl like her?

Suddenly, Ava was looking at him and blinked. He forced a smile and walked over, his case under his arm.

'Ava. It's nice to see you again.'

Ava stood up. He tried to think of something to say but the words just floated around his head. Nothing seemed suitable. Nothing came to mind. She laughed, a nervous laugh. She then took his hand, her touch light and delicate, and shook it.

'I think there's a free room over there so we can have a word. Mam, come this way.'

John followed the two women across the corridor into the room. Its only contents were a table in the centre with four chairs around it. Ava and her mother sat down. John put his case on the table and fished out the papers he had collected, wondering what on earth he was going to say.

Chapter 12

The large rectangular room was light and airy. Tall, arched windows to one side, reaching from the floor almost to the ceiling let in the sun. The decorative carving around the edges of that ceiling gave the room a majestic aura, reinforced by the crest behind the raised dais directly in front of him.

Two of the windows had been opened slightly and a gentle breeze ruffled the papers set down in front of one portly man at the end of the long bench behind which John was sitting. The black-gowned usher had fetched John from the room where he had been with Ava and her mother, and led him to the front of the vast room. A number of other men were already there, all older, all wearing morning suits. At least he'd got that bit right. Ava was directly behind him.

Chattering from the public benches at the back of the room floated to the front. John felt the eyes of the crowded public benches at the back of the room bore into his back. He turned to his left at the sound of laughter. One of the men he and James had seen talking to Ava was laughing and pointing in his general direction. John stared at his papers, laid on the desk before him.

As it turned out, he'd not had to say a great deal to Ava when the three of them were alone. Ava's mother had not been slow to give her opinions and had dominated what conversation there had been. It was the 'newspaper talk' rather than her daughter's appearance at the inquest that seemed to cause her the most grief. On John raising the subject, Ava had simply asked why would she not give evidence. She had done nothing of which she should be ashamed and there was little point in her being here if she did not get to say her piece. John had gazed into her pale blue eyes, any kind of rational thought an impossibility. Before he could utter anything, the usher put his head around the door to say that the coroner wanted everyone in early to ensure proceedings would start on time.

Suddenly, the words 'all rise' came from the back of the room. The hum of conversations stopped and chair legs scraped along the floor. John followed everyone else in getting to his feet. A door to the side of the dais opened and the coroner strode in. Dressed in a black morning suit, the coroner's dark eyes scanned all those on the front bench. Tall, with black hair, greying at the temples, he sat and glanced at the papers on the desk before him, keeping everyone on their feet. John felt his pulse quicken.

'Be seated, everyone.' His confident tone boomed around the room. 'This is the resumed inquest into the death of Mrs Edith Harris. At the initial hearing, I heard evidence only as to identification of the deceased and the date and time of death, and adjourned for the police to carry out enquiries. There are just one or two preliminary issues which I will deal with before we re-commence.'

He looked around the room. His audience stared in silence. John sat rigidly still, afraid less any movement would break the spell and bring down on him the wrath of this man in whose court he sat.

'I am aware that Mrs Harris's death has led to a degree of interest from the newspapers, both those local to this city and the nationals. I have listened to the representations of the Press Association and have made provision for twenty reporters. Given the complexity of these proceedings, I have taken legal advice myself. As a result of that advice and given the circumstances, I have decided that a jury is required and I have asked my Coroner's Officer to select a jury. This has been done and the members of the jury will now enter.'

A jury! He had not realised there was to be a jury. As the eight men entered and filled the benches by the window, John's mind scoured the reading he had done over the past week. He had consumed every piece of information he could lay his hands on about coronial law and procedure. He knew there could be a jury. Why had he not realised that there would be a jury? His chest pounded, the weight of the masses behind him pressed in. He needed more – more time, more knowledge, more experience, more…more gravitas. He should not be here and—

He felt an elbow in his side but it was the coroner's voice which he heard. 'I said who represents Miss Brownlie? I would appreciate it if we could all pay attention.'

'Th…that's—'

'Stand would you.'

'Th…that's me, sir. F…Farrelly is the name.'

'Solicitor or Counsel?' barked the coroner.

'Err…s…solicitor, sir.'

The coroner obtained the same information from all of those sitting on the same row as John before continuing 'I've directed that those people who are represented should be. Counsel for Doctor MacPherson and Mr Jobson the chemist will simply hold a watching brief. Representatives for the other participants in these proceedings will be at liberty to adduce evidence from their clients after my questioning and may also cross-examine other witnesses.'

He stopped and now shifted in his seat so that he was turned towards the sombre faces of the jury. 'Gentleman. Before we start to hear the evidence, a few words about your role and duty. You are here to establish how Mrs Harris came about her death. It is not the purpose of this inquest to try any person or persons although this may inevitably form part of your deliberations. To confirm, however, these are not criminal proceedings.'

He turned and looked to the row of advocates. 'Now, Mr Preston, you represent the police in these proceedings. I understand that there is a problem in relation to two of the witnesses I had indicated I wished to hear from?'

The stout man stood, a sheaf of papers between his podgy fingers, his waistcoat straining against his girth. 'Sir, the proprietor of the nursing home in which the deceased stayed prior to her demise, one Dolores Roberts, has influenza, as has her husband. Neither are in attendance this morning.'

'Can they come tomorrow? Or perhaps the following day?'

'Sir, apparently not. The medical evidence as to their condition is from another witness in these proceedings, Doctor MacPherson. Apparently, it will be at least seven days before they would be in a state when they would be able to attend. Can I say that from the police perspective, the evidence collected thus far would indicate that Mrs Roberts did not take the lead role in the deceased's care and her evidence at this place in these proceedings may not be of the greatest import. We would invite you to proceed with the inquest.'

'Very well.'

A Doctor Birkenshaw came first. He told of his initial conclusions from the post-mortem to the effect that heart disease was the primary cause of death brought on by pneumonia and congested lungs. John took a detailed note of the evidence, scribbling frantically for page after page on his legal notepad. To John, none of this evidence did any harm.

'Why did you send off the deceased's organs for analysis?' John looked up following the coroner's question.

'There were signs of the use of morphia and for the sake of completeness, I felt other possible causes of death should be ruled out.'

John's occasional and secretive glances in the direction of the jury revealed one or two puzzled expressions. He would have liked to have asked for more simplistic explanations to some issues and some of the terms but feared the response of the coroner. It seemed as though the experts with their expertise, the Coroner with his medical knowledge and the other advocates with their experience were in a bubble of their own. They communicated in a secret language, only allowing outsiders, such as John and the jury and those like Ava who might be affected, an occasional glimpse into their world. Perhaps all would be revealed in the end.

Following the science was not his only difficulty; there was the intoxicating presence of Ava sitting behind him. On the one occasion he needed to turn to her for a whispered conversation about a particular piece of evidence, his attention to her answers was distracted by her perfume. And as he spoke quietly into her ear, he could not keep his eyes off the flawless white skin of her slim neck rekindling the memories of their night together, never far away at any time.

The next witness said his name was Doctor Rhodes and that he was from the Home Office. In a flat emotionless voice, he told of analysis bags and their references and their date of receipt. He was going on about morphine. Grains of morphine. Morphine found in her heart, in her liver, in her lungs. John's mind whirled; words like 'cyanosis' and 'chlorodyne' somersaulted around his head, cartwheeling over and over. Poison, that's the word he used. He said the word and stopped for a second, leaving it hanging in the air like some kind of accusation. Death had been caused by being poisoned. Poison was evil, John thought. Evil was perpetrated on a human being by another human being. And if that had happened, had not Edie been murdered? The doctor's words hammered home. Six times the amount expected. A heavy hit likely just before death. John felt perspiration trickle down his back.

'Any questions, Mr Farrelly?'

Had he any questions? What could he ask? What did he know about morphine? Should he have investigated? John hauled himself to his feet. The eyes of the world bore into him.

'Well?' John cowered under the coroner's impatience but suddenly heard his voice puncture the silence. 'Err...D...Doctor

Rhodes. You cannot be certain when the deceased actually ingested any of the morphine found in her organs, can you?'

'No,' came the assured reply, 'it is not an exact science. My feeling is that there was a heavy dose shortly before she died that caused or at least contributed to her death but I agree, I cannot give that opinion with any certainty. Whether that dose was intended to bring about that death is of course not a matter for me.' He glanced in the direction of the jury.

John sat down and leaned back in his seat and gripped the edge of the desk to still his trembling hands.

Doctor MacPherson came and went. Dementia and Multiple Sclerosis were words which floated around the court before fluttering away. Prescriptions were produced. Morphine had been obtained from Jobsons the chemists. Did he know who for? Yes, they looked like his signatures. Old Mrs Briscoe, she'd needed morphine. Dear old Ethel. He thought that the morphine not used had been returned. Hadn't it? That is correct, it had been a bad time for him. His wife had died after a long illness and he supposed it had been wearing. Yes, that may be true; he may not have had the attention to detail that he should have.

Miss Brownlie? John looked up. What was the significance of this? John felt her eyes in his back.

Yes, the shaking voice of the doctor went on. He was aware of her working at the home. Had he helped her get the position? What were her qualifications? He really couldn't be sure after this time. Perhaps Nurse Dolores may be able to help. No, that's right, morphine could not be administered by a member of the nursing staff without his express approval. Had he given authority? No, he wouldn't. The very suggestion! Yes, he had been confused on other matters but this? No, he wouldn't. It went against everything he believed in. It would be a totally improper practice. No, on that point he was certain.

John felt the touch of Ava's hand on his shoulder. Thoughts of the last physical contact between them again floated into his mind. He turned leaned towards her. She reached up and whispered into his ear, her soft breath stroking his face like a gentle caress. He closed his eyes, forcing his mind to stay in the present, to understand her instructions but, like a mischievous puppy chasing a ball, his thoughts strained to get away, to go back to that night.

He dragged himself back to face the witness. Did they really dispute what had been said? The witness had not said that Ava had administered any morphine. Was there anything he could usefully ask?

'Err…I've no questions of this w…witness, sir.'

'Are you sure?'

John scrambled through the notes he had taken. His handwriting had suddenly become illegible. Scribbled words floated up in no rational order. There was something he had missed. Why had the coroner queried his decision not to ask questions?

'We've not got all day, Mr Farrelly.'

'Yes…err…no…err…I have no questions. Thank you, sir.' John sat down, his eyes still skimming over the notes he had taken.

He looked up as the next witness was called in. After a number of confident answers in response to the coroner's first few questions, there was a gasp from the back of the room when Grimes told the inquest about the value of the estate. Pens scratched and note pads rustled at the benches occupied by all those reporters. Miss Brownlie, he said in his matter-of-fact delivery, was the beneficiary, as things presently stood. More fevered scratching. John felt Ava shifting in her seat. He wanted to sit next to her, to tell her it was alright, to say that it made no difference to how he felt. He glanced to his side. One or two jurors were looking at Ava, blank expressions on their faces.

Grimes's voice droned on answering each question precisely, painting the picture, never giving away anything else. The police were doing this, doing that, concentrating on the events leading up to Mrs Harris's admittance to the home on Sherwood Avenue. Yes, there was a son who was simple and had little understanding as to why his mother had gone into the home. One of the curiosities was that the deceased seemed to have taken against her son. Whether there had been any influence by others in this turn of events was one of the lines of enquiry. No, the police still had an open mind but would continue to investigate the matter.

'Miss Brownlie!'

John heard the swish of her skirt as she stood and inhaled the fragrance of her perfume as she edged past the knees of people sitting on her row. There was a perfect silence as she took the seat at the front of the room and smiled tightly at the usher as she took the oath before her eyes scanned the masses crammed into the courtroom.

She turned to her side as the coroner spoke, his voice softer than it had been. 'You are aware that you are under no obligation, none at all, to give evidence. The jury will not think the worse of you should you decline to give evidence.'

'I'm quite happy to answer your questions.'

'Speak up, young lady.'

Ava repeated what she said.

'You've had the benefit of legal advice?'

'Yes, I suppose so.'

'You've been advised that any evidence you give today, in this court, can be used in any further proceedings that there may or may not be?'

She nodded and her evidence began, her soft voice floated over the room. The room suddenly sank into shadow as the sun slipped behind a crowd and a sharp April shower drummed on the window. All eyes stayed trained on her, oblivious to anything outside. It was Doctor MacPherson who had helped her get the job. He knew she had not done anything like this before, everyone did. Is that a problem? She had come to feel very close to Edie. Edie said she was pretty, reminded her of herself all those years ago. Edie was lovely. She had learned all about Edie's life with her husband abroad. That was before Edie had Denis. He was with a cousin now, kindly Doctor MacPherson had told her. No, she didn't know how he knew. Edie was upset because Denis didn't visit but what could she do, she didn't know Denis or where he was. Edie told her all about her jewellery, how nice her diamonds would look on her. She liked Edie, she could talk to Edie. She had no idea how much she would get until today, there was no way she could know, it was in the hands of the solicitors, but it didn't matter, not when it was that much. Yes, she did inject Edie, to make her easy. Doctor MacPherson had shown her how. Dr MacPherson had prepared the syringe. So, what was the problem?

No one moved, no one coughed, pens were laid down.

Chapter 13

John stood by his window. An incessant swirling drizzle smeared his vision of all those scampering across the Market Square. How he envied them, those whose greatest concern was not being soaked by the rain. People scurried under the verandas, into Lyons tea shop, into department stores. What kept them awake at night? What would he not give to have nothing to worry about save for the endless rationing? The pile of messages laid on his desk remained untouched. Inertia now ruled his life. He dared not read them for fear of what was there. But the longer he delayed it, the more the fear grew and the more there was to fear. The one thing he had done was to stash all his files away in his filing cabinet; out of sight out of mind. And, worst of all, James had not spoken to him, not since it happened. He really would—

He started at the tap on the door and turned. 'Shirley, it's you. Any problem?'

'Mr Farrelly would like to see you. He…uhm…he said you were to go straight away.'

'Oh. Right. Thank you.' As the door was gently closed, John shut tight his eyes. It really couldn't get any worse. He slowly put on his jacket.

'Come!' The command would have echoed throughout the whole office. John slipped through the door. The dark oak panelling dominating the room, a larger version of his own, complemented the grey day. The open fire to his left would have been made that morning on account of winter's final embrace. John yearned to take off his jacket as its heat and the cloying sooty smell added to his discomfort. The reflection from the flames could be seen in the glass door of the cabinet to his right, a cabinet housing his father's life history – his medals, a black and white image of him shaking hands with the Lord Chief Justice in 1932, a framed parchment evidencing the Law Society's gracious permission to practice, numerous photographs of civic functions and, in the corner on the bottom shelf, the stilted pose of his family, taken at a time when there was no reason for four dour faces.

Occasional spitting of coal and the ticking of the clock over the mantelpiece was all that could be heard. His father was behind his huge oak desk, scribbling notes as he perused a conveyance. A pile of files stood neatly to his left. A folded document, maybe a set of plans, lay to his right, weighed down by the gold figure of a Tommy, the inscription along its base extolling the bravery of the Sherwood Foresters during the Great War. His father's war.

John's eyes were drawn by movement over his father's shoulder in the luscious green garden attached to the offices. A man in a glistening yellow sou'wester was raking up cut grass from the pristine lawns. What cares did he have? What worries were there in tending to the garden? He'd have to think about the timing of the summer's first trim and that would be it. When had John ever told his father that he wanted to be a solicitor? He hadn't. This was the course that had been chosen for him. That's what you got for cowardice, that's what you got for not having the spine to make your own way. That was just one of the many differences between him and James. Maybe it was his own fault that he was standing here, having no idea what his father wanted, not even daring to sit down. There was no maybe about it.

'I need to discuss with you a particular matter.' John flinched as his father's words bounced around the room, breaching the silence. A vision of his bottom drawer, the drawer he kept locked, the drawer in which he had stuffed all the files that his father couldn't be allowed to see, sprang into his mind. These were matters which needed time and concentration, neither of which he seemed able to find, matters which taunted him with his own incompetence, matters which proved he had no right to be working for his father. Old Albrighton's lease on his butcher's shop should have been renewed weeks back. He daren't ring the Council, terrified of hearing them say they wouldn't now agree the renewal, terrified of his father's response on learning that one his oldest clients had to find new premises. That was just one of many. And now his father had found the drawer. That must be it. How could he be so stupid? Nothing moved without his father knowing. Every time limit was imprinted in his father's head. He not only knew about the drawer he knew about every matter, every sign of abject failure hidden from the world.

'Ava Brownlie! I believe the name means something to you?'
John stared at his father.

'Well?'

It must be some reporter. Had to be. Or her mother. He hadn't been able to face her afterwards and had shot away without a word. That night he had resolved to visit her. Explain what had happened to Ava. He had promised God that he would go the very next day. The resolve had melted the following morning when the reality of having no answers to give her hit him.

'Has the cat caught your tongue, boy?'

'I was…err…just about to…'

'You were about to do what exactly?'

John said nothing.

'Nothing! You were about to do nothing!'

His father's face had almost taken on the colour of beetroot. A drop of spittle from his father's mouth landed on the pristine white ink pad in front of him. He'd not spoken to his father; there had been no point. Mercifully, the feeding frenzy as the local and national press picked over every word had not resulted in any mention of him. There were other, more salacious details better deserving of their attention than her nondescript, incompetent representative. It was only during another sleepless night that it had occurred to him that as the story became stale, there may be a telephone call – or worse still, a visit – to the office by reporters seeking to give the story the oxygen of a fresh angle. On arriving each morning, he had expected to be met by rain-coated reporters seeking his take on what had happened whilst photographers thrust cameras in his face, scatter gun clicking raking over him like bullets.

'For pity's sake, say something, boy!'

He had no words for his father, any more that he had words for her mother. He was stuck, mesmerised by the enormity of it. His heart raced and he blinked, realising that the tears pricking the corners of his eyes would only enrage his father further.

'Pater, old boy, shouting will achieve nothing, now will it?' John froze. James had not been in the same room as their father since the argument all those years ago. Yet the voice from behind him was that of his brother.

'Sit down, Johnny boy.' James emerged from behind the door which had concealed him as John had sidled in. John felt a hand on his shoulder as he was pushed into the chair in front of his father's desk. James walked round and perched himself on the edge of the desk. He lit a cigarette and looked down at John, shaking his head but smiling.

'Bit of a mess, eh, old chap?'

His brother's words, his brother's smile, sucked him in, into his world, where a touch of fairy dust would soon put everything right. John had not spoken of the matter to anyone. He had been powerless to prevent this huge mass building up in his mind, powerless to stop it surging into his every waking thought and now he was quite unable to think of anything else. It was always there with its taunts, its mocking. But what was it? It was the monster from his childhood nightmares, come to eat him alive, destroy him. That was until James's smile and velvet tone made it shrink to a size where it became manageable.

And now his mind had space to turn to other, more immediate matters. He stared at his brother and then at his father. His mind slipped back to that Christmas, five years ago, the last time that the two of them had spoken.

It wasn't what James had said at that time, although that was bad enough, it was the look on his face. The superior arch of his eyebrows, the lips threatening to break into a smile, the gentle stroking of his chin, they were all there. James could have been describing a scene from *Gone with the Wind*, he could have been mimicking Clarke Gable, he could have been recounting an amusing incident at Oxford. But he was doing no such thing. He was telling his family over Christmas dinner that he'd managed to blag his way out of National Service. The whole shebang was not of his making. He'd decided to be a conscientious objector and the damn fool tribunal had swallowed it hook, line and sinker. No death in foreign fields for him. No service to King and country in some Godforsaken jungle or desert.

Their father, absurdly still sporting an orange paper hat, had got to his feet, ripping his napkin from his buttoned collar, apparently oblivious to his tie flirting over his shoulder. Red faced and unable to form his words, spittle landed amidst the table decorations. Charging around the table as quickly as his bulk would allow, he grabbed James by the shoulders and forced him out of the room and out of his house. 'Nazi', 'absolute disgrace', 'I and millions like me fought in the trenches for the likes of you' were words which John recalled although whether his father had actually spluttered them at that point he could not now be sure. It was later as everyone sat with heads bowed that their father had uttered, with a breaking voice, that to have two sons not do their duty was more than any father could bear. No one had said that John's poor eyesight was not of his making. But that is not what occurred to John at the time; his only thought was that this was the first time he had ever seen his father show any emotion other than anger.

His father stood up and walked to the window at the back of his office. James blew smoke into the air. 'Father dear. As I say, shouting and screaming will not solve our difficulties.'

'Our difficulties?' he replied without turning, emphasising the first word.

'If you really were of that view, I wouldn't be here, now would I?'

Nothing was said. The clock ticked, the fire spat.

'Err…p…perhaps someone c…could tell me what's happening.'

'Quite right, Johnny boy, and so I shall. We, and by that I mean your father and I, have been to see the poor creature. Suffice to say, you are now instructed in the defence…oh, don't look like that. This time there'll be a King's Counsel to do the difficult bit, such as the talking so nothing to be afraid of. All you have to do is to tell him all about it. What could be simpler? Father, dear, if you would be so kind to return as to the table, perhaps we can discuss the next steps?'

He complied, glaring at John. 'I'll overlook the conflict of interest, given the circumstances. You'll do the leg work, boy. This mess isn't of my making. I've never touched a criminal case in my life, let alone a capital case. I'll front it so far as the girl is concerned. Just remember – you don't so much as have a thought about all this without telling me. Do you understand? You tell me everything.'

John nodded. James smiled and, once more, slowly shook his head. 'Now John, I would love to hear all about the inquest. It would appear that it all became rather eventful.'

John looked at James, the events still raw, like a bleeding wound. Her screams had sliced through him. Her large, round blue eyes pleading for him to do something were still etched in his head. But now he could start to face them.

'It…err…all started when the j…jury c…came back and said that they had come to a v…verdict upon which they were all agreed.'

John felt the eyes of his brother and father boring into him. 'They said that it was w…wilful murder and…and that it was A…Ava. At first no one said anything. Time had stood still. It was when the officers there arrested A…Ava that it all started.'

John looked down. 'She s…struggled but there were three of them. I couldn't get to see her afterwards. I tried. Honest I tried.'

'I'm sure you did, Johnny boy. Not to worry, eh?'

'Not to worry! I really don't think you have the slightest idea as to the seriousness of all of this!' John shrank back in his seat, as if forced back by his father's voice.

'Oh, but I absolutely do, Father dear. It's just that I for one have absolute faith in my brother. There could be no better person for the defence.' James beamed at one, then the other.

'Well, we'd better ensure that the fool that you have such faith in understands the position and understands fully his role.'

'Quite, Father. I'll let you deal with the legal bits.' James slid off the desk and went over to the window.

'Right. I'll tell you once and once only, boy. After the jury had come back with its decision, the girl was arrested on a coroner's warrant…look, don't you think you should be noting this down?'

A podgy hand with thick fingers slammed a piece of paper onto the desk in front of him. 'This power apparently exists if a jury returns a verdict indicating a criminal offence by a particular person. She's been charged with Mrs Harris's murder and will be before the police court next Monday morning for a committal to the assizes. It's a capital charge so we have leading counsel and will be paid from the public purse. Understand thus far?'

'Y…yes.'

'Yes, sir! The man leading us is Mr Randall. First-class chap. Lieutenant Colonel. He was a brave, brave man. We went in together as officers and by some miracle came out together. He'll look after us. The junior he's recommended is Mr Sprite. He'll be there for us on Monday – see the way the winds blowing. So, if you could turn up and make yourself useful, perhaps take some notes. Reckon you can manage that?'

'Err…yes. Will…err…'

'Yes,' said James, 'Ava will be there. As I said, we went yesterday to sort things out with her. They've put her in Winson Green – it's the prison in Birmingham where female prisoners are sent. Obviously, there's scant chance of bail. She would like you to deal with the paperwork…don't look like that Johnny boy. She now accepts it wasn't your fault.'

'There's one thing you going to have to take note of, boy.'

'What's that…sir?' said John.

'Your brother has been telling me about this oaf, Grimes. He's been sniffing around causing trouble, insinuating your brother knows something about the whole sorry business. When you brief Mr Randall, you make sure he knows that this family is not involved, eh? I will not tolerate any scandal. Now I suggest you go and see your client's mother. We don't want her going elsewhere…well, get going then!'

As John grabbed the doorknob, he turned at his father's booming voice. 'And get old Albrighton's lease sorted, will you?'

'Catch you soon, Johnny boy.'

John was finally able to leave.

Chapter 14

The pubs and inns had long since spilled out their customers into the dark streets. The ornate orange globe on the top of the Palais de Danse would finally be in shadow. Even the drinking clubs hiding in the narrow lanes and nooks and crannies of Broad Marsh had had their fill. Nottingham was asleep. Only those who embraced the darkness and the rats were abroad.

A full moon rendered the scudding clouds almost white against the night sky. The black waters of the Leen shimmered in its light, just for a moment, through a rapidly filled gap. The railway was now silent. The grey-bricked bridge supporting it provided shade from the moon. He stopped under its arches and listened. Nothing. So he was right. He put a cigarette in his mouth and struck a match, knowing its fizzing yellow light would act like a beacon. If there had to be a confrontation, so much the better here. With his friends; the darkness and the rats.

Footsteps echoed on the towpath. He walked on – having drawn him into his lair, he would drag him further, away from the hovels which bordered this part of the river, to a place where humans seldom went, to a place where it would be days before anybody would be found. To follow him would be bravery or abject folly. For James, it mattered not a jot. But it would tell him what he wanted to know. The footsteps continued as if they were both linked by rope. Finally, he stopped and turned.

Grimes emerged from under the shadows of the bridge and stopped, five or six yards away. Far enough to be able to get away, thought James. The other man lit a cigarette, his eyes concealed by the brim of his hat, his collar turned up. Finally, he looked at James and spoke. 'Mr Farrelly, what a dance you lead us.'

'Why are you following me?'

'You didn't think I'd follow you here, did you?'

James said nothing.

'You see, with you, here, I feel quite safe. You can't harm me, can you?'

James screwed his hands in his pocket into tight fists, the nails cutting into his palms. He pictured the other man's face just below the river's surface, far enough down for the filthy water to flood into his lungs but near enough to see his bulging eyes as he realised that he would be held there for as long as it took. The longer the better. James shook the image from his head. Concentrate. He had to concentrate.

'You weren't at court the other day. I'm sure you're aware that she was committed to the assizes for a trial.'

'No reason why I should be there, dear boy. Contrary to what you and your Keystone Cop chums think, this all has nothing to do with me.'

'So you say, Mr Farrelly, so you say. I beg to differ.'

The moon came out, again just for a moment. The officer took a step forward, still staring at James, a sneer on his lips. This had now become personal and that is what worried James. That element was something that he had not factored in.

'You're not a stupid man, Mr Farrelly. Quite the opposite in point of fact. And whatever you may think, that is something I respect you for. I don't for one minute believe that you thought that no one would guess. It's as plain as pike staff to me that you're somehow involved. How else would you get the estate? I confess that at the moment I haven't got the evidence to prove it. That's what you're banking on. But I'll get what I need. Do you know why, Mr Farrelly?'

James stared at him.

'Because there is a weak link or links in every crime. And I will find your weak link. That I promise you.'

James's heart raced. He couldn't work out how much was bluster, how much this was designed to cause panic and miscalculation. There was no evidence. He'd made sure there was no evidence.

'Make no mistake, she will hang. Poisoners always do. Even pretty young mothers. There will be no reprieve. But, Mr Farrelly, I have a problem. I just cannot get rid of this idea which has grown and grown. It has swilled around in my head, always there, telling me I'm missing the obvious. It's the notion that you are involved. You must be; she couldn't have done it without help. Everything in this whole sordid business ends up with you. It's quite simple when you think it through; you're in this together. If not, why is your name in the will? There's only one possible explanation for your name in the will and that's because you've put it there. But there's more than that.'

James blinked.

'The sad thing, you know, is that she's still smitten. Smitten with you. That much was obvious when we questioned her. It's just a pity we didn't know about your duplicity at that point. But she'll get to know all about it at the trial. Then we'll see what she says, when she sees she's being stitched up.' He took a final drag on his cigarette and then threw the nub end to one side.

'Anyway, I reckon this is the way you think it'll all work out. She's acquitted, she inherits and you both end up with the money. Or she is convicted, she therefore cannot inherit and who then gets Edie's fortune? Why, James Farrelly of course. She's reprieved and she's out in seven or eight years. Still young, got her looks and you both live happily ever after and again you both get to enjoy the money. God, she must trust you. But then I've thought a little more. It doesn't matter to you, does it? She doesn't get the reprieve – you don't even have to share it. Who gets all that money? Well, dear old Mr Farrelly still does, doesn't he? So, it's either both of you or just you. But, one way or another, that means it is you. And it might suit you just fine if it is just you.'

Still James said nothing.

'And that's where we come to the weak link. She doesn't get reprieved, as she won't. What happens then? Are you just going to stand by and let the law take its course? You know, I reckon you would. But she won't go meekly to the gallows. She'll talk. She'll talk to save her neck. If that doesn't work, she'll talk so that you get the same.'

The moon came out from behind a cloud. Grimes looked down at his feet, nudging a small stone around with the toe of his shoe.

He looked up again. James saw the eyes, sparkling in the moon's light. He saw the yearning, the desperation, of the hunter as it sought its quarry. 'But that's not your only problem. That's not the only weak point…nothing to say? Obviously not. As I was saying, I'm quite safe here. You can't do anything. If anything happens to me, it'll show I'm onto something. To answer your question, I'm following you because you're guilty of murder. I still reckon the girl's involved. But maybe, just maybe, this is all your own work. Perhaps you've duped her like you've been duping everyone else for years. And you're quite happy for someone else to take what's coming. So I will keep following you. Every step. What I am going to prove, I promise you, is that you are involved as well. That's a problem to you. But we'll let her have her trial, shall we? Rank up the pressure, eh? See what comes crawling out.'

'As I say old chap, nothing to do with me.' James walked past him, towards the lights of the city without looking back.

*

'It's no use looking at the door. Your father is on the golf course and won't be coming back. I'm right, aren't I?' Grimes laughed, a deep laugh that filled the office. He stepped towards the fire, rubbing his hands. 'Good God, it's cold for the time of year. Don't you reckon, laddie?'

He didn't wait for an answer but walked over to the cabinet. He tilted his head to one side, reading the titles on the spines of the books.

'I...err...I'm really not sure it's r...right that you should be here.'

'Oh, and why is that?'

'You're investigating a matter where th...this firm is in...instructed in the defence.'

Grimes walked over and lent over John, his fists pressed into the desk. 'I'm not here to discuss the niceties of a criminal trial, laddie, I'm here to talk about the witness statement that you have given.'

John felt a small amount of spittle land on his cheek. He looked away, stood and went to the window.

Grimes spoke again, this time without the hissed menace. 'I just want to check one or two things. Make sure we've got our facts straight.'

He took a small notebook from an inside pocket and nimbly flicked through the pages. 'Now, you've said you were with your brother on the night Mrs Harris died?'

John looked back at him, his hands in his pockets, recalling all too readily the alibi but straining to remember the detail. The truth was so much easier. It was there, like a slab of concrete, never changing. But lies changed to suit their purpose, like a chameleon changed its appearance. 'Y...yes.'

Question after question was asked, some several times, different angles but amounting to the same thing. John blocked them all...it's in my original statement...yes...that's right...no there are no doubts.

'The new will you drafted. What was in the old one?'

'Err…everything went to my b…brother.'

'Did you prepare that will?'

'No.'

'Who did?'

'Err…I don't know to be honest. I've t…told you all this b…before.'

'Did you not need to see the old will?'

'Not really, any new w…will w…would revoke all previous testamentary dispositions.'

'Were you not curious why the previous will contained a disposition leaving everything to your brother?'

'Well…he told me that he f…found it professionally embarrassing and it w…was at his r…request that I drew up the new w…will.'

'So why is he mentioned at all in the new will? No reason that I can see.'

John said nothing. It was a question that had hovered in the periphery of his mind at the time. His answer now if pressed was that it was none of his business. John turned and faced the window. He closed his eyes as he asked himself why he had not prepared some kind of explanation.

'We've spoken to Edie's solicitors, the firm who dealt with her affairs up until you drafted the will. They are not impressed, to put it mildly, at your involvement. But that's of no concern to me, not for the moment anyway. They know nothing of a will leaving the estate to your brother. They have a will in their safe leaving the bulk of her estate to her son. Most surprised to hear that there have been two wills after that. Anything to say?'

'I w…was acting under instructions from a woman who I w…was told w…was seriously ill.'

'And a woman who had dementia and who was disinheriting her family. And before you say you didn't know who was in her family, you never bothered to check. Anyway, how well do you know your brother?'

John turned around. 'W…what do you mean?'

'I mean as I say, Mr Farrelly.'

'He's my b…brother so—'

'He's a doctor, isn't he?'

'Yes, as you w…well know.'

'He wasn't in the forces as I understand it?'

'Err…no.'

108

'At Oxford, learning his craft. Is that it? Is that why he wasn't pulled in like the rest of us?'

'Yes. Yes, that's right.'

'Strange that. Our information is that he was there a week and left.'

'Pardon.'

'Some misdemeanour or other. Doesn't really matter what. But…suffice to say, he has never qualified. Not as a doctor anyway.'

John stared at the other man. He felt his legs go weak under him as if one of the pillars of his life was crumbling away. He took off his glasses. 'No, that cannot be right. He's got p…patients and is in p…partnership w…with D…Doctor MacPherson. I don't know w…where you have got your information but you're w…wrong. Q…quite w…wrong.'

Grimes smiled and turned John's chair so that it faced the window. He sat in it, slowly shaking his head. 'No, John. There's no mistake. I can assure you.'

John looked away. 'How…w…what…'

'You're not the only one who's been fooled, believe me. He's also been going around saying he's older than he is. For what it's worth, I don't see how you could know. He's managed to con an old drunk like MacPherson and God knows who else. I'm sure he has enough idea of medical matters to be able to trick most people but…'

Grimes shook his head slowly and smiled. 'John, let me put my cards on the table. I need your help here. I'll be quite open with you – I think James is involved in Edie's death. And I think that he went round to the home on the night she died, in fact I'm certain of it. The nurse at the home – Dolores is it? – and old Ernie – who I know of old – deny seeing him. I've been to see Ava who says she didn't see him that night. I think he broke in. Perhaps he'd a key. But you've given me a statement saying he was with you. Now John…as an officer of the court I do not need to remind you of your duty to tell the truth. When all's said and done, you're a man of the law, a member of an honourable profession. I know therefore that you wouldn't knowingly lie. But isn't it possible that when you were sleeping off the beer, he slipped away? Could he have done that without you knowing?'

John closed his eyes watching the pieces of the jigsaw floating before him. This time they gently fell to the floor in their correct places. How often had he been brushed off when he asked about James's job? Why was it only when James wanted something that he would humorously describe an incident that occurred when he was working? MacPherson was incompetent. Everyone knew that. So it all could be true. And then there was the image which stuck in his mind; James moving serenely across Sherwood Avenue on that foggy evening, the evening when John had told the world that they were together.

But James was his brother. His brother needed help. His brother might be in trouble, serious trouble. How many times had his brother helped him? Got him out of a spot? And just because he was there that night, it doesn't mean he was involved.

'John, you should know that we've found no one who actually saw you and James together that night.'

He swallowed. His mind raced as pieces of conversations slipped into his mind, visions of people, things he had seen, what he had said, what would happen if he now said something different.

Grimes's soft voice merged with everything else in his head. 'And what about Ava? She is going to stand trial for her life. You wouldn't want to be caught up in a miscarriage of justice that leads to an innocent young woman losing that life.'

What about Ava? Her words at the inquest hammered against the inside of his head. She had not known what she was injecting. His heart lurched with a pang of jealousy as he thought of MacPherson, probably just as besotted as himself, preparing syringes, making excuses to see her. But supposing James was found to have lied about being there that night? It might give her a defence. At the very least it may provide a reasonable doubt as to her guilt. And that's all she needed. But there is the will. Jesus Christ – the will. Why hadn't he spotted it? It was now so obvious. She's convicted, she can't inherit, he does. The wording – Ava's gift goes to James *if it should fail for any reason.* James had insisted on that wording. A murderer forfeits a gift in their victim's will. If Ava is convicted of murdering the old woman, she's not entitled to the legacy. But, the wording in the will means that, in such an eventuality, the legacy to Ava goes to James. That is virtually all of the estate. He's planned all of this. He's fooled everyone.

'Mr Farrelly...John. If you say there was some period during the night when you were asleep and cannot account for your brother's movements, that'll do for a start.'

He had to tell the truth, just had to. He could not stand by and—

The *thud* made him start. He looked up as the door rocked gently on its hinges to see his father's bulk filling the frame.

'What the blazes!' was his cry. Perspiration was running down his cheeks. He moved towards Grimes. 'Get out! Get out of my office, I say! Get out this minute!'

Grimes slowly stood, grim-faced and glanced at John. It was a few seconds before he replied. 'What a pleasant surprise, saved me an extra journey.'

'Just get out! Your Chief Constable is going to know about this, I can assure you!'

The officer took his hat from John's desk and slowly backed out, his eyes flicking between John and his father. 'I will need to see you again John, I'll—'

'Get out! Go with him. Make sure he leaves.' John had not realised that Shirley had followed his father into the room. She scurried out and they were alone.

'What did you tell him?'

'Err…'

'Spit it out, boy.'

'I…err just said w…what I'd said before.'

'That your brother spent the whole night with you?'

'Yes, that's r…right.'

'Is that true?'

'Yes…yes. Why can't anybody believe me? W…why is everybody asking m…me all these questions? It's just not fair!'

'Why didn't you throw that odious police officer out?'

'Err…'

'You're lucky, boy. Very lucky. If I hadn't been delayed and Susan or Shirley or whatever she's called hadn't had the common sense to tell me what was going on, he'd still be there now, grinding you down. His type can smell weakness, boy. Now pull yourself together and stick to the story. Do not deviate from what you've said. Do you understand?'

*

The embers in the grate were now just a dull glow. Shirley had long since put her head around the door and mouthed 'good night'. Save for that, he had been left alone. Alone to think and contemplate and ruminate. And as he did, the dilemma grew into something monstrous, something bigger than him, something that would swamp him. Neither sitting at his desk with his head in his hands, nor pacing up and down his room, had come near to presenting him with a resolution. As the sky outside had darkened, as the furniture in his room had formed black shadows, so his despair had grown.

He was defending the woman he loved in a case where he had told a lie, a lie that made her conviction all the more likely. And there was no way out. He had veered from walking away from the case completely and letting down Ava to walking into Grimes's office and speaking the truth, thus condemning James when his presence at the home that night may have been totally innocent, nothing more. Each position was intolerable, an offence to all he should stand for.

Leaving the office into the dark night, a swirling, moaning wind blew clouds across the night sky and hurled litter across the Market Square. As the chill air buffeted and cooled his face, he closed his eyes, relishing the freedom from the four walls of his office, savouring the solitude. Here, he was free to live his own life. Here, there was no one telling him what to do, and worse, what to think.

He walked around the square and then walked further, out of the city and onto tree-lined avenues. On and on he walked. It was as he found himself back on the city's deserted streets that he finally came to a decision of sorts. It occurred to him as he unlocked his car, knowing his father would have retired to bed and he could go home, that it was the same decision that he had been making all his life. He would do nothing. It was not a decision in point of fact. It was a way forward allowing him to keep face with both. He would do everything he could for Ava, everything in his power to help her. And he would say nothing to Grimes. He was doing his best by both of them. He was not doing the best by himself. But this is something that he would steel himself to live with. And he would hope and pray it turned out alright. Because hope was all he had. He could no more control events than he could stop the wind blowing the litter around his feet.

It was only as he lay awake in his bed, listening to the wind rattling the window panes, that it truly dawned on him that he should include in those prayers a request for the strength of mind not to think about what he was doing.

Chapter 15

The day had finally dawned. John was standing outside the door to court number one, peering through the milling throngs, seeking out Randall or Sprite. Two large files containing just part of the paperwork the case had generated lay heavily in his arms. A third file was wedged into his brief case at his feet.

It was the day he had dreaded, but a day he wanted over and done with. He knew that it was only after the trial, when all this was but a memory, that he could start the process of emptying his mind of it all and getting back to his ordered, beautifully mundane existence with or without Ava. The knot in his stomach, the fear of the telephone ringing, the endless study of unfamiliar law and procedure would not leave him until it was all over. But the day had finally arrived. Today was the day when the trial would start, the trial which would culminate in twelve people, good and true, determining Ava's fate. And his own.

It was a day when the sun seemed brighter, as though that sparkling brightness was trying to provide an antidote to the first nips of autumn in the early morning and late evening. It was the day when his mother had handed him his coat as he left. The last time had been the day that she had decided that spring had finally overcome the winter.

Today's events, set up last June when she had been arraigned in the assizes at Nottingham's Shire Hall, had come around quickly. Since then, he had buried himself in his duties such as they were; collecting evidence and any number of character references, consultations with junior counsel, drafting the brief to king's counsel. He still tortured himself at his momentary initial flush of pleasure when his father had finished reading the twenty-three-page document and had complemented him as to its thoroughness and detail.

As the trial had loomed, like a brooding storm on the horizon, he had swayed from despair to outrageous optimism. His worst times, usually staring wide-eyed at the ceiling in the early hours, invariably had him convinced of the inevitability of her conviction and trying to think of the words he would use if asked to explain why he had given information to the police that made his job preparing her defence more difficult. His best times, which were generally in James's presence, had him visualising the jury foreman saying they had unanimously found her not guilty. Such fantasies did not end there. They usually unfolded into the perfect life as a so grateful Ava accepted his proposal and had them making a home together in blissful happiness. At such times, he even had names for their four children. But even then, even as the euphoria of her inevitable victory was at its sweetest, the thought of James on that foggy evening slipped into his mind and he would look at his brother fearing that all his illusions were about to be smashed.

There had been two meetings with her when, chaperoned by his father, he had tried to ensure that he had collected all of the evidence that Sprite thought might help. She had seemed so small in the grey, austere room. Dark roots showed starkly against her scalp. He'd replied to her request by saying that of course he would ensure that her mother could have permission to hand in her hair dye and best frock for the trial. She had kept the conversation going. What was happening on the outside? Were people talking about her? Were her photographs in the papers the good ones? As her words floated over him, he yearned for the intimacy he dreamed would be theirs. Her soft voice enveloped him, caressed him so that he heard it but not her words. For brief moments he could even forget his father's presence, forget the stony-faced warden standing in the corner of the room, forget the bars in the window and the screwed down table and chairs.

As they had left on the second occasion, she had thanked them for coming and for their help. For a second he thought she was going to kiss him on the cheek. With a hand laid on his, she craned her neck forward but stopped as the warden made a step forward. She glanced at his father before turning back to John, flashing a tight smile. In truth, it was at that moment that the magnitude of it all had swept over him, like the sea taking a swimmer who was out of his depth. It was then that he could have slumped to the floor, crushed by the weight of her predicament and his part in it. But God had answered his prayers in part; he stayed on his feet, the tears stayed within, his face didn't crumple, his upper lip stayed ramrod firm. God had given him the strength of purpose to carry on, enabling him to function, at least to the outside world.

At a third meeting, just last week, this time accompanied by Sprite, there had been no such attention. A brief shake of the hands was all there had been. Perhaps the meeting with junior counsel had reminded her of the closeness of the trial. That must have been it.

On arriving this morning, he had pushed his way through crowds congregating outside the court. Queues, women wanting to show support for one of their own or men wanting retribution against one who had dared to want more than her due, had snaked around the side of the court building. Reporters had collected at the large swing doors, snapping all who entered. Ava's story and the forthcoming trial had rumbled on in the press throughout the summer. Such comment as was needed from the firm had, mercifully, been dealt with by his father and John himself had been left alone. He had hoped that by arriving so early this morning he would have avoided them. By hiding behind the large frame of a uniformed police officer, John had slipped in unnoticed, retaining his anonymity.

Now, black-gowned and bewigged figures, their instructing solicitors and clerks in tow, sped here and there. Ushers with lists on clipboards, similarly gowned, barked directions. There was still no sign of counsel instructed for the defence.

John's vacillations as to whether to enter the courtroom or not were finally resolved by a bushy eye-browed, grey-haired usher. 'That man! Don't block the doorway!'

As he entered, his heart lurched, his stomach churned and he stopped still, forgetting momentarily the weight of the files. Dark oak surrounds, rising high above him gave the court a box-like shape. A scent of lavender hung over the polished gleaming wood of benches running across court number one. White light shone brightly on the elevated empty judge's chair, the deserted witness and jury boxes and the vacant dock. But it could not repel the shadows in the corners. This was a place where daylight never came, where it was not welcome. How apt. Even here, in this courtroom, where God would hear proclamations that the truth and nothing but the truth would be told, there were secret places, out of sight, where the barristers and the judge would not probe. None of them had any interest in what had happened. Their collective attention was drawn to what could be proved and where did the truth come in deliberations of that nature? Not even a poor second. The truth here was simply a victim of the system and the system's need to be seen to work. In his Cambridge days, John may have participated enthusiastically in mock trials in which such matters would have been pored over in the minutest detail. Now he cared not one jot. It was all about the result. His role in the process was not as a representative. He was a party, a relation, a friend. That was the role he had assumed. And then, there was more; he was a witness. Not that he would have to enter the witness box. Not that his statement would be read out. Not that the press and the public, ravenous as they were for all the gory detail, would know anything of it. He swallowed as his conscience once more spoke to him. It wasn't that he was no better than the rest, he was worse than the rest.

What would she feel as she was brought up into this enclosed, forbidding space? Would she feel his terror, or welcome the attention? Hadn't she once told him that one day she would be famous? Maybe that was the difference between them. She would embrace her role. He would not.

'Ah! There you are Farrelly, my good man!' Randall's voice seemed to carry to all parts of the court. His white, pristine wig fitted snugly on his large head of curled sandy hair, perhaps once a fiery orange. A big nose and big mouth dominated his flushed face. His flowing black gown just added to the impression of size. He was the colour in a black and white world. John felt large eyes bearing down on him from a great height. 'Don't just stand there, man.' Suddenly the whole appearance dissolved as a smile broke out. 'Let's take up our allotted places, eh Sprite, my man?'

'If you say so, Mr Randall.' The smaller man stepped out of the Randall's shadow. About John's size, his hangdog expression in a long, acne-ridden, clean-shaven face was the antithesis of Randall's bonhomie. Black cotton hung from the worn edges of his gown. His wig had lost its sheen. A grey mark down one side seemed to mimic the hair on which it lay.

'How's your father, young Farrelly?' boomed Randall. 'Top fellow.'

'Oh, he's…err—'

'Are we being graced with his company today?'

'Err…n…no, he's…err…tied up with—'

'Pity. I'm only involved in this rather unpleasant business as a favour to him. We served together, you know. In the Great War. I've got some tales I can tell about those days. Both officers. Sherwood Foresters. You did your bit, I understand, Sprite, old man?'

'I got through the last two years. It's…err, not something on which I speak of.'

'Well, young Farrelly, I'm sure we'll have chance during a break to discuss all of this. Now, not totally familiar with the

116

business of today. Civil litigation's my field. Sprite here is the criminal man. That's right, isn't it, Sprite, old man?'

'I have spent many a long day on these benches, Mr Randall, if that's what you mean.'

Sprite led them over to the front benches indicating the place behind where John should put the files. Sprite then looked around and beckoned John and Randall towards him.

'I've had a quick word with Preston. He mentioned a couple of things. If our girl was to plead guilty, he thinks old Stoppard would put in a recommendation for a reprieve. Preston reckons she'd be out in ten to twelve years.'

Each word was delivered slowly, as if allowed into the open only after great thought had been given to its suitability.

'Stoppard's our judge, as I understand it?'

Sprite nodded at Randall.

'Well,' said Randall, his face once more dominated by a wide smile. 'Isn't that our answer? The last championship match of the season starts today. Three days at Trent Bridge would be just what the doctor ordered. Shall we go and talk to her?'

'Now let's just stop there a minute, Mr Randall,' said Sprite. 'The prosecution case is compelling but by no means free of difficulties. They have to prove that Miss Brownlie was responsible for the deceased's death with malice aforethought. I think that they have a reasonable chance of successfully arguing that Miss Brownlie could have been responsible. But that's a world away from proving beyond a reasonable doubt that she was responsible. It's all rather circumstantial, and Preston knows it. That she may or may not have had a motive is no evidence of murder. In any event, this is a poisoning case. A recommendation from the trial judge can be influential with the Home Secretary in many cases, but poisoners generally are not reprieved whatever the trial judge may say.'

'So what are you saying?' asked Randall, a frown lining his forehead.

'I say we take our chance. Stoppard is straight down the line. If he thinks they can't prove it, he'll withdraw it from the jury.'

John's mind raced, trying in vain to think of something that might add to the conversation. But he had warmed to Sprite; here was someone who was at home in this arena. He thanked God for that at least.

'So what's the girl saying,' asked Randall, 'when arraigned, I recall that she was non-plussed by the whole thing.'

John butted in. 'She denies it all. She d…doesn't know how Mrs H…Harris died. It was nothing to do with her.'

'Right,' said Randall, sighing.

'The other thing, rather curiously,' started Sprite, 'is that Detective Inspector Grimes has been taken off the case.' He lowered his voice. 'Apparently, it's caused quite a rumpus on the prosecution side. Grimes evidently was convinced that others were involved, in particular a Mr James Farrelly, who has been running around masquerading as a qualified doctor without a letter to his name. Preston did say that it had occurred to him that there may be something in it. The clause in the will to the effect it all goes to him if Miss Brownlie can't inherit for any reason is curious, to say the least. It seems as though he gets the lot if the girl goes down.'

'He's your brother, young Farrelly, is he not?' asked Randall.

'Yes, but—'

'Your father took me to one side and tipped me the wink on this. The confounded fool Grimes was making a perfect spectacle of himself. Not a shred of evidence against your brother, according to your father.'

Sprite looked at John, studied him. 'Mr Farrelly, I know it puts you in rather a tricky spot, but it is your statement that totally exonerates him. Preston has asked me to check that you stand by it. If so, they'll leave it and their case is the girl's acted on her own. There's no possibility that you're mistaken over dates or times are there?'

John felt Sprite's eyes gazing at him. The vision swept into his mind, the one that refused to be bottled up. Once more he saw the dark but unmistakable form of his brother emerge from the shadows into the mist on Sherwood Avenue before disappearing inside the pebble-dashed house. His brother or the love of his life? The question he had buried deep inside, the question he had avoided asking, had been drawn to the surface for examination by all present. But the choice was not so stark. Sprite had said that the prosecution thought they may be in difficulty in proving their case. There was no decision that he had to make. Was there? Was there? The words screamed in his head. But. But. What was so wrong with just telling the truth? Could he not say he had been mistaken? Sprite had reached over with the olive branch, showing him the way out. Things were now crystal clear; to tell the truth created the reasonable doubt that someone with a motive other than Ava could have been involved. Yet it went nowhere near proving James was involved. That surely must be the right thing and that's—

'You look rather squiffy, young Farrelly. It'll be the lack of air in these damn places. Take a seat, eh?'

John looked up at Randall. His heart was beating, his pulse raced. But the moment had passed.

'As I say, your father assured me that there is no possible way that any member of your family can possibly be involved. Sprite, when we start, just slip a note to that effect to the Crown, there's a good chap. Let's move on, shall we?'

Sprite glanced at Randall and then looked back at John. 'Very well, Mr Randall. The Crown's case will therefore be that she was on her own and that she did it for the money. Mr Farrelly's statement stays out and we don't suggest that James Farrelly was involved,' said Sprite. 'Undoubtedly our main difficulty is that there's no one else with any motive who could have committed this offence.'

'Your father was particularly eager that we should ensure that your family name is not dragged through the mud,' said Randall. 'Well, young Farrelly, you can advise him that victory on that score would appear to be ours. I'm sure you'll both sleep a little easier tonight.'

John saw that Sprite appeared to be about to say something when the sound of footsteps against the wooden floor and the scraping of chairs made them all look to the front.

'All rise.' A voice boomed out and John stood in the well of the court behind Randall's large back looking as the judge, resplendent in a blood-red gown and white wig, slowly took his seat. Horn-rimmed glasses framing a thin, bony face peered over those present as he placed his papers before him and unscrewed the top to a pen. John followed everybody else and sat.

Looking around, he saw that the public gallery was now full. There was no space on the hard, uncomfortable bench on which he sat or the bench in front where the barristers were competing for space. Things proceeded slowly as the jury was sworn in, counsel whispered to each other, the press scribbled on pads in front of them until, suddenly, there was total silence. John closed his eyes and mouthed a prayer.

Clicking heels on concrete, far away at first, then louder and louder could be heard. John opened his eyes and turned in the direction of the dock behind and above him. A door swung open and Ava, his Ava, strode into the apparently spacious dock. All eyes in courtroom one were turned towards her. She grasped the bar running along the front and looked around, a tight smile on her face, before gazing at the judge straight ahead.

John felt a light tapping on his shoulder. He found himself looking into Sprite's face. Several spots seemed to be in the verge of erupting. John breathed in his stale breath as the words hit him. 'Who on earth is the fool who arranged for her to have her hair done? A peroxide blonde on trial for her life is not a cocktail I would generally advise. As much as anything else, looking like that in front of a jury could do for her. She looks like a tart.'

John stared at him, feeling a blush creep up his face. Before his head could fully take in Sprite's comment, he turned as another voice echoed around the arena. The clerk, sitting in front of the judge, read the charge and asked her how she pleaded.

'Not guilty. Definitely not guilty.' Her tone was strong, confident. As the eyes of those present turned towards Preston who had risen to his feet with a flourish, John stared behind him at Ava. She swept her skirt up from behind and sat down, still smiling.

So, now the trial was to start. And smiling was the last thing that he felt able to do.

Chapter 16

John's hand was on his office door when he heard the roar. His heart sank at his father's bellowing command ordering him to go and see him without delay.

'Trying to avoid us, eh boy? Thought by creeping in when everyone's gone home you wouldn't have to report back to us? Is that it, boy?'

John shook his head and looked at his feet. Earlier today his intention had been to ask his father at some point why they had got leading counsel who did not specialise in defending people charged with criminal offences. As he looked into his father's eyes, he realised his error in not coming straight to his father. And now was not the moment to raise the matter.

'Right, then. What's happened?'

James stood at the window, his back to them. 'Before you start,' he said, turning, 'you've said nothing which contradicts your statement?'

John stared at him, hooked by his brother's wide, haunted eyes, his grey pallor. The whole expression was not one he had ever seen before.

'N…no. Of course not.'

James closed his eyes and breathed out. He then smiled. 'Never crossed my mind that you would, Johnny boy. So what's occurred? Sit down, eh?'

As he did, John thought back to the day's events. The legal argument in the absence of the jury that morning had been one that in different circumstances he would have found interesting. Now, like everything else in the case, it wound his stomach into a knot. Travelling back by train from their visit to Ava last week, it had become apparent that the point had occurred to both him and Sprite. If the prosecution could show that she had knowingly injected morphine but could not disprove any assertion on her part that her intention was to alleviate pain, she was surely not guilty of murder. Yet, her stance was that she had not realised she had injected

121

morphine if that's indeed what it was. But, as Sprite had said, you have to think of all the possible scenarios.

Randall had said that the argument was better put forward by Sprite. Sprite and Preston, together with the judge, spent most of the morning considering this before coming to the tenuous conclusion that the issue was in fact one for the jury. If the prosecution could show that she had administered morphine which had resulted in death and that the intention was to shorten life then the jury was entitled to convict and Stoppard would direct them accordingly at the appropriate time. If there was a reasonable doubt as to this intention, the matter would be different. Stoppard's aside during the exchanges as to whether pain relief to the degree administered was required was something that had jarred in John's mind and still did. Sprite had mumbled over lunch something about that being as good as it was going to get on that matter and the trial proper started after the jury had trooped back in at that start of the afternoon.

The opening speech by Preston had been short and to the point, reinforcing the simplicity of the prosecution case. Ava stood to inherit the vast estate of a woman who had died in suspicious circumstances whilst in her care. Ava had accepted at the inquest having responsibility for the care of the deceased, had agreed that she had administered injections and the prosecution case was that she had shortened that woman's life to get her hands on her vast estate. What other explanation could there be? It really was that simple.

Just two witnesses had been heard during the rest of the day. The first, Mr Jobson the chemist, had given largely uncontested evidence to the effect that he had provided morphine, and a considerable amount, as a result of prescriptions signed by Doctor MacPherson, to be used over the last few months for a variety of patients at the home. It had generally been collected by Nurse Dolores or her husband although the prisoner had been twice in the weeks before Mrs Harris's death. Further than that, he had no knowledge of events at the home. On being told by the judge at the conclusion of his evidence that he may leave, he had scuttled away clutching his trilby, tripping on a step as he went.

The other witness, that dreadful nurse, had spent her hour in the witness box pointedly not answering the questions posed, but providing the information that she felt relevant. Had she been responsible for the deceased's medication? No, that was Miss Brownlie's job. She'd come highly recommended by Doctor MacPherson. No point having a dog and barking yourself she'd added, to laughter from the public gallery. John had noticed that one or two on the jury had smiled. Given that the rest of her evidence could be summarised as her and her Ernie losing the fees of a very generous and loving patient and what had she to gain from her dear old Edie's passing, the court was none the wiser as she strutted out. Save, thought John, it was one less person who may have been involved. And that was why the prosecution had bothered calling her. They would soon show that Mrs Harris had died from morphine poisoning, that Ava had been the one administering it, that she would benefit from her patient's death and therefore must have knowingly caused it. As John was relating to his father and James what had happened, it suddenly all seemed so simple. And so hopeless.

He closed his father's door behind him and the pessimism which he had felt on occasions before the trial now returned with a black edge which dogged him through the evening and night. Whichever way he looked at it, he could not see how the jury would not believe Ava was guilty. But they did not know her, not like he knew her. Intentionally harming another human being was something that she would never entertain. The proposition that she may do what the Crown said she had done was utterly preposterous. But they weren't getting the full story, were they? As he lay awake that night, his statement crystallised into a document exonerating James at the expense of Ava. He had burned his bridges on that. The relative tranquillity he had enjoyed before the trial was explainable, partly at least, by the fact that at that time his position was not final. He could always go back and say that he had been mistaken. Now, that point had passed. He would now have to live with the choice he had made. Or, to put it more accurately, to live with his indecision. And if this sleepless night was any indication, living with that was something he was going to find impossible. His final thought as he drifted into a light but dreamless sleep was the look on James's face in his father's office that evening. Now, as sleep finally overcame him, he understood. Fear. No, more than that. Terror. And it was not on account of Ava.

*

'Morning, Farrelly.'

John turned towards Randall's thunderous voice.

'Had your father on the line last night. He was still a little concerned that your brother's name might get dragged in. This business about practising without the necessary qualifications or whatever. I think I've been able to resolve that little matter. Kindly tell your father that Preston has agreed not to bring it up. It's not germane to the matter before us. Preston doesn't want Stoppard jumping on him for confusing the jury.'

Sprite wandered up. John was beginning to realise that his dejected expression was a permanent feature rather than an indication of his present disposition. 'They're calling Roche before MacPherson. Apparently, they think it'll help if Roche explains how the old girl died before MacPherson confuses everyone. We'll see I suppose.'

Visions of the inquest slipped back into John's mind. At the time, he had barely taken any notice of any of the witnesses. He would have been unable to describe any of them afterwards such had been his torment. Now, despite being sick with nerves, but with the responsibility for testing the prosecution case resting on the shoulders of others, he found himself taking note of those in the witness box. A small, grey-haired, bespectacled man stood there, blinking.

Having established that Doctor Roche was the Senior Home Office Analyst for matters such as this, and that the organs he had examined were those of the deceased, prosecuting counsel carefully went about extracting the required evidence like a vulture might pick at its carrion.

'What, in your opinion, was the cause of death?'

'Oh, poisoning. By morphine or heroin. I understand that Multiple Sclerosis had been diagnosed and there was some mild dementia but these conditions did not contribute to her death.' Roche's quiet voice suited him, but the impact of his words bounced off the walls of the court.

'Can there be any doubt?'

'Oh no. There can be no doubt. None at all.'

'Given the diagnosis of Multiple Sclerosis, would that have caused death in time?'

'It may shorten life but to no great extent. The reality is that but for the morphine, more likely than not, she would have gone on for years.'

'Would the body exhibit any visible signs, of the morphine, I mean?'

'The deceased, as I understand it, prior to her death, developed a blue bordering on grey pallor. It's called cyanosis.'

'As you understand it?'

'Yes, that's what Doctor Birkenshaw told me. That's why I was asked to take a look.'

'And who is Doctor Birkenshaw?' interjected the judge, peering over his glasses at Preston.

'He carried out the post-mortem, My Lord,' replied Preston.

'Is it intended that this Doctor Birkenshaw should give evidence?'

'No, My Lord, his health is a matter of concern presently but—'

'Well, how can this witness give evidence of what he has been told?'

'The actual cause of death is not disputed, My Lord, therefore—'

'Is that right?' The trial judge stared at Randall.

Randall stood and looked down at Sprite who quickly nodded. 'That is correct, My Lord.' John noticed how of all those who had spoken, Randall's voice was by far the loudest.

'Well,' said the judge, 'if that is the case and it helps the jury to understand the trail of events, I suppose it does no harm.'

'Doctor Roche,' continued Preston, 'would you enlighten us as to the effect of morphine on the body. As simply as possible, if you would.'

John noted the look Roche gave Preston, recalling that of a second-year tutor when he had been unable to accurately explain the difference between a misdemeanour and a felony.

'Yes. It is a drug which is directed at various sites in the central nervous system. The usual purpose is pain relief although it has no local anaesthetic properties.'

'Every type of pain? Is it used for all pain?'

'No. Generally it's prescribed for chronic pain in its severest form.'

'How does it lead to death, generally speaking?'

'The effects, whether given by mouth or by hypodermic injection, are rapid. There can be a period of excitability followed by deep sleep, moving into a stupor and then coma is common. The pulse is initially rapid but irregular and then quickly slows as the patient slips into the coma. Breathing can be noisy. Death from morphine poisoning is as a result of respiratory failure. Generally, death occurs within six to twelve hours of a toxic dose. I should add that the effect can vary widely from person to person and different patients will exhibit different symptoms.'

'Let us turn, if we may, to the results of your investigations in the present matter. Again, as simply as possible, what did you find?

I'm sure if you wish you may be allowed to refer to any notes you took?'

'Do you want to refer to notes?' asked the judge of Roche.

'Yes, it would help. I did make them immediately after I carried out the necessary tests.'

'Very well.'

Roche continued. 'The deceased's stomach contained 3.28 grains of morphine. Her heart just under a fifth of a grain and her kidneys had three quarters of a grain. Her liver had a small amount.'

'Can you explain what all this means?' asked Preston.

'Yes. In effect, the deceased was riddled with the stuff. I would estimate that her body contained in all over four grains of morphine. Almost certainly, the deceased was given a significant amount a few hours before she died which led to congestion and then to her death. Death was therefore as a direct result of the administering of morphine.'

'In layman's terms, how much morphine?'

'Put it this way; had she taken this in liquid form, she would have had to have consumed five or six twelve-ounce bottles. One grain could be sufficient to account for someone not accustomed to the drug.'

'You mentioned heroin at the outset. Did you check for heroin?'

'I did, but you asked me to keep things simple and it's no simple task to detect heroin. Heroin is a diacetyl morphine and, when in the body, quickly changes to morphine. It is hard to say whether heroin had been administered. But whatever was in the body should not have been there in anything like those quantities. It's that which effectively killed her.'

Preston thanked the witness and sat down. Randall slowly rose, turning the pages of the notes he had taken. John noticed him glance down at Sprite who turned away. He flicked over more pages before saying he had no questions.

Stoppard smiled at Randall, stood up and announced that this was a good time for lunch.

*

As MacPherson shuffled towards the witness box, John thought back to their first meeting. James had tagged along with John during the long summer holidays to meet George, the kindly old doctor's only son. For John, the friendship he had formed with George at Cambridge had been deep and longstanding.

At that first meeting, on his manicured lawns, Doctor MacPherson had thrust a copy of a magazine – he couldn't recall the title – in John's face, pointing at a photograph of a smiling man in a white coat with a cigarette held in mid-air.

'See this, young man!' He swept a strand of dark hair away from his shining blue eyes. 'See the title! "More Doctor's smoke Camels than any other cigarette." How can they be allowed to print such nonsense? Mark my words; there will come a time when such drivel will be viewed as an anathema to the medical profession.'

Even James had stubbed out his cigarette. John could picture now the look in the Doctor's eyes as he had touched his wife's hand, no doubt his way of saying thank you for bringing out lemonade on that hot afternoon. He remembered how he had called over the gardener and asked him to sit with them as he sipped the drink put in his hand. And he remembered the Doctor's kindly eyes looking at whoever was speaking, as if what was said was the most important thing in his life at that moment.

The afternoon had shot by as they were regaled with stories of travelling around Europe, Jazz clubs in London during the twenties. He'd said nothing about the war; the Great War, his war. John had spotted the black and white photograph standing at the back of a shelf of the Welsh dresser; khaki dressed sombre soldiers in a line, the haunted expressions on their unlined faces not dimmed by the passing of the years and the fading of the photograph.

George junior's death in an air raid the following autumn had started the downward spiral. The death of the Doctor's wife at the Christmas, said to be caused by her overwhelming grief, had finished the job. Alcohol had quickly moved in to replace all he had lost. The general consensus was that he had been saved by James's generous agreement to become junior partner in the practice.

Now, the unkempt mop of grey hair and matching bushy eyebrows and the red hue of tiny veins criss-crossing his bulbous nose and cheeks told their own story. A light grey, crumpled suit seemed at odds with the shadows of the courtroom. Even from where he was sitting, John saw that MacPherson's bow tie was not straight and fancied that he could make out a stain of some kind on his white shirt. As he clutched the bible and stammered out the oath, John thought once more of the photograph. The once distinguished features now bore frowns as he stared at the words of the oath. His skin clung to his cheekbones giving him a haggard look. The dull, blue-grey eyes were now a pale imitation of their former selves.

Stoppard asked straight away if he would like to give his evidence seated to which MacPherson mumbled his thanks. Preston's initial questions were general and MacPherson was able to deal with them with little apparent difficulty. His voice shook and there were several occasions when Stoppard asked him to repeat his answer and to speak up. The court was told that MacPherson had first come across the deceased at Nurse Dolores 's home.

'How long had she been a resident there when you first saw her?'

'Well, I...err...don't keep records, so I could not be certain on that point.'

'What was wrong with her?'

'Well, it was...err...quite complicated. As I recall, she...err...had a number of complaints.'

'How did you treat her?'

'I do recall that I prescribed a mixture of Kaolin.'

'And what's that?'

'Well, it's a mixture of sodium bicarbonate with peppermint water. It just would make her a little more comfortable. It comes in twelve-ounce bottles.'

'Did you prescribe morphine?'

'Err...no, I don't think so...no. Definitely, not.'

'We've been given copies of the prescriptions that you signed. They were collected from Jobsons, the chemists nearest to Sherwood Avenue, I'm led to believe. I note here that you appear to have signed a prescription for chlorodyne.' Preston brandished a piece of paper. 'I understand that this is a tincture of chloroform and morphine.'

'I don't recall that.'

'Take a look at this, Doctor MacPherson, if you would.' The prescription was handed to the older man by an usher. 'Is that your signature?'

'Yes. Yes, it is. I'm sorry, I forgot about that. It would just have been to make her a little more comfortable.'

'Now, Doctor MacPherson, we must—'

'I've just remembered. Barbiturates. To help her sleep. I prescribed that as well.'

'Yes, we've got the prescription. Can I ask you about some of your other prescriptions? They show that for a considerable period of time, both before and after the deceased's arrival at the house, you have prescribed a significant amount of morphine.'

'No…no, not a significant amount. There may be the odd one. There were some unfortunate patients who did need strong pain relief.'

'Mrs Harris?'

'Err…no, I wouldn't have said so. There was a Mrs Briscoe. Ethel Briscoe was her name. A sweet old lady. I do specifically remember seeing her before Christmas when she was in quite acute pain. I think she had gangrene in her lower legs. She had morphine. I'm sure of it.'

'Yes. You signed her Death Certificate. A stroke. That's what you said.'

MacPherson stared at Preston, open-mouthed. 'Oh. That had slipped my mind, I'm afraid. I really don't recall that. It's so difficult…' His voice trailed off. John bit his lip, once more thinking of the summer's afternoon. MacPherson's eyes remained fixed on Preston like a drowning swimmer staring at a far-off lifeboat.

'Anyway,' said Preston, throwing him a lifeline, 'Mrs Briscoe's death has no bearing on the instant matter, so perhaps we may move on. Are you saying you were not responsible for all of these prescriptions?'

'Well, I …err don't know. I don't recall.'

'Do the prescriptions contain your signature?'

'Well, yes. It appears to be me.'

'Let us move on to the prisoner. We heard from Nurse Dolores yesterday. She said that you recommended the prisoner?'

'Did I? Well, if that's what she says, that must be right, I suppose.'

'How did you come across the prisoner?'

'I'm afraid I cannot remember. One meets so many people, you understand. I do remember her being in my surgery. She said she had done nursing work in the past and I think that would be at the time Nurse Dolores needed some help.'

'How did you know she needed help?'

Randall quickly stood, grabbing hold of the table as he did. 'My Lord, are we not drifting off the point? We are here to determine how the deceased met her end, not to discuss the staffing of an unregistered nursing home.'

Stoppard looked at Randall. 'I suppose you're right, at least about the home…although I feel that the jury ought to be made aware of how the prisoner managed to acquire employment as a nurse with, as I see it, precious few qualifications.'

Preston responded, 'My Lord, on reflection it's not disputed that the prisoner was employed as a nurse. I would like to conclude the evidence of this witness today if possible, so perhaps I might move on.'

'Very well,' said Stoppard.

'Doctor MacPherson,' continued Preston, 'It is abundantly clear to me that you have prescribed a significant amount of morphine.'

'Yes, I have to confess that does surprise me. But you have to remember that Nurse Dolores took in a number of patients who were coming to the end of their days and who would be in pain. When...err...you've seen what I've seen...the trenches were desperate places, you understand...pain is something that you do try to alleviate.'

'I'm sure. You don't keep records of who the morphine was for, do you?'

'No, I'm afraid not. When my dear wife was here, she used to deal with that side of things.'

'Did you show the prisoner how to administer an injection?'

'Yes, I believe I did. Somebody asked me to, the nurse I think or now I come to think of it, it was Doc—'

'We need to know why rather than who. Why was that necessary, to show her how to administer an injection?'

'I...err—'

'I'm not sure this witness can be expected to answer that question,' interjected Stoppard, 'surely that is something within the knowledge of the prisoner.'

'Very well, I'll move on. Did the prisoner ever tell you that the deceased was in pain?'

'I...err... I don't recall.'

'Did the prisoner ever ask you to prescribe morphine?'

MacPherson suddenly put his head in his hands. For a minute, he said nothing. Suddenly, the only sound that could be heard was his sobbing.

'Is this a good time to have a break?' asked Stoppard.

'My Lord,' replied Preston straight away, 'There's nothing more I wish to ask. I'm anxious that this witness should be spared the ordeal of having to return tomorrow. Perhaps my learned friend could commence his cross-examination now with a view to finishing as soon as possible?'

'Mr Randall?' said the judge.

Randall stood. 'Oh...err...right.'

Sprite turned to John and rolled his eyes. It was forty-five minutes later when Randall finally sat down. His line of questioning, drawn up during a lunch-time conference with Sprite to which John had been invited, had become bogged down like a tank in the Flanders mud as MacPherson floundered between not remembering and not knowing. When it was put to him that the prisoner had never spoken to MacPherson about morphine or pain relief generally, MacPherson simply mumbled that he could not be sure of anything after all of this time. There had been a similar response to Randall's suggestion that MacPherson himself had prepared the syringes used by Ava.

After Preston had announced that the prosecution case had been concluded and as papers were swept up at the end of the day, Sprite suggested that this would be a good time to discuss whether any evidence should be called by the defence.

'You m...mean Ava not giving evidence?' asked John.

'Exactly,' replied Sprite.

'Doesn't that look as though we've something to hide?' asked Randall.

Sprite stared at Randall. 'Let's talk about it tomorrow.'

Chapter 17

MacPherson trudged out, closing the door softly behind him. His pathetic bleating that he could not do without him, how he would never be able to cope, that they would sort out a role for him, that he would help him qualify, was the price of hearing about today's events.

James picked up the Enfield, the hand gun he'd discovered in that old man's effect the previous day, something to add to his collection. His finger ran along the sleek, black barrel, as he visualised a bullet emitted from it, twisting and flashing through the air, its target already selected, marvelling at its ability to kill.

He pulled a bottle and glass from a drawer of his desk and poured himself a large whisky. He switched off the light and sat down. The glass cabinet with the medicines, the glass ashtray on his desk, the dark tiles around the fireplace, the body charts on the walls all shimmered in the light from the street lamp outside his rooms.

He closed his eyes, yearning for absolute darkness. Finally alone and with glass in hand, he relaxed. Sleep was unlikely to come, now or during the night. He sensed that this was a pivotal moment. If his plans continued to roll out as he anticipated, he would soon be able to see the inevitable conclusion. Tomorrow was key.

His mind began to drift. He slipped back to those long-gone days and to the cupboard under the stairs. The kitten, all stiff and stick like, all bone and matted fur, lay cradled in his arms. He breathed in and could almost taste death's sickly, pungent perfume. Darkness put its arms around him, comforted him.

Here, in his cupboard, time had stopped. Here, he could think. And plan. And reflect. And his mind hovered over the whole matter, checking for weakness, ensuring all was as it should be. But tomorrow was key. What a clever, clever man that chap Grimes was after all. How surprising. Utterly wasted in the police force. It had never occurred to James to have a wife, or soul mate, whether male or female. It was not something he did or would ever do; the thought of touching someone, something alive was something that, to him, was absolutely repugnant. He shuddered. And so when the dear man had been pontificating, it had opened up a new world, new possibilities, new strategies.

And sometimes, just sometimes, one needed that flexibility of mind. One needed to be able to stand in another's position and see things from another perspective. And so he had visited her last week and talked of their future, talked of a future envisaged by Grimes. How she had glowed. He had never realised that declaring undying love, that bearing your soul, could be so easy. Even in the dank room with the bars, he could sense her heart beating under the grey prison garb, could see the pulse beating against that slim white neck.

How they had talked, the whispered plans they had made. They were plans that would come to pass – that was so because that is what he had said. He could still hear his voice, as if it had been another person talking; 'don't fret my dear, even if it should all go wrong, pretty young things in your position are reprieved.' They always were. She could rely on him. That's what he had told her. Her eyes had melted into his. Her intensity, her longing, had hammered against him. Why, even as she had placed a hot hand in his, he had kept his composure, had squeezed back, had not retched. She was his. Without any doubt, she was his. Totally his.

And what would they do with the money? Country houses, a pied a terre in London, maybe somewhere in the south of France. How she lapped it up, like the cat that had the cream. Of course, he would stand by her, that's what he had said. It would be for but a few years. Then they would set her free, set them free. They would still have their youth, their looks. And the money, all that money. And think of her fame. She would be someone, someone who would be noticed. Someone who had risen from the gravest peril to the highest of the highs. But fame needed oxygen. It needed the oxygen of her story. It needed her own words. She had to tell her story. The world needed to hear it.

Yes. Yes. She had whispered it breathlessly. She would do it. She had to do it. Even if it were to go wrong, how could they later prove her innocence if her story stayed within her? She saw that. She had to give evidence.

But the thrill. This had taken his cravings to a new level, to a heightened exquisiteness. The irony. He was sending someone to their maker with the power of his mind, with the power of control. There would be no injection, no fabricated death certificate. The law, with its pathetic majesty, its all-consuming power, would take its course, would do his work. But only because he had made it so. His power was the greater. All he had to do was think, and plan and reflect. He thought of the *Punch and Judy* shows on the pier, John's rapt features entranced by it all, mother's smiling face. It was the operator that had always fascinated him, the one that controlled it all, out of sight. And here he was. The proprietor of his own *Punch and Judy* show. A show for the whole world.

His heart beat, his skin tingled, that all too familiar feeling was here as he encountered death but there was more. Now there was that element of personal danger; an extra aspect. Grimes had proved to be an opponent who deserved respect. The fear that James had felt, that stomach churning dread of a knock on the door, had been genuine. It was only now that he understood the full nature of the risk he had undertaken. But it was something he embraced. It was something he recognised would be a necessary ingredient to whatever he did in times to come.

He opened his eyes and breathed out, gazing at the gun and caressing it once more before putting it in the bottom drawer of his desk. Biting his lip, he prayed that he was right and she would do as she had been told.

Chapter 18

'Well?'

Randall's voice boomed through the empty courtroom. John and Sprite were sitting at their allotted places.

It was Sprite who answered. 'She wants to give evidence. I saw her last night and she was adamant. I took young Mr Farrelly this morning to see if we could change her mind. Had she not given evidence at the inquest there would have been little evidence that she had administered anything and we could have given firm advice not to give evidence.'

John looked away.

'It's not necessarily such a bad thing if she gives evidence, is it? I spoke to young Farrelly's father last night and he was of the view that she should,' said Randall.

Sprite's glum expression stared at Randall. 'Depends what she says, I suppose, and how she says it. She did enough damage at the inquest by admitting the injections. I can't see how telling the world and his wife what was in her mind when she did it can make it any better. I have to be honest – I think it's a bad idea.'

Fifteen minutes later the expectant courtroom was full. The only sound as she made her way to the witness stand was the clicking of her heels on the slabbed floor. Wearing the same clothes as on previous days, her hair had retained its peroxide sheen and stood out against the dark wooded background, drawing all eyes towards her.

As she took the bible in her right hand, John noticed her red nail varnish and was taken back to her cold, spartan bedroom all those months ago. Then he could reach out and touch her, such was her proximity to him. There he could speak her name. There he could tell her about his day. Now, she may as well be on the other side of the world. Shaking her head as she was offered the small white card by the usher, she mouthed the words of the oath. John gazed her at her slim neck, the flawless skin of her face, her lips as they delivered the words, her pale blue almost colourless eyes, yearning for them to catch his as they raked over all present. Finally, they rested on Randall as he asked her for her name.

The first few questions were answered in a firm voice and with a smile. She corrected Randall's mispronunciation of the Nottingham suburb of her birth. She spelt the letters for the judge. All stared, entranced. Her words of that morning came back to John.

'One day I'm going to be famous. You see if I'm not.' Those words ricocheted around his head. Here he was, stomach churning, his heart beating against his chest so loud that he was certain she would hear it and finally look in his direction, and her words had come true. And she was actually enjoying it.

'Tell me how you came to obtain employment with Nurse Dolores.'

Randall's question brought John back.

'I was looking for work and Doctor MacPherson told me of the post.'

'How did you know him?'

'D…a mutual friend introduced us.'

'What experience have you?'

'I've no qualifications as such, but I have worked before doing something similar.'

'And when did you start?'

'That would be the 15th January this year.'

John realised that here at least Randall was in his element. Evidence was evidence whatever the area of law and, as the table tennis like exchange proceeded, so the foundations were being laid upon which Ava could stand and tell the world that she had done nothing to hasten anyone's death.

'Edie was a lonely old soul. She just liked to talk. And I suppose I was the only one who had the time. She could be confused about the here and now but she was better when she spoke of the past. She often told me about her holidays before the war when she had her family with her. She missed them, she really did. Do you know she had three stillborn before Denis came along? Denis was her pride and joy. That's why him putting her with Nurse Dolores really upset her. And then, he never came to see her. I was upset for her.'

John was brought back once more. The eyes of all those present were staring at the vision. Even the judge, not slow to intervene until now, was ensnared. Occasional glances at the notebook in which his fountain pen recorded the evidence were the tiniest of interruptions.

'Doctor MacPherson? He was a kindly man. I liked him. If I told him I was on the early shift, he would often pop in. Nurse

Dolores was often out on her errands and I would make him a cup of tea. He told me about his wife. He was lonely, like poor old Edie, I suppose. He just wanted someone to talk to.'

John glanced at the jury box. Twelve faces all looking in the same direction, trapped by her words, softly given, taking in what was said like a sponge. She was dragging the whole thing round. Not by legal argument, not by taking a point of law but by being herself. Randall had simply created the stage where she could play her part, and that part was the easiest one of all for her. She was just being herself.

'Doctor MacPherson showed me how to do an injection. He said it would make her more comfortable, help her sleep. I would never have harmed a hair on that lady's head. You see, she was just so kind. I even began to look forward to going in.'

Paper rustled from the other end of the benches. Preston, frowning, and those with him were flicking through paperwork. A whispered word could not break the spell that Ava had created.

'Did you inject her with morphine?'

'Of course not. Barbiturates, that's what Doctor MacPherson told me it was. To help her sleep. Just to make her easy. I just wanted to make things better for her.'

'What about the money? The money left to you, I mean?'

'I had no idea. I knew something was happening about her will. I didn't know she was rich and she didn't say anything about leaving any money, at least not to me.'

The will, the will that he had hurriedly drafted, slipped into John's mind. This was just one more piece of the jigsaw, the jigsaw that James had produced. It was only when each piece was in place that the whole picture could be seen. But the picture's accuracy was dependant on every piece being included; any missing piece distorted the picture. As Ava's words drifted over the courtroom, John looked briefly once more at the jury, praying that the absence of the piece he had hidden, the piece that supported her story, didn't render that story incapable of belief.

Randall sat down and Stoppard said it was time for lunch. Sprite opined during the break that the morning could not have gone any better but the true test was still to come. It was only after the cross examination that they would have a proper idea about Ava's performance. Randall supposed it was similar to assessing a wicket. It was only after both teams had batted that a proper assessment could be made. John thought it nothing like, but kept quiet.

Preston drew himself to his full height. 'So, Miss Brownlie. Tell us about your nursing experience.'

'Well, it's not experience as such, but I helped look after my grandmother a while back, before she passed away.'

'You accept you've no qualifications?'

'No, but I can do the job alright.'

'I take it you've never worked in a registered nursing home or a hospital?'

'No, but—'

'In fact, your only experience is in Nurse Dolores 's unregistered home?'

'Yes, but—'

'A home which takes in the elderly and infirm for money without any authority ever vouching for the standards of care being exhibited. Did you lie about your qualifications?'

'Well, I wasn't really asked. I think Doctor MacPherson vouched for me.'

'And how did you meet Doctor Macpherson?'

'Doc…a mutual friend introduced us at the club.'

'The club?'

'Yes, it's the Blue Lamp Club, it's a gentleman's club. I worked there.'

'And what were your duties at this club?'

'My job was to ensure that the gentleman had drinks and what have you.'

'You made sure they spent money?'

'Well, if you want to put it like that.'

'In fact, you are a prostitute. That's right, isn't it?'

'No—'

'I'm sure Doctor Macpherson had no knowledge of what was going on but you were working in a brothel, that's right, isn't it?'

'No, that's—'

'Anyway, let us move on. So you had no idea the deceased had left you this money?'

'No, I had no idea.'

'This lady who was quite happy to talk of tragic events in her life—'

'Yes. We became very close.'

'You must have learned something about the type of life she led?'

'I don't know what you mean.'

'Was she a local woman?'

'Yes. I believe so.'

'She lived here, in Nottingham?'

'Yes.'

'Looking after her son, Denis?'

Ava suddenly smiled. 'Yes, her pride and joy.'

'Did she talk about their activities together?'

'Yes.'

'What did she say they did?'

'Oh, this and that.'

'Holidays?'

'Yes, I believe they had holidays.'

'Where?'

'Err, I think she mentioned Great Yarmouth. She went there a few times.'

'Yes, Miss Brownlie, Great Yarmouth. And where did they stay?'

'I'm not really sure, she—'

'Well, what did she tell you about the holidays?'

'About what they did, about the problems in looking after Denis. She often said she needed to protect him. People would make comments when they were out and…well that's why she was so hurt when Denis didn't visit her.'

'Problems when they were out? People making comments? Didn't this cause a problem in the hotel or wherever they stayed?'

'Oh, they stayed…'

'They stayed where Miss Brownlie?'

'In a house.'

'Which house?'

'I don't know.'

'It was a house she owned, wasn't it?'

'Err…I think so.'

'So you knew she had an estate which included another property as well as her home in Nottingham?'

Ava said nothing.

'You spoke at the inquest about jewellery. Diamonds in point of fact. I'm going to suggest that you knew or at least strongly suspected that Mrs Harris was leaving an estate of a significant value.'

Ava said nothing.

'She had no close family, other than Denis, did she?'

'Err… no, I don't think so.'

'Surely Mrs Harris told you what was in her will?'

'No, not at all.'

'Oh, come, Miss Brownlie. As you say, something was "happening" with her will. In other words, she was changing her will. You had become, by your own admission, close. It simply flies in the face of common sense for you to proclaim that you did not know she was leaving you her estate.'

'Well, it stood to reason that Edie would want to leave something for Denis.'

'Why did it? According to you, she placed the responsibility for being in the home firmly at the feet of her son. Her resentment – a resentment that we only know about through you – was deepened by his refusal to even visit her. Why did you presume that she would leave anything to her son?'

'Well. I—'

'There was no one else it could realistically go to. She is changing her will. You have become close. The only possible reason for changing her will is to disinherit her son.'

Ava said nothing.

'Miss Brownlie. It's perfectly obvious to me that you were well aware that you stood to inherit an amount of money that would have been beyond your wildest dreams.'

'No, that's not right, you're twisting what I'm saying.'

'Let's move on. You were responsible for the deceased's treatment, were you not?'

'Yes, Nurse Dolores told me—'

'Nurse Dolores did not treat her?'

'Well…not while I was there but—'

'Did Doctor MacPherson ever treat her in terms of actually injecting or medicating her?'

'I…err don't think so.'

'Did the deceased ever say she was in pain?'

'No, no she never did.'

'So why were you injecting morphine, a drug designed to kill pain?'

'I didn't think I was. I didn't know it was.'

'Do you dispute Doctor Rhodes' evidence to the effect that – let me look at what he said – the deceased was riddled with morphine?'

'I…err don't know.'

'If you weren't giving her morphine, who do you say was?'

140

'Well, Nurse Dolores was there most of the time and I heard her complaining about Edie.'

'Let me make sure I understand what you are saying. You are asking the jury to believe that a nurse who has nothing to gain from the will and in fact loses nursing fees as a result of the deceased's death was in fact responsible for that death.'

'Well…Doctor MacPherson prepared the syringes or whatever you call them.'

'So, now you are suggesting that the family doctor is responsible for the death?'

'I—'

'You have no answer to give. We know that the deceased met her death through morphine poisoning because that is what Doctor Rhodes told us. We know that you are the only person who accepts injecting the deceased. We know that you stood to inherit a fortune as a result of that death. I've no further questions.'

*

John stood at a first-floor window on the Shire Hall, watching Nottingham's traffic flow by. He had returned following a telephone call to his father and taken in fresh air after the bear pit of the courtroom. He looked at his watch. The jury had been out for two hours. Sprite had ventured that the longer they took the more pessimistic he felt. John pulled a cigarette from his jacket pocket and, with trembling fingers, lit it. He couldn't turn around; he might catch the eye of her mother and have to say something.

Each question Preston had asked felt like a punch in the stomach. As the slaughter played in his mind, each answer seemed more pitiful. Like prey in the jaws of a wild beast, she had been given no time, no leeway, no sympathy.

Two hours five minutes. Time, like the criminal process, moved slowly.

'I've sent Mrs Brownlie out for a cup of tea.' John jumped as he felt a hand on his shoulder. 'She's not bearing up too well, as you might imagine. The usher knows where to find her.'

John thanked Sprite for his thoughtfulness. Sprite walked off and John looked at those milling around the waiting room, wondering who they were. Were they friends? Family? How little he knew about her.

Two hours twenty minutes.

And yet she had placed her life in his hands, his and those who had spoken on her behalf in court. It was a trust he had abused whatever the result. He had provided information which stopped the prosecution from proceeding against the person who may be guilty of this crime or at least knew a great deal more about it than he had revealed.

Two hours thirty minutes.

And where was James now? Keeping well out of the way, that was for certain. John had not seen his brother for the past two days. Perhaps a manifestation of guilt, perhaps he had done his work. Then again, maybe Grimes was wrong, maybe James had done nothing other than try to help Edie. Maybe John was forcing the pieces into the wrong places.

'The jury is coming back. The usher has gone to fetch her mother.' John followed Sprite back into the court, head down, throat dry, lips silently moving as he prayed for one more favour.

Chapter 19

The most perfect of perfect days has finally arrived. Sunlight, like ripened lemons, bathes everything in its fairy dust. The sapphire sky in which it hangs gleams, as if buffed by the long-gone winter storms. Clutching their pink and white invitations, the privileged few mingle. Ladies in never before worn frocks of crimsons and blues and yellows and greens, gentleman in sharply cut suits of light grey with handkerchiefs peeping out of breast pockets and neck ties in matching red, create a riot of colour at one with the happy occasion. Faces, awash with expectant smiles, look expectantly down the lane. Laughter, like a tinkling piano, blends with the murmur of polite conversation.

White blossom floats slowly from leafy apple trees to the manicured verdant green lawns where they stand. A gentle, tepid breeze ruffles the orange, cherry and yellow rose petals in immaculately tended borders. Their spring fragrance merge with the exquisite perfumes worn by the ladies. Luscious, deep green ivy clings to the slate grey walls of the country church, an otherwise picture postcard building nestling in the rolling Nottinghamshire countryside.

John's new morning suit, a darker grey to that of the others, creaks as he glides from guest to guest. The Mayor, his glinting golden coat of arms lying on his rounded girth, slaps him on the back, uttering words of congratulation, telling him that a career in local politics is a sure-fire route to greatness and, as the country struggles to its feet after the hardships and sacrifices of war, young men with vision and vitality are needed to guide and energise the recovery. And how good it is to see the county's finest settling down with the support of a good woman.

High-ranking officials of the Nottinghamshire Law Society shake John's hand, asking whether it is in order to arrange appointments on his return from honeymoon to discuss possible roles on the committee and saying how wonderful it is to have something to celebrate after the dark days of the war. And how splendid that justice has prevailed and that his bride can now carry out her worthy work in the newly formed health service and take her rightful place alongside him in the highest echelons of county society.

The rector with his white hair and bushy eyebrows, wishes him all good fortune, adding that it is gratifying to see young men such as him leading the rest of us, using God's words as their guiding principles. And, of course, behind every great man stands a good, Christian woman. It is days like today, celebrated in the eyes of God, that provide the perfect antidote to the hangover from the war.

Just as the last of them walk away, John feels a hand on his shoulder. There stands James, dressed in attire matching his own, telling of his pride at being John's best man and how he and Ava will reap the happiness which everyone knows should be theirs. John shakes his hand, any doubts he may once have had over his brother now, like the winter's frosts, a distant memory.

Finally, his father approaches, his mother a few steps behind. He places two large hands on John's shoulders and whispers words describing his pride and voicing his belief that the firm can be in no safer hands as it strives to take advantage of the opportunities presented by the recovery from war.

A car, matchbox like in the distance, can be seen on the lane winding its way towards the church. John smiles as the gleaming black Bentley glides to a halt at the bottom of the path. Feeling butterflies tingle in his stomach, he enters the cooling, dim interior of the church, leaving James to usher everyone in. Candles, standing head height in ornate golden holders each side of the aisle, create an intimate atmosphere in keeping with the day. Flowers of reds, whites and blues, hanging in baskets, make a vibrant backdrop to the taking of the vows. As he takes his pew at the front John kneels down and then looks up at the cross, dominating everything. Gazing at Christ, John mouths his thanks. His prayers have been answered, all of them, and John will show his gratitude in the good works he will undertake for the rest of his life.

The shuffling of the feet of people entering and the low purr of conversation is drowned by the organ as it announces her arrival at the top of the aisle. John stands and allows himself a glance over his shoulder. A slight, momentary concern – who is giving her away? – is swept away by the vision that is Ava.

Her white dress and hair the colour of summer hay shimmer against the dark background. As she glides forward, her features became clearer through her headdress. Their eyes meet, his lock into the pale blue of hers, her face lights up and John, for the first time, tastes perfect happiness.

Ava. His Ava.

'Come on, John.' On hearing James's voice and feeling a hand on his shoulder, he turns and moves forward, waiting for his bride to join him by his side.

'Come on, John.' More tapping on the shoulder.

'John!' There's now an urgency to the voice. But it is not James who is speaking.

'Come on, John!'

He's coming. There's no need to shout. How can he miss the happiest day of his life?

'Wake up, John!'

His eyes edged open. He turned to his side, seeking out Ava's smile. Darkness. Nothing.

Fingers gripped the top of his arms. Pulling him. Dragging him up.

'Wake up, John. Please. You've got to wake up.'

The side of his face lay squashed against something hard, cold and unforgiving. He forced his head up. Shirley. Shirley? A frown creased her forehead. Concerned, watering eyes looked into his.

'Your mother telephoned my mother last night. She was worried sick as you'd not gone home. I've come in first thing. I thought you may be here.'

The world spun around his head. He said nothing.

'Look, you were lying on the desk. The papers have gone everywhere. I'll tidy them up in a moment. Come on, no harm done, let me get you some tea.' John felt himself pulled gently to his feet. A wave of nausea broke over him. He clamped his teeth together fearful of retching. His eyes caught the dead ashes in the fireplace and he shivered. A bitter taste – stale beer – made him swallow. Another wave as remnants of the previous evening sitting upstairs in the Trip, the argument with the Landlord in the Salutation and being sick in the toilets somewhere or other replaced the dream in his head. Shirley took his tie in her fingers and drew it up to his neck.

'You'll do.' She smiled. 'Your father will be in in a few minutes. Tell him that you spent the night in my mother's spare room. The last thing you need is a dressing down from him.'

She smiled once more. 'I'll get the tea. You look as though you could do with it.'

145

John slumped into his chair, as if pushed down by the cares of the world. Out of the corner of his eye, he saw the screwed-up ball of paper by the side of the waste paper bin. He reached down and picked it up. Flattening it out with the ball of his hand, he forced his eyes to take in the typed words, words on a telegram from Randall telling him that the Court of Appeal could find no error of law and that her appeal had been dismissed.

He looked at the flipchart calendar and pulled off the top page. Today's date stared at him in large, red accusing figures. One week today. That's when it would happen. That's when the state would kill her in cold blood. Unless he could do something to persuade powerful people that it shouldn't.

He ought to build the fire or get someone to do it. He lent back in his chair and closed his eyes. There was no point. It didn't hide the stench of smoke and beer and it didn't stop the hammering in his head. And it didn't help her. Nothing could.

*

'And where the blazes were you last night?'

His shirt and trousers seemed to stick to him. The heat from his father's fire burned his face. 'I…err…spent the night at a friend's. I…err—'

'Oh, don't waste my time with your facile explanations! You look absolutely dreadful. Had my father seen me in that state he would have kicked me out without hesitation, I can tell you. I would just add that upon my return from London yesterday, I found your mother in the most frightful state, worrying about you. Just pull yourself together, boy. This is a difficult time for us all you know, not just for you.'

'I—'

'I suppose you know what's happened. Inevitable according to Randall.'

Even now, having had the night to digest it, the reminder that this latest part of the process had failed and that they were one step closer made him want to run away, escape to a time when such burdens were alien to him. Panic threatened to overwhelm him as his helplessness stood before him, oblivious. Tears were forming, he had to say something. 'I really don't see why I couldn't have gone?' Even to John, it sounded pitiful. The time his mother had cancelled the annual trip to the circus because he had caught a cold crept into his mind.

'For the love of God boy, we've been through this! You're too heavily involved...you've no objectivity. In any event, who was going to run the office in my absence? The tooth fairy? And please remember that this whole mess is of your making!'

'Yes, but—'

'Right, this is where the real work starts, according to Randall that is. The jury's recommendation for mercy will not be lost on the Home Secretary. Representations need to be drawn up. If you want to make yourself useful, get on with that. Randall said something about a petition to highlight the sudden change in public opinion. Get that sorted. And for God sake, wash your face!'

He turned and walked to the window. Rain from a grey sky pattered against the glass. When he spoke again, it was as though John was not there and he was giving voice to private thoughts. 'Never ceases to amaze me. During the trial, when the whole story is trotted out, there is no sympathy whatsoever. Now you'd think an angel had fallen from heaven. Doesn't alter what she's done.'

He turned back. 'You still here, boy! Haven't you any work you should be doing?'

Chapter 20

A white frost twinkled in the light of the half moon. Its reflection trembled in the inky waters of the Leen. James stepped from under the bridge and gazed at the pin-pricked stars, lying across the night sky like spilt salt. They had been there for thousands of years and would be there thousands more. He just needed four days. Four days and it would be over. It was then that the state would do his work. He shivered, but not because of the cold night air.

For once, the old man had been right. The visit today had been productive. He thought once more of her sitting in the chair, hands squeezed together on the table, as if in prayer. Dark roots stood out against her white face and blonde hair. She really could have done with those seeing to. She seemed to have lost weight; her skin clung to prominent cheekbones. Frightened eyes looked into his, desperate for assurance. He smiled.

But assurance is what he had given her. The appeal? Don't worry about that, my dear. They never work. Now, let's keep our voices down, eh? The warden in the corner can't hear us, but we need to keep all of this to ourselves. So not a word to anybody, eh my dear? The reprieve? That's what will work. It will be late, very late, and therefore spectacular. How the world will rejoice. Had she not heard? Her face was in all of the newspapers? Her name was in headlines? She was famous. Her name was being mentioned in Parliament, even at this very moment. And when the reprieve came, when it was acknowledged that she had nearly been the victim of a gross miscarriage of justice… well, then her name will be engraved in the hearts of all, never to be forgotten. Why, her name could by synonymous for evermore with the abolition of this medieval ritual. And then, well then they would be together, together for eternity. Yes, of course we would see that her family was alright. Yes, her mother was bearing up. But let's talk about our life together when all this is sorted. Let's talk of how we will spend the money. How you will be feted wherever you go. How we will live without a care in the world.

On his leaving, there was a slight flush on the cheeks of her face. She had smiled and moved her lips towards his. Fortunately, the guard had quickly noticed and she had recoiled at her sharp words. 'Move away! No touching!'

At this very moment, she would be lying there, her nerves calmed by his pledges that it would all be alright. Yes, the old man had been right; keep his damn fool brother away and go and see her. Tell her it was all under control. Just to keep her quiet. We can't afford to let her blabber. That is what his father had said. Wise words. Because once it was done, once it was all over, then he was safe. The state would not countenance the idea that anyone else may be involved because that would mean it might have done away with an innocent person. God forbid.

He smiled again as he watched a rat scurry towards the water's edge. Once more the death of another under his own direction made his body tingle. He was the puppeteer and doing a damn fine job. Four more days. All he had to do was wait.

He wondered at John's sudden zest for life this evening. Standing in the now deserted Market Square, the workers had long since caught their buses home. James had looked up into John's second floor window, yellow against the darkened evening. He wandered forwards until he stood underneath the open window. Even from that distance, James could hear his little brother striding around the office barking orders to Shirley, or whatever her name was.

James bit his lip. Whatever happens, Ava could not be allowed to see him. There was no way that she could be allowed to see him.

*

Wind whistled around the Market Square. A cold, bright sun ducked in and out of the scudding white clouds. John ran between those whose only thought was to get back to work or to catch the trolley bus back home. 'Madam, please sign the petition. It's to stop the murder of an innocent woman in two days' time…sir, add your voice to the clamour for a reprieve…help stop a grave injustice.'

Most had signed, some had even sought him out to sign. Newspaper billboards blared out her name. The nationals had taken up her cause. He had even spoken over the telephone this very morning to a reporter from Fleet Street. The reports in the locals had the added spice that this was one of their own, from their neck of the woods. The whole world had only one name on its lips.

Even his father had been swept along. Just yesterday morning, he had knocked on John's door and sat down on the opposite side of the desk encouraging him to get himself out into the city to drum up support. He had said that John had no time to see her, that wouldn't help her now. No days out in Winson Green. He would be able to see her after the reprieve. But for now…fortified by his resolution to do something positive and by his father's words, John had cancelled the pointless visit and here he had been since.

'John.' A rasping voice from behind made him stop.

He turned and found himself looking into an ashen face, an aura of illness reinforced by several days of stubble. Bloodshot eyes peered out of dark hollows. Uncombed hair lay lank against the scalp. John took a pace back as he was hit with the stench of stale beer.

'John. There's still time.'

'Detective Inspector Grimes. I hardly r…recognised you. Are you…are you alright?'

'He's going to get away with it.' Grimes grabbed John's arm. 'I tell you, he's going to get away with it!'

The slightly slurred words sounded like sandpaper against his throat. John gently took his arm away. 'Look. You look in a b…bad way. Let me buy you a coffee.'

The nearest café, by chance, had been the venue for that first date with her. Forty-eight hours ago, maybe less, such a visit was one he could not have contemplated. Now, he had a purpose. No longer was he standing by the side, watching others. Now he was actually doing something that may be useful. And, all of a sudden, he seemed to be functioning. How many signatures had he got? Well into the hundreds, maybe more. Surely that together with the newspaper clamour may be enough?

Grimes, sitting opposite, had not taken off his coat. A film of grime coated the collar of his shirt. His tie hung loosely to one side. He pulled a packet of cigarettes out of his pocket and took out the last one. With trembling hands he lit it, sucking greedily, before swallowing half of the mug of coffee John had placed in front of him.

John welcomed the warmth as he sipped his own, thinking of something to say to fill the awkward silence. Suddenly words tumbled from the man opposite. 'It's not too late. You can still save her.'

'That's what I think. W…with the newspapers on our side and w…with all the support from the people of Nottingham, I'm beginning to feel quite confident.'

'Petitions! Are you mad! Do you think anyone actually looks at them?'

John ignored the glances from people at the neighbouring tables. 'Keep your voice down.'

'There'll be no sympathy for a poisoner. Poisoners don't get reprieved. Her only hope is for evidence casting doubt on her conviction. And you already have that, you know you have.'

'I don't know w…what you mean,' said John, the reminder of his statement dousing his better frame of mind like rain on a trip to the seaside.

Grimes looked round the room, wild eyes raking the whole scene. 'The more I think, the more certain I am that she's not responsible.'

'You w…were responsible for prosecuting her.'

Grimes looked around again and then lent forward, whispering. 'You know I was taken off the case?'

John nodded. 'Yes, I heard.'

'This is between me and you. It goes no further. Right?'

Again John nodded and leaned forward himself.

'To what extent she was involved, I cannot be certain. But I am sure that brother of yours is. It's the only way it all makes sense. She did not have the knowledge or expertise. Not to act alone, anyway. Your brother either acted alone and has duped everyone into thinking she did it or, less likely in my view, they were in it together. And if she swings, we'll never know. I took all of this to my superiors but they weren't interested.' He looked down at his hands, forming a tight-fisted ball on the table. 'A little bird told me they won't prosecute a medical man.'

'I recall that you took g…great d…delight in telling me that James is not a qualified doctor.'

'Makes no difference. They need the co-operation of the medical profession to make sure that the new system of free treatment for all coming in next year is not scuppered. Any prosecution of a medical practitioner, whether qualified or not, where pain relieving medication has led to a death would scare doctors rigid. There but for the grace of God go I; that's what they'd think. And then there's your father. He was quite vocal in his criticism of me when I was trying to put the frighteners on your brother. So, they only went against the girl.' He now looked up, his eyes staring at John. 'When I said we should go against your brother, I just had your statement thrown in my face.'

'I'm desperate to save her but conspiracy theories w…won't help, of that I'm sure,' said John, deliberately ignoring the reference to his evidence.

'Agreed.' Grimes once again grabbed John's arm. 'But there is another way, a way which will work.'

John stared at the other man.

'Write to the Home Secretary. Tell him you were mistaken. Or at least say you could have been mistaken. Allow for the possibility that your brother is involved. At the very least it will give us time.'

John left Grimes in the caféteria. As he walked through the city streets, he didn't notice the sharp shower that led to umbrellas being raised. He didn't notice the people. The need for signatures was something which no longer occupied his mind. His strides grew longer, his pace quickened as he made his way to the office. There he threw his hat and coat to the floor and pulled headed paper from his drawer. His pen flowed fluently over the paper as he set out how he saw James entering the home during the evening before Mrs Harris died and that any statement he had made to the contrary was in error. He signed the letter and lent back in his chair. He closed his eyes feeling cleansed, as if a thunderstorm had blown away the mugginess of a sticky summer's day.

Hearing his office door swing open, he opened his eyes and covered the letter with his arm.

'You're back early, boy. Did the rain get in the way?'

'Err…yes, that's right,' he muttered, realising that concealing anything would attract his father's interest.

'Who are you writing to?'

John looked up at his father, desperately trying to think of an answer.

'Let me see, boy.'

John had little choice but to let his father to read the letter and sat back waiting for the explosion.

'Well, if that's what you're saying.'

John stared at his father, open-mouthed.

'Look, we need to work together on this. You get back out there. Get as many signatures as you can. I'll draft the request for a reprieve based on the new evidence in your letter. Be back here by five o'clock and I'll catch the night train to London. If I pull some strings, I think I'll be able to see the Home Secretary tomorrow and do what I can…well, boy, what are you waiting for?'

John smiled at his father and left the office, finally free, free of the lies the deceit. Now, for the first time in months, he and the truth, he and justice, were on the same side, they were bedfellows, not walking on the opposite sides of life's road. He could now face the world head on. And so he hunted down signatures with a renewed vigour and determination which did not take 'no' for an answer.

Chapter 21

He sat, elbows resting on his desk, head in hands, utterly numb. He knew the pain would hit him, that he was in that brief period when the trauma had occurred but his brain was yet to take it in. The time he had stubbed a toe on a doorframe on his fifth birthday running from James came into his mind. There was that moment of acute clarity, that sliver of time, when he acknowledged the force of the blow and knew that the pain was hurtling in his direction. His eyes slid to the clock. Ten minutes to nine. She had just ten minutes. And now there was nothing they could do. All efforts were spent. All efforts had been in vain.

The waiting yesterday, locked away in this office, desperate for news, seemed so pointless. The day had been spent staring at the telephone, gazing out of the window, staring at files, unable to turn his mind to anything. Momentary hope had come about five o' clock when his father's telegram had arrived. 'Still here. Reps being considered. Hopeful for audience this evening. Will return by early train tomorrow.'

But as time slipped by with no news, so the doubts grew. And it was as he heard his father's ponderous footsteps mounting the office stairs this morning, as John tore out of his office, as he saw his father's blank face, that he realised that there was now no hope, that they had failed.

'I was coming to see you. I've been to see her mother.' Further words were unnecessary. John had turned slowly and pulled his office door shut behind him. He sat at his desk and opened the file on top of the pile before pushing it away. He stood and walked to the window. Stick like figures in the square became blurred blobs in his tears. He sat down once more, drew his sleeve across his face and stared in front of him, seeing nothing.

A knock on the door. He blinked. Then whispering and footsteps shuffling away. His eyes automatically sought out the clock. Two minutes past nine. It had happened. It was over. Why hadn't he felt anything? How could the moment have passed without him realising?

A grey man in a grey suit in a far-off city had ended a life. Deliberately. Intending to do so. Because the state had told him to. The state had directed him to, even though it now knew that she probably wasn't guilty. He couldn't feel anything. Not at the moment. But the anger, the wretched bitterness would come. He knew it would come. Just like he had known that his toe was going to hurt.

The telephone rang. He automatically lifted the receiver from its cradle and held it against his ear. 'Mr Randall for you.' He heard the click as Shirley put down the receiver.

'Morning, Farrelly. Thought I'd give you a call. Thoroughly bad business. Don't feel responsible, whatever you do. There's nothing more you could have done. Absolutely nothing. These things happen. As barristers and solicitors, there are times when you have to accept that the law will be applied in a way which may not meet our approval. And when...'

John stared in front of him. The voice on the other end of the line droned on. The words bounced off, not penetrating. Finally, a gap appeared. The silence meant that Randall was expecting him to reply. He ought to really. It was decent of him to ring. But there was nothing to say. There was nothing he could say.

'This is your first, isn't it?'

There was no point in replying. There was no point in anything anymore.

'You will get over it, old boy. It takes time. Take a couple of days off then back on the horse. Best way.'

More platitudes filled the silence.

'Not that it doesn't affect us all. I suppose you learn how to deal with it. That all comes from experience. We all have our different methods, you know old boy. Your father came over yesterday afternoon. I think he just needed to parley. I know we both had one whisky too many and it dragged into the evening, but it was a comfort. For us both, I suspect. The peace of the Lincolnshire countryside, away from everything, is probably what we both needed.'

Yesterday afternoon? Yesterday evening? The words hung there, waiting to be claimed. Why did it matter? He tasted salt on his lips. Gradually the words and their significance acquired a meaning. He looked at the clock. Its hands were blurred.

'Yesterday? You saw my father yesterday? Yesterday afternoon? Yesterday evening?' He didn't recognise his own voice.

'Yes. I'm sure he'd have asked you to come had he thought. During the trial I'd said he should come over for a catch-up. Last night was the only time he had any spare time. In other circumstances we would have had a pleasant evening, reliving the old days. The trenches were awful, I don't mind telling you. But we got over it, and you'll get over this. We both had a skinful so I put him up. Pass on my regards and tell him I hope his head's not too bad. I—'

John slammed the receiver down and stood up. The world span. The contents of his office, his father's portrait on the wall, files, books from the cabinet, swam around his head. He gripped the edge of his desk and finally retched over the papers before him. The fury was coming, at first like far off thunder, then louder, then louder still until it burst into his head. He pushed through his door, stumbled down the corridor and kicked open his father's door.

'What! This may be a difficult morning boy, but that doesn't mean you can come bursting into my office. Knock and wait to be admitted, will you?'

His father's dark eyes looked up from behind his desk. As John met his stare, those eyes retreated into the folds of flesh, finding refuge on the piece of paper in his hand. James was standing by the lit fire, papers between his fingers, looking from one to the other.

John's head was suddenly bereft of the clutter. Now, he saw it all, the whole jigsaw, each piece merged with its neighbour, their edges obliterated. The responsibility was so obvious. Momentarily, he was stunned. Stunned by the duplicity. Stunned by his own naivety. His hand yanked the piece of paper from his father. His eyes stayed fixed on his father. He did not need to read the letter in his hand. He knew what he had written. The words of his confession were words he could never and would never forget.

Sparks and crackling drew his eyes to the fire. Names, hundreds and thousands of them, were browning and curling in the flames. James brought his hands away and looked at John. It occurred to John that he heard never seen his brother blush before.

'Families have to come first, boy.'

John looked back at his father.

'She was going to blabber. I…we had no choice. No choice at all.'

'That's right, Johnny boy.' John turned towards his brother. 'I'm sorry. But we really had no choice. There was never any chance of a reprieve. What was the point in dragging me in?'

'You needn't look so righteous boy!' John's eyes were dragged back to his father. 'You're as involved in this just as much as anyone. More so in some ways. You could have stopped it at any time. All you had to do was tell the truth. But you lied, boy. And that girl's blood stains your hands as well as ours.'

His father stood, drawing himself to his full height. John stared at him. His father looked away and then walked slowly to the window, his hands behind his back.

'I've agreed to pay the girl's mother an allowance. It'll help her...well, it'll help. She seemed almost grateful. She's going to move away. I advised her it was for the best and that she should never speak to anyone about the matter. With all the talk there'll be, it's the only way she'll get any peace.'

His father laughed, the humourless laugh of one who was used to getting his own way. 'You, boy, are going to get back to work. You are going to forget about this. And, like the girl's mother, we are never going to speak of it again.'

John stared down at the letter held in the fingers of his hands. He thought of the future, a future denied to Ava. He looked at his father's back. He looked at James, his brother's arm draped over the mantlepiece, his unsmiling face betraying no emotion.

John would tell the authorities what had happened, his part in it, his father's part in it. And that his brother was a murderer. Yes, that's what he would do. It was the right and proper thing to do.

Who was he kidding?

They were the actions of a brave man. He was not a brave man. Never had been, never would be. No, whilst brave deeds swept through his head, driven by an anger at himself, he knew that his father was right. They would never speak of it again. And, if the story was not spoken of it would die. But John, his father, the firm would continue as they had before. The days, weeks and years lay before him, tied to a profession which he had entered at the behest of his father.

He picked up the gold Tommy, standing on the corner of his father's desk. He let it lie in his hand, surprised at its weight. He turned to his right and hurled the commemoration of battles won by brave men through the glass door of the cabinet. After the shattering of the glass, a total silence reigned. John stared, eyes wide open, hand trembling, at his father's medals, the photograph of him with the Lord Chief Justice, the scroll evidencing the permission to practice and the family photograph, all lying haphazardly on glinting shards.

He looked at his father and then at James before turning and going back to his own office.

Part Two
July 2005 – Nottingham

Chapter 22

The trial may as well have been taking place in IKEA. Gone were the days when courts conjured up fear in the hearts of those unfortunate enough to be dragged there. Light, airy spaces; that's what you got these days. The crest, attached to velvety-mauve curtains, hung behind three middle-aged faces sitting behind their bench on a raised, light oak dais. In the well of the court stood several more rows of benches, all but the first two empty. Large windows with fitted blinds, magnolia walls and a wall-to-wall colourless carpet completed the calming aura. Even the perspex dock to one side could have passed as a greenhouse.

At one end of the front bench, facing the magistrates, stood a power-dressed prosecutor, clutching a statement from which she plucked snippets of information allowing her to frame her questions. He was sitting at the other end, as far away as possible, trying not to retch at her overpowering perfume which hovered like a pea souper fug over the whole shooting match. The firm's three-monthly figures, masquerading as papers connected to the case, lay between his fingers.

Finally, he'd had enough and drew himself to his feet. 'Your worships, I wonder if I may interject just for a moment and ask the prosecutor to pose her questions in a way that doesn't lead this witness. It won't have escaped your attention that the witness is a serving police officer who I am quite certain is capable of telling the story without being spoon-fed.'

The middle of the three faces smiled at him. 'Yes, Mr Farrelly, that had occurred to me.' The magistrate looked at the prosecutor. 'Don't lead the witness.'

Dust motes hovered in the slatted rays of golden sunlight sliding in between the plastic blinds. A reporter to his left doodled on her pad. If only she knew. The scoop she had been waiting for all her life was passing her by. A probation officer bent down and whispered in the ear of an usher before scurrying out. The usher followed at a more leisurely pace.

Having shown his client that he was still awake, he went back to the rows of numbers. The text that had lit up his phone ten minutes ago, telling him that the bank wanted to see him within the week, still screamed out. An unpleasant vision came into his head – Rod Chisolm's beady eyes gleaming at him through folds of pasty flesh. A Managing Partner, someone to deal with the tiresome administration, attend to staffing matters, had seemed a good idea five years ago. It allowed John to concentrate on his passion – his clients. Now, it seemed as though he was having to put as much effort into protecting his staff from the Managing Partner as he did in fighting for those clients. The unexpected downturn in profits this past six months had spawned a desire on the part of Chisolm to scrape away anything that resembled fat. John liked the money as much as the next man, but ridding the firm of its strength, namely the people who brought in fees, seemed just wrong. He read for the tenth time his text to Chisolm; 'partners meeting first thing Monday morning, no dismissals before then, let's get tonight out of the way.' His forefinger flicked over his phone from letter to letter. It bought him time but did not smack of complacency. It would do. His hand hovered, just for a moment, before he pressed down on the word 'Send'.

Suddenly, words floated over the court which captured his attention. No one else would have noticed, but he did. It was the slight hesitation, the way she dragged out the sentence as if giving herself time to think. He glanced to his side, hearing the rustling of papers and watched her slim fingers flicking through her notes of evidence. Years of experience told him what was going through her head; she was asking herself what she had missed, whether there were any gaps, whether she had asked all the right questions. Finally, she announced to the world that the prosecution case was closed and that there were no more witnesses the Crown wished to call.

No engagement ring. No wedding band. It was the way nowadays, his Isabella being an obvious example. Prosecutors seemed so young. Perhaps it wasn't the way they looked; maybe it was the way they acted, the way they conducted themselves in court. Sharp suits with padded shoulders were no compensation. Inexperienced. Yes, that's how he would have described her. No problem with that. It was not realising: that was the issue. He thought of Isabella in the remand court downstairs, fighting to persuade the bench to give Jake Simmonds bail. This was the sixth time this year he'd been pulled for taking without consent –

'twocking' the youngsters called it. Isabella would do a far better job than the girl to his right. He'd taught her and she was learning and learning quickly. Isabella reminded him of himself once he'd found his feet in the magistrates' court and that's what he loved about her.

He looked up. The magistrates were staring at him, expectantly. The result here would be, from the prosecution point of view, the wrong one. Another guilty person getting off. Not with a murder or rape. But another case where justice had been thwarted. What did the powers expect? They send a wet behind the ears girl, fresh from college. And the irony was that old George was sitting on the bench behind her, an absolute gentleman out of court, but a prosecutor who for decades had been prepared to prosecute his granny. Appraising her; whatever that meant. Had the old bastard been prosecuting this trial, it would have been so very different.

So what? He was defending, when all was said and done. Business was business. Had it been the other way round, had this been the conviction of an innocent person…well, that was something that he would have fretted over for days, weeks even. A bad conviction could linger, fester in his mind, wake him up in the still of the night. He still shivered at the thought of young Stephen Smith last year, charged with slapping the mother of his children. No one had seen through her lies. Why would they? No one believed Stephen's ramblings about her new boyfriend and her wish to get Smith out of her life. It had sounded incredible, even to John. But he was acting for the boyfriend in other matters so he knew. And couldn't say anything. Smith had refused to be represented by anyone else. And the boy had not seen those children since the inevitable conviction. Then, there was Amy Jones, the young nurse fitted up last October by some vile detective constable whose advances had been spurned. The cocaine slipped into the glove compartment of her car had finished her career and just about finished her. Arthur Spratt, the veteran haunted by the ghosts of dead soldiers from the Iraq conflict and whose only crime had been to steal a loaf of bread when he'd lost his job, slipped into his head. The three-month sentence had been wrong, just plain wrong. There would have been others, those who had not got the justice they deserved, those who had been let down by the system.

They were outweighed by the hundreds of cases which he had pushed in the right direction, cases where the best result possible had been obtained. And then there were the bad acquittals, like the present case. They didn't matter. Cases like that were soon forgotten, once the Legal Aid Board had paid the bill, that is (unless someone else was paying a fat fee, like today). It was the injustice to ordinary people whose lives had been blighted by the abuse of power by the state and those that fought the state's battles that drove him on, even after all of these years. Of that there was no doubt.

'Mr Farrelly?' said the chairman of the bench, the middle of the three faces.

He touched his bow tie with his finger and thumb in that way he had and once more drew himself slowly to his feet. With one glance and one smile, he caught all three magistrates in his web, like a spider catching a fly. They were now his, unable to withstand the gentle oratory, the irrefutable logic of properly constructed legal argument that they were now going to hear. Such was his reputation; a reputation he had earned, a reputation he knew he deserved. He was about to earn that fat fee.

Not that he had been constructing anything. Random words swirled around his head, waiting to be picked. His words would not be as a result of any conscious selection exercise, but he knew as he started to talk, in the disarmingly soft court voice he had lovingly developed over the years, that what emerged from his mouth would be no different than had he spent an hour painstakingly preparing the application. He could not remember a time when he was not able to do this. It was as if his subconscious had been working on the matter throughout the whole monotonous morning as several police officers had given the court the benefit of their recollections. Or, he thought, their collective recollections.

'Your worships,' he heard himself say, 'somewhat unusually, I do not intend to call any evidence on behalf of the defence for the present. I do intend, however, to ask you to dismiss the prosecution case at this point. And the reason that I am making such an application is that there is an essential part of the prosecution case upon which you have heard no relevant evidence. In short, I am making a submission that there is no case for my client to answer. If you agree, and I am going to argue that you have no choice but to agree, this ends the matter and you need hear no evidence from the defence.'

He smirked inwardly as, from the corner of his eye, he saw the prosecutor look up at him. He could sense her terror, visualise her pale face, her wide-open eyes as she resumed her frantic perusal of the notes she had assiduously been taking all morning, searching for what she had missed. He picked up his own legal pad; he may as well look the part. He didn't look at it, there was no point. He'd not written anything, not one word.

'Before I come on to the deficiencies in the prosecution case, let me set out the legal framework that you need to consider when you retire to deliberate on the application. Firstly...' His words continued, flowing from him whilst his mind flicked over anything but. He thought of his client, that pretty young thing, sitting behind him, no doubt staring at the back of his head, oblivious to what was going on. He'd not told her he would be making the application. Why would he?

But hers were not the eyes he felt boring into his head. The man in the corner of the public gallery was the one he had to consider. After all, he was the one paying his fee. The newly married and newly elected Labour Member of Parliament, holding a small majority in a normally safe Conservative seat, and who had been elected on a manifesto of family values and zero tolerance to crime, had every reason to be concerned if the prosecution case was not kicked out and she had to give evidence. Then, that reporter wouldn't be doodling because his client would have to tell the court what had happened to her that night at the hands of the holier than thou junior minister.

His mind slipped effortlessly back those few months to the night of the call, the night when the about to be duly elected representative for that nondescript seat in one of Nottingham's better areas had telephoned, tearfully screaming that his dressing-gowned mistress had crashed into a nearby tree when fleeing him after receiving his drunken slap across her face. The police were crawling all over her RX8 and she was pissed. Sort it out he had shrieked. 'My career's on the line here! For God's sake sort it out!'

Those three faces looked at him expectedly. 'Let me come to the crux of the application. My client faces an allegation that she drove her car with excess alcohol in her blood, in other words that she was driving with alcohol in her blood stream that exceeded the amount allowed by law. Common sense suggests that the prosecution have to produce evidence that my client had alcohol in her blood that was indeed in excess of the prescribed limit.'

His eyes flicked over the magistrates, catching their eyes in turn, ensuring that each would feel that his words were unique to them, were personal to them.

'So, what evidence is there as to this essential component of the prosecution case? Your worships, the evidence as to the amount of alcohol comes from a statement by Doctor Simon Preston who just happened to be the consultant in charge in the accident and emergency department at the hospital to which my client was taken that night. It is a statement that I have not objected to being read because we, the defence that is, accept its contents. The statement is factually correct. You will see from that statement that it was Doctor Preston who took the blood from my client allowing for the alcohol content to be assessed.'

His mobile shuddered on the desk in front of him. Inwardly, he scowled; a conversation with a human being was so much more preferable to a text scrawled in broken English. The usher walked slowly back in before taking his seat and finding something of interest in the list of cases to be heard that day. The reporter doodled. But the magistrates listened.

'Now it is at this point where we encounter the problem, and I am going to argue that it is an insurmountable problem that the prosecution face. You will see that there is a second statement from Doctor Preston. It is a statement that I handed in this morning, a statement the prosecutor agreed to read out. It therefore forms part of the evidence that you should consider in the same way that you would if Doctor Preston had been here to tell you about it himself. It simply states that he, Doctor Preston that is, had responsibility for the clinical care of my client that evening and that he was asked by the officers in the case to take the specimen.'

A phone trilled from the public gallery. He ignored it and the resulting trawl through pockets and bags before the offending item was silenced. His eyes stayed trained on the magistrates; his spell was not broken, the web remained intact.

'I remind you at this point that by section 7A of the Road Traffic Act 1988, a request on the part of the police for a sample of blood to assess the amount of alcohol in that blood shall not be made to a medical practitioner who has responsibility for the clinical care of the person said to have driven whilst over the prescribed limit. In short, the request should not have been made to Doctor Preston. It was. The resulting specimen is thus inadmissible.

Once more he watched his phone vibrate against the desktop.

'Your worships. I am quite certain that the consequence of this unfortunate faux pas on the part of the prosecuting authorities is now all too obvious to you. I will however spell it out for the benefit of all others present. Quite simply, the evidence before you indicates that the sample was obtained illegally. As such, it is evidence upon which the prosecution cannot rely. It cannot be taken into account. You must disregard it. It follows that there is no evidence of the taking of the sample and thus no evidence of alcohol in excess of the prescribed limit in my client's blood stream. Consequently, this poor lady, who has had the full might of the state against her, has no case to answer. I simply ask you to dismiss the case at this point.'

He sat down and flashed a smile at his young opponent, noticing tears which had formed in the corner of her eyes and the blush which had swept over her face.

'Have you anything to add?' The chairman of the bench looked at the prosecutor. She shook her head and looked down. 'We will retire to consider Mr Farrelly's application.'

As they trooped out, he sat down and picked up his phone. He then turned, feeling a sharp slap on his shoulder.

'John. I've not seen you since I heard. Many congratulations. An OBE. Thoroughly deserved.'

'George! Long time, no see. And thank you.' He stood up and they shook hands. 'Have they stopped you prosecuting? It must be at least six months since you graced us with your presence.'

'Management now, I'm afraid. They've decided up on high that they have better use of my thirty years' experience than conducting cases.'

'So you look after the young ones?'

'Sort of.' He lowered his voice. 'I have to prepare a report on the performance of kids such as young Miss Potts here.'

'You've got your work cut out. She looks the part but not much experience. And drink driving trials against the likes of me are not the ideal places to acquire it,' whispered John, smiling.

'Her lack of experience didn't stop you ambushing her, I note.'

'Your management role doesn't mean you put her right, I note.'

They both laughed. Those nearest in the courtroom, the usher, the pretty young thing and the prosecutor looked round.

'As I see it, that's not my role. The fact that she gave you the opening by agreeing that the statement could be read, and is about to lose the case, is something which goes in my report.'

Neither said anything for a moment. John glanced at his phone, remembering that he had received two messages.

'Still working all hours God sends?'

John smiled. 'Someone has to.'

'How's Shirley? Still complaining about the hours you put in?'

'She understands. Most of the time anyway. She's presently deliriously happy because of the announcement last week that the Olympics are coming to London. Part of my retirement will apparently be spent going to see any number of things of which I have no interest. As a gesture of peace, I have in fact got her tickets for the first day of the test match at Trent Bridge next month. The only downside is that I will have to accompany her. Utter waste of time in my book.'

'Well, she'll enjoy it even if you won't. Last time I saw her she was complaining that she was feeling old.'

'She is getting old, just like the rest of us. Between me and you, George, she has managed to convince herself that her mind is going. Her mother had dementia and she thinks she's going the same way. Things slip her mind of course, happens to us all. She was seventy-five last birthday.'

'Well, pass on my regards. You're eighty-two and from your performance today you don't seem to be having many problems.'

'It's work. Keeps me young. George, you are coming tonight, aren't you?'

'Wouldn't miss it for the world. The whole of Nottinghamshire's prosecution service is looking forward to getting drunk and gorging themselves at the expense of Farrellys.'

John laughed. 'Yes – fifty years since I took over. It's something Brian, in particular, wanted to mark. And then there's the presentation.'

'That's what comes of having your only child as a partner. Anyway, to be still in practice at your age is an achievement in itself. And to receive an award from the Law Society for services to the vulnerable as well as the OBE is no small feat. You should be really proud. I'm looking forward to it. Presumably anyone who's anyone will be there?'

'So it would seem. I've got to talk to the world and his wife. Marketing and all that.' He rolled his eyes.

'Why are you still killing yourself, John? You've made your money. You've sealed your reputation. Slow down, take it easy. Spend some time with Shirley in that mansion of yours. Enjoy your Bentleys.'

'One day perhaps, but work still gives me a buzz.'

'I can't see the point of owning a Grade 2 listed Manor house in the wilds of Derbyshire with more history than any respectable museum and spend your time down here scrapping with kids a third of your age.'

'If I didn't know you better George, I'd wager that Shirley's been bending your ear,' replied John, smiling despite his irritation.

'How is the old place?'

'Finished. The ballroom has finally been restored. We're opening the gardens on two Sundays this summer. Shirley's done a marvellous job ordering around the workmen, I have to say. I think having something to do has been good for her.'

Neither said anything for a moment. The other man looked at the ground. When he spoke, John sensed that he had come to a decision.

'Is everything alight? At the office, I mean.'

'Couldn't be better...why?' replied John. 'What have you heard?'

'There's talk on the street that you're struggling, one or two problems. The word is that Farrellys is not a happy ship at present. One of your young solicitors has been sounding us out about a job. Redundancies are apparently in the offing and—'

'Who's been talking?'

'John, keep this to yourself but your Mr Chisolm is going around saying there's no future in legal aid and, in particular, there's no money to be made defending criminals. And other firms are lapping it up. John, you're not daft. You've made enemies, you know you have. You don't become one of Nottingham's biggest and most successful law firms without making people jealous.'

He smiled. 'It's nothing, just a few staffing issues. And a Managing Partner who is rapidly coming to the end of his shelf life. Between me and you – and I know you'll keep this to yourself, George – I've perhaps not been keeping my eye on the ball, what with the reception tonight. Mind, do you know that at the last count we were employing sixty-three lawyers throughout the various departments so it's getting harder to keep an eye on everything? And then there's the support staff. I can't trust Chisolm to run it, Brian's not up to it, so it's down to me. One thing I won't stand is people who've been loyal to me being laid off. We'll get this party out of the way and then I'll sort it out.'

'Good. You know if you need a word, someone away from the office to bounce ideas off...?'

'Thanks George. To be honest the houses make more than the firm these days.'

'How many have you got now?'

'Twenty-three at the last count. And we're completing on two more today. Some let to students, some to ordinary families, some to those just needing an address for bail. All mortgage free and all managed by me. That's where the money is.'

'Has Harry gone then? I thought he managed them?'

'Oh no. He still keeps an eye on them for me. Deals with day-to-day issues. He's my driver as well.'

'I always wondered whether there was a conflict – you providing accommodation to your own clients. Supposing they don't keep to their bail conditions? Do you report your own clients if there's a problem?'

'It's not a problem. The property company is totally separate from the law firm. Harry sorts it. Nothing to do with me.'

After a moment, John continued. 'We go back a long way, don't we? I defended your first trial. A good while back that is.' He laughed. 'Look, could you look out for Shirley tonight, make sure she doesn't feel neglected? There are some important clients coming who'll need some attention. I've not told anyone about…you know, her memory. Can you just check she's okay every so often?'

'Of course. I…John, I think that man in the public gallery is trying to attract your attention.'

'Right, duty calls, I suppose.'

John walked towards the back of the courtroom, indicating with a flick of his eyes that the ashen-faced man should leave the court.

'What's happening?' demanded the man as they found a small interview room. His voice was trembling, his hands shook.

'Relax, Will.' If you can't stand the heat, don't play away, he thought yet again. 'If they go along with it, which they will, the case is kicked out and she doesn't have to give evidence. She therefore says nothing about you and your secret is safe.'

'And if they don't?'

'If they don't, she has to say where she'd been that evening and that she had to drive away to escape your violence and we've an excellent matrimonial litigator, a partner of mine.' John smiled.

'That's not funny.'

'Come on, they're coming back,' said John as the usher tapped lightly on the door.

*

John shook the hand of the pretty young thing, murmuring his congratulations, and noticed that she shot out the foyer of the court without glancing behind.

'Odd,' said John as he walked up towards the smiling Member of Parliament. 'She might have thanked you for paying my fee.'

He said nothing, simply took John's hand in both of his and shook vigorously. 'Never again. I've learned something over this. Thank you so much. It…err…won't come out, will it?'

'Don't see why it should. She won't want to advertise the fact that she's got away with drink driving and no one else knows.'

'Thanks once again, John. Send me your bill and I'll see you tonight, eh?'

As he walked away, John heard a familiar voice. 'Granddad!'

'Isabella,' he whispered. 'It's Mister Farrelly when we're at court. How many—' Her round, plump face creased into laughter and he smiled.

'Get him out?'

She looked at him, her light blue eyes sparkling. 'Yessss,' she hissed through gritted teeth, clenching a fist as she did. 'Cause I did. It's taken two months but he's one happy punter.'

It had been a good morning. 'I thought you would. Where's he gone?'

'Bluebell Street. Harry said we're full up everywhere else.'

'Yes. I got the texts. And what colour do you think you are today?'

She took her shoulder-length, rusty-coloured hair in her fingers and mumbled some colour which he'd never heard of. 'Like it?'

'Not particularly. I'm not sure this articled clerk you insisted we get is a good influence. And Rod's giving me grief over it. Something about standards.'

Isabella put her arm through his and laughed as they walked towards the large swivelling door.

'Oh, don't worry about him; it's your firm, Granddad. Anyway, they're called trainees nowadays. As you well know. And Libby works very hard. Just because she's got copper-coloured hair does not mean that she doesn't do a good job. And, it was my idea.'

'And while I'm on the subject of your acquaintances amongst the staff, a little bird tells me that you've been socialising with a secretary.'

'Oh, it's only Sarah. She's a laugh.'

'Isabella, suppose we need to sack her or make her redundant at some point? There has to be a divide between ourselves as owners of the firm and those who serve us.'

'Granddad, don't be so pompous,' she replied, laughing.

'Just don't make it too obvious, eh?' he said quietly, as if to himself. 'Lift back?'

'Please.'

'Right, then I'm off home to make sure your grandmother is ready for tonight. Tell your father, will you?'

As they emerged out of the air conditioning and into the blinding sun, they passed two uniformed police officers with the prosecutor, one pointing a finger in her face. He looked away. As he and Isabella stepped through the rear door of the Bentley, held open by his valet, he wondered whether it had been necessary to humiliate her, thinking momentarily of his own unsteady first few steps in the magistrates' court. The thought soon passed as he told his granddaughter how he'd saved the career of her Member of Parliament.

'Harry, drop Isabella off at the office and then take me back to the Manor, if you would.'

Chapter 23

Tepid tap water jetted over John's fingers as he bent over the sink. He stood, wiping his hands, and stared into the mirror. He'd heard it said that as you got on, as the years shuffled past, that it was your father you saw in the reflection. Not with him. With a full head of hair, admittedly now completely grey, most people said that he passed for sixty-five. Light brown eyes gazed out of his tanned face. Lines from his eyes had the slight indentation of a life of cerebral activity and luxury, rather than the deep furrows of hard labour and worry. The goatee beard, also grey, had been Shirley's idea. He slipped in his contacts, blinked, adjusted the black bow tie, and nodded. He would do.

Like he would do for a further ten years. Isabella's whispered words were still bouncing around his head. Delivered as she burst into his office immediately on his arrival twenty minutes ago, her eyes bright, anger tumbling from her mouth, she had repeated the conversation she had overheard between Chisolm and his ally, Victoria. The one area he'd left with Brian was new partners. Not who – but if. That was five years ago when thoughts had briefly turned to his retirement and paying him off; thus a need for fresh capital. John had stayed on having agreed with Brian that the day to running of the firm could be delegated to someone with experience in management. Chisolm, a civil litigation lawyer, was duly appointed. Their initial plan to let him do the menial stuff and keep the major decisions to themselves had proved optimistic. As Chisolm grew into the role, so the bullying side of his nature became apparent. Now they were saddled with a civil litigation partner and matrimonial partner with their measly five per cent equity in the firm and their petty demands. Why did they stay? Why couldn't they go somewhere where they would be appreciated?

That wasn't altogether quite fair. Victoria was an adept matrimonial lawyer albeit ridiculously shy. They had worked together constructively whenever their respective areas of specialism had crossed. Rod Chisolm was simply a horrible little man. If ever there was a person who was suited to civil litigation, it was him. As Isabella had relayed the conversation, he could easily visualise the pit bull like face spitting out his view that John was past his sell-by date, that the firm was not the cash cow it should be.

Anyway, that was next week's problem. But, as he gazed at his reflection, an idea was beginning to form. Something that would have happened at some point. Maybe it was time to hurry things on a little. Once more he touched his bow tie, closed his eyes and breathed deeply. After a final look into the mirror, he pushed open the door, walked through his wooden panelled office and headed downstairs in the direction of chattering and cut-glass laughter, his eyes flicking over those already present as he did.

John wanted a quick look around the parts of the ground floor where those invited were likely to wander. He moved down the large staircase and into the foyer, ensuring that the foot of the stairs remained roped off as he did. The foyer itself, a resplendent square-shaped area of high ceilings with their ornate decorations, antique furniture and lush carpets, was in order. The magnificent dark oak front door, leading to a grassed area and then onto the street occupied only by the professional classes, was open. Two young waitresses stood either side holding glasses of champagne, tonic water for the few that didn't drink. He nodded and smiled at two young women as they entered, looking around, each taking a glass. All the doors to the rooms leading off the foyer were closed and locked save for the door to reception which he had decided could be left open to be used by anyone who needed facilities for a private telephone conversation. A quick look told him that the room was in order. The foyer led towards the back of the building which was dominated by a large boardroom and steps into the gardens. This is where he wanted everybody, in one area where he could move from one person to another, giving sufficient attention to the would-be clients, slightly less to his competitors, a little more to those who may be of use – prosecutors, barristers – in short, an area where he could work 'the room'.

Everything downstairs was just as he had ordered. He mouthed 'good evening' to a young solicitor from the criminal department, a legal pad pressed against a wall, a phone welded to her ear, as she took down the details of a new arrest needing their help. He entered the boardroom and smiled on seeing Shirley talking to Isabella and the group of young female members of the workforce who seemed to trail after her nowadays. He noted with approval that even the spotty geek who ran the computer system had put on a tie. He beckoned Isabella over to him. May as well tell her now.

The boardroom, a large rectangular room on the ground floor where partners' meetings were held, was dominated by a large portrait hanging over the traditional fireplace. From that canvas, John's eyes followed all who entered. Out of habit, he glanced up, saw the black dinner jacket he had worn for the sitting blending with the dark background, ensuring he and everyone else was drawn to his slightly arched eyebrows, the hint of a smile. His hands clutched Shirley's shoulders as she sat in front of him, in the way a father might cling on to a young child at the side of the road.

A Queen Anne ebony-striking clock, which had set him back £10,000 at Christies last year, sat on the mantelpiece. On the two other walls were the portrait of his father that had at one time been displayed upstairs and one of Brian. The montage was completed by photographs and prints of legal luminaries from different eras, all signed by the subject. An original dark beamed ceiling gave the room an antiquity which John would have said was at odds with the firm's business ethos but consistent with a respect of tradition. But for that day's celebrations, the Victorian oak dining table which, when extended to its full length, could seat twelve people would have sat proudly in the room's centre. It was John's avowed intention that he would never see it at its full length during a partners' meeting. It could seat eight when not extended but John had secreted four of the seats in other offices.

The fourth side was comprised of large set of French windows opening out onto shallow steps leading into the gardens. A number of people milled in the boardroom but most had spilled out and down the terraced steps into the gardens and the heat of the evening.

A catering company had provided the waiters and waitresses, all in matching white shirts or blouses, carrying silver salvers with flutes of champagne or glasses of a light Burgundy or a dry Chablis followed by the canapés. John had quickly snuffed out Chisholm's suggestion that using the firm's support staff to serve drinks and canapés would save money. Tonight was the real deal; the night when the legal world, and anyone else that mattered, saw that he and his firm were very much top of their game.

He caught sight of Chisholm's thick neck perched on his barrel-like torso. Leaning against a wall, a tin of beer in his hand, he was letching as usual over his secretary. John walked over. 'Good evening, Rod. Can you mingle? Remember, tonight is a marketing opportunity. Hello, Sarah. Have a nice time, won't you.'

John moved away, smirking at his admonishment of Chisolm in front of his secretary, before moving slowly down the steps, nodding to one or two familiar faces, a quick word here, a quick word there. Longer conversations could wait until more alcohol had been consumed. He took a glass of sparkling water, brought to him especially by a white-bloused young girl, and turned to survey the scene.

Tables with white cloths had been placed strategically, encouraging people out into the gardens. There were no chairs; John didn't want anyone sitting and out of reach if he wanted to talk, do business or whatever. On each table stood a candle, to be lit at 9.15pm as night took hold. This was not a function which was going to end any time soon. The money handed over to the firm of landscape gardeners had been money well spent. The luscious, verdant grass gave just slightly under his feet as he stood on the perfectly manicured lawns. The evening sun, a deep orange orb sinking in the western sky, bathed the gathered throng in its mellow warmth. The lengthening shadows of all those present had the appearance of laid down Lowry figures. Green leaves and pink, red and yellow petals of the immaculate roses set in flawless borders rustled in the tepid and gentle breeze which now helped provide welcome relief from the burning heat of the afternoon. The riot of colour was completed by the reds, greens and blues of bespoke Dahlias of various types, Pink Lightening, White Dwarf Hybrids to name but a few – John having sanctioned the cost.

John thought of the weekend he and Shirley had spent poring over lists of business acquaintances, those who they wanted to come under that umbrella and those at other law firms it was politic to invite. The resulting gathering showed that that was time well spent; the great and the good of the whole city had collected to experience the opulence that was Farrellys, Solicitors. He spotted and headed over to the representative of the local law society, her chains of office glinting in the sun, and thanked her and her entourage for coming.

As ever, the lawyers were to be found huddled in groups, allowing few others in. Their garb indicated that they had come straight from their respective places of work; perfectly pressed suits and the occasional wing collar of those who felt it necessary to advertise their appearance in a court of greater importance than the magistrates. Most smiled sweetly at the clean-cut waiters and waitresses. All secretly envied their youth and looks (but not their wages).

Other professionals would not easily breach the solidarity, the togetherness that a group of lawyers produced. In truth, the lawyers were happier in their solitude. This allowed them to wallow in their collective isolation and engage in legal gossip without having to make the effort of ensuring an outsider felt included. This tribalism extended to the lawyers' husbands, wives, partners and the like. The lawyers were only truly at ease when only they were present and they were free to enter into a dialogue which was comprised of their own language and where they were able to say what they wanted, knowing that nothing uttered would go beyond the pack.

Thus the lawyers spoke with each other amiably, their courtroom and conference-based arguments of the day swiftly and easily put to one side. They may have been competitors in business, may have fought over clients as though their last meal depended on it, may have entered into arguments on behalf of clients that were far less fair than a bare-knuckle fight, but none of that endangered in any way the closeness that bonded them together. All of this, John understood. He was, after all, one of them.

Only those who practised in the magistrates' court knew him personally. It was the magistrates who dealt with the mish-mash of social problems which manifested themselves into crime, or activity treated as crime, whilst the proper crime was hived off to the Crown Court. Given his dominance in his arena, reflected by his knack of winning instructions in any matter likely to attract the attention of the press, John knew that George was right and that he had few genuine friends among the legal population. Most, he suspected, would have spoken of a grudging admiration; envy, however, was never far away. Those fortunate enough not to engage in criminal litigation knew of him simply by reputation, the reputation being of a survivor, a man who had battled to drag his firm into the present day but a man who had never forgotten the vulnerable. And when anybody had reached their eighty-second year, was still practising with the zeal of those a third of his age, and had received honours that seldom reached those lawyers wading through that mish-mash of magistrates' courts business, such an event had to be marked. And if it was being marked in a way that cost nothing to the other firms in the town, few were going to miss out. And if it was marked in a way which told the lawyers of the city and anybody else who was worth knowing that Farrellys and John Farrelly, in particular, was still alive and kicking and making money, he was not going to miss out.

The low hum of conversation was occasionally interrupted by the strident ringing of mobile telephones. The genuine calls were taken. Those that had simply been pre-arranged to quench the craving to appear needed were ignored with a throw away comment that people really would have to learn to cope. The shrill northern accent of a young girl bemoaned the fact that as duty solicitor for the day she may have to leave for the police station and, as like as not, would be there until the early hours. Sympathetic noises from the non-contentious crowd around her did not mask their wonder that anybody ever allowed themselves to be sucked into the whirlpool that was criminal defence. John watched the girl glancing at her phone, checking her texts, begging it to ring.

Eight-thirty. John sought out Shirley, finding her engaging in small talk with the most recent appointment to the conveyancing department. Taking her hand, he walked her over to Brian. A touch on his elbow interrupted his son's explanation as to why the clause dealing with Capital Gains Tax in a particular deal was so important. The woman he had been talking to flashed a smile at John and moved away.

'Oh, is that the time,' said Brian, watching her retreating back. 'Of course.'

John looked around as his only son mounted the steps to the boardroom, stumbling once, and turned round at the top. Tall and thin, some would have said gangly, a touch of grey at the side flecked his short dark hair. His black-rimmed glasses gave him the aura of an accountant. Or at least that's what John thought. Brian's divorce, seven years before, had not surprised John. The original marriage certainly had. He'd managed to hook a client. John had been happy to stamp out the gossip; any port in a storm had been his attitude. Both John and Shirley would have liked more children, Shirley because she liked children, John because he would have liked to have got it right if there had been a next time. Their son was the only thing John and Shirley had disagreed on over the years. To Shirley, he was a gentle, hard-working man who was the perfect role model to Isabella. To John, he was spineless man who had never learned to control his nerves and who, to John's disappointment, had chosen commercial property as his specialism rather than criminal defence.

The tinkling of Brian's pen against his glass brought the purr of conversation to an end. John felt Shirley's hand on the inside of his arm and glanced in her direction. Her dyed blonde hair was cut fashionably short. Her makeup, professionally applied that afternoon, augmented her permanent tan and blue eyes. And, he thought, gently squeezing her fingers, she still looked good in that black dress. Getting old? Who was she kidding?

Brian looked over the scene, blinking several times. 'Err…ladies and gentleman, if I could have your…err attention just for a few moments.' As silence finally reigned, he unfolded a piece of paper taken from his side pocket. He looked over those assembled once more and blinked twice more before starting to read.

'On the fiftieth anniversary of my father taking over the firm, I would just like to say a few words to…err mark the event as it were. It is nice to see so many old friends here tonight and that reminds me of my father's achievements. Not just in making Farrellys the nationally renowned firm that it is today, considerable though I believe that to be. But, from 1955, when my father took over from my grandfather, Wilfred Farrelly, the original founder of the firm, he started the process of creating a law firm with the cutting-edge technology of the day and modern business practices without forgetting its roots and its obligation to help the vulnerable in society. From representation in the police station around the clock before it was fashionable to do so, to establishing an expertise for helping those with mental health problems, to purchasing a portfolio of properties to be used as a bail address for those who would otherwise be sent to custody, my father has shown that it is possible to run a profitable general practice without compromising his ideals. I would like to propose a toast: Dad, many more years.'

'Many more years,' chorused most of those present.

'You didn't repeat it, darling,' John pulled Shirley towards him, squeezing her arm and whispering into her ear.

She pecked him on the cheek. 'As you well know, I would like you to retire. Or at least give me some indication as to when we will spend more time together.' She put a finger to his lips as he was about to speak. 'Hush, dear. That lovely woman from the Law Society is going to say some nice things about you.'

Brian stood to one side as she took her place. Her words were measured and beautifully delivered. This was no well-worn speech frequently given. She spoke of the society's pride in one of their own receiving an Order of the British Empire, no less, for services to the legal profession. John, she said, was a man years ahead of his time. At the cutting edge since legal aid was introduced by the Legal Aid and Advice Act enacted in 1949, John had devoted his life to providing legal help to those who otherwise would have no recourse to the law and all this at a time when such work was not fashionable.

It was what everyone who entered the profession sought in those idealistic times before the responsibility of running law firms took over. But John had not succumbed like the rest of us; he had shown what being a solicitor should be, what could be attained.

John felt Shirley's fingers grip his arms. The applause at the end of the speech was warm and genuine. By popular request, John said a few words, Shirley by his side. Nothing memorable; thanks to all for attending – he was genuinely touched by the good wishes of a profession he was honoured to serve – thanks to Shirley, thanks to all the people who had worked with him. He had to stop at that point. To his surprise, he felt tears pricking the corners of his eyes. George's comment that morning about the county's prosecutors drinking at the expense of Farrellys had been said in jest, John realised that. But he could now see that those present wanted to be there. For the first time, the extent of his achievements became apparent. It dawned on him that he had achieved something during his working life. George was right; his reputation was sealed. The slaps on the back, the vigorous shaking of his hand, were truly meant.

Shirley's words interrupted his thoughts. 'Now go and have your important conversations. And as it's beginning to get dark, I'll ask the caterers to light the candles.'

'I'll see you for the fireworks,' he said, squeezing her hand.

The puzzled, questioning look on her face showed she'd forgotten about the fireworks. John watched as she walked away, wondering why she'd not remembered the conversation that morning about that very subject.

'John. Nice of you to invite us. Congratulations. And I mean that.'

'Robert,' replied John, shaking hands with a man now in front of him, 'thank you, good of you to come. It's only right, the years we've been arguing over clients.'

'Don't know how you can afford all of this,' said the other man, looking around, 'not the way that things are now.'

'No one's finding it easy, Robert. The attacks on legal aid will get more and more swingeing. The one advantage we have is that we have a strong non-contentious side. General practice. Diversify. That's the future.'

More desultory and pessimistic talk followed before the other man walked away mumbling about needing a drink. John smiled to himself. Why the misery? Business was what you made it.

More people were seen, more clients drawn into the firm's clutches, more prosecutors buttered up. John was at his best, swooping here and there, mentally ticking off his targets in his mind. He suddenly noticed that the light of the sun had been replaced by light from candles positioned at various parts of the garden. He thanked God that the weather had been perfect, that the balmy evening was just so for being out of doors. He watched the shadows of the candles bouncing on the now flushed faces of those present as alcohol was consumed and the talk became more animated. He sipped his water and moved in the direction of the one reporter who had been invited, the cost being a full-page article and Brian's short talk reported in full. John had the original in his pocket to hand over, its length tailored to the space available on the paper's pages. He was just sorry that he hadn't had advance notice of the other speech.

'John! Many congratulations, old boy.'

John turned as he felt a hand on his shoulder and found himself staring into a ruddy, smiling complexion. 'Simon,' he replied, shaking the proffered hand, 'glad you could make it. How's the hospital? As chaotic as ever?'

'What do you think? Too much work, too little time off. Nice evening, you must be pleased.'

'Oh yes. Very. We've been lucky with the weather, of course.'

'By the way, while I've got you for a moment, I've been meaning to ask, what was it with your rather mysterious call that night asking me to tell the police that I would take blood from some drunken fool of a woman who'd driven into a tree? I'd forgotten all about it until I received your email last week asking me to put my moniker on a statement.'

John led him by the elbow to the shadows at the side of the lawn away from the crowds. 'Oh, just a bit of creative defence. Look, come round for dinner one night and I'll tell you the whole story. Just for tonight, I'd be grateful if you'd keep stum about the whole business. There's one or two from the CPS here and I don't think they'd understand. Thanks for the help, though.'

The talk became more raucous, the laughter louder. Estate agents were seen, commercial clients flattered, the reporter reminded of the agreement, the managing director of a nationally renowned haulage company advised of the High Court's latest decision on an obscure tachograph point.

John strolled over towards a lone, tall, thin silhouette on the edge of the lawn. 'Victoria. I hoped we were going to meet this new man we've been hearing all about.'

'He couldn't make it. Business.'

'Sorry to hear that.' John found himself looking up at her. Her short mousey hair framed her round, pretty face. She looked away. He fancied he saw the glint of tears in her eyes. 'Maybe some other time,' he added. 'Victoria, this isn't really the time and place but I want to give you a head start on Monday's meeting. I've given Isabella ten per cent of my share. I know you talk to Ch…Rod. I'd be grateful if you kept this to yourself for tonight. He'll know next week.'

She said nothing for a minute. 'He was hoping tonight might be the time when you allowed him…well, us actually, to buy a further share. It's been five years and we're no further forward… and…oh what's the point?'

She began to walk away and then turned. 'Look! If you thought telling me tonight would somehow divide us, you are mistaken!' She then strode away. Some people looked in the direction of the shouting. John stepped back further into the shadows, cursing Brian, letting them return to their conversations.

The darkness of late evening had now conquered the bright day. Stars were beginning to win their nightly battle with the city's lights. John felt Shirley's fingers on his arm, delicate as a feather. 'Hello, darling,' he began, 'Have you had a nice…whatever's the matter?'

'Nothing, Nothing at all.'

'You're crying,' he whispered.

'Hush now, let's watch the fireworks. They're about to start.'

He took her hand in his, conscious of Brian's slightly slurred voice from the boardroom urging people onto the lawn. John's mind swept back across the evening straining to find the moment he had got it wrong, when he'd inadvertently brought her to tears as only a man in two marriages can. That the other marriage paid for the houses, the holidays, the expensive lunches with her friends and God knows what else that gave Shirley the idyllic lifestyle she craved had always been his excuse, his plea in the court of matrimonial warfare. Not that he would ever ask her; he was afraid of the answer.

He watched as her eyes rose upwards at the first whoosh followed by the myriad of white sparkling, flecks of light falling like snow towards the ground. A swish from either side of the lawns made him jump. Red and green stars mingled like a fan over the night sky before slowly dissolving into a nothingness. Oohs and aahs merged with the whizzes and hisses. He put his hand around her shoulder drawing her closer. She did not resist and he kissed her on the cheek. 'A holiday. That's what we need. Just the two of us. Two or three weeks at the house in Burgundy? Maybe a villa in Tuscany if you fancied a change?'

She put her arm around his waist and he smiled, relieved he'd dealt with the tears. He was happy she was here, grateful she'd spent her life by his side. He thought of Victoria, her endless singles clubs, the irony of a blind date remaining unseen and thanked God. He saw the copper-haired girl, in the shadows, talking to the computer geek. Perhaps problems such as her should not take up his time at the expense of his wife. As oranges and yellows and reds and greens shimmered across the whole sky, as the whistles and swishes blended with the chatter and talk of the people, he'd been lucky, so very lucky. He turned and took her by both shoulders and then took her face gently in his hands. 'I'm sorry.'

She smiled, her watery eyes glistening, 'don't be silly, what on earth for?'

'I just want to say that—'

'Dad, I need a word.'

'Brian, can't you see I'm with your mother.'

'Hello, Mum.' Brian turned back towards John. 'It's Diana, she's just told me she's getting divorced from Jeff. You know what this could mean, don't you?'

John felt Shirley's arm slide away. He watched her walk back towards the boardroom. 'Who the hell's Diana?'

'Coltrons Properties, Estate Agents and Developers. Thirty-five per cent of my fee income. That's who.'

John looked at his son, his mind calculating the consequences.

'Granddad, there you are, I've been—'

He turned around to find Isabella's flushed features in his face, a glass in her hand.

'Not now, Isabella, I'm with your father.'

'Granddad! I just want'—

'Isabella, I said not now!' John made a note in his head to sort whatever it was she wanted over the weekend. If she was going to be foisted on Chisolm and Victoria at the meeting on Monday, he didn't want or need her to have any distractions.

'Sarah! Tell him.' John looked at the tall, blonde-haired girl standing behind. The look appeared to be enough. Any secretary at Farrellys who had any sense would not utter a word to him in these circumstances.

'Issie. Don't be silly, come on. Let's go. Mr Farrelly, I'm sorry.'

John watched as Isabella was dragged away. It was then that he saw the girl with the ridiculous copper hair, hiding in the background. He really needed to do something about it. She couldn't be seeing clients like that. But, this minute, other matters required his attention. He turned back to Brian. 'Is Diana the MD?'

'The very same. The one who'll close the company rather than let her stay-at-home, useless husband support his failing computer business with her millions.'

'And if she shuts down, you lose—'

'Exactly.'

'Isn't there a pre-nup?'

'Not sure.'

'Didn't you ask her? It's the first thing I'd want to know.'

'I thought Vikki could sort it out. I'm just worried about a third of my practice disappearing.'

'I'll deal with it for the moment.'

'You've not done matrimonial for years.'

'You'll see at the meeting on Monday why I don't want Victoria running a case like this, not for the present. She can do the donkey work once I've started it off but I'll front it. So, who left who?'

'Neither yet. But the text she's just had from him has confirmed what she's suspected for weeks; he's having an affair.'

'I'll ring her next week. Right, I'd better find your mother. By the way, do something about those girls that your daughter has had in tow all night. One of them has copper-coloured hair – not something we want at Farrelly's. He turned, looking for Shirley, his eyes only finding the managing director, of an advertising company who needed some attention.

Chapter 24

She really shouldn't be alone, she thought, pushing her way through the milling, chattering crowds searching for the tall, blond waiter with the blue eyes and the white wine. Tonight of all nights. She'd known all along she'd be given equity. It was obvious. To Granddad, family was everything and that meant her. Revolting Rod, he of the wandering hands and bad breath, and the insipid no-man Victoria, were toast. This would soon be all hers. Her grandfather wouldn't be around forever and Dad would be better off lecturing something obscure rather than practicing law. If he hadn't been so afraid of making a living off his own bat, he'd have moved on years ago. Well, she would release him from his purgatory. And then she could do as she pleased.

But there should be somebody. Twenty-six; it shouldn't be like this. What was the point of a career path wending its golden way like the yellow brick road to the perfect future if it was just her and her cat? As her eyes flicked over those assembled, all she saw were the same old faces, those where she had been already and those who were attached, the thought of extra-curricular activity as abhorrent to them as a rumble with Rod would be to her.

She cursed her grandfather. To dismiss her as if she were some flighty and irrelevant secretary, and in front of Libby and Sarah, was just not on. Was it too much to let her ask Harry for a lift up to Mansfield? Maybe Sarah had been right; just leave it. But her unfulfilled promise meant that Sarah's brother and, of greater importance, his two friends were tantalisingly out of reach. Unless. Unless…

'No taxis for an hour.' She turned on hearing the words and looked into Libby's sullen face.

'I'll get the keys for the Audi.' What Granddad didn't know wouldn't hurt him.

'Haven't you drunk too much?' Large round eyes peered from behind Libby's glasses.

She gazed at her oldest friend. The light from the fireworks gave her copper hair a metallic sheen. It looked good. And there she was again, looking out for her. Once in power, once she was it, Libby was going to get a fizzing pay rise and the pick of the male secretaries Isabella was going to employ. She smiled and wrapped her arms around Libby's thin frame, carefully holding her glass in one hand, her clutch bag in the other. If she was going to drive, the remaining two mouthfuls were going to have to be her last. If another glass was put in her hand, she would down the lot.

She suddenly giggled. 'Libby, darling. Because you're my friend, because you're my bestest friend, I'm going to get you a shag tonight. Because that's what friends are for, isn't it?'

'Issie, are you sure?'

Isabella smiled at the girl standing at Libby's shoulder. 'Yes Sarah, darling. It's crap here. Come on, let's get out before Daddy asks me to talk to some goddam boring client.' She put her glass on a tray held by the blue-eyed Venus and, grasping his neck and pulling him towards her, kissed him on the lips. Laughing at his open-mouthed stare, she winked and put her arms around the shoulders of Libby and Sarah and marched them out.

'Hold on a minute.' Libby shot through the roped off area and upstairs as they entered the foyer.

'Come on Libs, I'll get collared if we don't go now.'

'Just one minute.'

Libby appeared clutching a large light brown envelope. Can you nip up Bluebell Street? It'll be on our way. I'll put this through the door. I need the defence statement back by Tuesday and I'm sitting behind counsel in the Crown Court on Monday so this'll save me coming in tomorrow.'

'Boring,' chorused Isabella and Sarah together before all three girls walked off giggling.

The keys were on the hook by a door leading to the car park at the side of the building. Isabella grabbed them, looking over her shoulder as she did, before slipping out with the others into the night sky. As the electric gates slid open, she cheered, 'Right girls, it's operation Libby shag.' They all laughed.

'And look what I have,' shouted Libby over the radio, leaning into the front seat and holding out two bottles of Chablis so that they glinted green in the glow from passing street-lights.

'Well done, Sister,' squealed Isabella. 'Where did you get them from? Shit, these lights are always on red.'

'I'd made myself known to blue eyes before you snogged the arse off him.' They all laughed.

'So if you'd collared him, why the need to shoot off to the frozen north to meet my brother's friends?' asked Sarah.

'I'm not that bothered about Mansfield, honest. I'd never be able to afford to get up there anyway.'

'Libby, darling,' said Isabella.

'Oh, remember to turn onto Bluebell Street, won't you Issie?'

'As I was saying,' said Isabella, looking into Libby's eyes through the rear-view mirror, 'they come to you, darling. I think you need a lesson on who's in charge.'

'Libby, what do you reckon?' said Sarah, 'when she's in charge, do you reckon she'll still be friends with us? I reckon she'll have parties with posh fireworks and no band and we'll be no further forward.' More laughing.

'You just wait,' said Isabella. 'We'll be the *Girls Aloud* of the legal profession, we…what does that fucking taxi think he's doing…we'll only have female fee earners, Sarah, I'll get you trained up. And we'll only have boys as secretaries. Only the best-looking ones, of course.'

'What about your dad?' asked Libby.

'Not good looking and no good at typing,' said Sarah. Again they laughed.

'He'll be out of it, the boring fart,' said Isabella. 'He hates it anyway. It'll just be me, me, me! Or us, us, us!' They all cheered, momentarily drowning the sound blaring from the radio.

'Issie, will you still do crime?' asked Libby.

'I'm not sure I'll do any fee earning. Do you know what I fancy?' Isabella glanced in the mirror and then to her side. 'I fancy managing. Getting everything sorted so that we make bucket loads of money.'

'It'd be you that would have to take the clients to all the posh dinners,' said Sarah.

'And you'd have to do the breakfast meetings.' The laughing got louder.

'Can you imagine, Libby?' continued Sarah, 'Issie up before half-nine? Eh, Issie you could call in on your way back after a night out.' Once more, they all laughed.

'Yes,' said Isabella. 'A little black number at eight o' clock and—'

'Issie!' screamed Sarah. The *thud* as the front of the car struck something was followed by screeching brakes. The car swerved to a halt.

'What the fuck was that?' asked Sarah, her voice trembling.

'There's something in the road,' shouted Libby, looking behind.

'Oh my God!' shrieked Isabella, staring into the mirror. 'It's a body! It's a fucking body! I've fucking hit somebody! I didn't see! I didn't see a fucking thing!'

The radio continued to blast out. Isabella slapped the button and there was silence. An absolute silence.

'Drive on!' said Libby suddenly.

'What?' sobbed Isabella.

'Drive away, I said. Quick! Issie, you've been fucking drinking. It's dark, no one saw you. No one's come out so no one's heard anything. And who's in on Bluebell Street on a Friday night? Drive away!'

Isabella sat there, tears dripping onto her legs, unable to move.

'Drive away!' shrieked Libby.

'Yes! She's right Issie! Let's just get out of here, quickly!' shouted Sarah.

As if their words had suddenly registered, Isabella suddenly turned the key and the car roared off. No one said anything as the car nosed back into Nottingham's late-evening traffic. The lights of the other vehicles were blurred in Isabella's tears. She looked in her mirror – no flashing blue lights. She frantically went back over the fragmented incident in her mind. Had there been anyone there? She didn't think so but…but, she just didn't know. Once more she looked in her mirror. Wasn't Libby right? Wouldn't somebody have come rushing out if they'd seen or heard anything? But that was an area where you minded your own business, where you didn't interfere. She grasped the steering wheel, wanting to stop her hands shaking. She had to focus, think clearly. Her mind had to be pin sharp. She turned off the main road, again glancing in the mirror, pulled to a halt away from a streetlight and killed her lights.

'Sarah. Get out and look through the gates, make sure no one's around.'

As she did, Isabella just hoped to God that the parking space she had left was still empty.

'Yes. It's empty.'

It was only as she entered the unlit car park at Farrellys and had parked in the space left only fifteen short minutes earlier that

Isabella turned and looked at the others. 'No one says a thing. Ever. Okay?' Her voice was hard, brooking no emotion.

The only sound was Sarah crying softly.

'Okay,' said Libby with a shaking voice.

'Okay,' said Sarah, as she yanked the door handle and pushed open the door before running off.

Chapter 25

John sat in his in his study and unclipped his bow-tie with one hand, a large whisky in the other. The *Pastoral Sympathy* drifted over the room. He did not particularly like Beethoven. In fact, he did not particularly like any music but it seemed to fill a space in his head, allowing him to concentrate on his thoughts. And it was something that he tended to play when he was pleased.

And there was every reason to be pleased. It had been all he wanted. He had taken his fingers off the pulse in the last few months. Maybe it was the party, maybe it was all the work at the Manor. Maybe he was just getting old. But tonight had shown the world that he and the firm were still here, still a force.

He felt energised, ready once more to thrust the firm forwards. And it wasn't just tonight's success that made it thus. His decision to admit Isabella to the partnership was a good one. He sipped the whisky, the warm glow as it trickled down his throat mirroring the expectation he felt as he looked forward to the look on Chisolm's face when he saw Isabella sitting in the boardroom at the partners' meeting first thing Monday. Yes, he was back in control, back at the top of his game.

He emptied his glass and switched off the study lights before making his way into the bedroom. If Shirley was awake, he would endeavour to make his peace tonight. If not, it could wait until tomorrow.

As he carefully pushed open the bedroom door, lest she was asleep, he found her sitting at her dressing table vigorously rubbing cream onto her arms. She looked in his direction as he entered, her face a blank canvas, not revealing anything.

'Did you have a good time, darling?' he asked tentatively.

'Very nice, dear,' she replied softly.

'I'm sorry that business took me away from you.'

'I don't mind. Honest. Brian needed a word. It's fine.'

John hung his trousers in the wardrobe. He slowly undid his cufflinks, suspecting it was far from being fine.

'Shirley. Out with it. What's up? What on earth have I done? Whatever it is, I apologise.'

He felt her eyes locking into his. Once more tears formed in hers. He pulled her to his feet, his heart suddenly racing. 'What on earth is it, darling?'

'It's happened again.' She bit her lip.

'What? What's happened again?'

'I've had another of those turns tonight. The ones that you keep saying I'm imagining. The ones where I suddenly can't recognise anybody or remember anyone's name. The one's where I hear things and see things but can't do anything.'

She started weeping. 'John. I'm absolutely terrified that I'm going like Mum. It's Alzheimer's. They didn't have a word for it in Mum's lifetime but that's what she had. I've…I've been telling you for weeks…months that I've got a problem.'

He sat on the edge of their bed and took her hand, pulling her down next to him. 'We'll sort it. Together. I'll get an appointment with whoever is the best person for it. Even if it is what your mother had, there's so much more they can do nowadays, medication and all that. I'll ring first thing next week. Promise.'

'Will you?'

'Of course.'

'Unless a client gets in the way?'

'Shirley, I'll make it my number one priority.'

'We'll see.'

He turned to kiss her. She pulled away. 'Anyway, I've got an apology,' she said quietly.

'Darling, you've nothing to apologise for.'

She leaned over and picked up her handbag. From an inside compartment, she fished out a letter. She looked him in the eyes. 'This.' She handed him the letter. 'One of the receptionists asked me to hand it to you last week when I popped in to see Brian about the party. I'm sorry. It slipped my mind. It's exactly what my mother would have done, forgotten it. This is what I'm like. This is how it'll be. It's going to get worse and worse.' Tears rolled down her face.

He smiled and kissed her. 'Don't worry about the letter. Can't be helped. Look, anybody can put something to one side and forget about it. I forget things. I promised Brian tonight I'd get him out of his latest pickle – but I've made sure I've noted it in my diary. If I didn't then I'd forget.'

She smiled, squeezed his hand and went back to the mirror.

It was as just Shirley had dozed off and John was lying back, his hands behind his head, just about to switch off his lamp, that he remembered the letter. He leaned over to his bedside table, mildly curious to see what rubbish was being advertised. He carefully opened it, glancing at his wife, making sure he didn't wake her. He would get someone to see her, just to tell her that she wasn't losing her marbles. Her mother had always been mad, not just in the later years and—

John's hand went to his throat, his heart stopped, his mouth went dry, blood froze in his veins. He flicked over the words again, willing them to change. This could not be true. Please God, let it be a sick joke.

Sleep certainly would not come now. He got up and put on his dressing gown. With a backward glance at a sleeping Shirley, he slipped out of the bedroom and into his study. He slid open the window. A full moon bathed the Derbyshire peaks in its silvery light. Two car headlights, pinpricks in the darkness, bounced their way along a distant country lane. A tepid breeze caressed his face. John breathed in the fragrance of cut grass. A dark shape shot across the inky sky. The 'ke-wick' he had heard during recent nights again rang out. A tawny-owl, Harry had said. Previous evenings he could have stood here for hours. Now, each sensation, each taste of the countryside on a summer's night was blurred, as if tarnished. His mind went over each word, again and again. He pulled shut the window and sat at his desk. Under the glare of the light from the lamp, he read and re-read the letter. No matter how many times, the letter still formed the same words and the words were in the same order, saying the same thing. After an hour, he went back to bed. He put it back in its envelope which he placed in the drawer. He lay down, his eyes wide open. Sleep was no more likely to come now. Not tonight. Perhaps not ever.

Chapter 26

Brian swallowed. His face burned. He forced his index finger between the collar of his shirt and the sweaty skin of his neck, loosening the stranglehold of the taut fabric. They had to be here, copies of the letters just had to be here. He frantically skimmed through the file once more, this time cursing at the clumsiness of his moist fingertips, praying that he'd somehow missed the letters and that, by some miracle, they were there after all. A large lump weighed heavily at the bottom of his stomach. Already his mind had surged forward, taunting him with the calls he was going to have to make, the conversations he was going to have.

He picked up his phone and jabbed three numbers with his finger, breathing heavily, trying to drag some composure from somewhere. 'Sharon. I've...err got the licensing file for the supermarket on Albion Road, the hearing's in two weeks and I thought I'd just check it. I...err can't find the letters.'

'What letters?' came the disinterested voice from the other end. Someone was laughing in the background. A phone rang.

'The letters sending notice of the application to the local paper and the police and what have you. The letter sending it to the court is the only one on the file.'

'They should be there. If you dictated them, I'd have typed them.'

Brian closed his eyes, telling himself not to shout, that it was alright, that the copies had simply been misfiled. 'Sharon, can you please check the post book. Do it now, please. Make sure there's a record of letters being sent two weeks last Monday to all the people that have to know about the application. Then ring me straight back, please. Thank you.'

He put down the phone and sat back in his chair, knowing that he would not be able to attend to anything else until he had had proved to himself that the correct procedure had been followed and all was as it should be.

Liquor licensing was a source of work that he had been getting in increasing amounts over the past two years, initially just a trickle but now a steady stream. It was an area he wanted to develop. Not for the fees, although the work was profitable and the money it brought in kept Rod off his back. It was for himself. It was his area, something only he could do. And thus he had cause to lock himself away for periods of time, his desk piled high with thick files, his floor strewn with plans of premises to be licensed, a barrier to anyone who entered his room.

It was his dependability that attracted the clients, or at least so he thought. Licensing procedure was a minefield; whenever an application for a liquor licence was made to the local magistrates' court, copies had to be sent to the police, fire-brigade and local authority amongst others. The fact of the application also had to be advertised in the evening paper. There were strict time limits which tripped the unwary. Failure to comply meant the whole process had to be started again with the loss of thousands in terms of lost sales of alcohol and the embarrassment of messing up. Methodically plodding through the minefield was something he found satisfying. To tick each little task as it was completed caused a flutter in his stomach, the warmth of a job well done. He never missed time limits, thus things didn't go wrong at court, and the supermarkets could open on their allotted days with their celebrities and balloons and banners and everyone was happy. That he periodically had to physically get the file out of one of the grey metal cabinets in the corner of his room to check that all was in order was, he guessed, something he had to do. It was the way he was.

That flicker of self-doubt was like an itch that just had to be scratched. He thought of the time during his training that he'd gone away with Mark Wilson from university for the thirtieth anniversary of the D Day landings in Normandy. It was when they were crossing the channel on the way out that the question had popped up in his mind; had he put the application into court to renew old Mr Marshall's tenancy on his hardware shop? He must have done. Surely. It wasn't in his nature to miss something like that. But the more he tried to convince himself that the application had been drawn up, been submitted, the court fee paid, the more the doubts grew. What had started as a fleeting question had grown through the week into a monstrous certainty. The question had beavered away all week, always there, always in the back of his mind, whispering to him. When he spoke to Mark, or found something interesting, it would nip at his ankles like a boisterous puppy. Could he have telephoned the office from France? This was of course in the days when a mobile telephone was something that you were only likely to encounter in a science fiction novel. The answer was a most definite 'no'. He was never going to do anything that would draw attention to any quirks in his character. His father wouldn't have understood and it would have been another cause of disappointment – the latest in an ever-growing list. Afterwards, he had reasoned that it was all about the consequences. If he hadn't put in the application to the court, the old man's lease could not be renewed and a business which had been alive and kicking for as long as anyone could remember would in all probability be blown away like withered and brown leaves in autumn. And so he had made an excuse on the Sunday evening of their return and scurried into the office, just to check. Of course, everything was exactly as it should be and the ruined holiday was soon forgotten in the bliss of sheer relief. He hadn't gone away again; Mark always seemed to be busy when Brian was free. That was a shame, he'd thought. They'd seemed to get on.

So when he had opened his diary first thing on this particular morning, a daily routine he had followed since commencing his training, and seen that the application was to be heard two weeks to the day, he simply had to check, just like he had to check he locked the front door when he left home each day three times, just like he had to check seven times that he had switched off the gas fire in his office each winter evening. He had to know that everything was as it should be and could not rest or settle until he had.

The ringing of the phone on his desk made him jump. 'Were they sent?' He could feel his heart beating.

'No, Mr Farrelly, there's no record of any letters going to the police, fire-brigade or local authority. Or the paper for that matter. I've checked the date you mentioned and the week before and the week after.'

Brian put the phone down, his mind racing. He gripped the edges of the desk, lest a full-blown panic attack kicked in. He had to keep calm, he had to think. It was a sacrosanct rule, punishable by immediate dismissal, not to record outgoing post in the post book. The post book was something that was always accurate. Any letter that left the office would be recorded in the thick journal.

He grabbed his diary from the corner of his desk and scrambled through the pages at the back, seeking out his list of useful telephone numbers. Once more he picked up the phone and, with a trembling finger, dialled the number. 'Is that Nottinghamshire Police? Err…can you put me through to the licensing department, please.'

His fingers drummed on the desk as he waited.

'Can I help you?'

'Err… yes. This is Farrellys solicitors. I'm just ringing to check you received a copy of the application we've made for the supermarket on Albion Road. We sent it a couple of weeks ago.'

'Wait a minute and I'll see.'

The line went dead and Brian was once again alone with his thoughts. He would not have forgotten to send out the copy applications. It was a mistake that he simply didn't make. It must be Sharon. She'd forgotten to put the copies of the letters on the file and therefore simply overlooked the need to note the post book. He closed his eyes and spoke to God. Whilst not a religious man, Brian did occasionally ask for favours; please God, make this alright and he would not tell Rod about Sharon's mistake. And he would go to church, and—

'No, we've not had it.'

Brian slowly replaced the receiver back in its cradle. Thirty minutes ago, he'd been alright – not looking forward to the partners' meeting – but alright. He'd survived Friday night, something he'd been dreading for weeks. He'd not made a fool of himself, the speech was adequate, which is all he had asked, and he had made passably interesting conversation with his own clients who had attended. Now, a problem had arisen which would dominate his every thought, fill every waking moment. Scratching the itch had opened a wound. But it was more than that. Even after the apologies, the recriminations and the general fall out were over, he would still have to look at himself in the mirror. And the self-loathing would be the worst part about it.

He dragged himself up and went to the window. The day was grey. Angry clouds hurried across the leaden sky, chased by the wind. Green buses plodded slowly around the rectangular paved areas of the Market Square, picking people up and putting them down. Others were striding here and there, some with umbrellas, some having dragged out their winter coats, most with mobile phones welded to their ears.

There was the irate client he would have to face. The hearing couldn't go ahead even if he sent fresh notices out today; the notices had to be sent out more than twenty-one days before the application was heard. The supermarket couldn't sell alcohol when it opened so it wouldn't open. The Mayor would be cancelled and told why. And the client would go elsewhere. One mistake and they always did.

And he would be forced to tell his father. The insurers would have to be informed straight away. The cost of this would be well above their excess and it was firm's policy that only his father could notify the firm's insurers. Telling his father. He put his hand to his mouth; retching on the carpet laid only last month would not help. Even now, could taste his father's disappointment. There would be no shouting, no angry recriminations. It may have been easier had there been.

Brian thought of his father working in this very room back in his grandfather's day. Brian had never met his grandfather, or at least if he had, he didn't remember. Wilfred Farrelly was someone who was only spoken of in hushed tones; perhaps the occasional story at Christmas or at some family celebration. No, his memory was now revered in the unsmiling, starch like pictures which adorned the office walls. He was part of the firm's early days, a period glossed over as if any achievements then could not hope to compare with recent triumphs.

Brian's father had taken Wilfred's larger office, the one overlooking the gardens, on acquiring the firm. Brian's mother had told him. Even when Brian moved in to this office on qualifying, his father had made no mention of the fact that this had once been his room. In fact, Brian would have known nothing about the firm and any history it might have if it hadn't been for his mother. She had often spoken of his father's zeal and energy building the firm. He'd wanted to prove something to his own father, Wilfred. At least that was his mother's explanation. She'd hinted one Christmas night, after a glass too many and when his father had had to nip – as he called it – into the office, that there had been issues from his past which had driven him on, made him strive to be the actual best, better than anyone else in town, as if trying to make amends for something. Next morning after Brian had had a sleepless night pondering what it all meant, she had clammed up and made it quite clear that it was a subject which would never again rear its head.

Brian was a chip of the old block; that's what she said. It's what she always said. That old block was a champion's hero, he was the man who had rescued hundreds from the full rigours of the law, a kind and gentle man. He was the man she had married and the man she still occasionally saw on those all too rare times when she could get him to forget, just for a little while, the cares of the firm that had evolved under him. Brian thought of the times when his mother held his face in his hands, tears in her eyes, saying that his father did love and respect him, was proud to have him as a partner in the firm. So why did Brian see himself as such a disappointment?

Brian turned at a knock on the door. His father walked in.

'Brian, what's this?'

His heart sank as his father sat on the other side of the desk. For a moment Brian thought that his father had already somehow managed to discover his licensing catastrophe.

'This came in the post this morning.'

No, this was something different. Brian, just for a moment, felt a twinge of disappointment. To have got his confession out of the way now would have been one thing not to worry about. His father may even have taken the whole matter on himself, not trusting his son not to make it worse. But as his father placed the letter he had been holding onto Brian's desk, Brian realised that other matters needed his attention.

He slid into his chair and read its contents, trying to concentrate, trying to take in the meaning of the words as his father sat opposite him. And as he did, his eyes widened.

'Well?'

This was ridiculous, absolutely ridiculous. He re-read the letter, conscious of a thumping heart, conscious of his father's presence, trying to make sense of the words.

'I…err…I don't know. I don't know what they're talking about.'

'Is this some kind of sick joke on your part?'

Brain looked at his father. The eyes were wide, the hands were clasped together. His father looked drawn, his features haggard. He was as dapper as ever, perfectly groomed, his grey beard neatly trimmed. Maybe it was the sickly pallor. He looked, Brian supposed, just tired. Perhaps the rigours of practice were beginning to catch up. There had been problems recently, nothing you could put your finger on, just things going wrong. Previously a bi-word in efficiency and good practice, entirely as a result of procedures installed by his father over the years, the firm now had the air of lurching from problem to problem. And now this.

'Someone has played a joke, a sick joke but nonetheless a joke.' It was the only explanation Brian could think of. It was common for the firm to be represented at the funeral of late clients. It was something Brian himself particularly liked to do. But for the personal representatives of such a client to receive an invoice for such an attendance was beyond the pale.

'Right,' his father said wearily as he looked up, 'we'd better get to the meeting.'

Brian suddenly felt sorry for his father. The lines around his eyes seemed deeper, the energy that put them all to shame seemed dimmed. He was carrying the firm. For the first time that Brain could recall, the weight was taking its toll. And now was not the time to add to the weight by telling him that some letters that should have been sent seemed to have vanished.

Chapter 27

John glanced to the side, distracted by a sudden gust of wind and heavy raindrops drumming on the French windows. Was it only three days since they'd been milling in the garden on a balmy summer's evening? Now, the brisk, unforgiving wind had blown in the clouds and Friday had proved to be another of summer's false starts. Two young girls, their blue kagools wet and shiny, hurried from table to table, piling trays high with plates and glasses. So Rod hadn't sanctioned overtime.

Empty bottles rested on their sides, glistening on the damp lawn. Screwed-up napkins, now a soggy white, pock marked the grass. One, he noticed, had wrapped itself around a rose bush, dropped there by a wind that did not care.

He dragged himself back to the business in hand. Four other people were sitting around the old antique table, their eyes set in ashen faces glued to the figures on the papers he had handed out. The clock ticked, mournfully knocking off the seconds of the remainder of their lives. Or so it seemed to John.

A sharp crack splintered the silence as Chisholm flung his papers down onto the table in front of him. 'Sod these,' he began, pushing the white sheets so they slid across the polished surface, 'what's she doing here?' A fat finger pointed in Isabella's direction. John felt dark eyes glowering from the deep holes in Chisholm's fleshy face.

Fetching the fifth chair should have been memorable, a rite of passage, something John had always intended to do himself to commemorate the event. He thought back to the number of times he had imagined this moment, his pride as a fourth generation of the family was brought into the partnership proper and became a part-owner of the business. But this morning he had simply told one of the office juniors to bring a chair. It was the letter, the letter that was stuffed into the inside pocket of his jacket, lying like a compress against his heart, preventing it beating properly. Every thought he had was reined in by its words, stopping him from functioning.

Even Isabella's squeals of delight on Friday evening when he told her of her newly acquired share seemed to belong to another period. Some of his best decisions over the years had been snap decisions. He thought of that morning all those years ago, a morning like any other, when he decided that Shirley would become the woman with whom he would spend the rest of his life rather than the girl who did his typing. Within a week they were engaged.

Isabella's promotion, based on a comparison of her development as a young advocate to that of the incompetence of the girl in Friday's trial, had brought to a head ideas which had been developing for a few weeks. And on being told by Isabella that Chisolm had once more been spewing his vile poison, he had realised that he was spot on. Giving his granddaughter a slice of his own share in the firm was providing him with an ally, someone who would fight alongside him. To give her eleven per cent and thus more than Chisolm's and Victoria's combined shares may finally convince them that they had no future at Farrellys – no future which would earn them an appreciable income at any rate. And the firm would be back in the family's hands – the way it was meant to be, the way it should be.

'Gentleman, and lady, of course, meet your new partner. I've given Isabella an eleven per cent share in the firm. She therefore takes her place, deservedly I might add, at this table.'

'Err…you said on Friday that it was ten per cent and now…' Victoria's voice petered out as John stared at her.

'There is a problem with this firm.' John turned towards Chisolm's growl.

'And what is that?' replied John, smiling sweetly.

'I reckon that every decision is taken at Sunday tea. Me and Vicki don't get a bloody look in. And with her in, I can only see it getting worse.'

John forced himself to concentrate, dragging his mind away from the letter.

'Have you seen these?' Chisolm picked up the papers and slammed them back down on the table. 'We've barely made a profit over the last three months. Every department is down on new matters. We've had cock up after cock up…'

John crossed his arms allowing the words to flow over him and away, not taking them in. He had intended to enjoy this meeting, revelling in his granddaughter sitting at the table. Now, struggling to concentrate, as he watched spittle from the fleshy, red-faced fool land on the table, he simply felt numb.

'…And all you can do is spend the money we do make on pointless evenings where we feed half of the city…'

John snapped. 'Can't you just keep your pointless rants to yourself just for once? Can we not just get on with the business of the meeting and we can all get back to making some money!'

Perspiration glistening on his forehead, Chisolm stood up, a squat, barrel of a man. 'And all that crap last week from tweedle-dee here about the houses.' He pointed at Brian. 'They're yours, if you hadn't noticed. The rent from them is making you rich, not us.'

'Leave. If that's the way you feel, just leave.' John felt his dark eyes staring at him. Chisolm slowly sat down, gripping the edge of the table, the tips of his fingers turning white.

'I'm the only one bringing in any fees! Leadership, John. That's what you're supposed to provide. And you're not.'

John ignored him. 'Isabella now has a share in the business and on behalf of the whole partnership, I offer my congratulations.'

No one said anything. He hadn't expected Isabella to wade in during that exchange but once she found her feet, it would be useful to have someone to do the shouting. John glanced at her. She was a ghostly white, her rusty hair like a beacon against her pallid expression. Maybe nerves. Unlikely. Perhaps too much to drink over the weekend. More likely.

'I called the partners' meeting to announce Isabella's arrival into the partnership and to confirm, which I do now, that there will be no redundancies for the present. Now, as no one has made any comment on that latter issue, I propose to end…' He stopped at a knocking on the door. 'What is it?'

John's eyes were drawn to her copper hair as the girl sidled in. 'Didn't I leave instructions that we weren't to be disturbed?'

'I'm sorry…err,' she looked at Isabella. 'We've had the police on. Jake Simmonds has been arrested for that hit and run on Bluebell Street Friday night. They want to interview him. He's asked for you. I…err…thought you'd like to deal with it.'

'Well, at least someone's getting some work in today,' said John. He looked at his granddaughter. She was staring at the girl, wide-eyed and open-mouthed. 'You'd better go,' he added, his eyes on her. 'I heard about it on the radio this morning, it sounds a decent job…are you alright?'

'Err…yes. I could just do with some fresh air. I'll be off then.' She scurried out of the room. John made a mental note to talk to her about her drinking. The weekend had clearly been heavy.

John caught Chisolm out of the corner of his eye touching Victoria's elbow.

'You didn't answer. Why has she got equity?' she asked.

'I told you, she deserves it.'

'And,' boomed Chisolm, 'any other junior solicitor in the criminal department who does not happen to be your granddaughter is going to be treated in the same way, I presume?'

'The criminal department will, in my view, be playing an increasingly important part in the future of this firm and—'

'This is ridiculous.' As he said it, Chisolm stood and walked out, followed by Victoria.

John and Brian sat in silence for a minute. 'Well,' said Brian, collecting his papers and standing up, 'I suppose I'd best be getting on.'

'Yes, you do that. Brian, you've really got to start saying something at these meetings. As far as I'm concerned, the experiment in bringing others in has not been a success. This is a family business. We – the family that is – have got to stick together and be seen to stick together.'

Brian looked at his feet before walking out, without saying a word. John shook his head. Once more he felt the letter in his pocket. Biting his lip, he left the boardroom and made his way upstairs to his own office.

*

At one time, it had been the office his father had used. The work done three years ago had brought it into the twenty-first century. The room was dominated by a large light oak desk at the back of the room upon which rested his monitor and the files for court that morning. Two photographs stood on the corner next to the state-of-the-art telephone system, a system he did not understand. One photograph, taken last year, was of him and Shirley, tanned, drinks in hand, smiling in a restaurant in Hamilton during their three weeks in Bermuda. The other was of a young John and Shirley bent over a bemused Brian as he tried out his first tricycle on a newly landscaped back garden one Christmas. Matching bookcases either side of the room contained every book any criminal defence practitioner could ever need. All were in perfect condition. John found that the answers he needed to any problem were rarely found in books. Careful thought and the calling in of favours generally bought results. A coffee table and two armchairs to the right of the door were used mainly when giving interviews to the written press, or increasingly nowadays to television, on a multitude of legal topics. Any spare wall space was littered with photographs of John – John shaking the hand of a sportsman he did not recognise, some silver cup or other in the foreground, John with the Lord Mayor, both holding drinks, any number of John with a variety of celebrities who had spent various Christmases working at Nottingham's Theatre Royal.

He slumped in his chair and immediately swivelled around so that he was facing the gardens. The squally rain had now subsided to an incessant drizzle. The staff had done their job; all evidence of Friday had disappeared. Harry was meandering along the borders, checking the roses, bending to pull out a weed that had dared to trespass. And, just for a moment, John wished that he was the one in the garden.

A light tapping on his door interrupted his thoughts. 'Come in,' he shouted, not bothering to conceal his irritation. He turned back round to see a tall, gangly youth with an unkempt mop of light hair. Casually dressed in light slacks and a plain blue shirt, John had never seen him in a suit. Presumably, thought John, he must have been distracted by something or other when he allowed that concession.

'Terry, I've only got a minute then I've got to get to court. What's up?'

'Just a quick word, Mr Farrelly. It's the problems we've been having recently, the system crashing twice, files being deleted.'

'Have you found anything?'

'No, I—'

'So can't this conversation wait?'

'That's the point, Mr Farrelly. I've found nothing. The only thing I can put it all down to is sabotage.'

'Sabotage?' John didn't attempt to hide the incredulity he felt. 'A bit dramatic isn't it? How would anyone get in here to sabotage our computer system?'

'They wouldn't. That's why I've come to see you. The only way anybody could have done all of this is if they were already here and could get access to the system.'

'You mean an inside job?'

'It's somebody who works here, Mr Farrelly. You mark my words.'

'I'd know.' John looked at the boy's surprised face. 'I'd know I'm telling you.'

John ran his hands down his face wanting to be alone. 'Just keep a close eye on everything, will you? Let me know if anything else goes wrong with the system which I recall we were sold because of its reliability.'

'Certainly, Mr Farrelly.'

Chapter 28

'I'll tell the custody sergeant you're here. Simmonds you say?'

Isabella nodded and moved away from the counter. An unshaven youth, thin and pasty-faced, lay sprawled across the two plastic seats screwed to the floor in the corner of the foyer of the police station. She leaned against the magnolia-painted wall, clutching a thick green folder containing every form any legal representative could ever need when attending the police station to represent a client. An old man pushed through the entrance, shaking his umbrella behind him. A gnarled hand fished inside his raincoat and pulled out various pieces of paper. Ashen faced, he looked around guiltily, before shuffling towards the counter.

'I've been told to bring these in,' he said, his voice little more than a whisper. The white-bloused receptionist opened the glass partition without any apparent interest and scooped the documents through before closing the window and disappearing through a door at the back.

Isabella stared at the old man's back, wondering at his anxiety. What problems could he possibly have that compared to hers? She thought back to the sunny Friday, three short days ago. Then, her main concern was getting a dress which fitted. Now, she felt crushed by seemingly insurmountable problems. She'd spent the weekend in bed, feigning a bug, but holding her breath whenever she heard the telephone ringing downstairs. She'd snapped at her father as he put his head round her door each hour to see if there was anything he could do. No, she certainly didn't want him to ask her mother to come and could he not just leave her alone? That was about as civil as it had been.

'Right. That's all in order, thanks.' The documents were pushed back through the window and the man turned, clutching them, and walked away, smiling. As the swing doors to the foyer bounced back and forth after he had left, the door opposite opened.

'Miss Farrelly. We're ready for you now. This way.'

Isabella pushed herself away from the wall and flashed the suited tall, balding, grey-haired officer a tight smile before following him down some stairs and into the bowels of the police station.

'This interview room is free. I'll tell you what it's about and then fetch young Jake. Seems he's up to his old tricks,' he said, holding open a door and allowing her to walk under his outstretched arm.

'It's quite simple really,' he began. She took off her raincoat and sat down. 'I'll be quite open with you, Miss Farrelly, the enquiry is in its infancy, we've no concrete evidence at this point.'

He ran his fingers down an unkempt, grey moustache. At any other time, Isabella would be trying not to giggle as she thought of the words she would use to describe it to the girls later on.

He opened a beige file and glanced at the two pieces of paper lying in it before starting his monologue. 'Hit and run Friday evening close to the house – I think it's some kind of hostel – your client is bailed to. We've had a call this morning – and in all fairness it's anonymous so we've no statement – saying your client's responsible. I've come on this morning and picked up the job and, to be honest, I'm not really up to speed. But as I say, because of the allegation, we've brought Jake in to see what he has to say. Nothing more to add really. I'll bring him here if it's okay with you so we don't lose the room. The station's quite busy this morning with all the crap from the weekend. Coffee?'

Isabella shook her head and the officer left. She leaned back in the wooden chair and closed her eyes, her heart pounding. Her blouse stuck to her back as she shifted in her seat. The small, windowless interview room with its walls of dark wood pressed in on her. The only furniture was the square shaped table she was sitting at surrounded by four plastic chairs. A tape machine with four decks stood against a wall on one side of the table. A red light beamed out accusingly, as if staring at her. She had once heard that these rooms were bugged so that the police could listen in to consultations between solicitor and client. Granddad didn't believe it; what was the point, he had said, they couldn't use anything they overheard as part of the case put before a court, it would be a flagrant breach of solicitor and client privilege. Isabella wasn't so sure; it may simply tell them if they'd arrested the right person. They could then build the case from there. She thought for a moment of confessing out loud. See what happened. Prove it one way or the other.

The door opened and in walked Jake followed by the officer who placed a steaming, brown plastic beaker on the table. Jake slumped into the chair opposite her.

'Sure, Miss Farrelly?' he asked, pointing at the drink. She again shook her head and the officer closed the door behind him.

'Issie, I've done fuck all! I shouldn't be 'ere! You've got to get me out! I've done fuck all! I've got…'

Isabella watched as the words flowed from his chapped lips. Brown, wild eyes, set in a white acne-ridden face covered by patchy stubble and a sweaty sheen, flicked around the room. Greasy, dark hair flopped persistently over his eyes. She grimaced as the stale odour of unwashed clothing hit her.

'Jake!' The torrent of words continued like a river that had broken its banks.

'Jake, just stop for a minute!' This time he stopped, took a gulp of the grey liquid from the beaker and pulled a face.

'It's about a driving accident outside the flats on Blueberry Street last Friday. Where were you that evening? About ten?'

'That's the point, Issie. I can't remember. I can't fuckin' remember. You got me out that mornin' and I went on a bender. The afternoon, after I'd bought my drink, and evening's one fuckin' blank. Woke up under a bench in the Arboretum when it were light and went back to the 'ostel.'

'The Arboretum?'

'That park off the Mansfield Road. Only place you can get any fuckin' peace.'

A way out slowly emerged, like a chink of blue sky amidst a raging storm. Her eyes locked on to her legal pad as she noted Jake's words, not daring to look up lest he saw the gleam in her eyes. She gripped her pen tight in moist fingers. 'What time did you leave your flat on the Friday evening?' she asked, straining to keep her voice neutral.

'It was in the afternoon. I went to pick up me key as soon as they'd let me out and went straight out. I'd fifty quid in my property so thought I'd have a drink.'

'Where did you go that evening? In a pub, a club?' She'd asked the questions too quickly, her excitement mounting.

'No. I were on a downer to be honest. I brought some super strength. It was a hot afternoon and I went and sat out of the way in Arboretum. I must 'ave fallen asleep there and that's where I woke up. I knew it 'ud be quiet there. I didn't want to see anyone. When you've been sharing a cell like…'

Once more his words flowed over her as the pieces of his jigsaw slotted into place. And she thought. And then thought some more. This was nothing to him. Another conviction at the end of a list that ran for pages. It wouldn't matter to him and, if it was put down to drink, wasn't there an argument for supervision with treatment? She could use this to get him the help which he clearly needed. This would suit them both.

'How serious is it Issie?'

She swallowed. 'It's…err, from what the officer says I don't think it's that bad, Jake.'

'Will you be able to get me out?'

Her escape route lay before her, an open door through which the sun shone over a world where her problems and worries no longer existed. She stepped up to the threshold. 'I…err, I'm not sure. There's not much evidence but if you don't answer their questions, you'll just piss off the officer and custody sergeant. You say you've no memory of the evening. Is it…err…is it possible that you could have nicked a car, driven back to the hostel, had the accident, dumped the car and went back to the park?'

'Honest, Issie. I ain't a fuckin' clue. But surely I would have remembered something about it, wouldn't I?'

Her heart was beating so quickly she thought she was going to faint. The warmth of the sunny day through the door was drawing her through. The words on her pad blurred. If she went through, she couldn't go back. But pure chance had given her an opportunity, an escape. She made a promise to God that if she walked through, she would not waste the opportunity. She would grasp the opportunity with both hands. She wouldn't drink. She would work so hard, so very hard. But it was wrong. So utterly wrong. She thought of Granddad's homilies, the words telling her to respect the profession she had entered. How many times had he told her that she couldn't knowingly let clients lie to the police or to the magistrates, how many times had he spoken of how a solicitor should act? Now she saw how right he was. But how could she break her granddad's heart by not seizing her chance? How could she look into his broken face to say that she was sorry; sorry for getting into the scrape and sorry for not having the courage to take her opportunity to save herself?

Without looking back, she crossed the threshold, knowing as she did that nothing would ever quite be the same. 'Jake. Listen carefully to me. There may be some mileage in saying that you accept that you were the person driving and put it down to drink. We then argue that you have a drink problem and try and get you some help. You'd get banned from driving but you're banned for years anyway.'

'Is that what you reckon is best?'

Her heart beat against her chest, her pulse raced. She wished she had some of the disgusting coffee; she could have done with something for her shaking hands to hold.

'I do think it's something to seriously consider, Jake.'

'Well, that's good enough for me, Issie. You've never let me down yet. Have you brought any fags?'

She looked at him and nodded. 'Yes Jake, I've got some fags for you. Let me just write down what we've said for my records then we'll get the interview out of the way and then I'll see about you having a fag.'

'Could do wi' one soon. I'm gaggin'.'

She recorded on her legal pad how Jake had been advised of the allegation he faced and the weight of any evidence against him. She set out how he had been advised of his rights not to answer any questions that may be asked of him and the consequences of not doing so. Finally, she recorded his decision to answer the officer's questions.

'Jake, can you sign here?' She handed him her pen and tried to control her breathing. 'Right, I'll get the officer. Okay?'

'Yes. And Issie?'

'What Jake?'

'Thanks for comin' out for me. It's appreciated. I feel as though I've let yer down what wi' yer getting' me out only last week.'

She swallowed. 'It's okay, Jake,' she whispered and slipped out to fetch the officer.

'I could do wi' a fag before we start, Mr Ibbotson,' said Jake as the officer walked in followed by Isabella.

'You can for me Jake. Provided that Miss Farrelly doesn't mind of course?'

Isabella shook her head, thinking that she would normally object to leaving the police station stinking like an ashtray. Today, it didn't seem to matter.

'Right,' said the officer once both he and Jake had lit their cigarettes. 'Let's get going, shall we?'

Isabella watched the officer's thick, calloused fingers, the cigarette wedged between two of them, as he grappled with the cellophane wrapping around the tapes and shoved the tapes into their respective decks. Flakes of ash dropped onto the table. Once the tapes were in, he swept the ash to the floor with his free hand.

She listened as the tapes whirred and the officer and Jake introduced themselves. She mechanically gave her name and advised that her role was to protect Jake's interests.

Cigarette smoke hung over the small room. Her clothes seemed to stick to her. It became unbearably hot. She needed to get out, get away. The red figures on the machine shining through the smoky gloom and which timed the interview seemed to grind to a halt. She fixed her eyes on the pad in front of her as she wrote down her own record of what was said. She wanted to be any place other than this. Her head began to pound. Is this what her bitch of a mother meant by a migraine? Nausea swept over her. Her stomach felt ready to explode. As her pen set down Jake's words to the smiling officer, as Jake said that if a witness said he had done it then that was right and as the tapes span round recording those words, she put her hand to her mouth, fearful that she was going to retch.

After what seemed like hours, the interview was drawn to a close. The tapes were wrapped up, signatures scratched on various pieces of paper. 'I'll wait by the custody officer's desk, Jake. Okay?' She looked at the officer. 'I presume that he'll be put back in his cell for a few minutes?'

The officer nodded as he collected the tapes and his notes and Isabella hurried out of the room and took a deep breath. She found the toilet and locked the door. A ghost-like figure she did not recognise stared back at her from the mirror. She splashed her face with cold water. It was no good. She could not wash away the dirt of the deceit against someone who she was here to help. She knelt over the toilet and vomited into the bowel. Tears filled her eyes. Her stomach heaved again and once more she was sick.

Finally, she hauled herself out into the crowded custody area where officers and representatives were striving to speak to the custody officer, a bearded man sitting behind the counter pouring over a custody record. On seeing Isabella, he broke off a loud discussion about bail conditions to shout across the custody suite to Isaballa. 'Detective Constable Ibbotson was looking for you, Miss Farrelly. Ah, here he is.'

The officer strode towards Isabella. His eyes bored into her as if reading every thought in her head. 'Miss Farrelly, there you are. I need a word. Step this way, if you would. What I have to say should be behind closed doors.'

To Isabella, the whole area was now silent. She followed him, feeling everyone's eyes in the back of her head. Her legs had all the strength of a new born lamb. The nausea returned.

'Sit down, Miss Farrelly.' He shut the door of a small room usually used for consultations between solicitors and their clients. 'There's been a development in this enquiry which I need to tell you about.'

Chapter 29

John pulled down the blind in his office to keep out a watery evening sun. The wind and rain of the morning had blown over by lunchtime. The whole building was quiet; the phones were silent, no one was there to pester him. This was the time of day he liked to lean back in his chair and close his eyes, just for a couple of minutes. It was time for himself; that window between the ending of the traumas of the day and the start of the journey home to make conversation with Shirley. Any tasks which trespassed on this time made his heart sink, made him feel that he was being short-changed. And his time this evening, before he went home, was going to be taken up with two particular jobs.

He reached into his bottom drawer and fished out a three-quarter empty bottle and glass. The whisky forged a burning path down his throat as he picked up the phone. He put it down five minutes later, realising that Diana's matrimonial problems, breathlessly revealed by Brian on Friday evening, were just that and were not an alcohol spawned storm which had been resolved the following morning as he had hoped (and expected). 'I want a divorce and I want it quick, John. And I'm sure you'll quickly disabuse my former husband of any notion that may be lingering in that otherwise empty mind of his that he'll be a kept man for the rest of his life.' He finished the conversation by giving her Victoria's mobile number and saying that whilst she would deal with the matter day to day, he would ensure that he was in overall charge.

He then closed his eyes. He could not leave it any longer. There was no other pressing business that required his attention; no letters to write, no trial to prepare, no accounts to ponder and fret over, no partnership matters that could not be put off.

He pulled the letter out of his jacket pocket and lay it down flat on his desk. He did not recognise the name of the firm. Then again, what did he have to do with London firms, prestigious or not? He had googled her name, first thing Saturday morning. She was a solicitor there, an assistant so not important enough to have been given partnership, but there was nothing more. Once more, his eyes were drawn to the words.

Dear Mr Farrelly

I have received instructions from the descendants of Miss Ava Brownlie (deceased). It is their contention that Miss Brownlie's conviction and subsequent execution amounts to a miscarriage of justice. My instructions are to ask the Criminal Cases Review Commission to review to Miss Brownlie's conviction and refer the matter to the Court of Appeal with a view to the conviction being set aside.

I understand that you were the solicitor instructed by Miss Brownlie in those proceedings. The family are of the view that the conviction was as a result of the negligent advice of you, your firm and/or counsel prior to and during the trial and of the negligent preparation of the case by you, your firm and/or counsel prior to trial.

You will be aware that the Commission can only review a matter and subsequently refer it for consideration by the Court of Appeal if it is of the view that there is new evidence or a new legal argument that was not advanced at trial. My instructions are to investigate the possibility that your and/or your firm's negligent conduct and/or the negligent conduct of either or both counsel amounts to new evidence justifying such a referral.

I did wonder, given the sensitive nature of the matter, if you would be prepared to let me view whatever papers you still retain on a voluntary basis. I am sure you may think this is preferable to the Commission calling for them. I would also be grateful if you would agree to see me to discuss the issues.

In the first instance, perhaps you might call me on my mobile number at the head of this letter.

Yours sincerely

JOANNA ALLUM (MISS)

SOLICITOR

That she had invited him to call her on her mobile phone was a something that he'd not noticed initially. It was as his mind pored over the matter during the day that it had occurred to him that it was somewhat unusual. Maybe she was going through the motions. Perhaps she realised that her task after all of this time was hopeless and that she just wanted to be able to tell her clients, whoever they were, that she had done all she could. A quick chat after close of business and then report back. It's too late, she would say. There's no evidence. The only person still living is the solicitor who you want to blame. He pictured Miss Allum – she was young, eager, just starting, desperate for something to get her teeth into – flinging the slim file on her desk, frustrated that she'd been given another pointless job. Or maybe she was an old maid, experienced, good with clients, given the job so as to let them down gently.

He thought about another drink. Just one more. No, that wasn't the answer. Maybe he could ring tomorrow, leave it for tonight, it had been a long day. So tempting – but not the answer. The evening stretched out before him. He could tell Shirley about the letter. On the other hand, he could endure the painful process of the truth being dragged out of him. Shirley could always read him; she would know that something was wrong. And he had to have something, something concrete, to tell her. He had to be able to provide some explanation as to why an icy, bony finger had emerged from the murky and long forgotten depths of the past and felt his collar.

And so, he wiped his hands on his handkerchief and picked up the phone.

Chapter 30

'Do you have to answer that? We were talking.' Her voice was always louder when she'd been drinking. And she drank when she was worried.

John switched off his phone without answering it and looked at his wife, sitting bolt upright on the other end of the black leather sofa, glaring at him through the muted light of the two lamps. The ticking of the grandfather clock in the corner of the wood-panelled room they called the parlour (for reasons which escaped him) was the only sound that could be heard.

'It's Isabella, I've been trying to get her all day,' he said.

'Who?'

'Isabella.'

She continued to stare at him, her eyes boring into his. She must have seen the expression on his face. She looked away. Anger was replaced by confusion. He could see her striving to make the link, the link between the name and the person she should know. And confusion was replaced by fear. He knew the look, he'd seen it before and was beginning to understand its meaning. He was going to have to accept that his wife did not recognise the name of their only grandchild.

'Well…whatever.' She stood up and walked away, taking her empty, stained red glass towards the kitchen. As she did so, John wiped away a tear. This was something he could ignore no longer. He turned back to the phone and rang his granddaughter.

'Isabella, my dear,' he started, trying to sound upbeat, 'I've been trying to get you all day. About the meeting this morning. Don't worry about—'

'Granddad, that's not why I've rung. I just need you to tell me I've done right.'

'Go on,' he replied, slowly.

'He's admitted it.'

'What! If he's done whatever he was arrested for, why was he answering any questions?'

He sensed the hesitation, the slightest of gaps before she answered. 'That's why I've called you. He said he'd taken the car and was just on Bluebell Street going back to his room when she stepped into the road. He couldn't remember much but he kept saying that he wanted to get it off his chest. He was so adamant—'

'Jake Simmonds! Adamant! He's normally too worried about getting his next drink to be adamant about anything. What evidence had they got?'

'There was an eyewitness. It was a good description. And it happened just outside his room. He said he was feeling guilty.'

'He's never felt guilty before. What's happened? Have they kept him?'

'Yes. He's been charged and will be in the magistrates' court in the morning. They wouldn't give him bail.'

'What's the charge?'

He thought he heard her catch her breath. 'Causing death by dangerous driving.'

'Death by dangerous?' He whistled. 'I hadn't realised there'd been a fatality.'

'Yes,' she whispered.

'Are you okay? You sound upset.'

'It was a bit of a shock. I hadn't realised she'd died.'

'What do you mean?' John stood up and began to pace the length of the room.

'The feds, they—'

'Don't call them that, dear. It makes you sound like a client.'

'They only told me after the interview that she'd died, so it took Jake by surprise.'

'And you, by the sounds of it,' murmured John.

'Granddad. I'm worried. I don't know whether I did the right thing. I couldn't stop him coughing it.'

'What's done is done. Look. I'll do the bail application tomorrow and have a look at the whole thing. I'll see what I can do.'

'No. No, there's no need. I'll do the hearing. Granddad, is he likely to be convicted? If he's admitted it, I mean?'

'Well yes, highly likely, as you know already.'

'I told him he'd get credit for being straight with them.'

'Well, he will I suppose. But he'll get some time for it. That's a decent client off the scene for a good while.'

'So the f...the police won't look for anyone else, will they?'

'I wouldn't have thought so if they've got their man. Why? Why do you ask that?'

'It'll be some comfort for her family, that's all. And Jake'll get some credit for that, surely?'

'Well, I suppose so.'

'I'm tired, Granddad so I'll—'

'Isabella, I can't do with you going soft on me about somebody, no doubt drunk, wandering into the street and being run over. I've got battles coming up and I need you and your father by my side.'

She said nothing. He thought he could hear a soft sobbing on the other end of the line. 'Yes,' she then said so that he could barely hear her, 'I know. Good night.'

'You just get your head straight. Okay? Right. Good night.'

'What did she want?' John looked up as Shirley emerged from the shadows into the light of the lamps. Her memory had switched itself back on as if someone had flicked a switch. She held the stem of a full glass between her fingers. The wine, a deep impenetrable maroon, sloshed from side to side, threatening to spill onto the cream carpet. John raised his hand in warning and opened his mouth but thought better of it as she slumped on the end of the sofa. Streaks of black mascara under her eyes gave her the appearance of a macabre clown.

'She's had a bad day in the police station. She's got to learn to toughen up.'

'You molly coddle her.' She was beginning to slur her words.

'Rubbish.' He looked away.

'She's your favourite. Everyone's talking about it.'

'Shirley! You're drunk! Why don't you just go to bed and sleep it off.'

'Sleep! Sleep you say? How can I get to fucking sleep when you announce that we're still not shut of that awful, awful job? After all of these years. You rang her, you were saying. What did she say? Tell me!'

John buried his face in his hands. He wanted, no needed, to be alone. His bones ached, his head throbbed. 'She says she wants to see me.'

'Oh does she now! Well she can take a running jump.' Shirley gulped down a mouthful of wine. A trickle ran slowly from the corner of her mouth. 'You did tell her, didn't you?' He looked at her, saying nothing, not wanting this conversation.

'Didn't you?' she screamed.

'Shirley, it's…it's not quite that easy. I can't just—'

'You've agreed to see her! Haven't you? You soft bastard! You weak, soft bastard!'

'Shirley, I had no choice, darling. Really, I didn't. Look. I'll deal with it. I promise.'

'I'm going to be there. I'm going to see her with you! This so-called fancy solicitor from London! When is it? When are you seeing the bitch? I'm...' She brought her hand to her mouth and swallowed several times. 'I'm going to be there. D'you hear me?'

He sat there, saying nothing, his eyes on the floor.

'Well? When is it? When are you seeing the bitch?'

'Next Monday,' he replied, quietly.

'Right. I'm going to be there.'

'It's here.' He looked across at her.

'What?' Her eyes, round and wild, looked back at him.

'It's going to be here. I told her to come here.'

'You're bringing the cow here? To my home? You're bringing that awful, awful job into our home! How can you be so fucking insensitive?' Suddenly she hurled her glass at him. He winced as it glanced off his shoulder. Red stains slowly spread on his white cotton shirt as if a bullet had sliced through him.

She started sobbing, little sniffles at first, getting louder and louder until her wailing echoed off the stone walls. John bit his lip. After a minute, he sidled over to her. He put his arms tentatively around her shoulder and, as her arms went clamp-like around his midriff, her nails dug into his back. Her face pressed hard against his chest and he felt her warm tears through his shirt.

Finally, she pulled away. Her eyes, watery and bloodshot, looked into his. Her hands cupped his face. 'Look what this did to you before.' More tears rolled down her cheeks. 'Your guilt, in those six months, a year, I don't know, after the execution. It nearly killed you. It was months before you were able to do anything other than lock yourself away in your office and drink yourself stupid. And that was when your father was there to shield you from all the talk, the press and all that was going on.'

'I was a young boy then, just a kid. I was dragged into something I wasn't prepared for. It's different now. I'm different now. And, I've got you. You're right. You always are. But I have got you now. I'm going to do nothing without you with me and I'm relieved, more than I can say, that you'll be here next week.'

'John...John.' She shook her head slowly and took her hands away. She bit her lip and her eyes watered again. 'You're not different. You're still the same sensitive man I fell for all those years ago. You were the boy in the office who daren't ask for a cup of tea. Oh I know you go strutting around the office giving out your orders to…to whoever, making people run around after you. But you don't even trust yourself to win a partnership argument without your granddaughter on board to do your shouting. You can no more deal now with the analysing of everything you did and didn't do, the disparaging comments and your eternal guilt than you could then.'

'That's not—'

'Let me finish. There's one thing that is different.' He felt her eyes staring into his. 'I know it's not something that you ever talk about, not properly that is, in fact not at all.'

'Not tonight, Shirley, please. I really can't cope with that tonight.'

'No, John. If you – no, we – are going to deal with this, we've got to talk about him. I'm not prepared to let him be the elephant in the corner anymore.'

John looked away.

'James! There. I've said it. I've said his name. James! James! James! Before, you had James. And you only came through the other side because you had James.'

He closed his eyes, saying nothing. He knew she was waiting for him to say something, anything. Words would not come. This was not a conversation he wanted, had never wanted and would never want.

She started up again. 'Now you don't have him. He's not here to get you through this now. You once told me I got you through those times. That's not true. It was James you turned to, James who carried you through. It was James who talked you out of your depression. It was James who picked you out of the gutter that night. Don't you remember?' She laughed, hard and bitter. 'Have you any idea how jealous I was? How on your worst days he was always there. I could never understand it, all the talk, the rumours about him and what he had done, how he had been involved – no, you don't need to say anything, I never believed them – but it was him you turned to.' She put her hands over his. 'I wanted to be the one. You've no idea how it ate me up.'

John stood up, walking up and down the room. His mother and father looked down at him from the portrait screwed into the slate wall above the wood burner. Other photographs – more of his parents, of Brian, many of Isabella, Shirley's parents, Shirley and, most of all, John and Shirley – adorned walls and every available surface.

'Mind, every cloud has a silver lining. Your father would never have let you marry someone like me otherwise. He once told me that

I was the only one who seemed to be able to make you forget. It was the only nice thing he ever said to me. But it was still James you went to.'

She stood and he felt her hand in his. 'Do you miss him? You must, he was your twin, but you never say.'

He pulled away without answering and walked to the window, lay his forehead against the cold dark glass and closed his eyes.

'John. James died in 1953. It's been…years, many years. To lose anybody, let alone a twin brother, is unimaginably awful. But it wasn't your fault. You were not to blame.'

Unwanted memories, sensations, perceptions that he thought had been long since vanquished scuttled from the corners of his mind into full view. Like a breached dam, out they came, one after another, oblivious to his attempts to stop the chasm. He tasted bile in his throat, his heart hammered against his chest as his powerlessness overcame him. He felt himself retch and put a fist in his mouth.

Suddenly, the maelstrom subsided and the whole panorama was dominated by one thing, the one constant. In his mind's eye, he could see James as clearly as if he was standing next to him at this very moment.

'James's suicide was a tragedy. But you cannot live your life blaming yourself for everything that goes wrong.'

He heard her words. They meant nothing. He had nothing to say. No words could ever come any more than there could be any photographs of James in the room. He felt Shirley's hands lying softly on his shoulders. He turned and held her close, looking over her shoulder.

'Come on, let's go to bed.'

He didn't reply, there was nothing he could say.

Chapter 31

John watched the small Audi winding its way down the shrub-lined driveway from an upstairs window as he knotted his tie. He glanced at his watch. Five past two; she was slightly late. As the gravel of the courtyard crunched under the tyres, he felt a fluttering in his stomach. Peering around the thick dark brown velvet curtains through the small leaded and darkened windows, he scrutinised her emerge from the driver's seat into the shade of the courtyard at the front of the Manor.

He saw her push her sunglasses onto her forehead as she stepped back to survey the front of the house. Her age was difficult to place at this point. Her clothes, a blue skirt, matching jacket and neutral white blouse were businesslike but did not indicate great wealth. The car was three years old and did not have a private plate. She leaned into the back of the car and brought out a small, black attaché case before disappearing under the porch to the heavy oak door. As the chimes of the doorbell echoed throughout the house, he went to the galleried landing, grasping the oak railing with moist hands.

The shoes of the cleaner he had asked to admit her and whose name he could not recall clicked against the stone flooring. The front door creaked as it opened.

'Hello. Joanna Allum for John Farrelly.'

Why did she seem so matter of fact? Why was he so nervous? This was against the natural order of things. He heard the cleaner's rustic Derbyshire voice asking the woman to come in and wait in the parlour and that Mr Farrelly would see her presently.

'Thanks,' was the accentless, murmured reply.

He didn't move, needing time to think. Let her stew in the dark, wood-panelled parlour for a few minutes. To be invited to a place such as the Manor would be unusual, not something which a solicitor in her field would generally experience and it would do no harm to ratchet up the apprehension she was surely feeling.

He'd agonised all morning over what to wear. In the end, the decision had been rushed. Shirley's desire to prepare something for lunch, saying cheerily that she was going to take advantage of having John at home for once, had ended in histrionics when she had drifted into the conservatory to phone Brian leaving simmering vegetables on the hob in the kitchen. The resulting steam seemed to have left its black odour throughout the whole house, although maybe that was something he was imagining. The fact that the house was now a place of calm and tranquillity was something which he considered to be a minor miracle. Perhaps everything was for a reason; this was a meeting in which Shirley may have been a distraction. She had not mentioned it throughout the morning; he thought miserably that it was a sign of her deterioration and its speed that he was by no means certain that she had remembered. It had taken him and the cleaner with no name, aided by a dose of sleeping pills, over half an hour to settle her and get her to bed. She should now sleep soundly for the next few hours. The decision as to what to wear, hurried though it was, had led him to wear a grey lounge suit, light blue shirt and matching tie. The quandary had been whether to where a tie – smart but relaxed was an impression he had considered trying to create. In the end, the fact that a tie may reflect the seriousness of the matter was the decisive factor.

He crept down the stairs, anxious not to give her any indication his entry into the parlour was imminent and stopped at the door, placing his ear against the cool wood. Nothing could be heard. He wasn't sure what he was listening for; she was hardly likely to put on a CD. He breathed in and then pushed open the door.

'Miss Allum,' he said, striding into the room, a wide smile on his face. She put down a magazine that had been on the coffee table and got to her feet. He laid his hands lightly on her upper arms and air-kissed both cheeks. Inhaling the cheap perfume, he stepped back. 'Thank you so much for coming out here. Quite a drive, I would imagine?'

'It's no problem, I left my flat at about nine o' clock. The roads were okay.'

He now saw that long dark hair flowed down her back as far as her waist. There was no engagement or wedding ring and no indentations on her ring finger. Her jacket lay across the back of the chair where she had been sitting. The white blouse and blue skirt rather dated her, he felt. Weren't young women into power dressing nowadays? Whilst not overweight, a diet would not have gone amiss. Brown eyes looked out of a heavily made-up face. Late twenties, not married, stuck in a London flat, still an assistant solicitor, John sensed disappointment, or at least she should be disappointed. Not for the first time since receiving the letter, John wondered if throwing money at the problem would provide an answer as it had on occasions in the past. His thoughts slipped back to Isabella's calamitous trusts exam at the end of her second year at University. A couple of grand to a friendly quack who prepared a report explaining her anxiety and inability to demonstrate her legal knowledge in an exam setting and a definite commitment to the Dean of her law school to give a talk on careers in the legal profession and the whole thing had been swept under the carpet.

'Let me show you the house. We'll start in the gardens,' he said. No harm, he reasoned, in showing off the rewards that a career in the law could produce.

'Err…yes, if you like,' she answered, as if surprised by the suggestion.

The sun was shining intermittently between white fluffy clouds. A slight breeze ruffled the roses in the square borders set between rows of concrete steps. As they moved away from the borders and onto lawns flanked by beech trees, John began the talk.

'We've had the gardens sorted over the last couple of years. The work was completed about six months ago,' said John. 'They're based on the original created in the early eighteenth century. The original was one of the first type of English gardens which replaced the French style which had dominated until that time. The idea was to present an idealised view of nature. Thus once we move away from the rose garden, we see the groves of trees and how the lawns sweep down to the lake over yonder. You can probably make out the recreation of a classical temple on the other side of the water. We acquired the place about sixteen years ago when it was in quite a state. It's taken a fair amount to get it into the condition that it is today but I don't begrudge it.'

In the distance could be seen the blue-grey of the tips of the peaks. 'The grounds to the north of the house stretch to another couple of acres. It's there where the maze which was featured on television recently is to be found.' He waved his arm towards the left. 'I don't know if you happened to catch it?'

She shook her head. He wanted her to ask a question or make a comment, anything to show she was taking an interest.

'We're opening the gardens up to the public later in the summer. If we turn around, you'll get a better idea of the size of the Manor.' The three-storey square building with two-storey wings each side stood before them. The shrubs and woodland at the front of the house tended to hide the fact that this was a country house in extensive grounds. John had been told many times over the years that it was only from here, from the gardens at the back, that one could truly appreciate Ilebeck Manor. She really ought to be impressed. 'I do take the view that owning a property such as this brings with it its own responsibilities,' he continued, sensing his voice was becoming more strident. 'The east wing to your left was just a shell when we bought it. It's now home to a ballroom, again based on the original plans.'

From the corner of his eye, he caught her glancing at her watch. The sun burned down and his collar and tie felt tight around his neck. 'The building to the right of the west wing is where my cars are garaged; I have a passion for classic cars. I do believe this profession can be very rewarding. So, Miss Allum. What brought you into the law?'

'A desire for justice, Mr Farrelly. And whilst walking around these gardens is not unpleasant, I'm sure you will appreciate that seeing them is not why I have come.'

'I understand that, Miss Allum. But I spend so much of my time in my office or in a stuffy courtroom. When there is the chance of a change of scene, I try not to lose the opportunity. I find it important to remind myself sometimes of the rewards that a career in the law can bring. You're not in partnership?'

'Err, no. Although I'm not sure why that is relevant to the matter in hand.'

'Maybe you should consider employment outside London; a better standard of living, better work conditions, better rewards. So many young people nowadays think the world starts and ends in London.' Even to him, it sounded desperate.

He felt her eyes on him as she spoke. 'I've left my papers in your study or whatever it is. Perhaps we might go back and get started.' She strode off, retracing her steps back into the house. John followed, almost having to break into a trot to keep up.

She sat down in the cool of the wood-panelled room and took two sheets of paper from her case. Nothing was said as her eyes appeared to flick over the first of them. John felt a lead weight in the pit of his stomach; this was not how it was supposed to be, this was not in the natural order of things. People coming here, and particularly a young solicitor who seemingly had no hope of a partnership, should be overawed. They were being confronted with wealth beyond their wildest dreams. They should reflect on their own position, ask themselves what was wrong with them? Why were they not in such a position? When this was followed up by the suggestion that there may be an opening at Farrellys for her with the hint of getting a share of that untold wealth, she should be his, like a fly caught in his web. And such a prestigious organisation which was providing that opportunity could not possibly have anything to hide. That's what should happen. And that is most definitely what was not happening. He felt out of control, unable to comprehend this apparent lack of interest in material advancement and having little experience in dealing with it. He searched for the right words, words to tell her that a desire for justice would remain just that – a desire – if the disadvantaged, the vulnerable, the needy were ignored. That's what drove him on and on, even now, after all of these years. Yet, for some reason, these were principles, dear to his heart, which he seemed unable to articulate. Was it her? Surely not; dealing with other professionals without any suggestion of being intimidated was something that he had done all his working life. The thought, like an icy wind, crept into his head. It was the case. It was the case that was overwhelming him. Something that had been out of sight for a lifetime had, most definitely, been out of mind. And now it had been plucked from the misty past and placed squarely in front of him. The tensions, apprehension and stresses of his early years returned like a long-forgotten childhood nightmare. Then, words were often elusive. Maybe he had not come as far as he thought.

She was still looking at the papers. The clock ticked in the corner. Now the past was here, it would not let him go. He was reminded of those times all those years ago, watching his father cross out large sections of a lease he had drafted with an extravagant swirl of a fountain pen. He needed to say something. The silence was overwhelming. Damn it all; he needed to show whose house she was in and who she was actually dealing with.

'Miss Allum, perhaps you would enlighten me with the nature of your business here today.'

She looked up, holding his gaze. 'You've received my letter, Mr Farrelly. I'm spending some time in Nottingham investigating the Brownlie case and felt it only fair to give you this opportunity to give me your version.'

'Why on earth should I, Miss Allum? I have nothing to hide, nothing at all and I fail to see after all this time what there is to, as you call it, investigate.'

'Don't you think that the execution of a young girl in questionable circumstances should be investigated?'

'Miss Allum, you don't see my point. You wish to look into a case which is well over fifty years old. I am the only one left from that period who can give you any information. Fifty years is a long time. You cannot expect to rely on my memory.'

'You have some papers from the trial, surely?'

'If we have, I've no idea where they are. I'm sure that you appreciate that Law Society guidance does not require us to keep papers for that length of time. Given that you have not given me any indication as to who has instructed you or what information you have received, I am not sure you can really expect me to turn out my whole office out on what I'm beginning to sense is a wild goose chase.'

It suddenly occurred to John that he had just described exactly what all this was. Make wild allegations about negligence, always an emotive word for lawyers, and wait and watch whilst he tried to justify his actions; they were her tactics. He had given her an opportunity, had invited her into his house and all she had was two sheets of paper – which, for all he knew, could be blank. He would not embarrass her by asking to see them. Her whole attitude this afternoon was aggressive and designed to intimidate.

'Miss Allum,' he continued, standing up, 'if there is nothing further, I'm a busy man. I categorically deny any negligence or wrongdoing on the part of myself or my firm at any time in connection with the tragic case of which you speak. Perhaps you would kindly relay that to whoever has given you instructions and I will bid you good day.'

'Mr Farrelly. Sit down, please.'

Who on earth was she to tell him to sit down in his own house? He stood there, arms crossed.

'I had hoped that common sense would prevail and that you would have provided me with a copy of your own file. You haven't and it seems it will be necessary to see you again. In Nottingham next time, please. That's where I am staying all of this week and I don't see the point in having to traipse all the way out here. Perhaps your offices would be more appropriate?'

He tried to think of something to say, conscious he was becoming angry. 'Did you hear what I just said?' He didn't like to shout, particularly at a woman. 'You have absolutely no information about this matter. You are clearly on a fishing expedition and this particular fish has not and will not bite!'

Once more he felt her eyes upon him as she looked up from the papers she still held. 'Don't you know?'

'Don't I know what?' he snapped, his annoyance suddenly replaced by fear. His heart beat quicker, sensing he was going to hear something he would not like.

'Grimes's widow died recently.'

Grimes! A name he'd not given any thought to for years. A narrow, sunken face, wild, staring eyes, swept into his mind. James's funeral, that's when he saw him last. They hadn't spoken, Grimes had scurried off at the conclusion of the service.

He was just about to ask what that had to do with him when she continued. 'You are obviously not aware that Detective Inspector Grimes kept detailed diaries of all he did and made copies of all the relevant documents. It seems that Detective Inspector Grimes went to his grave certain that there had been a miscarriage of justice. He died in 1953, just after your brother. By coincidence another suicide. According to his widow, it was the Brownlie matter which killed him. More particularly, it was the failure of the prosecuting authorities to prosecute your brother that he couldn't get over. And I suppose, he must have felt guilty having been involved in the prosecution of, to him, an innocent woman who was hanged. Sit down, Mr Farrelly, please.'

John duly sat down.

'As I'm sure you can now guess, Detective Inspector Grimes's widow left all of those documents to the family of Ava Brownlie. I've no idea why she didn't pass them on when her husband died. Maybe she wanted nothing to do with the whole sorry business. Suffice to say, the family now wish to challenge the conviction, thus my involvement. Let me place my cards on the table. All the family require from you is an acknowledgement of your fault in the process. Such an admission will lead, I'm sure, to the Court of Appeal setting aside the conviction. Give me that admission now and I need not trouble you further and can leave you to your busy life.'

For the first time, she smiled.

John thought of the crate of papers, kept out of sight in the corner of the storage room in the attic at the offices. He would need to get them out, read them, ponder them.

'Mr Farrelly?'

Or did he? Did he really need yellowed, dusty papers to remind him what happened during that time? Weren't those events imprinted on the back of his mind? If he thought, truly thought, he could remember every fact, every utterance, without any prompt.

'Mr Farrelly. I'll take your silence as a refusal to give the admission my clients seek. When I contact them, they will be disappointed, I'm sure. In fairness to you, I will come to see you in your office at two o'clock Wednesday afternoon when I'm sure our conversation will be a little more fruitful. I'm afraid I'm not free tomorrow.'

She got up and left.

Chapter 32

At any other time he would have enjoyed the journey in. Summer was always the best of times. Sitting in the back of whatever Bentley Harry had selected for use that particular day, the commute took him from the vivid green and the peaks and hollows of the Derbyshire Dales, through to Nottingham's tree-lined avenues and grimy housing estates giving John a complete panorama of Britain's better parts and those areas which spawned a lot of his repeat business.

Sometimes he initiated a conversation with Harry, sometimes he did not. Harry would never start an exchange. Hiding behind thick-lensed dark glasses and a full grey beard, it was never easy to discern his thoughts on any particular topic. But his quiet manner, good humour and even temper were traits which John had come to value. A widower with one grown up son living in Brighton, John suspected that the job suited Harry. For a small wage and free accommodation in one of the houses, Harry was just asked to be available during the working week to ferry John around and to do any necessary odd jobs. That included dealing with any day-to-day issues in the houses. And watching the green fields and chocolate box villages with their traditional pubs slide by had grown into part of his daily routine. It was a good way to start the day.

It was a start that had often been denied to him this year. It seemed, these past couple of months in particular, that he had passed the journey engaged on the phone sorting out the variety of problems that had befallen the firm. Today, his phone may be silent but yesterday's meeting was playing in his mind. He'd left Shirley earlier still in her dressing gown sweeping up more broken glass and trying to find a way of getting a wine stain from a hessian rug, all before the cleaners arrived. That followed his attempt last night to tell her what had happened. Broken glass and stained rugs could be mended. If necessary, throwing money at it would provide an answer as it so often did. Buying Miss Allum off was something that, until yesterday, he would have considered if all else failed. Everyone had their price, even solicitors, or so he had thought.

Bringing her to the Manor away from the prying eyes of the firm was to give him a better chance of seeing how the land lay in that direction and work out how much advice to her clients not to pursue the matter further would cost him. That was now out of the question and John was in foreign territory. Money, his ultimate method of control, was something that was not available to him. That he could not understand why was, to him, as big a problem as it not providing an answer.

As the car glided into the car park adjacent to the office, John realised that the greenery of the Derbyshire countryside had long gone without him even realising. 'Harry,' he said on stepping out, 'have the car ready for me at two o'clock if you would. I'm not going to court today and this afternoon I'll work from home.'

'Very well, sir.'

John's heart sank as he pushed open his office door to see the back of Brian's head. He could not remember the last time Brian had crossed the corridor and ventured into John's domain. Brian's modus operandi, to John's knowledge, was to stay well out of the way of everyone else, if possible. As he walked around the desk, it suddenly hit him. Hadn't he been exactly the same with his own father? But he wasn't his father. He was inclusive, welcoming, empathetic, wasn't he? Maybe he wasn't. This is what dragging up the past achieved. It created doubt where there had been none. Today of all days, however, Brian and Brian's problems were something he could do without. Christ! Isabella! He had completely forgotten her phone call the other night. He didn't know what had happened yesterday although would have been amazed had Simmonds been granted bail by the magistrates. More importantly, he'd not rung her, just to see how she was.

'It's Isabella, isn't it?' he said as he sat down.

'Isabella? No. It's not Isabella. Why?' He blinked.

'Did she speak to you the other night?'

'No.'

John tried not to be annoyed, irritated as he was at the all-too-common puzzled look on Brian's face. 'So, what can I do for you?'

Brian stood up and started pacing across the room. 'We've got a problem. I had Diana on the phone at midnight. Her husband's left.'

'Brian. I spoke to her last week. I know she's having problems but I don't need to be informed about every single development. Now if you don't mind, I've things—'

'No. You don't understand. You don't see, do you?'

'To be honest, no.'

'The woman her husband has left her for. Diana found out last night who it is.'

'And?'

John's telephone rang. 'Yes.' He groaned as he was told that she was already marching up the stairs. As he put down the phone, his door burst open. Standing there was a short woman, mid-forties, no more than five feet two inches. Lank, hay-coloured hair reached her shoulders. Her blotchy complexion highlighted the lack of makeup. Her dress, something in green that Shirley would have worn, was one she had been wearing at the party. Its crumpled state was such that John wondered if she had not changed out of it since. Blue, tired eyes shot over both of them. It was Brian she spoke to. 'So! This is where you're hiding.'

'Diana. Thank you for popping in. Can we get you some coffee?' he asked.

'Coffee! I've not come to drink bloody coffee!' She suddenly turned towards John. 'Has he told you?'

'Diana. Told me what exactly?'

'About my husband! Why else would I be here this time in the morning?'

John's phone rang again. He picked it up. 'Can't you just take a message?' He put down the phone carefully, his mind racing, and turned back to the woman standing by Brian. 'Now, Diana. I do understand that this is a particularly difficult time for you. Just take a seat and tell me all about it.'

'I'm not staying and this is most definitely not a social call. My husband has run off with another woman.'

'Diana, I have every sympathy and we will protect you from all of the legal consequences of this unfortunate turn of events but we obviously cannot be responsible for—'

'Don't you two clowns ever speak?' She glared at Brian. 'You've not told him, have you?'

'Told me what, Brian?' asked John, turning towards his son. Brian's reluctance to pass on bad news was a constant cause of irritation. John was reminded of the conversation yesterday with Brian's secretary. That was when he had learned about Brian's failure to notify the appropriate authorities of a licensing application.

'Err...I was just getting round to it when Diana joined us. Diana's husband has, by a most unfortunate coincidence, started a relationship with Victoria.'

'Victoria! The Victoria who works here?'

'Yes!' screeched the woman, 'that Victoria! The bitch who is apparently dealing with my divorce. And unless I get a very good explanation as to what's going on, you can rest assured that neither me nor my company will send any further instructions to this firm and will not pay one penny of any outstanding invoices.'

She marched out, slamming the door behind her. Neither John nor Brian said anything. John drew his fingers down his face. A dull pain throbbed in his head.

'So,' said John eventually, 'how much do they owe us?'

'At any one time, the outstanding fees amount to about twenty-five thousand.'

'But that's not the problem here, is it?'

'I…err, don't understand.'

'The problem is that she'll take her work elsewhere if we can't sort out this problem. And the problem is obviously Victoria, the woman who you were so keen to introduce to the business.' John stopped, knowing that blaming Brian for anything would only lead to a crisis of confidence from which recovery would be measured in weeks.

He stood up, having come to a decision. 'Deep in the partnership deed is a clause allowing us to dismiss a partner from the partnership if and when that partner's fee income falls below a certain level in the last financial year. If you bother to check, you will see that this is the case with Victoria. You'd better arrange a meeting of the partnership. Chisolm will moan but I can live with that. And you'd better tell Diana what we are doing.'

Brian left. John looked out of the window onto the garden. Once more Harry was there, this time slowly and methodically mowing the lawn. Stripes in shades of green formed perfect lengths. He was now wearing the old threadbare jacket he had worn as long as he had worked for John. Professional gardeners came in but Harry had always said it was a task he was happy to perform. As he strolled along the lawns, carefully lining the mower, John watched, this time envious, not just of Harry's job, but his way of life. There was more to it that that; he was jealous of his peace of mind.

His phone rang and he turned back. 'I'm really sorry to disturb you, sir, but I think you need to know about the call earlier. It was from a Detective Constable Ibbotson. I've got his mobile number. He said it was a private matter.'

John punched in the numbers. 'Doug. I've only just been told you rang. I've not been told what job you wanted to discuss.'

'John. Thanks for returning the call. I suppose I'm ringing in a private capacity and it's probably nothing but I thought I'd let you know as a matter of courtesy. I've come back from leave this morning and been asked to look into a report of registration number of a car said to be involved in a traffic matter. I've just checked with the DVLA and the vehicle's registered to something called Farrelly's Properties Limited which I think is you is it not?'

'Err, yes, it's the property side.'

'As I said, I'm sure the witness has made a mistake over a digit or something but I may need to take a quick look. You've no objection, have you?'

'No. But it sounds serious, what's the problem?'

'Oh, it's nothing to worry about. It's just something that I have to eliminate from our enquiries.'

'Right,' said John, doubtfully. 'If you need to have a look, just ring and ask for Harry and he'll make the car available.'

John put the phone down and bit his lip, wondering whether there really was nothing to worry about.

Chapter 33

The whole morning had slipped by. He had been stuck in the attic, a dusty fourth floor backwater, hidden away behind the locked door in the corner, alone with his thoughts and with his past. He had ventured through a door which until today hadn't been opened for nearly half a century. As if complaining about being roused from its slumber, the door's lock had groaned as he had forced the key to turn and its hinges had squealed as he had pushed. Coughing as he breathed in the billowing dust, he gingerly took the bulky files out of the boxes into which he had stuffed them back in the days when his misery was so acute that he could have sworn that he would never again feel pleasure in anything.

Even now, fifty-eight years on, a knot formed in the bottom of his stomach as he ran his fingers over the buff cardboard files. He'd found an old desk, moved there years before, and slowly opened the first, peering through the half-light which fought its way through the grime-crusted windows looking over Nottingham's rooftops. Copy letters on tissue like carbon paper, linked together in the top left corner by green treasury tags, the brief to counsel still tied up in its fading pink ribbon, the tens if not hundreds of hand written statements, all passed through his hands. As his eyes flicked over matters that had been written in a different era, he realised that he had been right; he hadn't forgotten anything. It had all been locked away in his mind just as he had locked away the files, so that as the years rolled by, he was able to turn his back and pretend to himself that it had never happened. As the paper evidence of his guilt lay before him, he found himself wondering – no, more than that, almost marvelling – that he had been able to think of anything over the subsequent years other than an innocent girl being sacrificed on the gallows in the name of justice before her life had begun. How could he have slept at night? How could he have ever concentrated on anything else? How could he ever have looked at himself squarely in the mirror? How could he have done any of these things when it was his lies, his cowardice, which had destroyed the defence that he, as her solicitor, should have laid unflinchingly before the jury?

That afternoon, back in his office, the sun streamed in and the fresh, delicate fragrance of newly mowed grass slipped through the open window. John sat at his desk, taking deep breaths as he prepared to face the woman who was responsible for spinning him round, forcing him to gaze on the horrors of his past. This morning, he had felt her hands on his arms, holding them down, stopping him from covering his eyes, compelling him to confront his crime. Now, he closed his eyes, forcing his mind to focus totally on the matter in hand. Just because people were guilty, it didn't mean that they had to plead guilty. He was entitled to make the prosecution to prove its case. That he was sure the case against him couldn't be proved without his admission was not the comfort it should have been. It simply meant that he had to make a decision. The decision was to admit nothing, it had to be. Whilst that would protect him from public ridicule, it would not protect him from himself. When this Allum woman had long since gone, he would be left with the carnage she had re-opened. He breathed out, touched his bow-tie and picked up the phone.

'Send her up,' he said quietly to the receptionist. But it was Chisolm who burst in just as he was wiping his hands on his handkerchief, knowing that he should shake her hand whatever he might think of her.

'What the hell do you think you're playing at?' Chisolm's bull-dog like features were the colour of an over ripe tomato. The collar of his white shirt cut into his thick neck.

'What on earth are you talking about?'

'You phone Victoria and accuse her of virtually bringing the firm to its knees by having a private life and within half an hour you've set up a partner's meeting with one item on the agenda, namely her dismissal over some trumped-up problem with her fees last year.'

'For crying out loud! You moan at every opportunity about your drawings and when I address the issue, you still aren't happy!'

A fat, trembling, finger hovered in front of John. 'For the record, she did not know where her boyfriend worked and had no idea that he happens to be the husband of a client.'

'Rod. Save it for the meeting. I—'

'You'll have to wait for your meeting. She's gone off sick. Stress. Here's her sick note.' Chisolm slammed down a piece of paper onto John's desk with the flat of his hand.

John rolled his eyes. 'I'm just about to see an important client and I'm busy and I would hope that the same goes for you so perhaps you would kindly get out of my office.'

Chisolm leaned over John's desk, his fists pressing into the wooden surface. 'If you so much as lay a finger on her!' He stared at John for just a moment, button like dark eyes gleaming, turned and strode out.

Whispered voices could be heard from somewhere before she walked in, without knocking. John tried to dismiss Chisolm from his mind, forcing himself to concentrate on the smirking woman as she sat on the other side of his desk. But that wasn't easy, something else had jarred in his mind, something that made no sense as perfunctory words about the weather were exchanged.

'You must have wondered?' Her question pushed Chisolm and everything else to one side.

John genuinely didn't know what she was talking about. He stared at her brown eyes. Her dark hair had been bundled into a ponytail and today the blouse and skirt had been replaced with a sharp grey suit. Her expression, that over confident, unworried, almost complacent look, had not changed. It had not occurred to him the other day, but he saw it straight away today; she was laughing. She was laughing at him. He should be mad, he should be furious.

'Wondered what?' he asked, remembering it was his turn to speak.

'Why James was not prosecuted, of course. It's one of the things in the whole matter which I find hard to understand.' She was staring at him, as though it had been his decision.

John wanted to slap her. He wanted to wipe that condescending sneer off her complacent face. She was sitting in his office having arrived five minutes late, he was giving up fee-earning time with no hope of any recompense, he had sent out the office junior to get something called peppermint tea, and all she could do was grin as she scribbled something on the legal pad lying on the desk in front of her.

'It wasn't my job to decide who should and who should not be prosecuted.'

'But it was your job to defend Ava,' she said, looking up.

'Obviously.'

'And emphasising that there was somebody else who had a motive and opportunity to murder the old lady was surely something that any reasonably competent representative would do?'

Her eyes strayed over his shoulder, as if fixed on the tops of the trees through the window behind him. 'Grimes had a view on the matter.'

John knew what she was going to say next. He thought of that morning in a different lifetime in the café, Grimes's haggard features breathlessly pouring out his conspiracy theory.

'Grimes thought their hands were tied by the powers that be,' she continued. 'The creation of the National Health Service was a major plank in Attlee's manifesto after the war. It was something that was not universally welcomed by doctors. And if they didn't play ball, the whole thing would be scuppered before it had got off the ground. The prospect of the state executing a medical practitioner, whether qualified or not, following the death of a patient under his care may have been the straw which broke the camel's back. It's just a thought but it makes some sense. Don't you reckon?'

'Miss Allum. I cannot possibly comment.'

'I think Grimes was wrong, on that point anyway. I think that other forces were at work,' she said.

'Oh?'

'Yes.'

He waited for her to continue. A ringing telephone could be heard from down the corridor. He felt her eyes staring into his. He stood up and walked to the window, not wanting her to see what was inside his mind.

'I know what was in the will. James wanted her to hang. It's as plain as anything. He'd then get everything. My guess is that he killed the old woman, in effect framing Ava.'

'Guess away, my dear,' said John, searching for a degree of bravado he did not feel.

She seemed to ignore what he had said. 'Why on earth did you feel that you could represent her?'

'Pardon?'

'There's a massive conflict of interest. You must have realised?'

He sensed her eyes on the back of his head. He took the handkerchief out of his breast pocket and wiped his forehead, hoping that she could not see. The heat was suddenly oppressive. He felt sick. Thoughts, possible answers, or was it miscellaneous words in no particular order, swirled around his head. It was different in those days. No one bothered about conflicts then. But he couldn't say that; it was tantamount to admitting he now realised he had been wrong.

'The evidence pointed at Miss Brownlie. There was no evidence linking my brother to any wrongdoing.'

'Not after you'd made a statement providing him with an alibi. Grimes was convinced that you were lying. Absolutely convinced.'

John came back to his desk and stood, looking down at her. 'Miss Allum. A rogue police officer did not agree with decisions made by other members involved in the prosecution. That does not mean the whole matter needs to be re-opened.'

'Mr Farrelly. The issue I've raised relates to your conduct. Let me spell it out. There's the ethics of representing someone charged with murdering your own client – you'd drawn up Mrs Harris's will, hadn't you? Then there's the statement you gave to the police exonerating a person – your own brother in point of fact – who stood to gain a fortune from the deceased's death and Ava's conviction. Yet you still represent her. It might be suggested that you didn't do enough for her. There will be those who might say you deliberately distorted her defence. And you get a result. She's convicted – your brother's in the clear with the money.'

He said nothing; no obvious answer coming to mind.

'Well?'

'It's just conjecture fifty years after the event.' It was the best he could manage.

'If the situation arose today, what would you do?'

He went back to the window, pressing his forehead against the cool glass. He could tell the truth, tell her that he had lied for his brother, tell her he would have walked over hot coals for his brother. Wasn't that the truth? Wasn't that what it had all boiled down to?

'I would do nothing differently,' he said.

'The statement you gave – Grimes said you were lying. His notes go on and on about it. He thought you were abusing your position.'

John turned round. 'So you've already said. It's a ridiculous suggestion anyway.'

'I don't agree. I think he had a point. You were – still are – a solicitor. Your word would be accepted. It wouldn't have occurred to anybody that you weren't telling the truth. I accept it's different nowadays, the word of any professional is more likely to be scrutinised. But in those days, if a professional person said something, no one would question it. And I think James had worked that out. You were the perfect alibi.'

'That's again pure conjecture.'

'No, think about it. James had told a lie, his whole life at the time was one monstrous lie. He was running around saying that he was a qualified doctor when he was nothing of the sort. But no one questioned him. To him lying in a professional capacity was second nature and all too easy. So, why not get another professional to lie? It works. He'd proved it.'

'The fact that my brother lied about his qualifications does not make him a murderer. And what has that got to do with me confirming he was with me that night?'

'Grimes was sure you were both lying. He was able to prove James was lying but only because he had documentary evidence of his lack of qualifications. No such luck with you.'

'I really don't see what point you are trying to make.'

'The point, Mr Farrelly, is that you should not have been professionally involved in Ava's defence. A different solicitor would have questioned your statement. Obviously, you didn't and no one else would. The result was that Ava was denied a fair trial.'

'Miss Brownlie made it clear that she wanted me to represent her.'

'But she wouldn't have spotted the point, would she? Is she likely to question you?' She stopped talking as though she had suddenly thought of something. 'Did she even know?'

'Pardon?'

'Did Ava even know that you had made a statement exonerating James?' She didn't wait for an answer. 'How could she? Who would tell her? Not you. By this time, she's been charged and Grimes couldn't see her. So he wouldn't tell her. I bet she never knew that her solicitor had given a statement exonerating the one other person who had anything to gain from Mrs Harris's death. She didn't object to you representing her because she had no idea you had a thumping great conflict. It wasn't as though your statement would be read out or referred to in court, would it? James's possible involvement and the reason why it was not brought up – your statement – was hushed up.' She stood up and started pacing around the room.

'I did my best for her despite overwhelming evidence.'

She continued, as if ignoring him. 'Following on from that, Grimes says that your brother's lack of qualifications was never brought out at the trial. By that time, Grimes had been kicked into the long grass. But his notes make mention of a colleague tipping him off that there was some agreement between prosecution and defence that it wouldn't be raised. Do you know anything about that, Mr Farrelly?' She sat down.

'It's a long time ago. You cannot expect me to remember discreet detail of everything that was said at her trial.'

'Have you not got your file?'

'No. It was destroyed a number of years ago.'

'Let me ask you again. Was there any agreement with the prosecution to leave any involvement that your brother may have had out of the trial?'

'No.'

'Are you sure?'

'Miss Allum, what is this? Do you not believe me?' He sat down, wondering if she was running out of points to make, hoping that was the case.

'Grimes's notes say that your father had complained to his superiors about him. In particular, your father said that he was harassing James. Grimes was "persona non grata" at the trial but, as I say, he had contacts within the force sympathetic to his view and was told that there was an agreement between prosecution and defence that the prosecution would make no mention of the possibility of your brother being involved in return for the defence making no mention of Grimes's activities. Did that happen?'

'That's preposterous! No, it most certainly did not happen!'

Did it happen? Was that why James was not mentioned at the trial? John had not thought about it in that way. He had never seen beyond the statement that he had made. But it made sense. It made perfect sense. Nowadays, a complaint about what police officers had done and had not done could be fatal to the prosecution. But it was not like that back then. Was it? In the deepest chasms of his mind, he recalled comments by leading counsel instructed by his father along those lines. Leading Counsel was chosen by his father. Suddenly, and with crystal clear clarity, John recalled the question he had intended to ask of his father but never had. Why had they got leading counsel who did not specialise in criminal defence work? They had been friends and had gone back a long time; they had served together in the Great War, had they not? He should have seen this at the time. It now seemed so obvious. His father had chosen counsel not on the basis of his expertise but on the basis that it gave him a measure of control over what the jury heard and what it did not hear. In particular, it now seemed blindingly obvious to John that his father's aim was to protect James.

241

'No Miss Allum, you are looking for controversy where there is none to be found.'

He stared at her. Slim fingers were flicking over scrawled notes. Had she finished? Was that it? Was that the case against him? He breathed out. His confidence that she could prove nothing was surely justified. She didn't have that much, just some random comments by an obsessed police officer who was told by his superiors to stay away from the trial.

'You represented Ava at the inquest, didn't you?'

He started at the sudden change of tack.

'Err…yes. And what is your point?'

'And it was straight after the jury's verdict that she was arrested?'

'Yes. On a Coroner's warrant, I believe.'

'And she was in custody until her trial?'

'Obviously. Given the charge.'

'How many times did you go and see Ava before her trial?'

'Oh, come on, Miss Allum. How the blazes do you expect me to remember details like that?'

'Winson Green, wasn't it?'

'Yes, I believe she went there.'

'Nottingham to Birmingham. Quite a journey in those days. I would have thought you'd have some recollection of making such a journey. And I'd have thought that you'd have been going at least once a week. Surely you'd remember?'

'I saw her obviously but please do not ask me to remember when and how often. Anyway, Miss Allum, Detective Inspector Grimes would know nothing of any arrangements I made to see Miss Brownlie. You are straying off your brief and I presume that we can draw this meeting to a close so that I can earn some fees.'

'Didn't I say? Grimes's notes aren't my only source of information. Sorry, I thought I'd said.'

John felt cold sweat trickle slowly down his back. He swallowed. His mind whirled as he tried to think of what other information there could be after all this time.

'Other evidence, you say.' He tried to keep his disquiet from his voice.

'Yes. Grimes's notes revealed a number of other enquiries which have borne fruit. My information is that you only saw her a couple of times between her arrest and her trial.'

John bit his lip. 'As I say, I simply cannot remember, and cannot be expected to remember, details such as that after all of this time.'

'Were you in love with Ava?'

'Sorry?'

'She was a beautiful girl.' She reached into her file and produced a black and white photograph, placing it on the desk in front of him.

He froze. His eyes locked onto the photograph. He flew through the years as if picked up by an unimaginably powerful force and flung back. He was in the club. Its dark walls pressed in on him. He grimaced as warm, weak beer made him gag. A smoky haze stung his eyes. An arm was draped around her shoulder. Her delicate fingers were wrapped around a drink on a table in front of her. She was sitting, looking up, directly into the camera. Blonde hair, as light as a summer's day, swept onto bare shoulders. Her colourless eyes, a flawless face, her skin as smooth as velvet, the merest hint of a smile on her lips made his heart pound. Short, sharp breaths struggled out of his mouth. With trembling fingers, he picked up the picture. He drew it close to his eyes. His stomach cramped as a long-forgotten sensation swept over him. He wanted her for himself, he wanted to grab her, pluck her from the pawing hands of those there. He wanted to gouge out their eyes so that they would never see her again. He pictured himself swinging a hammer into their leering mouths; no more would their lips have her. And for a second, just a second, he realised that such feelings had never been roused in fifty years of marriage.

'Mr Farrelly. You've gone very pale. Are you alright?'

'It's…it's…just a bit of a…a shock to…err…see her, after all of this time.'

'I asked you if you loved her.'

He put the photograph on the desk and dragging his eyes away looked up. His voice was a husky whisper. 'Everyone loved Ava. Everyone.' With the tips of his fingers, he pushed it towards her. She picked it up and put it back in her file.

'I'll ask you again. Was it appropriate to represent her?'

He shivered and breathed out slowly through pursed lips. 'Sorry?'

'I said, was it appropriate to represent her when you had feelings for her?'

'Err…I did not mean that. The murder was out of character. She was most certainly not that type of girl. Everybody agreed. That's what I meant.'

She stood up and gathered her papers. 'Right Mr Farrelly. Thank you for your time. I have a good idea as to her representation.

I will need to see you again to discuss the trial. With that, I'll bid you good day.'

She left the room.

He had been sitting there for five minutes, staring into space, when the phone rang. 'Mr Farrelly, I have someone on the line who will not give their name but says it's urgent. I've explained you're busy but they say they must speak to you.'

'Eh? Err…okay, you had better…err…put them through.' He sat up. 'John Farrelly here.'

'You're a bastard, Farrelly. Read the papers. Very carefully. You'll find them of great interest. Not long now.'

The phone went silent. 'Who is this?'

No answer.

'Who is this, I say?' he asked, louder this time.

Still no answer. John slowly put the phone down and slumped forward, his face in his hands.

Chapter 34

She could have passed for eighteen but the nameplate on her door had said that she was a consultant something or other. Then again, everyone seemed younger nowadays. Or maybe he was just getting old. He certainly hadn't expected a woman, particularly one in jeans and a shirt which had seen better days.

He glanced at Shirley, sitting to his left, her hands in her laps, staring at the desk in front of her, expressionless. The office was bright; dazzling yellow walls, sky blue carpet, a large window giving out onto the gardens and allowing in the sun. It was saying something – we're happy to be here and we want you to feel as comfortable as possible. Maybe he should do something like that. Perhaps the uniform magnolia and grey carpet throughout the office didn't create the right impression and maybe that was why misery blanketed the office like a shroud.

She must be thirty; the youngest of the two children in the photograph on her desk was at least five, the other probably seven. There was no ring on her wedding finger but fresh cut flowers sat on the windowsill. They were expensive, she'd not brought them herself and they would not have been sent by a patient. Her patients did not get better – the best that she could do was to stop the decline – and people who did not get better did not send flowers to their doctor. Yes, they were from a husband or boyfriend. Husband he suspected, the photograph would generate questions about her family and she would only want to answer if she was married. Comments about it being time to tie the knot did not sit happily with single professional women, or at least that was his experience.

She was too thin to be considered attractive. Dark hair was plastered tight to her head before forming a short ponytail. Brown eyes stared out of a narrow face onto a computer screen. She wasn't wearing makeup, her child like complexion was too young, too clear to need it. Thin lips round her small mouth reminded him of a character in an Enid Blyton book although she hadn't seemed unfriendly when she shook his hand as he'd entered. Mind, there was no reason why she should be; he was paying her fee, or at least that's what he presumed Shirley had arranged.

She looked at Shirley and smiled. God, this doctor was surely too young to know what she was doing. 'Now, Shirley. How have you been since I last saw you?'

John sensed Shirley stiffen. He ransacked his memory trying to think. What the blazes. What last time?

'Shirley, are you alright?' asked the young girl straight away.

'It's…it's just that…' She started snivelling, small tearless sniffs at first, then louder sobs.

'Shirley, pet!' For the first time, he noticed the hint of a Geordie accent. She leapt up and darted around the desk. Crouching by her chair, she took Shirley's hand. 'Now what's the matter, there's no need to be upsetting yourself so. Eh, pet?'

Shirley bent over in her chair., openly weeping Large teardrops fell onto her knees. Her body convulsed as the bawling became strident. John turned to his side, his hand hovering in Shirley's direction, trying to think of something to say, unsure of how he should act when his wife was crying in public.

'Now then, pet,' started the young girl as she stood up and bent over, her arm round Shirley's shoulders. The crying finally subsided. 'John doesn't know you've been to see me before, does he? It doesn't matter, honest love. It really doesn't matter. What matters is that he's here now.'

Shirley nodded and fished around in her handbag, bringing out a tissue. 'I'm sorry. I'm so sorry. It's just that…oh I don't know.' She blew her nose and then pulled a small mirror from her bag. 'Look at me now. What a state I'm in.' She laughed, a humourless laugh, and then looked at John. 'You've been so preoccupied recently. I've tried to tell you so many times but you just don't take any notice.'

He looked back, open-mouthed.

'Shirley,' said the young girl, 'why don't you wait next door for a little while and I'll bring John up to speed, eh pet?'

Shirley walked out with a final long look at John. He couldn't tell what she was thinking. He had always thought her so predictable, so dependable, so safe. Never before had she done anything without telling him. He told her everything, absolutely everything. That was how it was between them. But suddenly a chasm had opened up in the ground – he one side, she the other. And he suddenly felt lonely.

The young girl took the seat, next to John. 'Don't look like that,' she said, laughing.

'So how many times has my wife been to see you?' he asked.

'She first came in January following a referral by her GP.'

'And what are you exactly?'

'I'm a consultant geriatrician, love. I deal with the elderly and their aches and pains but I have a particular interest in dementia.'

'You don't look old enough,' he said. 'Sorry, perhaps I shouldn't have said that.'

She laughed, a high-pitched giggle. 'Oh you're a sweetie, pet, you really are.' Before John could respond, she spoke again, this time her tone serious, any levity gone. 'Shirley has dementia. She's worried about it, naturally, and she's worried about you.'

'Me?'

'The reason my secretary phoned you and invited you here is because Shirley doesn't feel able to talk to you about the matter or, to be more accurate, doesn't feel that you listen whenever she broaches the subject, she—'

'That's nonsense. Only last week I said I was going arrange for her to see somebody.'

John felt her hand close over his. 'John, that was the night of the party, wasn't it?'

He nodded.

'That was nearly two months ago, pet. You can't blame her for feeling that her illness is less important to you than whatever's happening at work, now can you?'

He didn't reply.

'From what Shirley has said, a lot of your time is spent at the office.'

'Shirley has a taste for the finer things in life,' he said quickly. She raised her eyebrows and he looked away. 'Well, I suppose we both do,' he added, quietly.

'Let me be candid if I may, John. I feel that Shirley's condition has deteriorated alarmingly, particularly over this past three months. Wasn't she doing something in relation to some gardens earlier this year?'

'She was project managing the restoration of the gardens. We have replicated the whole area to the west of the Manor to how it was in the—'

'Well, that's all very nice but the work, as I understand it, was completed some six months ago. I've noticed in many patients that when they stop work or lose a reason to use their brains it tends to bring on the symptoms and I think that's what's happening here. From having something to think about, she's gone to a situation where she drifts around the house during the day. She told me that she wanted to plan the party but you took that out of her hands and—'

'No, that was—'

'Hear me out John, I'm not saying you were being unkind. I'm saying that she doesn't have a great deal to think about. I suspect she feels isolated living in the country. She's afraid now to drive anywhere in case she gets lost and apart from a cleaner has little human contact. Had you not noticed?'

He looked out of the window. The truth was that he hadn't noticed. The running of the firm seemed to take up so much time. It was so much harder than it was than even five years ago. Problem after problem landed on his desk and no one else seemed to want to take any responsibility.

'I had noticed that she was becoming a little forgetful, but she is getting on a bit, we all are.'

'It's been more than that, John.'

'What can be done for her?' he asked.

'Two things. Firstly, I'm going to write to her GP and ask that her medication be increased. She's on five milligrams of aricept per day. I'm recommending it should be increased to ten.'

'What will that do?'

'There's no cure,' she replied quickly, holding his gaze, 'not yet anyway. But increasing her medication may slow down the deterioration. One of the things you need to do is watch out for possible side effects, which can be quite unpleasant. She seems to have been alright up to now but she may become nauseous, have diarrhoea, abdominal problems. Bad dreams can be a problem.'

'Right.' He stood up.

'Sit down, John. That's not all. Not by a long chalk, pet.'

He slowly sat, wondering if he could glance at his watch without her noticing.

'Don't worry. You'll be out of here in half an hour. Medication is all very well, and it'll certainly do no harm, but Shirley needs more than that. Having little to do all day and little company will make things worse. Shirley says that you've spoken on occasions about slowing down, handing over the running of the firm to your son. Did you mean it or were you fobbing her off?'

Once more he looked out of the window. The roses stirred silently, as if caressed by a gentle breeze. All was bathed in the shimmering light of a golden sun. They'd not had such a conversation for several months, he was sure of that. Of course, he'd been fobbing her off, as this young girl had put it. But if they had the same conversation now...well, it may be different. The problems at the office were always there, ready to sneak up on him whenever he had a quiet moment. Troublesome partners, irate clients; there had been a time when he could have dealt with them in the same way that he could flick a fly off his jacket arm. Somehow it seemed more difficult now. And there was one matter which was always there, always ready to pounce. Ava Brownlie was someone who had been dragged from the depths of his mind. It had been several weeks since his second meeting with that Allum woman and he had heard nothing since. But her questions were something which would not leave him alone. He hoped that Allum would go away and thought she might. But even if she did leave him in peace, he knew Ava wouldn't. His bones ached, his mind was dulled, unable to find answers. Maybe now was the time to slow down, spend proper time with his wife. Quality time; wasn't that what it was called nowadays?

The young girl's voice, quiet and soft, broke into his thoughts. 'It would be a shame if you only slowed down after Shirley's illness prevented you from spending some proper time together.'

God, could she read his mind? He turned on his chair towards her. 'I had been thinking...' he stopped and pulled his buzzing phone from his pocket. 'It's Brian, my son, he's texted me, he needs to talk to me urgently. I...err really need to deal with this.'

She looked at him, a sad smile on her lips. He suddenly thought of his mother, all those years ago. She'd had that look one year when he only got sixty-nine per cent in Latin. 'I'll go and see how Shirley is. I'll be back in five minutes, okay?'

'Thanks,' he whispered as he jabbed the number two on his phone. 'Brian, what's the matter?'

'Dad, where are you?'

'I'm with your mother. What's so urgent? I'll be back in an hour.'

'The police are here with a warrant.'

'What!'

'Well, were here. They've taken the Audi. Evidence apparently.'

'Evidence of what?'

'They've left a piece of paper but one of the officers said that they thought it was the car that was involved in that hit and run on Bluebell Street.'

John looked around on hearing a knock on the door. 'I'll be back as soon as I can,' he hissed.

'Right, John. I want…is everything alright? You look as though you've seen a ghost.'

He put his phone in his pocket in his pocket. 'No, everything's fine.' He felt her eyes upon him. 'No, really.'

'Come on in, Shirley.' His wife followed the young girl. John could see that the handkerchief was crunched up into a ball in her fist. She smiled weakly at him. The young girl dragged up a chair so that they were all sitting in a tight-knit circle.

'Right, John.' He looked up. 'Shirley needs to be with people during the day. You have to decide what's going to happen about your work. You're over eighty now, pet. I can't tell you what to do but most people would be retired. While you sort yourself out, I'm recommending that Shirley spends two or three days each week at a day centre. You'll find that there are people there who are far worse and it may be that Shirley can help out. The staff, wherever you decide to go, will be able to assess that. Shirley thinks it's a good idea. What about you?'

It was a good idea, wasn't it? The image in his mind was of the Audi being towed away. Did the staff know? What did they think? We're a firm of solicitors for God's sake. The police did not execute warrants at a solicitor's offices. Or should not.

'John?'

'Yes, that sounds perfect.'

'Right. Good.' John watched as the young girl took his wife's hand. 'We've got to find somewhere suitable. I can recommend a number of places but you also need to think about how you will get there. You ought to be thinking of somewhere close to home or perhaps somewhere near John's office.

She looked at John. 'Will she be dropped off and if so, who'll do it?' 'Don't you have a chauffeur?'

Something was there, in the corner of his mind, nibbling away, preventing him from thinking clearly. How did she know he had a chauffeur? Shirley presumably. How long had they been talking behind his back, planning this and planning that? Suddenly his heart stopped. It hit him. He felt clammy. The palms of his hands were moist. His shirt collar dug into his neck. He had to get away. It was Isabella. She was dealing with that job. Her client had admitted it.

And she had been at the interview. Had Simmonds taken a car belonging to the firm? That would be one mighty coincidence. All the pieces of the picture were there but he couldn't put them in the right order.

'John? Are you alright?'

'Yes. Yes, it's all a bit of a shock, that's all. A chauffeur? No. I'll take Shirley there. Each morning. And pick her up. If you can send me a list of places you think suitable, I'll work on it. Come on Shirley. We have some work to do.'

He took her hand and they walked out.

Chapter 35

They'd had the car for two days now; should he ring? If he did, his anxiety would be revealed and anyone interested would think he had something to hide. Whether he did have something to hide, or anything to worry about, he couldn't be sure. But until he knew, he wouldn't be able to concentrate on anything. Someone had once said that the cure to all fear was knowledge, or something like that. He was inclined to agree. He'd not spoken to Isabella; maybe he was afraid of what she might tell him. His fingers had twitched, hovering above his phone several times. She'd distanced herself from the office, her presence apparently required at the Crown Court although she would normally have sent a clerk to act as servant to the barrister entrusted with the case. After telling Brian that there was nothing to worry about, he'd spoken to no one.

He walked over to the window. The garden, an immaculate riot of colour against a leaden sky, lay below. Harry wasn't there. Perhaps he'd taken umbrage at being told that he would not be needed as a chauffeur on those mornings that John was to take Shirley to whatever day centre he was going to have to magic out of yellow pages.

He thought of his father. His father had probably stood on this very spot, looking over the lawns, as they then would be, finding answers to his own problems. Just recently, John had frequently found himself slipping back to the past. Perhaps things were less complicated in his father's time. Maybe life was easier for him. Then, the police did not seize cars belonging to the firm; members of staff did not have affairs with the husbands or whatever of clients. His father wouldn't have had to deal with the consequences of the actions of young members of staff.

It wasn't just because of Ava, this tendency to drift back, although she was someone who was now firmly fixed in his mind. That was different; Ava was the past coming to find him. As he stood looking out, he was conscious that he was looking back, searching for something, searching perhaps for a form of peace denied to him these past few months. Maybe he was looking for someone to sort everything out, make it better again. Maybe he was looking for his father.

He turned around on hearing a light tap on his door. 'Enter.' Terry's mop of unruly hair walked in followed by Sarah. John had to think for a moment before remembering that she was Chisolm's secretary, or personal assistant as they were now called. Terry was not wearing a tie, again.

'Mr Farrelly. Sorry to disturb you but I think there's something you should know.'

'Is this something that requires my attention at this moment? I really have a full day and—'

Terry nodded.

'You'd better sit down,' said John, glancing at his watch and wondering why no one ever approached Brian. This was going to be another problem that he was expected to sort out. 'Is this something that…err…'

'Sarah? Yes, she's the one that's told me about it.'

'Go on,' said John wearily, 'what's the problem?'

'It's the diary.'

'What do you mean, the diary?'

'The system the civil department use to record time limits. They're all recorded on the system.'

'What's happened?' John became uneasy. He was too old to understand 'the system' as it was called and detested the smug look on younger members of staff who seemed to have been born with a mouse welded to their hand. But time limits had always been a solicitor's nightmare.

'Well, personal injury actions have to be started within three years of the date of the accident and—'

'Terry! I do not need and do not have time for a lecture on civil procedure!'

'Mr Farrelly, hear me out. Sarah here has discovered this morning that all the records have been wiped.'

'What? They've just gone?'

'Yes, Mr Farrelly. There are no computerised records. Someone's got to go through each file and manually record the limitation date.'

John looked at Sarah. 'Is that right? The dates aren't written in any diary?'

An attractive girl with blonde hair and a pleasant oval-shaped face with honey-coloured eyes, she glanced at Terry, her hands held tightly in her lap.

'Yes, it's the first of the month and Rod…Mr Chisolm likes to have all the dates for the next month just to make sure we've issued proceedings where we need to and when I looked this morning, well there was nothing there. Nothing at all.'

'Where's Mr Chisolm?' asked John, recalling Terry's original suggestion that sabotage was behind all of this.

It was Sarah who answered. 'He's taking a few days off, Mr Farrelly.'

John leaned back in his seat and momentarily closed his eyes. Hadn't he made his money? Why was he killing himself over problems which should long since have fallen to others to solve?

'Right,' he snapped, leaning forward. He looked at Sarah. 'Go through each file in your department and create a manual diary which is not vulnerable to the whims of a computer system. Any matter which requires immediate attention, bring it straight to me. When you've created the new manual system, which you should be able to complete this morning, bring…no, contact Miss Farrelly and ask her to return from the Crown Court as a matter of urgency and tell her to come and see me to discuss the issue and how we ensure that we don't have problems of this nature again.'

He watched as she stood and scuttled out of the office. Turning to Terry, he asked, 'how has this happened?'

Terry looked away. 'Mr Farrelly, I'm really sorry. I wish I knew. I know there have been problems recently and I know it reflects badly on me so I've been really careful. I've watched everything like a hawk. The only possible explanation that I have is that it's a deliberate act. But I honestly haven't a clue how.'

'Terry.' John lowered his voice. 'This conversation is strictly between me and you. Okay?' The other man nodded his head, sweeping away a lock of hair which fell over his eyes. 'Mr Chisolm will be leaving the firm in the near future. Have you any reason to believe he could be responsible for this?'

John was breathing quickly, the palms of his hands moist. As he had uttered the words, it seemed that they had not been his, as though someone else was speaking. He had never before spoken about the firm like this to anyone other than Brian and only then when he had come to a decision. Something had changed, it would never – no it could never – be the same again.

'Look, don't breathe a word of what I've said to anybody,' he added hurriedly.

'No, Mr Farrelly,' Terry replied, eyes like saucers. 'Of course I won't. In answer to your question, I don't see why Mr Chisolm would want to deliberately harm his own department.'

'No, you're right. Of course, you are. Look, just forget I ever said anything. Keep an eye out, will you?' John opened a file, any file, needing time on his own. 'Was there anything else?'

Terry had remained seated. 'There is one more thing, Mr Farrelly, something of a personal nature.'

John sat back and braced himself. This was what you got when you crossed the line that there should always be between you and those who you paid to make money for you. Now, this young oaf had already forgotten about the chasm that lay between them. Now, he was going to start to talk to his betters as though he was their equal. Maybe the time was coming when someone new was needed, someone with fresh ideas, who would come to him with answers not problems. Looking for Terry's replacement could be one of Isabella's first tasks as an owner of the business. Not yet though; he still needed Terry to look after the computers. It wasn't like getting rid of a conveyancer or a litigator. Half the firm could do their jobs; replacing the one person who understood the infernal system needed a little more patience and cunning.

'Well?' he said as the unkempt youth looked to the side, appearing to have second thoughts.

'I know it's hard to find somewhere, Mr Farrelly, somewhere you feel they'll be happy. It's particularly hard when they can't tell you.'

'Terry, I haven't the faintest idea what you're on about.'

'Mrs Farrelly. We've seen she's not been well and…well, Mr Farrelly, to be honest everyone knows and is upset about it but I'm sure it'll be better all round. For everyone.'

'Pardon?'

'What I'm trying to say, Mr Farrelly, is that finding a care home for a loved one who can't look after themselves is hard and finding somewhere for them during the day is no easier. My mother goes to a day centre each day, she's got Alzheimer's. The place where she goes is excellent, really good. It's on your side of town as well. I just thought that you might want to consider it for Mrs Farrelly.'

'Terry, how do you know about my wife?'

'Word gets around, Mr Farrelly. We'd all seen that Mrs Farrelly was becoming a little forgetful and…well, when old Harry asked if there was anything he could do because he's not going to be driving you around, well, it was fairly obvious.'

'I'm not sure that I like Mrs Farrelly's condition being the subject of office tittle-tattle but what you say is true; I am trying to find a suitable place for her to go just for a couple of days during the week. Where is this place?'

Terry explained that it was just off the ring road and John quickly saw that it would only require a detour of about five minutes from his normal route.

'What's it like?'

'Mum likes it, as far as I can tell. There are lots of activities, always plenty going on and the staff are friendly. I'll email you the number so that you can arrange to go and see it with Mrs Farrelly, if you like.'

'Err…yes. Okay.'

The phone rang. Terry stood up. 'Righto, Mr Farrelly, I'll do just that.' He turned to go.

'Terry,' said John, his hand over the phone.

'Yes, Mr Farrelly,' Terry answered, turning back round.

'Thanks. It's…, well, I appreciate it.' Terry smiled and left the room, closing the door quietly behind him.

'Call for you, Mr Farrelly,' said the receptionist, 'he wouldn't leave a name although he's rung before.'

John swallowed. His heart missed a beat as he heard the click as the receptionist put down her phone. The voice on the other end spoke before he could utter a word. 'Forgotten me, had you? You bastard. Make sure you read the papers. It'll…' John slammed the receiver into its cradle. Blood pumped through his veins. He stood up and backed away from his desk, staring at the phone, as though scared it would jump up and crack him in the face.

It rang again, its shrill jingling bouncing around his head. On and on it went. He was willing it to stop, not daring to pick it up. Still it continued. Finally, he pulled a handkerchief from his pocket and mopped his forehead. It could only be reception. The only people who could bi-pass reception were Shirley and Brian. What was there to fear? He was in control. He could simply refuse to take calls unless he knew who they were from. He sat down, still breathing heavily, and picked up the receiver once more.

'It's a Detective Constable Ibbotson, Mr Farrelly.'

Relief momentarily swept through him. 'John. Morning. Can I see you at some point? In private. I need a word.'

It was the car. He wanted to speak about the car. The relief was replaced by a dread of what he was about to hear. 'Yes. Of course, Doug.' He made an effort to portray a nonchalance he did not feel. 'Can you tell me what it's about?'

'I can't really speak now. How about the snug in the Bell? Five o' clock?'

'Err…yes, fine. Doug, can't you just tell me what it's about?'

'No. Five o'clock.' The line went dead.

Chapter 36

John turned up the collar of his Burberry trench coat, a present from Shirley two winters back, as he walked across the Market Square. Autumn had crept up unnoticed and pushed summer away. Already a few dead leaves were scooting across the slabbed square, thrown around by the stiff breeze. The grey sky threatened rain. People strode this way and that, making their way to the car parks or the buses or the most recent form of travel, the trams that had opened for business only last year. All would be going home to their semis and their orange-bricked council houses to tell their husbands and wives about their mundane days. Queues trailed from bus stops, parents struggling to contain the excitement of children as they waited to be taken to the Goose Fair.

At that particular moment, John would have gladly given up the Manor to be one of them. The afternoon's cases, three guilty pleas to be sentenced following the preparation of probation reports, had been dealt with as if on automatic pilot. None of those being sentenced had been locked up. As each person shook his hand vigorously, thanking him and telling him that he was the only person who could have kept them out, he had simply smiled and made an excuse to get away. Small talk with grateful clients, normally something in which he eagerly engaged, recognising it was a sure way to repeat business, was out of the question. His mind was not capable of dealing with clients wanting his time when thoughts of a secret meeting with a police officer would not leave him alone. As the day had dragged on, John had convinced himself that its clandestine nature could only mean that something serious was afoot. But he had guessed that already. Calls to Isabella still were not being answered, despite the increasing desperation in the messages he left. The fact that Ibbotson wanted to meet him away from the police station and away from his office simply confirmed it.

He arrived ten minutes before the agreed time. As arranged, he sat in the corner of the small, intimate room off the dark corridor which led up to the larger and more populated lounge. Black and white pictures of scenes of old Nottingham filled most of the spaces on the walls. A small bar opposite the door formed part of a passageway which led into the lounge enabling one person to serve both this room and the lounge during less busy periods. A tall, acne-ridden youth wandered in behind the pumps at the counter but soon disappeared on seeing that there was no new business. An elderly man hunched over a newspaper and a middle-aged couple deep in conversation, obviously not married thought John, were the only other people in the room. With his tonic water in front of him, he was able to look through the window at those outside passing by and at anyone who entered the pub. It was fifteen minutes before Ibbotson finally arrived, glancing behind him as he slipped out of the cold and across the threshold.

'So why here?' asked John as the unsmiling officer placed a pint of something dark and unappetising on the table in front of him and sat down. Ibbotson said nothing as he pulled a packet of cigarettes out of the inside pocket of his brown leather jacket and lit up. His long, thin face was dominated by a thick, grey moustache which had the unfortunate effect of drawing attention to a wide bulbous nose set in the middle of pale, sickly looking features. From the length of time John had known him he would be in his mid-forties but he looked older. His greying hair, thinning on top, could have done with a trim, its extremities just touching the collar of his shirt. He slowly pulled loose his tie and undid the top button with his free hand. Finally, his dull brown eyes rested on John.

When he replied, his voice was little more than a whisper. 'I shouldn't be here and this conversation is not taking place. If anyone asks, this is two old friends meeting for a drink after work, right John?'

'Yes. Okay.'

'That's why we're meeting in the middle of town – less suspicion,' he added as if needing to provide further explanation.

'So what's this all about?' said John, Ibbotson's words simply confirmed that there was something to worry about.

'You know about the Bluebell Road job – the hit and run.'

'Yes, as you know we're acting for Jake Simmonds who has admitted it, been charged and remanded in custody.'

'What's he going to plead?'

'Doug, I can't tell you that as you well know. But you've got his tape-recorded interview so you can probably guess.'

'John. I'm worried that someone's locked up who shouldn't be and that your firm, or at least that granddaughter of yours, is getting into something really deep.'

John's heart lurched. His hunch that evening, when Ibbotson asked if he could look at the car to eliminate it from his enquiries, was turning slowly into a cold, horrible certainty.

'You've read the papers relating to the case?'

John nodded. He had spent the evening before last going word by word through his firm's file and then the prosecution papers which included statements from the witnesses and the summary of Simmond's confession. It had seemed straightforward. A down and out had stumbled into Bluebell Street and been mown down by a vehicle which didn't stop. Simmonds, a notorious car thief, was living at Farrelly's hostel on Bluebell Street. Isabella's written record of her attendance at the police station after Simmonds arrest contained a note that she had told him that the evidence against him was non-existent and that he had only been arrested was because he was a person with a record for stealing cars who happened to be living in the vicinity. She had gone on to record that he had told her that he been drunk that evening but remembered something about an accident in a car. Her advice had been not to answer any questions. Finally, her note set out his wish to admit the offence as he was feeling guilty. The squiggled signature under the note was presumably that of Simmonds, acknowledging the fact he had been advised that this was a course which he should not follow.

Yes, a straightforward matter. If so, why had a car with a connection to Farrelly's been seized? Had Isabella been aware of that at the time? Presumably not or she would have made a note on the file and declined to act. If she'd answered her phone he could have asked. If she'd answered her phone, he could have sorted it out.

'We've had more information,' Ibbotson's words were like a stake through John's heart.

'Oh,' he replied, feigning a nonchalance he did not feel.

'Another witness has come forward – a resident at the hostel you have on that road.'

John swallowed.

'The car's tyres screeched,' continued Ibbotson. 'The witness looked out of the window, drawn by the noise. Three people were in the vehicle. She is sure that the driver was your granddaughter.'

'Well, it can't be true,' spluttered John, 'it would have been dark, it—'

'She knows your granddaughter having been represented by her on a theft charge a month ago. We've checked the court entry and your granddaughter was acting for her. The witness got some kind of probation order and has to live at your hostel.'

'As I was saying, it was dark, and she's a thief and—'

'The street lights are quite good there.' Ibbotson raised his hands, the palms facing John. 'Hear me out John. I agree that identification would have been difficult and that the witness has convictions for matters of dishonesty but you should know that a passer-by who was walking his dog recorded the registration plate and the registration plate is of an Audi A3 which is registered to Farrelly Property Services. We've examined that vehicle. An attempt has been made to clean it but I was told this morning that a trace of the deceased's blood has been found in the headlight casing.'

John leant on the table, his head in his hands.

'We're carrying out further tests on the car but the intention is to arrest your granddaughter for perverting the course of justice. Damn it, John, it's clear that she coerced young Simmonds, scrote of this parish he may be, into admitting an offence that she committed. And a bloody serious offence at that.'

John thought of the night of the reception, that glorious summer's night, when Isabella came up to ask him something. He could have stopped it then. At least he could have asked what she wanted.

'You're probably asking yourself why I'm telling you this.' John looked at the other man; it was something that had not occurred to him. 'Simmonds has his first appearance in the Crown Court next week. Last week our barrister was contemplating threatening to up the charge to manslaughter if there was a not guilty plea. Your granddaughter is in this up to her neck but I wouldn't want you to allow her to make matters worse by persuading or at least allowing Simmonds to plead guilty to her offence.'

'Right, John,' he said standing. 'I'll take my leave. As I say, this conversation never happened.' Ibbotson then left.

John looked out of the window. Drops of rain were rolling down, fragmenting the lights of the square. The early evening sky would soon have given way to the night. He picked up his coat and walked slowly out.

Chapter 37

'So where is she?'

John stared at Chisolm. Chisolm's eyes shone brightly. 'Who?' replied John, knowing full well who he meant.

'Your granddaughter, the future of the firm, of course.'

John felt Brian looking at him. Victoria's bloodshot eyes stared in front of her. John's fingers drummed quietly on the table in the boardroom. He had envisaged at one point that Isabella would have been here to support him in his attempt to get rid of Victoria. That was now out of the question. She couldn't be seen anywhere near the place. John momentarily wondered why Chisolm had asked the question. He couldn't know; John had only told Brian. He could hardly have done otherwise. After leaving the bar last night, he'd gone straight round to the house Isabella still shared with her father.

'This is an unexpected surprise, Dad.' Brian stared at his father, frowning. He would have been wondering what was going on; hardly surprising given that John had never visited his son without Shirley since their son had left home some twenty years ago.

'I need to speak to Isabella. Get her, will you, please?'

'She's gone to bed.'

'It's only eight. Get her up. It's important.'

'She's come down with a bug. She's not been very well these last couple of days.'

'I bet she hasn't. Just fetch her! Please!'

The resulting conversation with his pasty-faced granddaughter had done little to settle the myriad of thoughts that had been swilling through his head as a result of his meeting with Ibbotson. In a dressing gown, unwashed greasy hair touching her shoulders, bereft of the greasepaint usually plastered on her face, she had clearly not left the house for days. Any hope that it was all a misunderstanding that he would be able to unravel had been dashed. Her meandering, confused cocktail of justification for her actions and excuses had all the appearance of downright lies. Damn it, after God knows how long listening to clients' efforts to extricate themselves from the truth, recognising a liar was one thing he could trust himself to get right. Her refusal to look him in the eye, the ringing of her hands, the sheer unlikeliness of what she said was all too much to ignore. To say that Simmonds must have somehow got into the firm's compound and taken a car was just implausible. Had a car thief wanted a car to get back home there were plenty of easier targets in Nottingham's streets that night. This being put to her had simply led to a flood of tears and Brian's remonstrations to leave her alone, the girl was clearly ill. The witness, screamed Isabella, was lying, lying, lying. And that was as far as John had got. His directive to stay away while he tried to sort it all out had been met with a sullen shrug. The possibility of her arrest was something he had not mentioned. There may be some strings he could pull there.

'She's ill,' replied John, staring Chisolm out. 'Now let's get on with the business in hand now that Victoria's finally graced us with her presence,' he continued, 'the matter of poor performance. Now Victoria, whilst the partnership deed is quite clear on the matter, it's only right that you should have an opportunity to give us an explanation as to what I have to say is a quite appalling performance in relation to fees brought in. I should add as well that your absence over the last two months has not gone unnoticed. It really—'

'Shut up, John.'

For a moment, John simply stared open-mouthed at Chisolm as his mind scrambled to find the words which might form a suitable reply.

'I beg your pardon.' It was the best he could think of.

'Vikki's got something to say.'

Everyone turned towards the only woman present. She blushed, just slightly, and glanced at Chisolm. He nodded, as if in encouragement.

'I'm…err…I'm leaving. With immediate effect. From now.' She bit her lip and looked once more at Chisolm.

'Well,' said John, the possible implications swooping through his mind. At least it may pacify Brian's best client. 'Your resignation is accepted. I think you've done the right thing. Perhaps you'd care to clear—'

'It's not quite that straightforward,' butted in Chisolm, his face suddenly bathed in smiles. 'Vicki's treatment over her relationship with a man who unbeknown to her was married to a client of this firm amounts to sexual discrimination. I do recall young Brian here married a client.' He raised his eyebrows and pulled an envelope from the inside pocket of his jacket, sliding it across the polished table towards John.

'What's this?'

A light tapping on the door stopped Chisolm answering.

'What?' said John. The door opened to reveal Libby hovering on the threshold, seemingly reluctant to enter. 'I thought I said we were not to be disturbed.'

'I'm sorry but I…I thought you should know that we've had a reporter asking to speak to you personally, Mr Farrelly. It's about some road traffic accident that you know about. He said that he wanted to speak to you and give you a chance to comment.'

John stared at her. How the hell had the press got to know about it. It had occurred to him as he lay awake in the early hours that at some point he would have to deal with the inevitable publicity, that he would have to protect Isabella, but a publicist would be employed as a buffer between the firm and the press as and when the need arose. 'Just tell them that we've no comment at this stage,' he snapped.

'What's all that about?' asked Chisolm.

'Nothing. So what is this?' John asked as he opened the envelope.

'I'm sure you're capable of reading it. But to summarise, Vicki is not resigning. The sexual discrimination amounts to a breach of the partnership deed and thus a breach of your contract with her. This letter is from her solicitors, James & Co from London, setting out her claim for breach of contract. I reckon when you take everything into account, the profits this firm ought to be making, her claim is not far short of a million.'

'You must be joking,' said John, realising that this was anything but a joke.

'Oh no, not at all. I've never been more serious,' said Chisolm, still smiling. 'And whilst we're all here, I'll hand in my resignation from the partnership.' He pulled out two letters from the other side of his jacket and all but threw them at John and Brian. I'm going to…err James & Co. I have to give six months' notice under the partnership deed we have here. Gentleman, it's been a pleasure.' He stood and motioned with his hand to Victoria to do the same. 'I can assure you I look forward to watching this firm career from crisis to crisis over the next six months. It is with some regret that I feel powerless to stop the demise of a once reasonable firm.' He then walked out, followed by Victoria.

John and Brian both sat, neither moving, neither saying anything. A telephone rang in the distance. The clocked ticked. A thought then hit John. His heart raced, blood pumped through his veins. If the press knew, if Isabella's scheming was in the public arena, any hope he had of persuading the prosecution that it was not in the public interest to end the career of an inexperienced girl would disappear. Once the matter was plastered over the newspapers, any prosecutor would feel that action was necessary.

'A million. We cannot afford it. Simply cannot afford it.' Brian's quaking voice broke into his thoughts.

'Eh? It won't come to that. And at least they're out of the way.'

'Rod's not. And I don't suppose he'll be putting in the effort he should during the next six months.'

Had the situation not been as serious, John could have laughed. His son, the person who he had hoped would hold the reins after him for just a short time before his granddaughter took over, had once again missed the point. The danger was not Chisolm pulling his weight; the fear was the damage that he may inflict – and what damage he had already inflicted.

A pattern, an intricate web of past conversations, small problems, little incidents, all inconsequential and seemingly unrelated at the time, began to form in his mind.

'Did Chisolm know the police had seized the car?' he asked.

'Well…I suppose he must have.'

'Has he mentioned it to you?'

'No. I've not really seen him to be honest.'

John ran his hand over his mouth. The bristles on his chin scratched the palm of his hand. Terry's original claim that sabotage was the explanation for computer problems that had infested the firm these past few months hung in the air before him. How long had Chisolm been planning his so-called resignation?

He would have known about the car. He would have spoken to the police and he had now tipped off the press. And how easy would it have been to wipe his own department's diary entries from the system and be conveniently away at the time he knew it would be discovered. He had now managed to coerce their former head of matrimonial, someone who hitherto would have walked to the end of the world rather than face up to conflict, to sue the firm. And…and there was something else, something that had puzzled him at the time but had been pushed away by the weight of other problems. The day Allum had been in his office, that minute before she came in, he had heard something – whispering. She had come across Chisolm. They knew each other. It was Chisolm who was responsible for whipping Ava Brownlie's descendants into a sudden desire for compensation. And it was Chisolm who had pointed them in the way of that foul London solicitor.

And all this because his own son had thought that he was a suitable partner.

'So what do we do now?'

John looked at Brian. Shouting would have been pointless. The poor boy knew his way around a lease and that was about it.

'You do your job and bring in some fees. God knows, we could do with someone making some money around here. But watch Chisolm if you would. Anything suspicious – and I mean anything – you come and tell me straight away. Do you understand?'

Chapter 38

Her hair was impeccably groomed, her makeup perfectly applied. It was the lipstick she'd forgotten. He'd not told her. Neither had the maid. He hadn't the heart to. He suspected the maid felt the same. And what did it matter anyway? She was slipping away from him, bit by bit. Today it was the eyes he noticed. The sparkle had gone. They stared in front of her, didn't flick from side to side taking in everything and everyone as they once had. Something that he had taken for granted not so long ago, something that he had loved her for, namely her zest for life, her vitality, was slowly disappearing. She looked through her handbag as she always had before they left the house. Now, it was habit, just something else that she did without understanding why or even perhaps realising that she was doing it.

'Okay, darling. Ready?' She smiled and walked through the front door.

'Have you remembered where we're going?' he asked as he slowed down at the junction of their driveway and the country lane that eventually led onto the main road towards Nottingham.

'John, will you stop treating me like a child? We're going to the day centre so that I can read to some of the older ones.'

'Are you looking forward to it?'

'I suppose so but that doesn't mean you're right. I'm quite capable of filling my own days thank you and don't need you to be watching over me like some mother hen.'

'Well, I heard about it and thought it's something you might like.'

'So you told me yesterday.'

He switched on the radio. The news would be no use to Shirley. Music helped, she liked music, big band mostly – it reminded her of their courting days, he supposed. It was in fact loud, modern stuff but she seemed happy enough and they descended into a companionable silence as the car swished along the wet, glistening roads.

Black, leafless trees stood silhouetted against the granite like winter sky, their boughs creaking in the ice-like wind. Fields, a lacklustre, dank green, flashed by. In them, cattle stood forlornly, heads bowed down, having scant protection against the incessant icy sleet drumming horizontally into their brown trunks. Mouldy-brown leaves lay mashed together on the edges of the road. The Mercedes glided in and out of the occasional branch which lay on the lane, dumped there by last night's gales and John switched on the main beam.

He wondered for how long he would make the journey into town. If he retired, he wouldn't need to subject Shirley to the ignominy of being put somewhere she didn't like. And all because she couldn't be trusted not to burn down the house, not get lost if she ventured out for a walk and not to forget the maid's name.

But he needed to work. He needed something to make him feel alive. He needed something to do. Looking after his wife, pottering around his garden in the summer wouldn't be enough. Not for him. The chance, awkward meeting yesterday lunch time sprang to mind.

He had been walking across the Market Square with a Christmas present for Shirley when they nearly collided. Will Aldwych, up until a few short months ago, had been the newly married and newly elected Labour Member of Parliament, holding a small majority in a normally safe Conservative seat, and who had been elected on a manifesto of family values and zero tolerance to crime.

Or so John's file had said.

Now, having resigned his seat, having been forced out of the half a million family home and not having shaved or, John suspected, washed in days, he was suddenly standing there, straight in front of him. The suit he was wearing was, to John's experienced eye, the same Saville Row number he had worn at the magistrates' court in the summer. Now, the crumpled jacket had a dark stain down the front, loose cotton hung where a button had seemingly been ripped off and the razor like crease down the front of his trousers had gone. His shoes no longer had their gleam and one of the laces had snapped, the remaining thread barely long enough to form a knot.

They both moved alternately to the right and then the left as they strove to step past each other. 'Will.' John had to acknowledge him, he could not ignore him.

'John.' Neither said anything more for a moment, both stopped the macabre dance and stood quite still as the lunchtime pre-Christmas throngs swept around them.

It was John, needing to say something, who finally spoke. 'Will. You look as though you could do with a sandwich and a hot drink, maybe something stronger. What about it?'

In some ways, it seemed a long time since those few days just a month back, when Will had been the headlines in the nationals, when ministers and even the Prime Minister could find nothing positive to say and when only his resignation had forced the hyena-like pack of journalists and paparazzi to move on to scavenge off their next victim. During that period, John had not answered Will's many calls and texts and emails. They had eventually stopped and John had not spoken to him since. Perhaps now was the time.

'I've nothing else planned and I've not eaten since last night, so why not?'

The press had rumbled Will. The not guilty verdict in the trial, the trial where John had successfully managed to hide the fact that Will's proclaimed family values did not extend to fidelity and did not prevent him from engaging in violence of a domestic nature, had proved to be a temporary reprieve. All that had been back in the halcyon and innocent days of summer, before events had hurled John to all the corners of his universe and then thrown him down like some rag doll. But there was always someone worse off he had always said, and that person was standing in front of him.

The copper-headed girl's interruption at Chisolm's grand resignation in the boardroom had turned out to be about Will, not Isabella. The morning after John's refusal to comment, the papers were awash with the fact that a source from Farrellys had leaked the truth and told the world why a pretty young thing in a dressing gown had driven her RX8 into a tree outside the house of a Member of Parliament. More of Chisolm's doing had been John's original explanation and Chisolm's subsequent half-hearted denials had done nothing to make him change his mind.

John led them into the King's Head, a cosy inn up a back street. A seat in the corner of the dark, wooden interior would camouflage Will from any prying eyes in search of a story. A fug of smoke hung over the bar above five middle-aged men in overalls sitting on stools, half empty pints in front of them, cigarettes perched between calloused fingers. A silver Christmas tree, about a foot in height, which John suspected had seen about as many Christmases as he had, stood forlornly on the bar.

John placed Will's whisky, his tonic water and a plate of sandwiches on the copper-topped, round table between them. 'So, Will. What are you up to?'

'I've just been to sign on. I never realised how hard it is to live on seventy quid a week.'

'Any chance of a job?' asked John, trying to be polite.

'I've got to look or they'll stop my benefit but my name's muck at the moment so nothing that'll get me back on my feet. I don't suppose there's any chance of—?'

'Sorry Will. I'm having to lay off staff, not take them on. Brian lost his best client a few months back and my criminal clients have been deserting me in droves since…'

An uncomfortable silence lay between them. It was broken when they both spoke at once. 'You first,' said Will.

'I never apologised for your business getting in the press. It was an appalling breach of confidentiality for which I am sorry. For what it's worth I've a good idea who it was.' John took a sip of his drink. 'You should have made a complaint you know. I wouldn't have blamed you.'

'I was sorry to read about your granddaughter,' said Will finally. John looked out of the window, feeling stinging tears in the corner of his eyes. 'I thought about getting in touch but there was nothing I could have done.'

They both fell silent. 'Want to talk about it?' said Will finally.

John looked at him, feeling suddenly surprised. Yes. Yes, he did want to talk about it. For the first time in his life, he had the need to talk to someone as opposed to feeling that he ought to talk to somebody. He couldn't tell Shirley; he and the maid had made sure she'd not seen or heard any of the news bulletins, which had seemed to feature nothing else but Isabella for about a week, and he had taken the newspapers with their graphic headlines to the office. Brian had taken three weeks off, another one absent with so-called stress. He was back this week but just mooching around, doing nothing useful. Isabella had eventually told her father what had happened and then stayed at home before finally texting John last week telling him not to contact her and not to go to her court hearing.

'She's going to have to plead guilty.'

'What's the charge?'

'Perverting the course of justice and causing death by dangerous driving. Eventually, she admitted it. It didn't help that she was with the articled clerk and some dim secretary when it happened. They

270

blabbed when the police came asking questions...to be fair they couldn't have done anything else.'

Isabella clearly blamed him. He hadn't quite worked out why. He hadn't protected her, he knew. He'd ignored her that night of the party and he'd not noticed how the Simmonds job had affected her. Finally, any idea of persuading the CPS to go light on her had proved ridiculously optimistic. But he'd not brought about the situation. Not that that mattered, not now. Isabella would get a sentence in years rather than months and whatever she did with her life afterwards, it would not be in the law.

'Funny how you do great things, help people, make a difference and it only takes one mistake, one error of judgement to wipe it all away.'

John looked at him. 'I would have disagreed six months ago. Now, I think your right.'

'What's made you change your opinion?'

'I've not told this to anyone other than Shirley.'

He stopped. He'd heard of people wanting to confess crimes to placate their conscience but had never really bought it. He thought of Isabella's phone call, the night she tried to justify somebody else admitting her crime to the police. She'd wanted reassurance. But now, John felt a pressure building up from within, a yearning to admit his own crime. He saw the man across the table from him. That was the man without the job, the posh house, the perfect family – he'd lost that. And what was left when the trappings of success were taken away was the actual person. He had no position to maintain, no one to impress; he could be himself, say what he thought. From his position today, as low as it possibly could be, he had a blank canvas. Once the furore had died down, as it would in his case, he could do as he wished. He could of course drink himself into oblivion. But he had a choice. And John was jealous.

'There was a particular job I was involved in when I was just a boy. It involved a young girl and went horribly wrong. Messy, dreadful business. I thought it long-forgotten. Certainly, I'd not given it any thought for years; I'd somehow managed to put it from my mind. Now I simply cannot understand how. It's there now, in my mind, never letting go.'

'So what's brought it back?'

'Her family. As I understand it, they see her and themselves somehow as victims.'

'Are they?'

John looked down and closed his eyes. He thought of that morning in the attic when he'd pored over documents that hadn't seen the light of day for over fifty years. It had all flooded back; the horror, the deceit, the worry. Allum's visit that afternoon and the defensiveness on his part that she had triggered soon helped him keep such emotions in check. But, having been let loose, they refused to return to the dark, hidden corners of his mind. In the night, as he lay awake, they returned to challenge him, to ask him questions to which he had no answer.

And now, as he looked into Will's bloodshot eyes, he knew that there was only one proper answer: 'Yes,' he said, quietly.

He'd acknowledged it to another human being. He breathed out, slowly, and sat up on his stool and told Will the whole story.

'I had a phone call from the family's solicitor a couple of days ago. She's coming to see me again next week and then I suspect it'll be an application to the Criminal Cases Review Commission to carry out a formal investigation as to whether there was a miscarriage of justice which there probably was. They will look under every stone, search in every nook and cranny. And the press won't take long to discover that the firm of solicitors which gets its clients to admit offences committed by its lawyers was also responsible for the execution of an innocent young girl. So, I'm going to tell their solicitor that I and the firm was horribly negligent, let them do their worst and bow out, any reputation I once had now in tatters.'

Will ran his fingers down his face and then slowly shook his head. 'John, learn from my experience. What's done is done. You falling on your sword won't alter anything. Admit nothing. Don't let fifty years hard work be ruined by something which happened when, as you say, you were just a boy. Then take your well-earned retirement still being able to rightly say that the world is a better place for you being here.'

As John swung the into the car park at the day centre, the discomfort he felt yesterday as he walked back to the office, having left Will in the bar with another drink, still hung over him. He had revealed something of himself. He had shown weakness. And it was not a feeling he liked. But he had also been given something to ponder. He shivered as the car slid between two white lines and turned towards Shirley. 'Ready?'

She looked at him, frowning. 'Why have we come here? This isn't my mothers.'

He smiled at her sadly and explained for the fifth consecutive day what was happening before getting out and trotting around the front of the car to the passenger door so that Shirley could not climb out and get away.

Reception was dominated by a large silver Christmas tree, bedecked with flashing white lights and baubles in all of the colours of the rainbow. A beaming young girl swept into reception, presumably alerted by a buzzer activated by the front door. Squat, the shape of a barrel, with unruly black hair pointing everywhere despite the valiant efforts of an elastic band trying to form a ponytail, she walked towards Shirley and took her hands. 'You must be Shirley! Wonderful to meet you! Come and have a cup of tea and meet everyone else.'

As Shirley was yanked through double doors and into what appeared to be an activity room, John followed, somewhat awkwardly. Shirley describing Brian's first day at school all those years back slipped into his head.

In a semi-circle of armchairs sat eight elderly people. All faced a large television which was attached to the far wall. Most were slumbering. John stared at one man in a brown cardigan, threadbare in the elbows, eyes tight shut, his head slumped onto his chest, saliva dribbling onto a dirty white shirt. One woman gazed at the television, her dull eyes not reacting as the auctioneer brought down the hammer with a loud rap. Another was singing quietly to herself, a lullaby John's mother had probably sung to him.

He hovered on the edge. Was he meant to leave Shirley and allow her to settle without his distracting presence? Or should he hang round like some spare part?

'Now then Shirley, you sit here,' ordered the squat girl, pointing out an armchair at the end of the arc in front of the television. 'Louise, this is Shirley,' she gushed, 'she'd like a cup of tea, wouldn't you, Shirley?' A young, thin girl in a light blue dress, sitting at a table at the back of the room, a sheaf of papers before her, slowly stood up and slouched away, presumably to make the tea.

John started as a wail blocked out the sound from the television, just for a moment. A woman in the centre of the semi-circle, thin white hair plastered to her bony skull, had woken. Louise came back and picked up a child's plastic beaker and inserted the spout with its three pin-prick holes into the woman's mouth. The wailing stopped and the woman returned to her slumber. Louise put the beaker on the floor by her chair and meandered off.

Suddenly, a high-pitched screech from behind punctured his ears. As he was about to turn, a thump in his back caused him the stumble forward, his fall broken by the back of an armchair.

'Betty!' It was the squat girl who had shouted.

He turned, his hands behind him gripping the top of the armchair. A spindly, grey-haired woman, rushed towards him, arms flailing like windmills. He cowered, trapped by the back of the armchair, as the woman thudded into him. Blows rained on the backs of his hands as he tried to protect his head.

'Betty! Stop it!'

John looked through the gaps in his fingers to see the squat girl and Louise, their hands around her arms, pulling the woman away. The woman seemed to be younger than the rest. Bright blue eyes glared at him from bony sockets, their hatred boring into him. What appeared to be her only tooth could be seen proceeding at an angle through her thin lips. As she was drawn backwards and away from him, she slumped, her head towards the floor, as though some kind of energy force had been shut down.

The two girls released their grip. 'Betty, love,' said the squat girl gently, putting an arm around her thin shoulders. 'There's no need for all this. This is just Mr Farrelly who has brought Shirley who'll be a new friend for you. Isn't that nice?'

The woman looked up, her eyes still burning brightly. Now free of any restraint, with another shriek, she burst forward again. A dirty nail, curling over the forefinger of her right hand caught him down the side of his left cheek. He pulled his head to the side but, on putting his fingers on the source of the sudden stinging, felt blood. The woman was still screeching something but he could not make out any words. He felt saliva land on his face, on the gash and in his mouth as he shouted, telling her to get off.

'Betty!' He looked up to see the woman being dragged away by a man in a white coat.

'Mr Farrelly,' said the squat girl. 'I'm so sorry. I don't know what came over her. She can sometimes be a bit funny with men but not like this. I can't apologise enough. She's had her medication, I gave it her myself, so I'm really at a loss to explain this.'

John was conscious of trembling. His legs felt weak and threatened to buckle. He turned around, looking for Shirley. She was standing, staring at him with big round eyes.

'Shirley, we're going! I'm not subjecting you to a place like this!' He took Shirley's hand and strode towards the exit, taking no heed of the comments of another man in a white coat, this man sitting in reception, to the effect that it was just a misunderstanding and would he be coming back.

Chapter 39

This time she was dressed in jeans and some sort of cape or shawl, the kind of thing Clint Eastwood wore in his cowboy heyday. She seemed to have less makeup, or at least there was a subtlety about it; it enhanced her features rather than hid them and rather suited her. The file she took from her case and placed on John's desk was now two inches thick. She flicked through notes scrawled on a legal pad and turned to a page about a third of the way into the file. As her eyes scanned the manuscript, the only sound was the moaning wind as it rattled against the windows and the rustling of the trees.

'I've got it.'

'What?' Sometimes, thought John, this infernal woman seemed to be speaking a different language.

'The transcript. Took some getting it, I can tell you,' she said, a smile of triumph on her face. John thought of Shirley's joy on acquiring the latest David Leapman, her favourite living artist, two years ago.

'Come on John, don't look so puzzled – the transcript of Ava's trial of course.' She laughed, that merciless, humourless laugh that, he felt, explained exactly why she was still single. 'Anyway, thank you for giving up more of your valuable time. Although, as I understand it, you've got a little more time on your hands nowadays.' Her lips again formed a smile. 'A little bird tells me that you've been having a few problems in keeping clients.'

'And that not so little bird goes by the name of Chisolm, presumably?'

She stared at him. 'I couldn't possibly say.'

'Right. Well. Let's get it over, shall we?'

'Very well. Last time, we talked about your involvement, in particular whether you should have been involved at all?'

He said nothing.

'I'd like to deal with the conduct of the trial itself and—'

'Don't you think that would have been a matter for counsel. We had experienced leading and junior counsel who had the responsibility for sorting out the tactics. Surely you can see that?'

'John, you seem to have treated this whole process as an attack on you personally. It's not like that at all. I'm here to advise the relatives whether there are grounds to refer Ava's case to the Court of Appeal as a miscarriage of justice. That could of course be as a result of errors made by counsel. The only person I can ask about that after all this time is you.'

'Well, go on then.'

'It struck me as odd that Ava gave evidence. I would have thought that it would be fairly usual in those days for the person charged not to give evidence so as not to be subjected to cross-examination.'

'It would depend on the facts of each case, I suppose.'

'Nowadays, if the accused does not give evidence, the court can infer that they're guilty, isn't that right?'

'Something like that,' replied John, happy to talk about the law if it meant they did not have to talk about the case. 'But it was still quite common in those days for the accused to give evidence.'

'But here, where the prosecution case taken as a whole was weak, surely Ava had little to gain in giving evidence?'

'She would have had advice from counsel about the pros and cons. I can't remember what that advice was after all this time but that was the type of thing the person conducting the trial would consider.'

'Yes, I suppose so.'

'If I remember correctly, she was adamant she wanted to give evidence.' Why? Why had she been so eager to give evidence? He hadn't fully understood at the time but that was something for counsel and not the mere instructing solicitor.

'You represented her at the inquest, did you not?'

'Err…yes, I believe I did.' John's heart sank, recognising where this was going.

'And she gave evidence then?'

'Err…yes, I believe she did.'

'When there was no compunction to do so?'

John said nothing.

'So why did she give evidence at the inquest?'

Why indeed? But he knew the answer to that. It had been James who had suggested that she should.

'I think she wanted to.' It seemed weak, so weak.

'I've got a summary of Ava's evidence at the inquest. Grimes made a note. It seems to me that by giving evidence she placed herself right in the middle of it.'

'Well, she didn't admit an offence.'

'She admitted injecting the deceased! A deceased who had died from poisoning from morphine! A deceased who had left her a small fortune!'

John said nothing.

'And having said that, I suppose it might be argued that she had to explain to the jury at her trial what she had meant.'

'She wanted to give evidence.'

'We only have your word for that.'

John saw the opening straight away. 'Isn't that your problem here?'

'What do you mean?'

'You have notes from a deranged police officer and the transcript of the trial. The only person who can speak of these events is myself. And I most certainly do not accept for one moment that Miss Brownlie did not have a fair trial. Quite simply, Miss Allum, this investigation of yours is going nowhere. I hardly need remind you that you owe a duty to your clients, whoever they are, to advise them that nothing can be proved one way or the other after all of this time and that they are simply wasting their money in pursuing this any further.'

'They're not wasting their money.'

'Oh, come on. You've been up here twice if not three times now to my knowledge on a very healthy London hourly rate to achieve exactly what?'

'You misunderstand me. I'm acting pro bono.'

'What? You're doing this for nothing?'

'Exactly.'

'Why?'

'I told you during our first meeting that it was a desire for justice that was my motivation to go into the law. I'm very fortunate to be employed by a firm of solicitors that shares those principles. My job is to help people get access to justice who would otherwise be denied such a basic human right by the unavailability of funding by the state and by a lack of personal resources. My clients are most certainly not rich although compensation is not their aim. They want an acknowledgement that what happened to their relative was wrong, very wrong.'

Hadn't that been why he had gone into the law? Hadn't he grasped such principles and held them forth like a sabre as he went into battle?

Who was he kidding?

He thought back to the days his father had decided his future. What he would have done had he not entered the law, he had no idea but at least it would have been his choice. He looked at the woman across his desk, a woman who strove to do justice for people for no monetary award. Her salary was not her reward; the money she made was just her means to exist. He had striven for justice, striven to help those he considered vulnerable but the act of achieving justice had been no more important to him than the monetary reward had been to Miss Allum. Did that make him any worse a lawyer? Were his achievements somehow less because his motivation had been personal reward whereas hers was altruistic?

'I'll let you ponder that a little while. Let's move on.'

He shivered and ran his hands down his face.

'A Doctor Roche gave evidence for the Crown at the trial, did he not? Wasn't he some big wig at the Home Office who had examined the deceased's organs?'

'You have an advantage over me, Miss Allum, in that you've read the transcript. After fifty years, the participants merge into one I'm afraid.'

'He seems very prosecution minded. He was adamant that, let me find it, "the deceased was given a significant amount a few hours before she died which led to congestion and then to her death. Death was therefore as a direct result of the administering of morphine."'

'If that's what it says.'

'Surely that would depend on how much morphine had been pumped into the deceased previously.'

'How do you mean?'

'If the deceased was not used to morphine, the dose given to cause death would not need to have been as great and could have been administered without any intention of causing death.'

'And?'

'There was no mention in the trial of her previous treatment. Roche wasn't asked about that. In fact, he wasn't asked anything at all.'

'I really fail how I can be held responsible for leading counsel's cross-examination.'

'Likewise, Doctor MacPherson wasn't really asked anything at all of relevance.'

'Again, how can I possibly comment?'

'Did you know Doctor MacPherson?'

'No. Not at all.'

'The nurse who ran the home seems to have got off relatively lightly. You didn't go after her.'

'I do recall her. She made some comment about losing money as a result of the death. I specifically remember her saying that she had nothing to gain from the death. I remember thinking that the comment was in bad taste. But it was clear that she had no motive so there was really no point in "going after her" as you say.'

'Was there any investigation into whether she had anything to gain? It seems rather convenient for the person running the home to say that she had passed on care of the deceased to a new girl who by common consensus had little experience.'

'I've already told you that we don't have our file. We simply don't have the space to keep files for longer than the Law Society say that we have to. I cannot answer that question. All I can say is that I've no doubt that all the necessary investigations were carried out.'

'You seem to have allowed the statement from the pathologist...' she flicked through the transcript, 'a Doctor Birkenshaw, to be read. Was there really nothing to ask him or her? A murder trial and you don't ask the person who carried out the post mortem anything?'

'The people you should ask, namely leading and junior counsel, are dead. I suppose it's a shame that Grimes chose not to share his papers and his thoughts with the world earlier.'

'The defence doesn't seem to have had any... energy I suppose is the word I'm looking for.'

'We did what was necessary. The jury heard the evidence and came to a conclusion. And remember in those days, given the sentence, the matter would be looked at thoroughly again.'

'Yes. I wanted to talk about what happened after the trial. I've read the newspaper reports for the period. It seems that public opinion changed after sentence had been passed.'

'Yes, I recall spending several days on the streets of Nottingham collecting thousands of signatures asking for a reprieve.'

'What happened to the petition?'

John leaned back in his chair, trying to look relaxed. 'It went to the Home Secretary, of course, that's once she had exhausted all her appeals through the courts.'

'Could you—'

'I also recall that my father went to London personally in an attempt to see the Home Secretary.'

'Did he see him?'

'Oh yes. The problem was that this was a murder by poisoning of course and there was an unwritten rule that poisoners didn't get reprieved.'

'What—'

'I've been in touch with the Home Office expecting that you would be asking these questions but unfortunately the one-hundred-year rule applies. We cannot get copies of what was handed in and the correspondence with the Home Office until the year 2047. Too late for me, Miss Allum, maybe even too late for you.'

'John, given the misgivings I have over the trial and the fact that I still have real concerns over whether you should have been representing Ava, would you not accept that her representation was inadequate?'

He looked to his side, at the photographs and the momentos in the glass cabinet and on the walls; evidence of a successful professional life, evidence of a reputation, evidence of a standing in the legal community and beyond. Of course, this damn woman was right. But so was Aldwych. Why should he be judged on just one job? If he accepted something went wrong in the trial and that he was responsible, that job would be his legacy. The thousands of people he had helped, the awards he had been given, the firm that had grown to be one that truly represented people from all walks of life; all of that wouldn't even get on the scales, let alone begin to tip the balance back towards him.

'I have every sympathy with your clients, whoever they are. The shadow across their lives even today must be difficult to bear but in all conscience, I have to say that my recollection at the time was that Ava had a fair trial. And I have to say that none of the points that you have made in our meetings have caused me to alter that view.'

'Could we agree some compromise? Would you not accept that whereas by the standards of the day the representation was adequate, it was not adequate when judged by today's standards and that on that basis Ava did not get a fair trial?'

'Miss Allum, now you are revealing your desperation.'

'Oh, I'm not desperate, John. But it seems to me that this is a matter which should be looked at again and that such a concession on your part may be sufficient to get the matter before the Court of Appeal.'

'You're asking me to say something which I simply cannot accept. Remember, Miss Allum, I was there. I sat through the trial. And what a desperate time it was, I can tell you. The evidence was compelling. The jury came, in my view, to the only decision that was open to them.'

She didn't say anything. Her pen drifted over the bottom of her page in an aimless doodle. John sat back. He had won.

'What do you intend to do now?'

'What?' Her question had taken him by surprise. 'What do you intend to do is a far more pertinent question,' he replied.

She looked at him, her face bereft of any emotion. She seemed, he thought, tired. 'I'll send a report to my clients.'

'But you don't think they've grounds to take this any further?'

'What do you intend to do, John?'

This was one question that he could now answer without difficulty. 'I've come to a decision. It's no business of yours but I'm quite happy to tell you that I'm going to retire. I'm hopeful that my son will take the firm forward. I suspect that he'll close the departments which rely on legal aid and concentrate on non-contentious work. So long as he adheres to the firm's principles of providing a good service to clients at a realistic price then I'm happy with that.'

'Won't you take a consultancy?'

'No. I'm getting out completely. I feel that I've done my bit…in fact, I've had enough.'

'And you can leave with your reputation intact?'

He felt a blush sweep over his face; it felt like an accusation. 'If you put it like that, yes. I've worked hard over the years. My firm's ethos has been to help the vulnerable whilst providing a good service to all member of the community. There are general practices although they are becoming rarer but I believe that the level of service we provided was beyond excellent. I want to be remembered for that.'

'And you're afraid that you'll be remembered for Ava's case, the epilogue to your career?'

John said nothing.

Chapter 40

John lay back against his pillow, his hands behind his head. Shirley was beside him, asleep. Her rhythmic breathing, interspersed with the moaning winter wind, was all he could hear. Sleep wouldn't come. Not tonight.

He slowly got out of bed, put on his dressing gown and crept out of the bedroom and into his study. He opened the window and allowed the glacial air to run over his face. Spots of icy rain landed on his face and hands, like the incessant tapping of a shower of pins. Thick clouds blanketed any moon that there might have been. Nothing could be seen, just an impenetrable blackness. He closed his eyes, breathing in the pure air from the hills, recalling with a smile the hardships of winters of his youth.

The night of the celebration swept into his head. That had been the high point. It was later, standing at this very spot, watching a summer night with all its foibles, that it started. There had been problems in the weeks and months leading up to then. But that was the night when the controllable slide down a slight incline became an uncontrolled somersault down a steep hill. That was the night he'd ignored Isabella and that was the night he had received the letter. So much seemed to have flowed from then. It was the letter that had opened up a chasm, a leap into unchartered waters, from which, for a while at least, he did not think he would emerge.

Now, he felt the warm and comforting glow of stability. The morning had started well; an email from Miss Allum saying that her clients had received her advice with disappointment but that she was not instructed to take the matter any further. He'd thought as much but confirmation had been gratifying and he replied, thanking her for letting him know.

It was just that afternoon, during a scheduled partners' meeting, that it had all been decided. John would leave once and for all at the end of January. With a neat and precise cut of the scissors, his ties would be severed, leaving no strands, nothing which could be used later to draw him back in. Brian, with a degree of reluctance it had to be said, had agreed to take over. With the agreement of those with whom such agreements were made, the contracts to do legal aid work that had been hard won were ended with a flick of the pen. From the start of Brian's reign, Farrellys was going to be simply a non-contentious firm. Any sadness that John had about the firm he had striven for with body and soul giving up the work closest to his heart was dimmed by his own bright future.

John had made peace with Victoria; she would receive the pittance that was her capital in the firm. She wasn't proceeding with the action, it wasn't something that sat comfortably with her. He had shaken Chisolm's hand but only because Chisolm had agreed to leave straight away. Given the trouble that dreadful man had caused – the sabotage, using Victoria to fire his bullets, stirring up the relatives of Ava Brownlie – getting rid of him now was the least he could do for Brian. Both their respective departments had more than able deputies, they wouldn't be missed whilst the existing jobs were concluded. And if the staff in the departments being closed looked for new jobs, they were welcome to take their existing files and clients with them.

So, for John, he had three more weeks; a period when he had decided that he would put in little more than token appearances. There would be no bitter-sweet finale. In many ways, July's celebration would be it. He wouldn't go to court again. He had telephoned several of the more senior figures in competing firms who had, to a man and woman, said he was doing the right thing and that they only wished they could do the same. It wasn't a case of him being remembered, because it was to be hoped he would keep in touch and attend all the social functions that the local Law Society would run. And yes, he would be leaving practice with the reputation of fighting tooth and nail for the vulnerable and running a modern legal aid firm as part of a general practice long before it was fashionable to do so. He was satisfied with that. He could melt away.

And then he would enjoy the fruits of his retirement. The houses would still bring in a far greater income that he needed; Harry would continue to look after them. A home for life on the top floor of one, a Bentley and reasonable salary had seen to that. John could than attend to his wife, something he wanted to do whilst there was time.

He thought of their conversation over dinner that night? How long would it be before she was no longer capable of talking animatedly about the future? When would it come to pass that she spent most of her time trawling her way through the past, only making occasional appearances in the present? But tonight was a night to cherish, making sure that each moment was remembered to be recalled in the hard times which he would no doubt encounter in the years to come. They'd talked of spending the summer in the house in Burgundy. How long had it been since they had spent anything other than a hurried weekend? They laughed, thinking back to the day – actually, several of them – John had spent in the adjoining barn, protected from the soft rain but able to get a signal on his phone to bark out orders to his staff. What about the round the world cruise that Shirley had craved for more years than John cared to admit? New experiences, new adventures; the doctors had told him that whilst there was no cure this would do no harm, no harm at all. The test match in Australia; how could her love of cricket have slipped his mind? He hadn't even been able to make the test match last summer. Now, it was going to be so different. He'd had his career, he'd made his money. Now she was going to have the time she needed and deserved.

The telephone rang downstairs, breaking into his thoughts. He pulled closed the window and looked at the clock on the wall. One o'clock. He smiled; it would be the police wanting to interview someone now and would he attend? There had been a time when he would have been dressed and on the way in five minutes. Now, as he padded downstairs, he was going to start his new life this very night and say that Farrellys no longer took on criminal clients and could they arrange for the duty solicitor to attend.

'John Farrelly here.'

'Sorry to disturb you, Mr Farrelly, but I think your presence is needed.'

'Sergeant, I'm afraid we don't undertake criminal work anymore—'

'No, you don't understand me, sir. This is Officer Phillips of the Nottingham City Fire Brigade. I'm afraid to have to inform you that your offices are on fire. We've three tenders at the scene. It's now under control but there's substantial damage. You may wish to attend.'

John put the phone down and closed his eyes, realising in a second what this meant. He only had three more weeks. Three more lousy weeks in which he had been going to blend into the background until he was invisible. No fuss. No drama. But now he had visions of scurrying around sorting out what could be saved, reassuring the remaining clients, sorting out the insurance. Brian wasn't up to it, certainly not on his own. And then, after those three weeks, he wouldn't be able to simply walk away. The mess wouldn't magically disappear. This was something that could take months.

He dragged himself upstairs and got dressed. Shirley lay there, oblivious. He bent down and touched her forehead with his lips before slipping out into the night.

*

John yawned. Last night's drive and subsequent meeting with the chief fire officer was taking its toll. A quick look around the steaming building had told him substantial damage didn't really do it justice. He had waited until broken windows had been boarded up and the smouldering building was secure before returning home, promising to be available the following afternoon for a meeting with the detective inspector who had attended. It had not taken the fire officers long to give their preliminary view that this was arson. Several petrol cans found in the debris and the stench of accelerants was testament to that. The preliminary questions from the police officer that night were all about who might have a reason to cause such damage.

Now, as the afternoon turned into evening, he was back. The morning had been taken up with the inevitable staffing issues. Snow had been falling for most of the day. It was only as the evening drew in that it began to settle. The fire had scorched a hole in the roof and flakes were falling gently through the gap and landing on the blackened interior. The police officer had come and gone. He was still waiting for the fire brigade's confirmation that it was a police matter, although there was no doubt. The insurance assessor had walked through the office with John, promising that they would sort the matter out as speedily as possible but that these things took time. His words drifted over John, unable to take in what was being said. A white-faced Brian had put in a brief appearance before leaving, saying he found the whole thing too distressing.

John was finally alone in the place that not so long ago had been his life. The structure of the building was safe but the fire had destroyed everything in its path. Although orange streetlights shone through the ash covered glass of what had once been the windows, the reflection of the snow lit up the scene in a grey-white glow. The choking stench of smoke clogged his lungs. He walked slowly upstairs, the sodden carpet squelching under his feet, and found his own room. The blackened walls made the room seem somehow smaller. Photographs behind broken glass lay on the floor. He picked up the charred remains of a textbook. The outside cover crumbled in his hand and he let it drop to the floor, the *thud* echoing round what remained of his room. Black dust billowed around his shoes. He pulled open the bottom drawer of his desk. The bottle of whiskey was still there together with a glass. He rubbed his handkerchief around the inside of the glass and poured himself a measure. Glass from the shattered cabinet crunched under his feet as he walked towards the window. Snow covered shapes of cast out furniture could be made out in the garden below.

He drifted from room to room, upstairs and downstairs, glass in hand, wanting to find something that he recognised. It wasn't his building, just an alien landscape, bearing no resemblance to the place he had thought of as home. Nothing was the same.

Pulling the keys out of his pocket, he walked through the foyer, approaching the main entrance. There was nothing for him here, not anymore. Before leaving for the last time, he turned around. Maybe the plans made yesterday had been premature. Brian's heart wasn't in it. The staff would find other jobs. Perhaps the firm had been finally beaten by the fire. The problems he had encountered had not beaten it, Ava Brownlie had not beaten it. But the fire probably had.

He thought of the office as it had been during the normal working day; people laughing, moving around, telephones ringing, Shirley's smile accepting his proposal, more recently Isabella's squeal on being told she was being admitted to the partnership. Now, save for the hum of the city's traffic, it was silent.

He stopped. And stood completely still, holding his breath. He'd heard something. There was something in the building. It sounded like scraping, maybe something being dragged. He began to walk back into the building. Then he heard it clearly: a voice. And the voice was calling his name; faint at first and then louder.

'John, John.'

The voice was that of a female. Isabella? Had she heard about the fire and come back? God, he hoped so. Maybe something could be salvaged, something more important than bricks, mortar and desks. His heart sank; she wouldn't use his first name.

He walked slowly in its direction, knowing where he was heading. He stopped outside the door leading to the boardroom. The door was closed but under it could be seen an orange glow. Once more, but clearer this time, he heard the voice. It was calling his name. For a moment, he thought that the fire was still alight behind the door. And that somebody was there. He pushed open the door.

His eyes were first drawn to a circle of candles; there were tens, possibly hundreds, around the room all lit, all dancing in a draught. Their glow together with the white sheen of lying snow in the garden produced a radiance that shimmered against the blackened walls.

It was only after a moment that he noticed it. And then gasped. His hand went to his mouth and he staggered back. His back thudded into the wall. He didn't notice that or the ash like dust which puffed into the air. He found himself sliding slowly until he ended up sitting on the damp wooden floor. Throughout all of this his eyes remained locked on the scene before him.

Chapter 41

She'd returned. She'd come back from the dead. And she'd come for him.

The ceiling had burned away from the beam. It was from the exposed but charred beam that the noose hung. His heart pounded, his chest felt fit to explode. His eyes stared, drawn to the scene, unable to move away as if wanting to torture him, to punish him.

He was witnessing a death that had occurred fifty years ago. At the end of the noose, hanging by her neck, was Ava. But it was not his Ava. It was Ava after the law had taken its revenge for something that she had not done. Her head was at a hideously distorted angle, her features contorted. Blonde hair lay against her shoulders. Eyes bulged from their sockets, staring at John, accusing him. 'This is what you have done,' those eyes were saying, 'this is the consequence of your weakness.' He tried to control his breathing, tried to think. This was a dream, just a bad dream. His back pressed against the wall, he finally closed his eyes, squeezed his eyelids tight, desperate to get away, to return to his own world. His mind slipped back to his firm before its problems, of Shirley directing workmen in the gardens, of Isabella's graduation. He was enveloped in the warmth and comfort of his old life, his real life. He violently shook his head, forcing himself to wake up and banish the nightmare and then slowly opened his eyes.

Still hanging there was the body of the woman he had put to death. He was conscious that he was whimpering but could not have said what he was saying. As her eyes bored into him, his fractured mind frantically tried to make sense of what he was seeing. She'd come back. She'd come back for her revenge. There was no other explanation. She wanted him dead, she was going to take him back and push him into the depths of hell. He tried to speak, say something, give her something, placate her. It was not her whose head should be in the noose, he knew that, he'd always know that. James should have been the one, and he wasn't because John had chosen his brother and not protected her as he had sworn he would.

That's what he would have said, but the words stuck in his throat, wouldn't emerge from his mouth, wouldn't save him.

Suddenly, slim hands emerged at her neck. Fingers forced their way between her neck and the noose. The noose was pulled away and the head resumed a natural position. Whatever it was jumped down, the eyes set in that leering face of utter perfection glued on him. This was it; she was coming for him, striding across the decades, like a comet shooting through space from the depths of time.

He gave up, he couldn't fight anymore. Amidst the scorched and blackened remnants of his life's work, the energy he'd used to build a firm which would draw admiration from the rest of the legal world, and in doing so banish her unseen and unremembered to a black hole in his mind, was spent. He slunk against the wall, defeated, eyes down, and waited for her to do her worse.

'John, how nice of you to come.' He looked wearily up. The snarl was familiar. The voice, he couldn't place it and yet knew it. It was Ava. Without a shadow of a doubt the spectre in front of him was Ava, but it wasn't Ava speaking.

Something moved in the shadows behind her, distracting him, just for a second. A second figure emerged into the half-light beside her.

'Terry?'

He was wearing a suit and tie and his hair was neatly cut. He seemed somehow taller than the unkempt computer man who had worked for him. But it was him.

'What…what's going?' John directed his question at Terry, taking some comfort from the familiarity.

'Stand up,' hissed Ava.

John pushed himself up with his hands and scrambled to his feet. 'Terry! What's happening? What's all this about?' he asked, instinctively rubbing dust off his hands as he did.

Terry handed something to Ava. She took it and strode over to John. 'Open your mouth!' He meekly complied and she stuffed the item she had been holding down his throat. He gagged feeling satin like strands of material clogging his throat. His chest swelled with trapped air. His hands went to this mouth, battling to pull it away. He gagged, wanting to retch. She was stronger, his efforts futile. His head began to spin, the scene before him blurred as his eyes closed. Suddenly, she pulled it away. He bent over gasping as trapped breath rushed from him.

'I suppose we ought to put you out of your misery,' sneered Ava. She threw the item that had been in his mouth at him. It hit him and fell to the floor. He bent down and recognised it straight away.

'Libby?'

'Oh, aren't we the clever one. The big man's recognised a copper-coloured wig. Nearly red to mark the blood you spilt, just in case you still haven't got it.'

She shook out her blonde hair so that it tumbled down her back. He stared at her, and suddenly saw what should have been obvious.

'That's right, Mr Farrelly.' Terry moved forward. 'I presume the penny's finally dropped. I've thought for a while that you should meet my grandmother's family. Ava was my grandmother, if you hadn't guessed. Of course, I never met her. You saw to that, didn't you?'

'I…err.'

'And Libby here is my half-sister. Libby, as I'm sure you've worked out, also never got to meet her grandmother. We were so pleased you were able to meet the rest of the family. Small that it is.'

'I…I don't understand.'

'You've met Mother. Let me explain – Libby and myself share the same mother. Different fathers. We never met either of our fathers, another thing we have in common.'

'I don't know what you're talking about. Your mother? I never met your mother, never.'

'Oh, but you did,' replied Terry. Libby started to laugh, a hyena-like bark that echoed around the shadowy room.

'You surely haven't forgotten the morning at the day centre so quickly,' he continued. 'I think Mother was quite taken with you. She has an odd way of showing it, of course. But when she was told that the man who had been responsible for her own mother's death had come to see her, I suppose it all became a little too much.'

'That woman. That woman who attacked me in that awful place was your mother?'

'Yes, Mr Farrelly,' replied Terry. 'That was our mother. And it's not the first time you've met her. Don't you remember?'

'He wouldn't, would he?' said Libby. 'Other things on his dirty little mind.'

'I…err, I really don't know what you are talking about.'

Libby marched up and slapped him across the face. 'Show some respect!'

John winced and put his hand against his stinging cheek. She was so close. God, she was her grandmother. The same pale blue, almost grey eyes, the same slim nose, the same perfect lips, the same flawless complexion. He slipped back effortlessly over the years. He inhaled her perfume, could her hear the slight American twang of her voice, could see her lips move as she talked. How could he not have seen it? How could he not see that he had employed the granddaughter of the woman he had loved and killed? How had he not seen past something as simple as a wig? Because he'd not been looking. They were right. Once the matter was over, once Shirley had dragged him from the gutter, it was part of his past.

'Mr Farrelly,' said Terry, 'let me remind you. There was a night, many years ago, that you spent with our grandmother. You remember, surely?'

Suddenly, as if the curtains had swished open on the first scene at the Theatre Royal, an image of a crying child, its fingers clasping the bars of its cot, a child waiting for its mother's attention was before him.

'Yes. Yes of course. The baby. The baby in pink. That was your mother?'

'Bravo,' said Libby, walking away, her back to him.

'So you've now met the whole family, the ones that are left, I might add,' said Terry. 'That's the woman who died because of you and the family left to pick up the pieces. Ava's daughter, Betty as she was known by the staff, we still think of her as Elizabeth, never came to terms with the shame. A prostitute, drug addict, homeless drop out. She was all those things. Little surprise that Libby and myself ended up in care, shifted from home to home, from adult to adult. Not together of course. Always alone. But local authorities keep good records so it wasn't hard to find each other when the time came. It's no life for a child, bouncing from home to home, you know. Or do you?'

He walked over so that his eyes were inches from John's. 'You profess to help the vulnerable. Quite apart from making sure she had no chance in her trial, you never gave any thought to her baby. Once they were out of the way, that was it. Your father bought off our great-grandmother and the whole matter was over, so far as you were concerned. Ava's family was certainly not going to intrude on your oh so perfect life.'

'I'd forgotten about her baby,' John said to himself. He felt his face reddening. 'I'd forgotten all about her baby.' He buried his face in his hands.

Terry walked away. Libby took his place. Hot tears burned a path down John's face. He took a handkerchief from his pocket and ran it over his cheeks.

'Crocodile tears, you bastard.'

The snarling voice, the contempt, the hatred. That's what was different. That's what living with a pernicious bitterness did for you. On the outside, no change. The features are the same. It's on the inside where the damage is caused. Years and years of battling in court. He'd been representing the outside, never given any thought to the person behind a legal aid certificate.

'You had your chance to admit your guilt,' she continued. 'Not me gov. That was your attitude, wasn't it?'

'I don't...I don't understand what you mean.'

'Joanna Allum spent hours with you, you worthless piece of shit.' Her eyes, those beautiful translucent eyes were pools of loathing. 'But even when it was all placed before you, all you could do was think about your reputation.' She spat at him. He felt spittle running down his face. 'But what about Ava?' she shrieked. 'What about anyone other than your fucking self? Why can't you just admit you lied?'

John said nothing.

'Admit it, you bastard. Admit you were responsible for the death of my grandmother.'

He couldn't. Simply couldn't. He couldn't tell the world what he had done, he couldn't reveal the secret he had hidden all his working life. He had to say something. 'Look. You've had your fun. I'll turn a blind eye to this performance and we'll say no more about it.' He moved towards the door but was blocked off by Terry.

'Let me out! Let me out now!'

'Mr Farrelly,' said Terry, 'do you really think we're going to allow you to leave and tell the world we set fire to your pride and joy without getting you to admit your offence.'

'You! You set fire to the office!'

'Mr Farrelly. I'm not saying that. But you might suggest that is the case.'

'The only person who's been damaging my firm is that bastard Chisolm.'

'Chisolm?' said Libby.

'It was Chisolm who damaged the computer system, it was Chisolm who was guilty of a gross breach of confidentiality.'

They both started to laugh and, as if egging each other on, laughed and laughed until they were bent double, clutching each other, tears rolling down their faces.

'Chisolm!' said the youth, 'he wasn't capable of using his mobile. You think it was him?'

John began to feel the stirrings of anger, a rage sweeping over him. These two young creeps who he had been good enough to employ had played an appalling trick on him and were now daring to laugh at him. He moved forward. 'How dare you—'

Terry pushed him back, splayed fingers prodding his chest. John fell to the floor.

Libby turned towards Terry. His chin was resting in his left hand, his right hand supporting his elbow, a smirk on his face. She whispered something that John could not hear.

'Oh, I quite agree,' he said, looking at John as he did.

Suddenly they moved towards him. He felt fingers digging into his arms, dragging him to his feet, and a hand pushing his back, his feet stumbling under him as he was moved towards the circle of candles.

'Look at it!' Libby's hot breath touched his neck. His hair was pulled and his head yanked back forcing him to look at the noose. The rope, rocking just slightly, glowed in the light of the candles. He gasped. Libby leapt on a stool standing directly under the noose, kicking away a cushion that had been lying there as she did. John felt hands forcing him up and pulling him onto the stool. Before he could do anything, the noose was around his neck, its coarse fibre cutting into his skin.

Libby jumped off the stool, causing it to wobble. John tried to shout. His feet lashed out seeking solid ground, gagging as the noose tightened. His heart raced and panic set in as the strain on his neck grew. The soles of his shoes slipped on the smooth wooden seat as the stool threatened to tipple over. His eyes caught those of Terry. Terry made a comment to Libby and they both laughed. Libby aimed a mock kick at the stool, laughing again as she did. Finally, his toes managed to get a grip on the stool. His breathing gradually slowed and he tried to talk.

'Let me down! For God's sake let me down! This is dangerous!'

'Mr Farrelly, our family is well aware of that. But whilst you're up there we can tell you all about it and then you have a decision to make.'

'You could kill me!'

'No great loss,' said Libby.

'Be quite apt,' said Terry, smiling, 'complete the circle when you think about it.'

'Of course, there is something you could to help yourself,' said Libby.

The pressure on his neck was growing, breathing was becoming impossible. His legs were beginning to ache. He put his hands to his throat, trying to force his fingers between the rope and his neck. Terry quickly moved behind him and pulled a piece of string from his jacket pocket. He pulled John's hands from the rope and tied them at the wrists behind his back.

'Mr Farrelly,' said Terry, moving around so that he stood next to Libby, facing John. 'Let me make it clear. We simply want an acknowledgement, in writing of course, that you made a statement to the police that was untrue and that as a result our grandmother and not your brother was found guilty of murder. It really is that simple.'

The words that he spluttered came out automatically, words his brain was programmed to use. 'I…I didn't lie. Let me down. Just let me down. Please. For the love of God. Please.'

'Tell the truth you bastard! Tell the fucking truth!' said the girl.

His legs were throbbing, his ankles hurt, his toes could not take the weight of his body much longer. The pain in his neck was acute. Their words continued to flow over him. His throat gagged; the words in his mind wouldn't form. Still they shouted at him. Slowly a darkness came over him. His eyes closed. He could no longer understand what they were saying. The pain seemed to drift away. It was as if the pain wasn't his any longer, as if it didn't belong to him. His mind became calm, he was able to think. The one emotion in his final moments that he was aware of was of sorrow. Sorrow that he was to die in this way. Sorrow that Shirley would be left alone. Sorrow that the months and years that they had left would be denied to them. Sorrow that it was all his fault. His mind reached out to God. He wanted to ask for forgiveness, forgiveness for his sins and forgiveness for not confessing his sins. But now it was too late. He clenched his eyes and simply asked for his end to be quick.

Part Three

27 July 2012 – Switzerland

Chapter 42

The pain, that almost exquisite hot poker like burning throughout every fibre of my body, is slowly beginning to ebb away, as my medication begins to nip. And as it does, other sensations tiptoe through me, taking its place. I feel a white light, bright and intense, beating against my hands and face as the sun's warmth washes over me, soothing me. A tepid breeze ruffles my hair, strokes me, buffs me. It carries the gentle fragrance of summer roses and the sharp tang of fresh apples and pears. The chatter and chirruping of the birds surround me. My efforts to stand prove too much and I slump back into my wheelchair. I force open my eyes to see, just for one last time, the blue of the sky, the green of the grass, the rustling leaves on the trees, the dazzling colours of the flowers, the blue-grey mountains in the distance, patches of snow at the summits as if applied with the flick of a paint brush. Life and all its beauty is laid out before me. How easy it is to take it for granted. How ironic that my appreciation is the greater on the day that I am to die. I want to make this moment last, I want it to stretch into infinity. But there's a darkness which edges in from the corners of my eyes, which is pulling on my eyelids, forcing them to close. The battle is so one-sided. I have so little energy; I'm so tired. The fatigue has prevailed again and I feel myself slipping away.

It's the voices that arouse me, concerned whispers from the corner of my suite. I do so like to be propped up here. I push open my eyes as a girl in a blue dress, pens in her breast pocket, hurries over. Deep, sorrowful brown eyes and a sad smile look down at me. 'John, you're awake. We've brought you in. Too much sun's not good for you, you know. The doctor's here to see you.' Despite her European twang, her English is perfect.

A suited man, tall and bronzed, with grey slick-backed hair walks over. He's smiling but I know he doesn't mean it. 'Good evening, John. Can you hear me?'

I feel refreshed, just a little. I'm in that little window before the pain returns but when the medication has worn away a touch and

I'm able to form coherent thoughts and able to assure him that it's alright. I nod.

'I'll be candid. We've got the latest results. They confirm what I told you last week. Your cancer's spreading, just like I said it would without effective treatment. We're doing all we can to alleviate the pain but the morphine you're having is the strongest I can prescribe. Do you understand what I'm saying?'

'Yes.' My voice croaks. 'I understand perfectly.' I need to limit my words, conserve my energy. Today of all days, I need to be able to think clearly.

'John. Let me put your mind at rest on one matter. Had you allowed us to give you anything other than medication to relieve the pain, you may have had a little longer but it wouldn't have altered the end result. And any extra time you had would have been measured in weeks. There was nothing that could be done which would have altered the course of your illness.'

'I know.' I steady myself, take a deep breath. 'And I'm grateful for your understanding.'

'Is it still your wish that it should happen tonight?'

'Yes,' I mouth.

'All right, it will be painless. Of that, you may rest assured.'

I try to smile. It's not easy but I manage it and he walks away, exchanging a word with the nurse. She comes over.

'I'll go to bed now, if you wouldn't mind. I'd like to be with Shirley,' I whisper.

'Okay, John, we'll get you to bed. Shirley's there and she's had her medication. She'll be asleep now.'

I feel myself being wheeled into the bedroom and lifted, like a feather into bed. My head is gently raised and two pillows are placed under my neck.

'Could you put the television on?' I ask.

'Don't worry, John. I've not forgotten. I'll put it on,' says the nurse.

'Shirley would have loved it.' I close my eyes, thinking of her excitement those seven years ago when she heard the Olympics were coming to London.

'I know, it's just starting. I can stay and watch it with you, you know.'

I shake my head and try to smile at her. My sadness is such that I cannot bring myself to thank her but I think she knows. I hope she does. She whispers, 'I'll be back when the anaesthetist is ready,' and leaves. She turns and walks back. 'And don't worry, Shirley will be properly looked after.'

Once more, I mouth by thanks and force my head around. I hear the door closed as the nurse leaves. Shirley is asleep. We are alone. I'd promised I'd put it on and it is. As the bright lights, the colours and the music, all that is the Olympics, floats around the room, I push my hand towards hers and take her fingers in mine. Yes, she would have loved it and I feel relieved and am settled. Now I'm just with the person I wish to be with, on this day of all days. There's nothing more to do. I'm ready and have prepared. The only thing I have to do now is to wait.

In some ways, this is my second time. Even now, riddled with cancer, doped up with God knows what, I can still feel the noose around my neck, can still feel the life being squeezed out of me. But they untied me and let me down. That much is obvious. Reprieved me: that's what they called it. A rational man would have known that that's exactly what they would do. They didn't want me dead; I was the only living witness to what happened. So if I went, so did the truth. And they realised that. But I am a coward, and cowards don't think rationally. With my neck in that noose, with life being strangled out of me, I realised that I did want to live. I wanted life so badly it hurt me. The reprieve came at a price. But in exchange for my life, once they had made me see how valuable to me life was, it was a price I was finally prepared to pay.

The price? Well, you've just read it: Parts One and Two, I've called them. My confession.

The terms? I actually think I got reasonable terms. But I suppose it suited both sides. Libby, or whatever her name is now, was wasted in criminal defence, she should have been in commercial property, negotiating deals. After I had scribbled a few sentences setting out what I had done, their insurance policy in case it all went wrong or I died before being able to write out the whole sorry tale, we thrashed the entire matter out. I set to work on the manuscript, containing my confession, a confession which is only to be published on my death.

The deal suited them. I used to advise people under arrest in the police station that the best evidence that the police get is what comes from the arrested person's mouth. How prophetic were those words. My confession is the best possible evidence of my guilt.

And the deal suited me; it's only after I'm no longer here that the world will know that Ava Brownlie had committed no crime, should never have been executed and my part in that miscarriage of justice. When I'm gone – well, whatever the fallout, I won't be around to see it. Whilst I'm alive, my reputation is intact. They now have the manuscript you've just read (they had the first draft within a few months but as the years have drifted by, I've made various amendments, sometimes after further consideration, sometimes after meeting somebody who gave me a different perspective); they can ensure they are happy with its contents and know that when it's published, I will not be here to gainsay its contents, claim that it was written under duress.

They even let me write it in the third person; it was my only stipulation. It helped; in many ways my near-death experience at their hands was quite cathartic. The person I wrote about did not seem to be me and I found it easier to see myself as someone else. Of course, I spoke to those still around, Brian and Shirley before her illness finally took over. Not that anyone knew about the agreement. I knew Isabella's story and, before he died, James had told me his. So, I believe you have an accurate and reliable account of the whole matter. And that's important to me.

Not that I found it easy to agree anything with them. Whilst fighting for my life with a noose around my neck, they had been gleefully recounting their activities. Obviously, it was one or both of them that set fire to the office. They eventually admitted as much. The police never discovered, not that the officers I spoke to had much help from me. I still had a lot to lose at that point. But it wasn't the fire that destroyed my firm; the destruction was down one particular factor to which I shall return. Libby and Terry would like to think that my firm's demise was down to their insidious campaign, a vendetta that infiltrated the organisation in the same way that my cancer has invaded my body.

Now I think of it, I should have spotted what was going on. As Terry said, not attempting to disguise his delight in the double bluff, he had told me that the computer system was being sabotaged. What he didn't say was that it was he who was responsible. Looking back, it's not hard to work out that one of them told Diana that her husband was involved with Victoria. What I didn't know was that Terry had known her husband through their respective work in computers and that he had set up a blind date with Victoria. I couldn't keep an eye on everything that went on. How could I have known? What could I have done differently to stop that happening?

I suppose I could also have guessed that it was Libby had informed the press about the private life of an MP who had entrusted such details with us. I should have recognised it was Terry's voice making the threats, on one occasion, within seconds of leaving my office. A mobile telephone was all that was needed. But I couldn't keep an eye on everything. Could I?

It wasn't difficult for Libby to destroy correspondence before it was sent out. Likewise, it was easy for her to forge letters that shouldn't have gone out.

These things don't matter in the great scheme of things, awkward though they were at the time. There was one more thing. Something that brought me to my knees, something that stopped me fighting, something that made me realise as I walked through the smoking embers that there was no point going on. Brian had never been the future. Isabella had; it had always been her to whom the baton was to be passed. There had always been a link between us; something you couldn't see or touch. But as Monday leads into Tuesday, as night merges into day, our minds, our heartbeats were similarly joined. And her demise was the beating of me. As the fruit was lopped off, the tree died, its purpose rendered pointless.

That was nothing to do with them. So they didn't finish me. I suppose therefore that Ava didn't finish me. And for that, at least, I'm relieved. It would be a sad state of affairs indeed if it was your one bad job which defines your legacy. Surely, that one matter has to be balanced against all the good?

I've not seen Isabella since. I was pleased, if not a little surprised, when she got a suspended prison sentence. But by that time, the damage had been done. Brian told me some years ago that she was planning to travel. After that no one heard anything from her.

So there you have it. A lawyer's story. My story – the story of how sixty-five years ago an innocent girl's life was ended. It's not for me to judge the full extent of my culpability but I accept my part. For what it's worth, I feel that my culpability was and is down to my flaws which I think can be described in one word: cowardice. Cowardice and weakness, actually. That's two but I don't suppose that will concern anyone.

Have I been punished, have I suffered as a result of my wrongdoing? Yes, the answer is without doubt a resounding 'yes'. I sweated blood and tears building up my firm, that very act helping me to banish Ava from my mind. I created something of which I was justly proud so that I can now tell myself that I had made amends. The firm I created set out to help the socially disadvantaged before it was commonplace to do so. For that at least, I am proud. Others will judge whether I did make amends. As I await my own

303

death, the answer I would give now is not the same as it would have been during those frantic years. Well, the firm I built has been destroyed – does that even it out? I hope so, I truly do but I confess I do not know. Irrespective of such matters, I have lost my beloved granddaughter. That to me outweighs the loss of a business. It outweighs it one hundred times over.

And of course, I've lost Shirley. Shirley's illness would have arisen, Ava Brownlie or no Ava Brownlie. That much is true. It's not Shirley's life that has been lost, it's the years when I was in the office, court, wining and dining clients and would-be clients, advising at the police station, and the rest of it. Instead, I should have given her something of me. By the time I had come to my senses, she had lost hers. That is my tragedy. Sadly, it's our tragedy.

Chapter 43

Two taps on the door tell me they're here. I know I've got five minutes. That's all. Muffled voices drift in from the corridor but I can't hear what's being said. That doesn't matter. I know what it's about. The morphine is beginning to wear off. I let go of Shirley's hand and pull myself onto my side so that I'm facing her.

A deep sadness sweeps through me. I reach over and place the tips of my fingers against her cheek. She's asleep; the stronger dose of sleeping pills has seen to that. I put my arm around her and lever myself further over. Her neatly cut hair feels so soft. The nurses I've been paying have done a good job in looking after her. I stroke her face and kiss her softly on the lips.

There is no reaction. There wouldn't have been had she been awake. That is how it is now. She has not recognised me for years. Dementia is an evil illness. It takes away the soul, leaving just the body, like a caterpillar leaving the skeleton of a leaf after slowly and methodically devouring the rest.

My time during these last few years has been spent in the Manor, looking after Shirley. All the feeding, cleaning, washing, wiping, preparing and what have you. I did all that. Pay-back time I called it; my punishment for the years of neglect has been years of total subservience. It completes the circle as Terry would have said. The occasional visitor we did have, and towards the end the only person who came was Brian, invariably said that the kindest act would have been a home. I disagreed. No one else could look after her with the same care and attention. It's been my job these past years, and I've not let her down. Where I am, she is. And that will not change as a result of my death. Shirley is coming with me. Together for eternity. I rather like the sound of that.

Even now, in this foreign land, as the Swiss doctors who I've paid to administer assisted suicide are outside, I find it hard to be brave. But I have to be. I push myself onto my elbow and place the pillow on which my head had lain over Shirley's so peaceful face. I then press my hands into the pillow, my tears falling onto and spreading slowly across the pillow, like a creeping paralysis.

She's not breathing. She looks no different now to the way she did five minutes ago. I whisper that I am so sorry and that I'll see her soon. Finally, I cover her face with the sheet under which she had been sleeping and put the pillow back, back on top of the letter I have already prepared, the letter in which I have explained what I've done. I had to do it. I had to make sure she was coming with me. For once, I think I've been brave.

I lay back. The doctors come in. Very soon they will have administered the injection that will put me into a sleep from which I will not awaken.

Finally, I can put down my pen. It will soon be all over. And that will be the right and proper end.

THE END

Epilogue
27 July 2012 – Derbyshire

Clair de Lune. The notes should drift into every corner of my mind, obliterating everything but the task in hand. It should have been special. It should have been perfect, so perfect.

I draw the needle slowly from my brother's arm. Perhaps I'm getting old, perhaps the cravings of one's early years abate as the years slip by, but I'm feeling curiously numb. It seems as though the injection was administered by someone else, as though I was looking down, observing the scene through the eyes of another. There was a time when such events were what I lived for. Mind, you know that don't you? John told you.

The Derbyshire countryside is as quiet as the grave. It's dark outside by the time I finish reading his final two chapters, then again I always did like the dark. It's something I've sought ever since I was a child. I switch off the lamp in John's study. I still feel a flutter in my stomach when I remember the room under the stairs. Oh the shenanigans I got up to in there, the plans I made, the schemes I hatched. Yes, my darlings, the dark has always been my friend, my comfort blanket, something to wrap myself in whenever I felt lonely. The only friend I've had, when I think back on my life. That and my brother of course. Twins are like that; joined at birth and linked through life, at least that's been my experience. And now together in death. How exquisitely appropriate. So why do I feel so empty?

But I cannot mope. I cannot tarry. I still have work to do. You've probably gleaned that John's manuscript is not likely to have comfortably prostrate itself on the altar of truth; thus my need to correct it, just in a couple of places. In fact, in more than a couple of places. He calls himself a coward and I suppose that where a man tells lies to suit his purpose, cowardice may be an appropriate label. My brother was a liar, some would say a compulsive liar. Do you know, he once told Ava that I was engaged; the very thought of it.

Poor old John; loyal to the end. The efforts the dear man has made to protect me. You know, I remember burying his hamster all those years ago. Did he tell Father? Not a bit of it. Later, he lied to the police, thinking he was saving me from the gallows. Capital chap. No matter to him that it led to the conviction and execution of another.

And then, when things were getting a little hairy back in 1953, he concocted my fictitious death. Well, Edie's money was beginning to run out. John had had his slice which he had used to buy dear old pater's share of the firm and I…well, let's just say managing my finances has never been a strong point. My past was catching up and…well, my apparent death was rather convenient. The undertakers who had assisted me in some of my earlier escapades at homes such as those run by Nurse Dolores had little choice but to arrange a funeral with a weighted coffin but no body. I was up to my old tricks; to the outside world, my death certificate was signed by Dr MacPherson (by that time, the old duffer really was on his last legs, doing little more than making the tea in a practice created under the newly formed National Health Service, sympathy having got him a position). John gave evidence at the inquest to the effect he had found me hanging from the upstairs bannisters at our father's home and my suicide was rubber-stamped. My funeral could then take place. My reputation was such that of the few who attended, only that sweet man Grimes, my dear old father and John's delightful wife didn't realise that it was only a piece of concrete that was carried into the church. And so James Farrelly was dead and buried and I was free to criss-cross Europe, drawn to the bright lights like a shark to blood, doing whatever was necessary to make myself a crust. Least said and all that.

I finally turned up on my brother's doorstep one wild and windy February night in 1982. A hedonistic lifestyle in Europe's hot spots can become quite a bore, even to one such as me. Plus, I was on my uppers. So here I was, happy to be home, missing dear old Blighty, quite oblivious to the problem I'd landed on my dear brother.

But once again, up stepped John, like my guardian angel, and Harry was born. A house was purchased and divided into flats. I took a room and other rooms were rented out. John saw an opportunity to line his pockets and bought another then another and another and by doing so created a role for me: managing the burgeoning property empire on his behalf. No one would recognise me after all that time. I have never resembled John and a newly sprouted beard and glasses ensured that James stayed dead and buried. I kept away from Shirley, although I was confident that even if she did see me, she would suspect nothing. If you're not looking for something, you don't see it.

It suited John to have a valet-like person to do his driving and to act as his eyes and ears. I was his spy. Whilst he lorded it, I was the one who tipped him off, a quiet word in his ear as to what was going on behind his back. When the boy who called himself Terry told my brother for the first time that the computer system was being sabotaged, John did not believe him simply because he expected that I would have forewarned him of any such dramas.

And that will tell you that my position within the firm, and I suppose my attitude, had shifted somewhat. It was the arrival of that sweet girl who called herself Libby, followed by Terry some six months later, that led to the first cracks in the entity that was John and Harry. Libby and Terry came with their own agenda and a fresh pair of eyes. Libby guessed my identity (Lord knows how, she maintained it was something to do with my eyes – I think she had correctly judged that as a lover of living, if not of prolonging life, my suicide was always a tad unlikely). This was not unduly problematic because I recognised her. And having done that and having seen her around the city with Terry, their purpose became all too obvious. Initially, there was a respectful stand-off, like cowboys prowling around each other before one draws his gun. Neither of us drew; what was the point? Respect grew into admiration and I began to see their point. That they thought I had killed dear old Edie was not their concern. They were not here to avenge the death of an old woman. It was my dear brother's actions, wilful or negligent, depending on your point of view, that had rattled their cage. And as we talked, I became sympathetic to their cause. Wasn't there an incident many years ago when a kidnapped person eventually came to see matters from the viewpoint of her captors? In one sense, that was me. In a rare moment of wit – inappropriate wit, I'll grant you, but it made me chuckle – Terry opined that I had been radicalised.

As time went on, I had become a little piqued at John myself. I was happy enough initially to have a roof over my head, a job, the chance to merge into the fabric of his firm and become invisible. What I found hard to stomach was the constant orders: Harry do this, Harry to that, Harry come here, Harry go there. Having to wear a chauffeur's grey uniform including matching cap was something which particularly grated. In public I was Harry. In private, I was still James but the dynamics had changed. No longer was I the brother to look up to. No longer was I the one whose favour was something to be craved. And no longer was he a stick insect to be pushed about. Out of my shadow he had flowered. I was the brother who was hidden away. And I suppose it was a change that I did not take kindly to. Throughout my life, to be the centre of attention, top dog, was something I yearned. To be John's gofer was not how I had envisaged ending my days.

And as my sympathy to the cause, as their purpose became known, and my disquiet merged, I came round to the view that John's conduct should not be allowed to go unpunished. Quite simply, I deserted. I became a spy in their camp. My brother was in fact placing reliance on a General in the enemy army, the existence of which the dear chap was deliciously unaware. He never guessed, that much I know. Libby was worried that he had observed her in animated debate at that hideous, so-called celebration with Terry. Whether he did or not, my dear brother had his attention diverted by other matters, matters more pressing than his responsibility for a death which he could have prevented.

It was Libby who came up with the idea of crucifying Isabella. It followed a chance comment by myself, something to the effect that she was the chosen one, the one who was to inherit his legacy. I hadn't realised that Libby and Isabella had a mutual history.

It came to pass that Libby had saved three months' pocket money, money given for her thirteenth birthday and the following Christmas; she was finally able to buy the tennis racket and pretty dress in the shop window. Her foster parents stumped up the weekly fees for lessons and Libby metamorphosed from street urchin to being a member of the local tennis club – just for a couple of hours each week, you understand.

There she encountered Isabella, a person who hadn't had to buy her own racket, who had the perfect dress, the most expensive tennis shoes. In her formative years, Libby wished upon a star for a mother and father as Isabella would wish for a sparkly new dress. But dreams only come true if you stamp your feet. Libby knew who Isabella was and her family's part in her grandmother's death; her mother's occasional lucid moment on the monthly access visits had seen to that. How many granddaughters called Isabella did John Farrelly have? Isabella didn't stay for long at the club, her interest soon forgotten in the same way that her grandfather would half drink and then forget his coffee on being distracted by something more interesting. But the brief meetings gave Libby a window into another world, spawning an acidic jealousy and firing a bitter hatred. They also hatched on Isabella's part an enduring friendship; for the first time in her life (and, I would aver, possibly the last) Isabella had found someone who genuinely seemed to like her. Libby, you see, and as you now know, could act. And so, they went to the same university, shared the same home while there, spent holidays together. Isabella persuaded her father to give Libby a training contract and, on qualifying, a job as assistant solicitor. Libby just bided her time.

How I rejoiced in their plans. How I delighted in being involved in their scheme. My niece was a spoilt, fornicating slut. Her seduction of anything male that moved made me to want to retch. She was a whore who had no place in decent company. Her treatment of me as her personal lackey mirrored the behaviour of her grandfather. 'Harry, take me here, pick me up from there, give young Jason a lift home, take me to see Kyle.' On such occasions, as I looked in the mirror, momentarily unmindful of the traffic, I would gaze at her face and visualise my hands squeezing her neck, her tongue protruding at an angle through her bruised and thick lips, her eyes bursting out of blackened and bruised hollows. Yes, I joined the mission to bring her down with absolute relish and a commitment that was total.

We had been waiting for the perfect opportunity, a little like a navy has to wait for the right weather condition before setting sail in pursuit of its conquest. The opportunity arose with breathtaking irony on the day of my brother's coronation, as we called that odious celebration It was Libby who texted me just as dusk turned to night to say we were ready to go. She had conjured up a spurious trip to meet some boys, always likely to arouse Isabella's interest, and contrived a shortage of taxis thus ensuring Isabella would be driving. A concocted reason to drive past Simmond's hostel and we were in business. It wasn't difficult to find a drunken no-hoper bailed to the home, her intoxication topped up by a healthy dose of morphine, just to ensure compliance, and I had a victim. We recognised the car – I'd driven it enough times – and a little shove on the part of Terry was all it took. My call to the police, naturally anonymous, advising that Simmonds was their man meant that it was almost certain that my dear niece would soon be in the police station representing a client arrested for an offence that she had committed. In such a situation, we reasoned that she was only ever going to put her own interests before everything else. And so it proved. Subsequent telephone calls, advising of the car's registration number and identifying the whore as having been the driver, completed the job. A few pounds slipped to a former client and we had a witness. Terry and Libby never told John about it – when all's said and done somebody had died. We hadn't intended that. But we were all responsible.

Nearly finished. I've almost put it all right. There's just a couple of things. What were they now?

Oh, I remember, my darlings. The final lie. And how typical of John. His request that I should provide the coup de grâce. The final blow. When he'd decided, once the manuscript was complete and when he was finally ready to die, that he wasn't going to fight the cancer, I suppose I was the obvious choice. His thinking, no doubt, was that it was an area in which I had some experience. How thoughtful that he should create a fictitious visit to Switzerland and Swiss doctors to administer assisted suicide. It is as farcical as it's untrue. No, my darlings, John's death is another one down to me, notwithstanding he had asked me. And, of course, that sweet old thing, Shirley. He couldn't leave her and he couldn't kill her. I could. So I did.

And talking of bringing life to a premature end, there's one more thing I really should say, just for Terry and Libby, or whatever names they are hiding behind nowadays. My mind races back, so easily, to that misty dank night, the night I slipped into the home, the night John had always presumed that I sent sweet old Edie to her maker. That I entered the place with that intention is something I cannot and do not deny.

But it wasn't quite like that. You see, my dears, we had drawn up our plans, Ava and I. Together. We were both in it. Ava was to admit administering Edie's injections, blaming dear old McPherson. It wouldn't have been difficult to get evidence of the old man's total incompetence. I was to dispense the lethal dose and all measures leading up to that beautiful moment. It's something I did so well and it guarded against mishaps. And, of course, it's something I so enjoyed. My passion, you could say. If she was suspected, she could blame McPherson and say what a tragic mistake it all was. That was a luxury not open to me – so the injections were all down to her, Edie's death is down to me. Edie is no more, Ava gets the money and we get to share it.

In the unlikely event Ava is charged, I'm there to organise the defence and, if necessary, the reprieve. My name had to be the recipient of the estate in case Ava was convicted and lost the right to inherit. Even if that was her fate, the state wasn't going to kill a young mother, especially a pretty one. She can't get the money, I can and we get to share it.

I was wasted as a doctor – or would have been had I hung around at college long enough to qualify – I should have followed the family route to a career in the law. And if I was charged – well, my dears, that simply wasn't going to happen because no one was going to suggest that I had anything to do with it. Although I have to confess that dear old Grimes caused me one or two anxious moments. But as plans go, not too bad, not too bad at all. And so Ava was prepared to put her neck on the line, or potentially through the noose as it were, for the man she loved. Yes, she loved me, with a passion that took my breath away. Ava trusted me with her life, literally. If you could not do it for your soul mate – who could you do it for? A capital plan, we both thought.

Actually, I have to confess that that is not quite the truth. Having criticised my sweet brother for having an aversion for integrity, it would be a little hypocritical if I didn't tell the truth, wouldn't it now? We'd dreamt up a plan, Ava thought it was a capital plan, that much is true. I thought it sucked. So, unbeknown to her, I had a slightly different plan.

Now that's more like it. We're getting somewhere now.

For that blonde slut to be by my side for eternity was a death sentence in its own right. For me, anyway. And so a scheme I'd had ever since that night when I poked my inquisitive nose into Edie's safe came into being. My plan was much the better because it involved me getting all the money and the state getting rid of Ava for me. How perfect. Now that's what I call strategy.

My plan crystallised when I convinced Ava that her route out of the squalor she found so distasteful was to rid ourselves of Edie and take her money. Over a light-hearted conversation in that hovel of a club, I gently broached the subject, ready at any moment to laugh away the whole thing as a joke. I was taking a real risk you know; had Ava been aghast at the very suggestion that something unfortunate should happen to Edie then it would have been rather difficult for me to act alone later on. I needn't have worried. I was pushing at the proverbial open door. Ava lapped it up like the cat that had found cream for the rest of its life and so we were on. What Ava did not know was that my plan involved ensuring her defence was scuppered and that any application for a reprieve went up in smoke – it actually did, you will recall.

To ruin any defence that she might have, I had to get John to believe in my guilt. How easy was that? Ava, rather unfortunately for her, paved the way in this respect. When John had let it known he was going round that fateful night, Nurse Dolores – as ever, well

313

aware of what was happening – let it slip to Ava who passed on that morsel of information to myself. How simple was it to enter the house at the very time John was there. Knowing that he was sitting in the car, all I had to do was slip through the front door.

Ava was charged so my job was to save her. She agreed that John was the perfect man to fight her corner. Who better to represent her than a man who was besotted? Her child-like conviction was that no one would think badly of a pretty little thing and even if they did, would not want to hang a young mother. This was a notion that, for obvious reasons, I was anxious not to discourage. The last thing she was going to do was to drag me in; when all said and done the agreement made sense. There was nothing to be gained in pointing the finger; she may be condemning her saviour. So she was never going to blab about me; we were partners and in the future were to be lovers. How the thought made me want to vomit.

What the dear girl, in her naivety, hadn't worked out was that I was a man who should not be trusted. I wanted Edie's fortune for myself and certainly had no need of a wife and all her demands. Thus I needed her to be convicted and executed, whilst apparently doing all I could to arrange for the opposite. All I had to do was ask John for an alibi and wait for him and dear old pater to come to the conclusion that I had done the old hag in. And, armed with that belief, nothing was more certain than they would conduct Ava's defence with a view to securing her conviction and her execution. They were going to save me and to do that they had to sacrifice their client. And nowadays, the lawyers talk about a conflict of interest. They don't know the half, my dears.

One more thing. I needed no saving. That has always been John's tragedy. As I think back to that night, I still feel, even to this day, the acute disappointment, that crushing sense of a thwarting of purpose. As I took from my bag the syringe, vial, needle, the liquid morphine – as ever my weapon of choice – as I stood over Edie and saw her bloodless complexion, the dull look in her lifeless eyes, I knew I was too late. Ava had beaten me to it. I was all for drawing it out, enjoying it. Not so Ava. Her eyes, wide as saucers, had been drawn to her inheritance, like a child spotting Santa Claus and she wasn't prepared to wait for Christmas morning. Perhaps she saw my procrastination as an indication of second thoughts; how was she to know I was savouring the task, relishing the anticipation?

What could I do? I could hardly go running to Grimes's chums calling murder most foul, now could I? But having deprived me of the role to which I was born, her fate was sealed. She had to be punished, punished for what she'd done to me. I still had the presence of mind to ensure that Edie's wish to be cremated came to pass. A cremation meant another doctor had to look at the body. This would inevitably lead to a post-mortem. And this meant that the cause of death was all too apparent. Just as I needed if Ava was to take the rap, as it were. My note – anonymous obviously – to the coroner alleging foul play ensured all this came to pass.

Not that Ava went kicking and screaming to her end. She was famous; just as she'd always wanted. How she looked forward to my visits when I could describe what the world was saying. Needless to say, I took the opportunity to assure her that the reprieve was around the corner. The later it came the better the story, the more spectacular the drama, the greater her fame. Well, that's the rubbish I gave her. I often think of her taking those final steps, still thinking she would be saved. The only person being saved was my good self.

And so, Libby and Terry, my dear chums. The jury was right after all. The court did its job. The right person was convicted. The only miscarriage of justice, as the lawyers love to drone on about, is that I didn't suffer her fate. Do I care?

I look once more at the two prone bodies.

No. Still nothing. I feel absolutely nothing. You know, I never have since I experienced the electrifying thrill of putting another to death with the power of my mind.

So what more have I to live for? I know the answer to that. That which drove me on has gone. There is nothing more to say. In a moment, I will put down my pen and leave my postscript to the story with John's final two chapters.

And then? Well, then I will put my hand in my jacket pocket and pull out the Webley I have brought with me, just in case either was more resistant to my dose than I had envisaged.

I would add, in passing, that my collection nowadays is rather impressive.

I will put the shiny nozzle of the revolver in my mouth. And I will pull the trigger. And, albeit belatedly, Ava will have her revenge.

And that, finally, will be the right and proper end.

THE END